W9-ATT-623

A Thread So Thin

Also by Marie Bostwick

A Thread of Truth (Cobbled Court #2)

A Single Thread (Cobbled Court #1)

On Wings of the Morning

River's Edge

Fields of Gold

"The Presents of Angels" in *Snow Angels*

"A High-Kicking Christmas" in *Comfort and Joy*

Published by Kensington Publishing Corporation

A Thread So Thin

MARIE BOSTWICK

KENSINGTON BOOKS

KENSINGTON BOOKS are published by

Kensington Publishing Corp.
119 West 40th Street
New York, NY 10018

Copyright © 2010 by Marie Bostwick Skinner

All rights reserved. No part of this book may be reproduced in any form or by any means without the prior written consent of the Publisher, excepting brief quotes used in reviews.

Kensington and the K logo Reg. U.S. Pat. & TM Off.

ISBN-13: 978-1-61664-342-3

First Kensington Trade Paperback Printing: May 2010
Printed in the United States of America

To my precious daughters-in-love

With thanks . . .

To Father Robert Tucker, of St. Anthony's of Padua church, for sharing his insights on counseling engaged couples. To Joseph Montebello and Davyne Verstandig, who are good writers, good listeners, and cherished friends.

To Brad, cheerleader, lover, husband, and best friend. To Betty Walsh, my first-round reader and in-house literary critic, for being an outstanding older (and much wiser) sister.

And to the team—Audrey LaFehr, Jill Grosjean, Nancy Berland, Sherry Kuehl, Adam Kortekas, and Molly Dane Skinner—for everything else.

A Thread So Thin

Prologue

Liza Burgess

By the time a person gets to be twenty-two years old, you'd think she'd be pretty self-aware. I always thought I was. But recently I learned something new about myself: I don't like surprises.

I don't like decisions, either. Until pretty recently, I didn't have to make many decisions, not important ones, not the kind that will change your life. When you're a kid, adults tend to make your choices for you.

Life is just filled with too many choices. That's what I think. Maybe I'd feel differently if my childhood hadn't been cut short by a few years, but it was. The way I see it, the older you get, the more chance there is that the choices you make now will screw up the whole rest of your life. Believe me, I know what I'm talking about.

My mom died from breast cancer at about the same time I graduated from high school. Just like that, I was alone in the world.

My dad is alive—at least I guess he is—but I've never met him and wouldn't have known how to contact him even if I'd wanted to. I knew I had an aunt Abigail, too, my mom's older sister, but I didn't want to contact her either, and for good reason.

Mom and Abigail hadn't spoken to each other since before I was born. Their falling-out was complicated and multifaceted, but it began because of my father, the man they'd both loved and, eventually, were both deserted by. But when my mom died, I didn't know that. All I knew was that Abigail had cut off all contact with Mom and, by extension, with me. She never called or came to see us, not even when Mom was dying. Abigail was the last person I wanted to turn to for help.

The person I did turn to wasn't even family. Not then.

I know people like to make jokes about lawyers, but they'd better not do it in front of me. When Mom died, Franklin Spaulding, our lawyer, was the only one on my side.

With his help, I sold our tiny town house, settled the estate, paid off Mom's hospital and funeral bills and, with the money that was left, went to art school in Rhode Island. Franklin helped me fill out the application and even wrote me a recommendation. And it didn't end there. He helped me move into my dorm and even showed up and took me out to dinner on Parents Weekend. Franklin is a great guy. I don't know what I'd have done without him. He called me every couple of months just to see how I was doing. I always said everything was fine. But it wasn't.

Even with Franklin's help, being an adult, making all my own decisions . . . well, it didn't exactly work out for me.

After three semesters, I flunked out, did something really stupid, and ended up in front of a judge. The judge didn't think I was the sort of person who should be "left to her own recognizance" (you think?), so he basically forced my aunt Abigail to be responsible for me.

To say I wasn't too happy about this arrangement would be an understatement. But now I can admit that a part of me was secretly relieved by the judge's order. I was only nineteen. Letting somebody else, even someone I resented as much as Abigail, be in charge for a while was an improvement.

But for a long time, the jury was definitely out on whether or not Abigail and I were going to work out. We loathed each other.

I was angry with the world as a whole and Abigail in particular. I went out of my way to do and think exactly the opposite of whatever Abigail did or thought, and basically I made her life hell. If Abigail said white, I said black, and vice versa, just so I could tick her off. It wasn't hard. She took the bait pretty easily.

But we eventually called a truce. It'd take a book to explain exactly how, but after a year of living with Abigail in her enormous mansion in New Bern, Connecticut, and many long, drawn-out battles, we worked out our problems . . . well, most of them.

Now Abigail is family to me—and all *that* implies. Sometimes I'd like to smack her. Sometimes I bet she'd like to do the same to me. But I love her and she loves me, even when she doesn't understand me, which is pretty much all the time. Still, in her own way, she's like a second mother to me—a caring, pushy, controlling, overbearing, and incredibly rich second mother.

After a lot of soul searching, I did decide to go back to school in New York, but once I got here, I didn't have to make too many choices. The curriculum for studio art majors is pretty well set, and as far as the other stuff—where I'd live and how much allowance I'd get, that kind of thing—I mostly leave that to Abigail. She's more than happy to take over, and I'm more than happy to leave it in her hands, so it works out well.

Like I said before, Abigail is rich. Really rich. Like Jimmy Choo, chauffeured limousine, Park Avenue penthouse apartment rich, and if I wanted all that, she'd be happy to get it for me. Heck, she'd be giddy with joy to get it for me. Abigail loves a project. But I don't want any of that stuff. It's just not me. I'm not glamorous. Never have been. Besides, I don't want to stick out.

When I came to New York to take another run at art school I wanted to fit in and be a regular student like everyone else: living in a crowded apartment with three other girls and sharing one sink, eating ramen noodles from the microwave and hot dogs off vendors' carts, getting woken up by the screams of sirens in the middle of the night or the shouts of drunks stumbling home after the bars have closed, sweating in summer when the window air conditioner breaks, getting soaked in the rain trying to hail cabs that shower you with water as they speed through puddles, slogging through the dirty slush of winter as the wet seeps in between the stitching of your boots and freezes your toes. If you're not glamorous, living in New York can be hard.

But I like New York. I like it a lot. I like the busyness of it, the way everything is always moving and changing.

But, that being said, New York isn't the center of my universe.

I'm here for a while, just till I finish my degree, and then I intend to go home to New Bern, where Abigail lives and where I live, too, or will, at the end of next term, when I graduate. Maybe you wonder what I'm going to do with a degree in studio art in a little Podunk village in Connecticut. The same thing I'd do with a degree in studio art in New York, or Paris, or anyplace else: work in retail during the day, and paint at night. You can be a starving artist anywhere.

It isn't like I've worked out a grand plan for all this; it's more that I don't have anywhere else to go or any other prospects. When all you're good at is painting pictures, your horizons tend to be a little limited. But the way I see it, limited prospects save me the worry of trying to decide what I should do with my life, you know? Everything is all settled. Well, it was . . . until tonight. But I'll get to that later.

The thing is, going home to New Bern is no hardship because, while I like New York, I love New Bern. I really do.

I love the way the hills are painted orange and yellow and red every fall, and how all the crocuses bloom on the same day in the spring. I love waking up early on the morning after a big snowstorm, going outside to get the paper from the box, and leaving the first footprints on the sidewalk. I love sitting with a picnic basket on the Green and listening to free concerts on Wednesday nights in summer, watching kids race around chasing fireflies while their parents lie on the grass and surreptitiously sip wine out of generic plastic thermoses because the Green is town property and you're not supposed to have alcohol on town property. And I love how, as long as people behave themselves, the police pretend they don't know what's in the thermoses. I love how everyone in New Bern knows everybody else's business and talks about it. And I love how nothing there, at least nothing big, ever really changes. But most of all, I love the people. New Bern is all about the people.

Evelyn Dixon, who owns the Cobbled Court Quilt Shop, has a job waiting for me when I come back. Evelyn's like my other second mother except that, unlike Abigail, she's calm, practical, and wise. And, most of the time, she does understand me.

Then there's Margot, who is like the big sister I never had: sweet and tolerant and smarter than me. Margot was a marketing executive in New York until she got downsized and moved to New Bern. Now she does all the marketing and accounting for the quilt shop, though a lot of the time she works selling fabric and thread. We all do that.

Everyone at Cobbled Court pitches in whenever and however they can. Ivy Peterman is in charge of order fulfillment for our telephone and Internet sales; Cobbled Court does a big online business. She's newer on staff but she fits in like she's been here from the beginning. Ivy's just a few years older than me but she has two little kids, Bethany and Bobby. She's had a hard life and can be pretty serious. I consider it my job to help her lighten up and remind her that she's still young. In other words, I like to tease her. She doesn't mind. We're friends. They're all my friends and, in a way, my family—Abigail, Evelyn, Margot, and Ivy. They're also the members of my quilt circle. I know, it's weird to think of a twenty-two-year-old sitting around with a bunch of older women making quilts, but what can I say? They're my girls.

And I love making quilts. Quilting is just another medium, another means for creating art. After I got tossed from school and nearly landed in jail, learning to quilt helped me realize that I really *am* an artist, a good one, no matter what those pruney professors in Rhode Island thought. I'm doing really well at my current school. In fact, I've got the highest grade point in my class. Not that grade point means so much in art school—what matters is the work—but I've produced some pieces that I'm very proud of and, if not for what I've learned about myself through quilting, I might have given up on art altogether.

So, you can see why New Bern has such a pull on me, why I spend as many weekends there as I can. But New Bern has another, very important, attraction for me: My boyfriend lives there.

Garrett is Evelyn's son. He was a programmer for a big company in Seattle, but he came home to help Evelyn after her mastectomies. He liked New Bern, and me, so he stayed. Now he takes care of Cobbled Court's website and is in charge of all the computer stuff. Garrett is a genius. He's also funny, and considerate, and absolutely gorgeous. He has the most amazing brown eyes. And he's taller than me by five inches, which I love. I'm five-ten, and I can tell you from personal experience, there's nothing romantic about being the girl who has to bend down to kiss her date good night. But that's no problem with Garrett. He knows just when to pick up the phone or send me an e-mail, and he remembers things like the anniversary of our first date. When he picked me up for that first date, he brought me one perfect pink rose and he's done the same for every date since. He's got romantic down cold.

Tonight, New Year's Eve, he went all out in the romance department. In fact, he went overboard. Before now, I wouldn't have believed that was possible, but believe me—it is.

1

Liza Burgess

Since it was New Year's and I wanted to look especially nice, I tried on all my jewelry before finally deciding to wear my new necklace to dinner with Garrett.

I make a lot of jewelry, but this was my best piece yet: five individual strands of slender silver beads that I'd joined into one necklace, twisting the strands together so they'd catch the light and make a statement. It would be perfect with the deep V-neck of the dress I planned on wearing. But when I was trying it on, I realized that the clasp was too flimsy for such a heavy necklace.

So I put on my winter coat and trudged ten blocks through the snow to the bead shop to buy a sturdier clasp. When I returned, I hadn't even put the key in the lock when the phone started ringing. I dumped my bag on the floor, pulled off my gloves, and ran to answer it.

"Where have you been all afternoon? I've been calling you for hours!"

"No, you haven't. I just went out to do some shopping. I've only been gone an hour." Abigail has a tendency to exaggerate. I like to call her on it when I can.

"Well, it seemed like hours. Listen, darling, I've only got a minute. Franklin and I are going to a party at the Guldens'."

Franklin Spaulding wasn't just my mother's lawyer, he was Aunt Abigail's, too, for years and years. A few months ago, he became her husband as well. He and Abigail make an odd couple, but they are perfect for each other.

"I saw Garrett, and he told me where he's taking you for dinner tonight."

"He did? He hasn't even told *me* where we're going for dinner tonight."

"I thought as much." She harrumphed. "Men always think women like surprises, but they're wrong. We pretend to like surprises, but what we really like is being prepared."

"That's not true. Women like surprises. I *love* surprises. Surprises are romantic."

"Of course they are, darling, as long as you're prepared for them. If you're not, they can be simply awful. Which brings me back to the reason for this call: What are you wearing tonight?"

I wasn't surprised by this question. Abigail is always quizzing me about my wardrobe. It's really none of her business what I wear, but I decided to humor her.

"Since it's New Year's, I thought I'd dress up a little. I've got that black jersey wrap dress. It's nice. Very New Yorky."

"It *is* nice, darling, but not quite nice enough. Not where you're going."

"Abigail . . ."

She sighed impatiently. "I don't have time to argue, Liza. Really, I don't. In a little while a deliveryman will be knocking at your door. I called to make sure you'd be there to let him in. I've sent you a dress. It's from my closet, but it should fit you perfectly."

Abigail and I are the same height and wear the same size, but she's sixty-five years old.

"Abigail, you've got to be kidding. You want me to wear one of your old dresses? On New Year's Eve?"

"Yes, I do," she said archly. "And you're welcome. Do you have any idea how much it costs to hire a messenger service to deliver from New Bern to Manhattan on New Year's Eve?"

I tried to interrupt, but she cut me off.

"Liza, *don't* be difficult. I haven't the time. Wear the dress, darling. Trust me. You'll be glad you did."

"But where are we going? Why would Garrett tell you and not me?"

She ignored my questions.

"Must run. Bye-bye. Have a wonderful time." She made two kiss noises into the phone and hung up before I could say another word.

The new semester wouldn't begin for a few more days. Two of my roommates, Kerry and Janelle, still hadn't returned from vacation. I'd been home in New Bern for Christmas but had returned to the city early because Professor Williams—Selena Williams, who headed up the art history department—had asked me to help her do some research for an article she was writing about the influence of Clement Greenberg on abstract expressionism. She's my favorite professor, so I jumped at the offer. Zoe, who slept in the bed next to mine, was the only other roommate in residence. She had gone home for Christmas, but Zoe's relationship with her mother—and her stepfather, one in a series of stepfathers—is pretty rocky. Consequently, Zoe never stays home one minute longer than she has to.

When I told her that Aunt Abigail was having one of her dresses messengered to me from New Bern and wanted me to wear it on my date with Garrett, Zoe made a face, stuck her finger in her mouth, and pretended to gag.

"Is she serious? Isn't your aunt older than the Chrysler Building? There is no way you can wear one of her old dresses out on New Year's Eve. She's probably worried you'll go out on the town with—horrors!—a hemline that's actually above your knees and that Garrett will be so senseless with lust at the sight of your bare legs that he'll put a roofie in your drink and take advantage of you while you're unconscious or something." Zoe ambled over to the tiny, cube-shaped refrigerator that sat between our beds, pulled out a diet soda, and popped the top.

I shook my head. "She's not like that."

She isn't. Actually, Abigail has very good taste in clothes. Unlike a lot of older women with money to burn, she doesn't go around buying fabulous designer fashions that were created for twenty-five-year-olds but look ridiculous on a sixty-five-year-old. Abigail says that at her age, "Beauty is a ship that has sailed. The most I strive for at this point is to be clean."

That's silly. I've never seen her look anything less than beautiful. Her clothes are *very* fashionable, great fabrics, but always age appropriate. When I'm her age, I hope I look half as good as Aunt Abigail.

But that's just it. I'm *not* her age. Abigail has great clothes, but I couldn't imagine that anything in her closet was going to look good on me. Especially not for New Year's Eve in New York.

"Just wait and see," Zoe said between slurps of soda. "Aunt Abigail's henchman is going to show up at your door with something that has long sleeves, a granny skirt, a turtleneck, and matching opera gloves. Something long and lumpy. Maybe a full-length snow parka. I'm telling you, Liza, she's just worried about you showing off too much skin. When the delivery guy shows up, let me answer the door. That way, you can always lie, you can say you had to go out before he came and never saw the dress."

Not so long ago I'd have had no compunction about lying to Aunt Abigail, but I like to think I've grown up a bit since then. Even so, when I heard a knock on our door, I let Zoe get to it first. I stood behind her, nervously eyeing the white dress box as she signed the delivery confirmation slip and closed the door.

Zoe carted the box into our room and tossed it on my bed. We both stared at it. "Well? Do you want to open it? Or should I?"

It was a big box, big enough to hold a lumpy, full-length snow parka. I hoped it didn't.

"No. It's all right. I'll do it."

Taking a deep breath, I took the box top off, pulled back the layers of white tissue paper, and gasped at the sight of the most exquisite evening gown I had ever seen in my life! The design was simple: a long, straight sheath of ivory silk, with a knee-high slit in one side. The fabric of the dress was covered with long, wavy lengths of thin silver ribbon, stitched with silver thread, making a subtle and beautiful pattern, like wind rippling over water. The ribbons ran vertically from the long hem up the full length of the skirt until they ended, cutting off at varying points along the tight-fitted, V-necked bodice, fading away one by one, so that the fabric at the shoulder seams of the sleeveless gown was a simple expanse of shimmering silk. It was the most beautiful dress in the world.

For a moment, we stood there, speechless, but Zoe found her voice first.

"Liza," she said, "I take back everything I said about your aunt Abigail."

"Yeah."

"Well? What are you waiting for? Try it on!"

It fit perfectly. When I went to zip up the back I realized it didn't have one. The fabric in the back of the gown scooped into three graceful folds that fell just to the curve of my hip.

Zoe whistled. "Liza, I'd kill to have shoulder blades like yours. They're gorgeous."

I turned around and peered over my shoulder to check out the view from the rear. "Thanks."

Zoe picked up some discarded tissue paper and went to put it in the dress box. "Wait a minute, Liza. There are shoes in here too." She held up a pair of four-inch stiletto sandals whose straps were strings of tiny rhinestones. They were perfect. I sat carefully on the edge of my bed, trying to slip on the sandals without wrinkling the dress. Zoe continued ferreting through the box.

"Oh, my gosh! And diamonds! Big ones!" I lifted my head and saw Zoe staring wide-eyed into a black velvet bag.

"Let me see that." She wasn't lying. I took the bag and pulled out an enormous diamond choker.

The dress and shoes were new to me—I'd never noticed them in Abigail's closet—but the diamonds I recognized. It was the choker that Abigail's first husband, Woolley Wynne, had given her as a wedding present. He died many years before, leaving Abigail a very wealthy widow. Abigail kept the choker in a safe deposit box and had shown it to me once when we were at the bank. Years ago, when she'd married Woolley, the choker had cost tens of thousands of dollars. I couldn't imagine what it must be worth now.

"Are they real? Maybe we should hire a security guy to go to dinner with you."

"Of course not," I lied as I held the choker up to my throat. The thought of having something so expensive in our no-doorman, no-luxury apartment made me nervous. There was no point in making Zoe nervous too. The dress and shoes were beautiful, but the diamonds weren't me. They were too much. Too glamorous. "Who'd be crazy enough to put diamonds that big in the care of some nameless delivery guy if they were real?"

Who? No one but Abigail.

"They're cubic zirconia," I continued. "Fakes." I stuffed the choker back into the velvet bag.

Zoe twisted her lips doubtfully. "Well, they're the best fakes I ever saw. Aren't you going to wear them?"

"Uh-uh. I've got something better in mind."

After helping me with my hair, Zoe headed off to Times Square to ring in the New Year.

"This is probably my last New Year's in New York. I figure you gotta do it once, you know?"

I nodded in agreement, but I was glad I wasn't joining her. I don't like crowds. Standing for hours, squashed between hordes of howling strangers in the freezing cold, waiting for a glowing ball to drop was not my idea of a great way to spend New Year's.

Garrett was right on time. I'd never seen him in a suit and tie before, let alone a tuxedo. He looked so handsome. I was glad Abigail sent the dress. And he was carrying not one rose, but an armful—two dozen long-stemmed pink roses tied with a white satin bow.

"They're beautiful," I breathed and buried my nose in the bouquet, the silken petals brushing against my skin.

"*You're* beautiful," he said. "You look like Keira Knightley. But taller."

I lifted my eyes from the flowers. "Don't tease me."

"I'm not. You look amazing. Like a movie star. Better than that. You look like you. Exactly like you. The dress. The shoes. Everything. And the necklace. It's beautiful."

"Do you like it?" I asked, fingering the silver beads. "I made it myself."

"I love it. I love everything I see," he said.

"Thanks."

Garrett and I've been dating for a long time, but I suddenly felt awkward. I went to find a vase so I could put his flowers in water.

"You look great," I called over my shoulder. "Where'd you rent the tuxedo?"

"I bought it. Had it tailored." He shrugged. "I figured I was too old to wear a rented tux. Who knows? Maybe I'll be able to use it again."

I laughed. "Planning on joining the country club, are you? Going to the charity galas along with Aunt Abigail and the rest of New Bern society?"

"There are other places to wear a tuxedo besides charity galas." He looked at his watch. "Ready? Our reservation is for nine-thirty."

"It is?" I plunked the flowers in water and grabbed my black wool coat. Not exactly the thing to wear with an evening gown, but it was the warmest one I had.

"You should have told me. It'll take forever to hail a cab on New Year's Eve. We'll never get there on time. Not that I know where we're going. Where are we going, anyway? Can we walk? If not, maybe we should take the subway."

Garrett held out his arm like a courtier asking for the honor of a dance. "Transportation has already been arranged."

My apartment is on the third floor of a five-floor walk-up on Eighty-eighth, between Second Avenue and Third. It's not the kind of place you see a lot of limousines idling in front of, but that was exactly what waited for us as we came out the front door. Actually, it wasn't quite a limousine, not one of those ridiculous stretch jobs they use for celebrities, weddings, or that groups of twenty kids pile into on prom nights. I'd have hated that. This was just a large and very shiny black sedan. A man in a black suit was sitting behind the wheel. He jumped out to open the door for me.

I looked at Garrett. "You didn't have to do this," I said, though

I wasn't sorry he had. Even if you're not glamorous, every now and then it's fun to pretend you are.

"I know. I wanted to. I want this to be a night we'll remember. Besides," he said, looking at my sparkling feet, "I couldn't risk you wrecking those shoes."

It was warm inside the car, so I slipped out of my heavy coat and scooted across the leather seat to be closer to Garrett. He put his arm around me. The chauffeur glanced in the rearview mirror and then pushed a button that raised a tinted glass window between the front and back seats.

I laughed. "That's what I like in a chauffeur—subtlety. What does he think we're going to do back here? Make out like a couple of high school kids?"

Garrett turned his body toward mine, running his hand under my hair, cradling my head in the hollow of his palm as I tilted my face up to his. The tips of his fingers were cool, but his lips were warm and soft and sweet. I liked the way they felt against mine, the way his bangs fell into his eyes and brushed my cheek as his head bent over mine, and the muscled weight of his body pressing me back into the smooth leather seat as we kissed and clung and glided silently through the streets of the city, past sidewalks full of smiling, laughing crowds, everyone happy and everyone hopeful, believing that maybe, just maybe, the best year of their lives was about to begin.

It's just not in my nature to look at things that way; I wish it were. But for a little while that night, my wish came true. With Garrett's lips on mine as I reached my arms up and draped them over his shoulders like two vines clinging to a strong and steady wall, something relaxed inside me and I believed it, too, that nothing but good was on the horizon. What lightness! I felt like I'd assumed a secret identity, put on a beautiful borrowed dress and shoes supplied by a good fairy, climbed into a pumpkin coach sedan, and suddenly transformed into a sanguine, faith-filled optimist. By the time the driver pulled up in front of the Carlyle Hotel and the maître d' escorted us to a VIP table near the stage, I was a new person. It felt wonderful. But it didn't last.

The fairy godmother gown, borrowed rhinestone slippers, champagne by candlelight, the pumpkin coach car—in the end, none of it made any difference.

When Garrett dropped to one knee in the middle of the dance floor at the Café Carlyle while the orchestra played the song he'd requested in advance, pulled a small blue box out of his tuxedo pocket, and asked me to marry him, the spell was broken. The optimistic, hopeful Liza vanished and the old Liza—the one who knows that happily ever after is only for books and that real life, the part that comes after the story ends, is hard and uncertain—was back in an instant.

Garrett wanted me to marry him. I didn't know what to say.

2

Liza Burgess

Garrett got to his feet, dusting off the knee of his pant leg as he did.

The ring of couples that surrounded us, peering hopefully at us a moment before, convinced they were at the most romantic New Year's Eve celebration in New York and ready to witness their approval of our engagement by a round of applause, shifted their eyes and began to dance again, pretending they hadn't seen Garrett's proposal or what, to their eyes, appeared to be my shocked and silent refusal.

"Come on. Let's go back to the table." Garrett grabbed my arm and I followed him, keeping my eyes lowered but feeling stares on my back as we left the dance floor, wending our way through the packed press of bodies. The crowd thinned as we neared the table. It was a quarter to twelve and nearly everyone was dancing, wanting to be near their beloved for the first kiss of the year as the clock struck twelve, balloons dropped from above, and the band played "Auld Lang Syne."

"You know, maybe it would be better if I took you home now. So we can avoid the traffic."

"But it's not midnight yet."

"Yeah. Well. Suddenly I don't feel like celebrating." He shoved his hands in his pants pockets and started heading past the circles of empty tables and toward the door, this time not bothering to grab my arm. Instead, I reached out to grab his.

"Hey! Garrett, wait a minute. Don't be like that."

He turned to face me, shaking off my grasp as he did. Unlike me, Garrett's got a long fuse, but he was angry.

"Don't be like that? How am I supposed to be? You completely embarrassed me out there, Liza. Now you think I should just stick around here so that everyone can stare at me?" His brown eyes flickered black.

"You were embarrassed? *You?*" I put my hands on my hips. "You weren't the only one out there, you know. Everybody was staring at me too. It was humiliating! Did you ever stop to think what a spot you were putting me in? Whatever gave you such a crazy idea?"

"Well . . . I . . . no . . . I . . ." Garrett sputtered and turned red. "This isn't just some crazy idea I cooked up on the spur of the moment, you know! Do you have any idea how long I've been planning this? You've got to call weeks ahead to get a table like this at the Carlyle, especially on New Year's Eve. I planned out the whole thing, but I wanted to surprise you! Is that so terrible? You always say you love surprises!"

"I do!" I shouted. "As long as I'm prepared for them!"

Somewhere in the back of my mind, I could hear Abigail laughing.

I closed my eyes, trying to calm down and collect my thoughts.

I've been trying to do a better job about keeping my temper and thinking things through before I react. It takes some effort, but I can do it if I focus. That's what I was trying to do: calm down, focus, and look at this thing from Garrett's point of view. But it wasn't easy.

I didn't understand why Garrett had decided to suddenly pop the question. No, that wasn't right. Clearly, he'd put a lot of planning into this evening. There was nothing sudden about his decision. And his intentions were really very sweet. But that still didn't make it a good idea. What was he thinking?

Why would he propose to me—crazy, hot-tempered, impulsive,

twenty-two-year-old me, who barely knows what she should do next week, let alone how she should spend the rest of her life and with whom?

On the other hand, did that necessarily make it a bad idea? I wouldn't always be like this, would I? I was a whole lot more mature than I'd been even a couple of years ago. The fact that I was holding my tongue and trying to look at this thing rationally instead of just freaking out proved it, right? And I wasn't so young. After all, I'd graduate in just a few more months, find myself out of the classroom and into the real world, and getting married was part of that, wasn't it?

Maybe. But maybe not. I didn't know. But I did know Garrett well enough to realize he hadn't meant to put me on the spot deliberately. That was just the way it had turned out.

I opened my eyes and looked at Garrett. "I just wasn't prepared, all right? This has been such a beautiful evening. Abigail wouldn't give me specifics, but she called and told me you were taking me somewhere really nice and advised me to step up my wardrobe. So I *was* expecting a special evening, but I could never have imagined this! The roses, the limousine, dinner and dancing at the most elegant restaurant in the city. . . . Thank you, Garrett. I've had such a great time."

"Right up until the part where I wrecked it by asking you to marry me, right?"

I pressed my lips together, annoyed by his petulant response. "That's not what I meant and you know it. I was prepared to have a lovely time with you. I always do, whether we have dinner at the Café Carlyle or a cup of coffee at the Blue Bean, but I never in a million years expected you were going to propose."

Garrett's eyebrows flattened into a line. He pulled his balled-up fists out of his pockets and opened his hands, jerking his arms in an impatient gesture. "Well, why not? You said it yourself. We always have a great time together. We're happy together, so why shouldn't we want to *be* together? What's so surprising about that?"

"Nothing, I guess. But you're making this seem like a perfectly logical, even obvious next step. I don't think it's as simple as that. If two people are going to spend the rest of their lives together, there has to be more to it than just enjoying each other's company, don't you think?"

Garrett's eyebrows drew apart, smoothing out the creases in his forehead. He relaxed his shoulders as if he suddenly understood everything.

"Well, sure. Of course there is! I'm sorry, Liza. I've never proposed before. Guess I was so focused on creating the perfect atmosphere that I left out the most important part: the actual proposal. Let me try again. I'll do better this time."

He took a step forward, took my hands in his, and locked his eyes onto mine. "Liza, I love you. You are the last thing I think about when I go to bed at night and the first image in my head when I wake up in the morning. You're the smile on my face when I go to work and the song I whistle as I walk down the street. You're the person I've waited for all my life. And now that I've found you, I want to be with you for now and forever. I love you, Liza. Please. Please, marry me."

His whole heart shone on his face, beaming a light that melted me. He was kind, sweet, and sincere. I was so lucky to have him in my life. I knew that. And this should have been one of the happiest moments of my life. I knew that too. So why wasn't it?

What was wrong with me? There couldn't have been a more perfect evening, or a more beautiful and heartfelt proposal on earth. And I'd never met a man who could hold a candle to Garrett. Not one of my girlfriends would have thought for two seconds before accepting. Why was I?

"Garrett, I love you."

His smile, which had widened with those first four words, faded as I went on. He knew. It only takes one syllable to say yes. Yes has no reservations. Yes doesn't need to explain itself. But I did.

"And I know you love me. That wasn't a surprise to me. I've known it for a long time. I bet there's not a man on the face of the earth who is more honest and open about his feelings than you. I'm not as good about that as you are, but I'm trying to be. That's why I can't just say yes to you. At least . . . not right now."

"That doesn't make any sense," he argued. "If you really—"

I held up my hand. "Stop! Just listen to me for a minute, okay?" He stopped, the petulant look returning to his face. I took another deep breath, trying to beat back my frustration before trying again.

"Garrett, I love you. So much. But marriage is—well, it's forever! At least, it's supposed to be forever. And if it's not, then I don't want to do it. I do love you. But . . . what if love isn't enough?"

"Liza, it will be!" he promised.

"How can you know that? How can you know that for sure? You love me now and you say you always will. I feel the same. But isn't that what everybody says when they get married? I suppose they must mean it. But if that's true, why is it that so many marriages don't last?"

Garrett frowned. "So you don't believe in marriage? You don't believe that love can last?"

"Why would I?" I asked, throwing up my hands. "I haven't seen many examples where it does. Have you? Your parents' marriage didn't last. And my father never even bothered to marry my mother. He lived with her for years and then, the minute she got pregnant with me, the second things got complicated, he took off."

"But that's exactly it!" he said urgently, grabbing my hands again and squeezing them. "Your father was never committed to your mother. Not the way I am to you. That's why he never married her and that's why he left. I'll never do that to you, Liza. Nothing will ever, ever change my feelings for you. Not ever. Believe me."

"I want to. I really do," I said. "I just don't know if I can."

He let my hands drop from his. My palms felt suddenly empty and useless.

"So this is a no," he said.

"I didn't say that. I never said that. What I said . . . What I meant . . ." I stuttered, frustrated with myself and with Garrett. He was always so understanding, so why couldn't he understand this? And me? Why was I such a complicated mess?

I didn't want to say no, but I didn't know how to say yes.

"Garrett, I need some time. I've got to sort this out in my mind. I know I love you. And I know that if I ever wanted to get married, it would be to you. But I also know that marriage scares me. No, wait," I said, holding my hands out to interrupt myself.

"That's not true. Marriage doesn't scare me, but divorce does. It terrifies me. The thought that in six months or six years you could wake up and decide that you don't love me anymore is more frightening than never having been loved in the first place. Do you know what I mean?" His expression told me he didn't.

"Don't look at me like that," I said. "You had a lot of time to make up your mind, first to decide you wanted to propose and then to figure out exactly how you wanted to do it. There was nothing spur-of-the-moment about this. You said so yourself."

His eyes were flat. I didn't know if he was angry, or hurt, or listening intently. I moved closer, reached out with one finger, and traced a tentative path from the elbow of his jacket down to his hand, letting it rest at the end of his fingertip.

"You've had weeks to plan this, but it's all new to me. Don't I deserve some time to absorb this?"

His eyes rolled up toward the ceiling, resting there a moment while he thought about this.

"You're right," he said finally. "It's a big decision. You should take some time. I want you to be sure."

"So do I. Thanks," I said, relieved. "I've got to ask you something. Did Abigail know you were going to propose tonight?"

"She asked me where we were going to dinner and I told her—after making her promise not to tell you and spoil the surprise, which obviously did a lot of good—but I never told her I was going to ask you to marry me."

I nodded. "Maybe it would be better if, just for now, we kept this to ourselves. You know how it is in New Bern. There's no such thing as a secret. I don't think either of us wants to deal with the pressure we'd be subjected to if people knew we were thinking about getting engaged."

"I guess." He shrugged. "But there's just one thing." He reached his hand into his pocket, pulled out the blue jewelry box, and opened it.

I'd been so shocked to see Garrett sinking to one knee when we were on the dance floor that I really hadn't had a chance to look at the ring. It was exquisite, a brilliant square-cut diamond in a simple, wide platinum setting, very modern and sleek and exactly what I'd have picked if I'd chosen it myself. Garrett knew me so well.

"What should we do with this? I know you don't want to wear it, but . . . do you think you might just want to hold on to it? For a little while. Just until you make up your mind?"

He held out the ring and looked at me with spaniel eyes. I knew it didn't make sense for me to take the ring until I could give him a definitive yes, but he looked so miserable. I just didn't have the heart to turn him down a second time.

"If you want me to," I said.

"I do." He took the ring out of the jewelry box and laid it in my open palm. It felt awkward, holding it without actually putting it on.

"Wait a minute. I've got an idea."

I handed the ring back to Garrett, dug into my evening bag, and pulled out a thin silver chain. "I had this left over from one of my jewelry projects," I explained before threading the chain through the ring and putting it around my neck. The chain was long, so the ring dangled just beneath my silver choker, almost like I'd added a diamond pendant to the silver piece. Later, I'd be able to wear it under my clothes. No one would know it was there and, for now at least, that's the way I wanted it.

"There!" I said after I fastened the clasp. "What do you think?"

"It's fine. Makes it look a little like we're two eighth graders going steady, but if you like it . . ." He shrugged noncommittally, but I could tell he felt a little better seeing the ring hanging around my neck.

"It's a gorgeous ring. Thank you." I reached out to squeeze his hand, wanting him to feel how much I meant what I said.

Taking in a deep breath and then letting it out slowly, he pulled his hand back and looked at his watch. "One minute to midnight. This isn't exactly how I pictured us beginning the new year."

"No? How did you picture it?"

"With you and me on the dance floor. Cheek to cheek. Lip to lip." He pushed his hair up off his forehead.

"Well," I said, slipping my arm under his and curving my body toward him, "there's still time for that. I know we made kind of a spectacle of ourselves before, but what do we care? We'll never see these people again. So what do you say? Do you want to dance?"

"Hmm," Garrett mused. "I don't know. Can I have some time to think about it?"

"Nope."

"Well, in that case, lead the way."

I did, holding his hand as we returned to the floor, wrapping my arms around his neck and lifting my lips to meet his as the bandleader counted down the seconds to midnight, and the balloons fell, and the crowd cheered, and I wondered what other surprises the new year would hold.

3

Evelyn Dixon

Depending on your point of view, January and February are either the best two months of the year in New England or the worst. Probably more people would opt for the latter than the former but, personally, I love this time of year.

Yes, it can be bone-chillingly cold, so cold that a lot of people book flights to Florida or the Carolinas and don't come back until March. And if it's an especially hard winter, they might not return until April or even May, kind of like the groundhog, Punxsutawney Phil, who pokes his nose out from his cozy winter burrows on February 2 and, depending on where the shadows fall, either heads back inside to hunker down until the signs appear more favorable or waddles out into the open and declares that spring has arrived.

Chilly winter weather tends to have an equally chilling effect on New Bern commerce. There are fewer people around to buy things, and those who are here tend to stay close to the warmth of hearth and home rather than brave freezing temperatures and the snow-heaped sidewalks of downtown New Bern, credit cards at the ready. Some stores, like the ice cream shop and the pool-and-patio store, close up for the entire winter. Most of the rest shorten their hours and stay closed an extra day or two during the week.

But that's exactly why this is my favorite time of year: It's the only time I can take a little time for myself.

This winter, I'm not opening the shop until eleven and I'm not opening at all on Sundays or Mondays. Charlie is closing his restaurant, the Grill on the Green, on Sunday nights, Mondays, *and* Tuesdays, and I couldn't be happier. Sure, it means less income for both of us, but after the spring tourist rush, followed by the even bigger summer tourist rush, then the fall foliage rush, and the holiday rush, it's nice to spend a few weeks of the year *not* rushing. This last year has been especially busy.

My best friend from Texas, Mary Dell Templeton, now the host of a very popular quilting show on cable television, decided to do a live broadcast from Cobbled Court Quilts during our third Quilt Pink event to fight breast cancer. For weeks leading up to the broadcast, the cable channel ran promotional videos about it and Mary Dell never missed a chance to plug it on the show. As a result, foot traffic in the shop quadrupled and our online sales went through the roof. It was a great event—hundreds of people participated and we made scores of quilts that will be auctioned off for breast cancer research—but it turned out to be more work than any of us could have imagined. I'm happy we did it, but I'm not sorry that things have calmed down a bit since then.

There's nothing much happening in New Bern now. Not a single charity auction, concert, or festival is scheduled during January or February—not a community obligation on the calendar. That suits me fine. Not that there's anything wrong with those kinds of events. During the rest of the year I participate in all kinds of community celebrations and I enjoy them. But I also enjoy this quiet season in Connecticut's quiet corner. It's like a long and lovely Sabbath rest, a day when there's plenty of time to read, to think, to plan and reflect, to finish up all of my UFOs—those Unfinished Objects that are the bane of every quilter's existence—and spend unhurried, unscheduled time with the people I care about, as long as they are among the hardy souls who choose to hold their ground and tough out the New England winter. Fortunately for me, most of the people I care about are very hardy souls indeed.

And then there's the weather.

I grew up in Wisconsin, so I know all about winter weather. When I was a kid I simply couldn't wait for winter. As soon as Halloween passed I'd polish up my sled and keep vigil in the front yard until the first snowfall. Sometimes the snow would come even before the end of October. One Halloween, I had to wear snow boots and a parka over my glittery fairy princess costume, which kind of spoiled the effect.

Lots of people born in cold climates like it as kids, but once they grow up and have to shovel driveways, pay heating oil bills, and jump-start frigid car batteries, the thrill of winter wears off. Those are the people who are first on the planes to Florida, the ones who don't even stick around for the Christmas and New Year's parties but get into formation and fly south the day after Thanksgiving. Not me.

The more it snows, the more I like it. After I married my husband, Rob, and moved to Texas, I didn't see a snowflake for the next twenty years. I missed it. Maybe that's why, after we divorced, I instinctively headed north—like a Canada goose making a beeline for the border—found my way to the village of New Bern, Connecticut, and never looked back. This is home now. Spring, summer, fall, and even in the depths of winter, this is where I belong. The way I see it, shoveling driveways is good exercise, and as for the rest of it? Fortunately, my two-bedroom cottage on Marsh Lane is so small that even when the oil prices spike in winter, the bill is still manageable. And living so close to downtown, I can walk to the quilt shop, which makes driveway shoveling less of an issue for me.

Today, the first Monday in January, I waded through a fresh fall of ankle-high snow, plowing a path between my house and the post office, where I picked up my mail and stopped in the lobby to say hello to Gibb Rainey.

Every small town has its share of eccentrics. Gibb is ours. I don't know how old Gibb is, but he's at least well into his seventies and possibly a lot older. He's friendly, likes college sports, and wears his UConn Huskies cap wherever he goes. He's also a loyal member of New Bern's Veterans of Foreign Wars post.

Years ago—no one has ever been able to tell me how many years ago, but many—near Memorial Day, Gibb was given the job of selling those little paper poppies the VFW uses to raise money for disabled vets. Because there are no mailboxes in New Bern and everybody has to go to the post office to pick up their mail, Gibb figured that would be a good place to sell his flowers.

He loaded a lawn chair into the trunk of his 1968 Chevrolet Corvair, drove downtown to the post office, and set up shop, parking his chair on the sidewalk, right by the post office door. Not only did he set a new VFW post record for money raised during the poppy sale, he had a great time chatting with the people who passed by. So much so that he returned with his lawn chair the next day, and the next, and every day after. You can't go pick up your mail in New Bern without stopping to talk with Gibb. In warm weather, he puts his chair on the sidewalk. And when it's cold, like today, he moves into the lobby.

A few years back, a new postmaster came to town. He said that Gibb couldn't loiter inside a federal office and made him leave. That lasted about a week.

Word of the postmaster's treatment of Gibb got around town. People started calling the office of the First Selectman, New Bern's version of a mayor, and even their congressmen. Before long, Gibb was back in his usual spot.

After talking to Gibb about the possibility of more snow the next day, I headed down the street to the Blue Bean Coffee Shop and Bakery, stomping my boots clean before going inside, happy as a kid on a snow day. After our usual early morning coffee date, Charlie and I are headed up to the local ski area to hit the slopes. I'm so excited!

But Charlie? Not so much.

"Remind me again," he growled as I came in the door and pulled off my gloves, "why it is we're going to go out in the freezing cold, strap two pieces of wood on our feet, and then plummet down a mountain until we reach the bottom, fall, or run into a tree? If we wanted to kill ourselves, wouldn't it just be easier to take off all our clothes, roll around in the snow, and wait for frostbite to set in?"

"Good morning, sunshine," I chirped and leaned over to kiss the top of his head. "Nice to see you too. Did you order my coffee yet?"

He shook his head. I looked over at Cindy, who was standing by a table, filling the sugar dispenser. "Can I have my usual?"

"Large skim latte coming right up, Evelyn. You want an English muffin with that too?"

"Hmm." I eyed the goodies behind the bakery counter. "Can I have one of those maple scones instead? And some butter? I can afford a few extra calories today. Charlie and I are going skiing."

Cindy grinned and screwed the top back on the sugar dispenser. "So I heard. He's been sitting here for ten minutes griping about it. I don't mind, though. When my husband gripes, it sounds like a band saw cutting through a piece of alder, but when Charlie gripes, it sounds elevated, almost musical. There's just something about that brogue. Everything he says sounds like poetry. It's that gift of gab, that's what. All the Irish have it. Charlie, Robbie Burns, and all the rest."

Charlie rolled his eyes. "Robert Burns was Scottish."

"Really?" Cindy deadpanned. "Well, in that case, I take back what I said before. You do sound like a band saw cutting through alder."

"Don't you have some muffins to burn or something? Where's Evelyn's coffee?"

Cindy winked at me and headed off to the espresso machine.

"I wasn't griping," Charlie declared after she left. "I was just pointing out the inherent dangers of the sport and wondering aloud how I let you talk me into this."

I pulled up a chair and sat down next to Charlie. "Stop fussing. It'll be fun and you know it. Besides, you were the one who said we should learn each other's hobbies, that it would bring us closer as a couple."

"Yes, but that was before I realized how dangerous your hobbies were. What I had in mind was *you* hanging around the kitchen with me, learning how not to over-poach a salmon, or you snuggling next to me on the sofa while we watch the complete James Bond film collection on DVD, or you taking up my interest in massage—"

"I didn't know you knew how to give massages."

"Strictly speaking, I don't. But I'm deeply interested in getting them. Now, if you'd just learn how—"

I clunked him on the head with a wet glove. "Very funny. So when you laid out your grand plan for us exploring each other's hobbies, what you really meant was *me* doing the things that interest *you?*"

"Not entirely. I reckoned you'd want me to try my hand at quilting, and I was willing to give it a shot. But once you saw how hopeless I was, I figured we could leave off and turn our attention to more interesting interests."

"In other words, *your* interests."

"Just so."

I put my elbow on the table and rested my chin in my palm. Cindy was right. Charlie did have the gift of gab, or at least the gift of repartee. He always kept me smiling. "You're a mess, you know that?"

"Yes," he said seriously and slurped his coffee. "You're not the first to point that out. So what do you say? Shall we go back to my house—or yours, I'm not particular—and work on our massage technique? I don't have any massage oil just now, but olive oil would serve, don't you think?"

"Sure, it would, if I wanted to smell like a Caesar salad *and* if I wanted to skip the ski date you promised me. Unfortunately for you, I don't want to do either of those things. Man up, Charlie. We are going skiing. You'll love it."

He groaned. "No, I won't. I'm an Irishman. We're more cerebral than physical, at least I am. The only sport I really enjoy is horse racing, and by that I mean betting on horses, not riding them. However," he sighed, "a deal's a deal. If you want me to ski, I'll ski. Not happily, but I'll do it."

"Good. We've got a beginner's lesson scheduled for ten-thirty. That leaves us plenty of time to eat and get to the mountain. Do you want to drive or shall I?"

"I will. I'm parked behind the Grill. Beginner's lesson? I thought you said you'd skied before."

"I have. Often. Mother and I used to go skiing every winter. She was really good," I said wistfully, remembering how trim and athletic she used to look in her tight black ski pants and bright blue parka, a white knitted headband holding back her thick mane of brown hair. In her day, my mother had been an expert skier and gave me my first lessons.

I remember how, when I was little, her arms wrapped strong around mine and how my skis were sandwiched between hers as she helped me catch hold of the rope tow that pulled us to the top of the bunny hill. In my mind, I can see her gliding down that gentle slope, effortlessly carving a path of wide, arcing turns across the mountain and calling back encouragements to me as I tried, haltingly and with considerably more effort, to follow. When I was older, we used to race to the bottom of the intermediate hill. Sometimes she would win and sometimes I would, though now I suspect that when I won, it was because she'd let me.

What a long time ago that was. How young, how strong, how agile she'd been back then.

She still lived in De Pere, Wisconsin, in the little house I'd grown up in and that she'd refused to leave when my father was killed in a car accident eleven years ago. I talk to her every Sunday night. She's as sharp and funny as ever, still my mother, but her voice is weaker now and sometimes sad. It seems she has less and less news to report every week, and when she does, it's usually news of another friend who has fallen ill or passed on.

Mother was one of the founding members of her church altar guild. They'd started with eight women, eight close friends who, like my mother, were experts with a needle and enjoyed serving the church by sewing new altar cloths, making needlepoint cushions for the kneelers, and keeping the church linens clean and in good repair. There are only two of those original eight left.

"Evelyn? Hello, Evelyn?" Charlie waved a hand in front of my face. "Anybody in there?"

"Oh, sorry, Charlie. I was just thinking about . . . nothing. Anyway," I said, shaking myself out of my reverie, "it's been a long time since I strapped on a pair of skis. It won't hurt me to have a refresher. Trust me, Charlie. You'll be fine. And I'll be with you the whole time. I imagine we'll both be on the bunny slopes for a while."

Cindy returned carrying my latte and a plate with two warm maple scones dripping with butter. "I heated them up for you. They're good like that. Brought an extra one, just in case. If you're going skiing, Charlie, you need to eat a good breakfast."

Charlie took a bite of the warm scone and moaned with pleasure. "Mmm," he said with his mouth full. "This might just be worth the pain of the ankle I'm about to break. Thanks, Cindy."

"You're welcome." She wiped invisible crumbs off the table and went back into the kitchen.

"So," Charlie said to me as he broke off another piece of scone, "what have you been up to? Everything fine at the shop?"

I nodded and took a sip of coffee. "Yes. Business has slowed, but that's all right. We had such a good fall. And online sales are still very strong. Margot and Garrett think we ought to create a catalog."

"Oh? How is Garrett, anyway? I haven't seen him around lately."

"He was in New York. He took Liza out for a very fancy night on the town on New Year's Eve. Dinner and dancing at the Carlyle."

Charlie's eyes sparked like two live wires. He leaned toward me, pushing his stomach against the hard table edge. "Really? Why didn't you tell me before? Did they have the red snapper with the truffled sunchoke mousseline? Or the rack of lamb with the eggplant cannelloni?"

People say that if you want to find success in life, you should follow your passions, do what you love. That's why I opened up Cobbled Court Quilts, because quilting is my passion.

For Charlie, it's food—buying it, cooking it, plating it, selling it, and making sure that it is offered and enjoyed in pleasant, relaxed, and elegant surroundings that make the simple act of eating an experience to be savored, an event that underscores the goodness of life. As sole proprietor of the Grill on the Green, New Bern's finest restaurant, Charlie has definitely found his niche and everyone in town has benefited. After all, there aren't many towns this size that have a restaurant to rival the best eateries in Manhattan. Even if I wasn't in love with Charlie, I'd love living just a short walk from a restaurant as good as the Grill on the Green.

But that doesn't mean I totally understand Charlie's devotion to food, the way his face lights up when discussing anything to do with recipes or menus. But then, he doesn't totally understand how I can get positively giddy over a new quilt pattern or why, though I already have more bolts of cloth on order than floor space to display them, I can never resist ordering just a few more. In our own weird way, I guess we're birds of a feather.

"Of course," he continued excitedly, "the Dover sole braised in champagne is excellent too—their signature dish—but, for my money, I'll take the snapper. Simply out of this world!" Charlie looked at me expectantly, waiting for a soup-to-nuts report on Garrett's dinner.

"I'm sorry, sweetie, but he really didn't say what they had."

Charlie reared back aghast, his face a mask of disbelief. "Seriously? New Year's Eve at the Carlyle, and Garrett didn't say anything about what they ate? There was probably a special offering for the occasion. Didn't he bring home the menu?"

"I don't think so."

Charlie sighed his disappointment. "Incredible."

"But that's my point," I said. "He barely said anything about the whole evening. That's not like him at all. Do you think something could have gone wrong between him and Liza? I know they're crazy about each other, but they're still so young . . ."

"Not so young. Garrett's twenty-six."

"But Liza's only twenty-two. And not an especially mature twenty-two. Don't get me wrong. I love Liza. She's like a daughter to me. But she still has a lot of growing up to do."

"Well, don't we all. Anyway, I think growing up is highly overrated. I've been giving it some thought lately and have decided against it." Charlie winked, trying to jolly me out of my mood.

"Quit worrying," he said. "I'm sure Garrett is just fine. If he wasn't, then he'd tell you, wouldn't he? You and Garrett are so close. Probably he's just tired after staying up half the night. Or maybe it's just the post-holiday letdown."

"Maybe."

Charlie opened an extra packet of sugar and poured it into his coffee. He likes it sweet. "So, do you think you're going to do it?"

"Hmm? Do what?"

"Start a catalog like Garrett and Margot suggested. It's not a bad idea."

I picked up my scone, broke it into four roughly equal pieces, and laid them at the north, south, east, and western points of the plate, making sure there was an equal expanse of space between each piece. It's an old habit. When I'm thinking, arranging objects into symmetrical patterns helps me focus. Even when I'm not quilting, I'm still quilting.

"Evelyn?" Charlie ducked his head down so his face intersected my field of vision. "The catalog?"

I jumped, a little startled to see his eyes so close to mine. "What?"

"I see Garrett isn't the only one who's distracted." He reached across the table and took my hand. "What's the matter? When you came in here you were all smiles, couldn't wait to hit the slopes. Now you're a million miles away. Did I say something to upset you? I was just teasing before. I'm happy to go skiing with you. I'm happy to go anywhere with you. If you wanted, I'd follow you to Siberia and back. You know that."

I lifted my hand from the table and Charlie's along with it and planted a kiss on one of his big knuckles. "I know. It's not that. I was just thinking about my mom, that's all."

"Virginia? What's wrong with her?"

Charlie has never met my mother, but they've spoken on the telephone. He likes her, and the feeling is mutual. Charlie knows how to make Mom laugh, and she thinks his Irish accent is adorable. Plus, he sent her a batch of homemade almond brittle for Christmas. That clinched the deal. She's been a Charlie fan ever since.

"You talked to her yesterday, didn't you?" Charlie's forehead creased with concern. "Is she all right?"

"She's fine. It's just that I was sitting here thinking about how we used to go skiing together. It's sad to think that she can't do things like that anymore, you know? I talk to her every week and she's always so glad to hear from me, but she sounds a little down." I sighed. "I always thought I wanted to live to be an old, old woman, but now I'm not so sure. It must be awful to see the people you care about die—first Dad, and now her friends. It must feel so lonely."

"True, but she's not alone. She's got family. You and Garrett. And she has a sister, too, doesn't she?"

I nodded. "Aunt Sylvia, yes, but she moved to California seven years ago. The winters got to be too much for her. They talk on the phone pretty often, but it's not the same, I'm sure."

"No. I'm sure," he agreed.

"I just hate to think of Mom being all alone with no one to talk to. When I moved to New Bern, I suggested she think about moving out here, but she wouldn't even consider it. Said she was perfectly capable of taking care of herself, thank you very much, and that she had no intention of moving halfway across the country at her age." I smiled to myself. She might be slowing down a bit, but Mom was just as opinionated as ever.

"How old is Virginia?"

"She just turned eighty."

"Eighty." Charlie clicked his tongue, impressed by the figure. "She sounds great for eighty. Say," he said, peering longingly at the last two pieces of scone I'd left on my plate, "are you going to finish that?"

"Go ahead."

"How long has it been since you've seen your mom? More than a year?"

I nodded. The years since my divorce have been so crazy. What with opening a new business and then dealing with breast cancer and my subsequent mastectomies, I'd barely had a chance to take a weekend at the beach, let alone get to Wisconsin. Mom never complained, but it had been far too long since I'd gone home.

"Why don't you hop on a plane and go out there?" Charlie said. "Business is slow right now. Margot and Garrett can keep an eye on the shop."

He had a point. This was the perfect time of year to go visiting. Of course, I'd have to call Mom and make sure I wasn't interrupting her plans, but somehow I doubted she'd have much on her calendar. It would be nice to spend some time with her, and it would give me a chance to see how she was getting along.

"You know," I said, brightening, "that's a good idea. I'll get on the computer later and see about booking a flight."

"Good! You need a break and Virginia will be glad to see you, I'm sure. And it'll be fun for you to visit your old hometown. Just promise me not to go falling in love with any of your old high school flames while you're out there."

"Not a chance of that happening." I laughed. "I went to my twentieth high school reunion and trust me, Charlie, you've got nothing to worry about. You're more and less of a man than any of those guys."

"More and *less?*" He frowned. "What's that supposed to mean?"

"It means that you've got more hair and less beer belly than any of the boys I went to high school with. And besides," I said as I crumpled up my paper napkin and laid it on my now empty plate, "there's not a one of them who knows how to make duck confit or macadamia butterscotch cookies like you do."

Charlie narrowed his eyes and nodded. "Oh, so that's how it is with you. You're just like all the others. You only love me for my cooking."

"Oh, no, Charlie Donnelly. That's not so. You're a fabulous chef, it's true. But that is only one of the many things I love about you. Though it's probably the lowest on a long list of very fine qualities you possess. There's not a man I know who can hold a candle to you."

I meant it too. I've never met a man like Charlie.

Upon first acquaintance, people tend to think that Charlie is tough, a grump even. It's an image he likes to cultivate, but he's never able to pull it off for long. Anyone who spends more than a day in his presence quickly comes to realize that underneath his prickly exterior, Charlie Donnelly has a heart as soft as a bar of chocolate left in the sun, and just as sweet. I love Charlie. How could I not? And yet, though he has asked me again and again, I'm not ready to marry him.

When I was a little girl, my father used to love Frank Sinatra. Dad was a history professor at the college in our town. Sometimes, after he came home for the day, he'd put Sinatra's "Love and Marriage" on the stereo as loud as it would go and invade Mom's kitchen, demanding she dance with him. She always protested that she was too busy for his nonsense but in the end, she always gave in, dancing around the kitchen with Dad while the rice boiled over or the pork chops burned. A lot of perfectly good meals got ruined as a result of Dad's antics, but I didn't mind. It was nice to see them whirling around the linoleum floor, locked in an embrace. It gave me a sense of security and a belief that love and marriage did indeed go together, that if you had the first, the second would inevitably follow, and love was a bond that cemented people together for life.

I believed that for a long time. I believed it when I fell in love and married Rob Dixon, and I continued to believe it through the ups and downs of twenty-four years of marriage. I believed it until the day my divorce papers were finalized.

I don't believe it anymore. I wish I still could.

The last few years have been simultaneously wonderful and terrible for me.

On the terrible side, I lost my husband, my home, and my health. On the wonderful side, I regained my health and found a new home and new friendships, the kind of friendships I never would have believed existed before I came to New Bern. I've recaptured the dreams of my youth, opening a successful business that brings me incredible satisfaction. And, most astounding of all, I've found love again.

I love Charlie, I do. But I'm not ready to marry him.

Life can be tough, and I've got the scars to prove it. Some of them are healed and some of them, like the scars of betrayal from my failed marriage, are still raw. I told Charlie that from the very first and he said he understood, that he was willing to wait as long as he had to. But after all this time, his patience is beginning to wear thin.

Charlie started to speak, but I interrupted him.

"And don't go asking me to name all those fine qualities you possess, Charlie. I won't do it," I said breezily, deliberately trying to distract him. "Because, as we both know, humility is *not* on the list. I'm not going to say anything that will make that ego of yours any more bloated than it already is." I forced a grin.

Charlie's eyes searched my face for a moment, wondering if he should call my bluff and demand an answer to the unasked question I was so bent on ignoring. The smile faded from my face.

Don't do it. Please, Charlie. Don't ask me. Not today.

He rubbed his fingers across the ridge of his jaw, the way he does when he's decided to change the subject, and put his fork down next to his plate.

"All right, then," he said. "If you won't tell me, then you won't. But you'd think that, every now and again, you might throw a fellow a bone. Just to keep his spirits up."

"Well, if you insist," I said with a smile, relieved to be treading on less serious ground. "In addition to the other qualities I mentioned . . ."

He pushed back his chair and got up from the table. I did the same. "You mean my duck confit, the absence of bald spots on my handsome head, and my trim physique?" He sucked in his stomach.

"Yes. In addition to that, you're an adventurous soul. Always ready to try new things. Sports in particular."

"Ha!" He laughed loudly and genuinely, and the tension between us dissipated, at least for the moment.

"Don't you try that on with me, Evelyn. I know your game. Flattery will get you nowhere. I said I'll go skiing with you, but don't expect me to enjoy it, all right?"

"All right."

Charlie dug some bills out of his wallet and left them on the table next to the check. I put on my gloves and stood by the door, waiting for him.

"Sure you wouldn't rather give the massage a try? Last chance."

"Make that no chance, Charlie. But I'll make you a deal. After we finish with our lesson and make a few runs, we can go back to my place. I'll make you some dinner and then afterward, if you're nice, I'll rub your sore muscles."

Charlie's face brightened. "Really?"

"Really."

"And you've got massage oil at your place? Or should we stop by the Grill and pick up my bottle of olive oil?" He raised and lowered his eyebrows suggestively and I laughed.

"Not that kind of massage, Charlie. I was thinking about something more in the way of a rubdown with some Bengay."

"Bengay? That sticky goo that smells like horse liniment?"

I nodded. Charlie walked over to me and put his arm around my waist.

"Oh well. It's not exactly what I had in mind, but I guess a fellow has to settle for what he can get. Come, my little snow bunny. Let's hit the slopes."

4

Liza Burgess

I rested my chin in my hand and stared, unseeing, at the faux woodgrain wall of the library study carrel, thinking, hitting the mental replay button on Zoe's tirade yet again.

"OMG, Liza! Are you kidding? You just turned twenty-two! Why would you want to tie yourself down like that now? Or ever? Marriage is a trap! A lure and snare instituted by men to ensure themselves a lifetime supply of sex! All men are misogynists, bent on forcing women into narrow roles of gender and . . ."

But what does Zoe know about it? She's had six boyfriends in the last two years. She's no expert on love and marriage. Why did I even bother to ask her?

I was so absorbed in my thoughts that at first, I didn't hear the soft tap-tapping of knuckles on the laminate wall.

"Liza?" I felt the gentle pressure of a hand on my shoulder. "Liza, are you all right?"

I looked up, startled to see Professor Williams standing over me. The fluorescent library light beamed through the unkempt tendrils of her brown curls, framing her face like a halo.

"Oh! Hi, Professor. I'm just trying to finish up the last of the research so you can have it before classes start."

She nodded. "I wondered. I walked by here a half hour ago and you were sitting in that exact same position, reading that exact same article." She leaned down to take a closer look at the magazine. "You're still on the same page. It's either so interesting you wanted to read it again, or so complicated you *have* to read it again, or you're distracted and thinking about something else. I'm putting my money on door number three."

"Guess I've got some things on my mind. Sorry. I'll get back to work." I turned to the next page of the article, but Professor Williams reached down and picked up the magazine before I could begin.

She laughed. "Liza, don't bother with it. Not right now. You've been working day and night on this. I think you need a break. Besides," she said, squinting as she scanned the page, "we won't need this one anyway. The Katzenburg essay makes the same point . . ." She paused to read a bit more. "And much more succinctly."

She made a disgusted face and mumbled to herself as she continued reading, "What a pompous blowhard this guy is.

"No," she said with a definitive shake of the head that set her curls bouncing, "we can do without this article. The Katzenburg is far superior. Not to *mention* that file of *personal* correspondence between Greenberg and Pollock you found in the museum archives. *That* was an incredible find, Liza! It's absolutely going to make this paper come to *life!*"

Professor Williams had a way of speaking, emphasizing certain words so that it was impossible to miss her meaning, like an anchorwoman reading the day's headlines. She was smart, thoughtful, and wildly enthusiastic about art history. And her enthusiasm was contagious. I'd taken other art history classes in the past and could take it or leave it, but Professor Williams's course had really piqued my interest in the subject.

When she asked if I wanted to be her research assistant, I didn't need to think two seconds before saying yes. The idea that I might actually be able to help her with something as important as researching a paper for publication was incredibly exciting. The more I study art history and the struggles of other artists, people whose work was never appreciated in their own lifetimes, the more I'm aware that I could spend my whole life painting and not know even the barest glint of success. I guess that's part of why I was so charged about the idea of researching for Professor Williams. Maybe I'll never be a well-known artist, but if I help her with this paper, at least I'll have accomplished something in the world of art.

"Really, Liza. Put away your work. It's so beautiful outside—cold and clear, and the sun is beating down on the snow so it glitters. You shouldn't be cooped up in the library on a day like this. That's the realm of dusty, musty old art historians, like me, not vibrant, young artists like yourself. You should be outside, seeking inspiration, searching for the muse. If you're going to be cooped up somewhere, it should be in an art studio, *doing* art, not reading about it. This is in my best interest as well as yours. After all, if young, creative people like you don't go out and *make* art, then what will dusty, musty old art historians like me have to write *about* art? Hmm? I'd be out of a job in five minutes."

I grinned and reached for the magazine. "All right," I conceded. "Let me just finish the notes on this article. I know it's not as good as the Katzenburg, but you might want it as backup later. Then I'll knock off for the day. I promise."

"Nope," she said and folded the magazine in half before tucking it under her arm. "I mean it. No more research today. In fact, no more research for the rest of the weekend. Go do something fun. You should get some rest and relaxation before classes start again."

"Are you sure?" I asked doubtfully.

"Yes. I am *sure*. In fact, I've rented a car and am heading out for the weekend myself, off to the Berkshires. I'm going to work on the outline for the paper and get in a little skiing while I'm at it. There's a lovely B and B in Lenox that I like to stay in for a few days every January. The eggs Benedict *alone* is worth the drive. That's what I came to talk to you about. You're from New Bern, aren't you? If you'd like to go home for the weekend, I can give you a lift. It's right on my way."

"Really? That would be great! I'll need a little time to get my things together. When are you leaving?"

"Not until one. Can you be ready by then?"

"Absolutely."

5

Liza Burgess

I clutched the armrest so hard that my knuckles literally went white.

Keeping a car in Manhattan is expensive. People pay hundreds of dollars to rent a monthly parking space. But public transportation is cheap and convenient, so a lot of New Yorkers don't own a car, they just rent them occasionally. Because of that, sometimes their driving skills get a little rusty. Professor Williams's certainly were.

As we headed north on the interstate toward Connecticut at a whopping thirty-nine miles an hour, blocking the way of every road-raging, horn-honking tailgater on the island of Manhattan, Professor Williams informed me she'd been so immersed in writing her paper that she hadn't been out of the city since October. My guess is that was also the last time she'd been behind a wheel. I glanced in the rearview mirror to see yet another driver barreling toward us, laying on the horn and making emphatic and meaningful gestures. Professor Williams seemed completely oblivious to the havoc she was causing and marched along to the funereal beat of her own drummer.

At that speed, the trip to New Bern would likely take two hours longer than it would have by train. But at that point, I was just hoping we'd get there in one piece. I mentally murmured a prayer, requesting the presence of a few guardian angels, and forced myself to look away from the mirror.

"I *wish* I could get out of town more often," the professor said as the blue Prius that had been tailgating us a moment before found an opening and sped around us, horn blasting. "You go to New Bern almost every weekend, don't you? To see your aunt?"

"And my boyfriend," I said, consciously loosening my grip on the armrest. "And my quilt circle."

"Oh, that's *right!* I remember that wonderful textile piece you had hanging in the student gallery. The quilted jellyfish. Beautiful piece, Liza. *Inspired.* Were you always a quilter?"

"Well, yes and no. I was always interested in textile as a medium, but I didn't really learn to quilt until a couple of years ago, when I moved in with my aunt. That's when I started to understand why textiles had such appeal to me. I mean, as far as color, you can do things with fabrics that you really can't do with paint—you can arrange and rearrange the fabrics and colors so easily. For me, it's like the difference between editing a paper on a typewriter versus a computer. It makes everything simpler. And in the process, you can experiment with subtle shifts in mood and voice. Changing even one color can alter the whole mood and composition of a quilt. And then there's the quilting itself. The threads you use, the direction and length and frequency of the stitches, make an enormous difference in the finished piece. It's subtle, you know? Kind of like the difference that various brushes or strokes have on the texture of an oil painting. But," I said with a shrug, suddenly conscious of how long I'd been talking, "like I said, it's subtle."

Professor Williams nodded intently as I spoke. That's one of the things I like about her: She has a way of making you feel that she's really interested in you. Or, as she would put it, *deeply* interested.

"So you took up quilting as a means of *informing* your art, bringing your work onto a wider plain."

"No." I laughed. "I started quilting out of revenge. Well, not completely but mostly."

Professor Williams glanced at me, clearly confused, which was understandable.

When I showed up at Cobbled Court Quilts for the first time—to make a block during a Quilt Pink event to benefit breast cancer research, the disease that took my mother's life—my motivation was almost entirely centered on vengeance, on humiliating Aunt Abigail and punishing her for neglecting my mother even when she lay in the hospital dying. I wasn't interested in quilting. I wasn't even that interested in helping raise money for breast cancer research. I was interested in forcing Abigail to face up to what she'd done—and not done—so much so that I blackmailed her. I gave her a choice: Either come to the Quilt Pink event with me, or I'd tattoo our shared last name on my neck in huge gothic letters and parade around New Bern letting everyone know we were related.

Sounds crazy, I know, but I'd have done it. I was that angry with her. Thank heaven Abigail agreed to my demands. If not, I'd have had to go through life with the world's ugliest tattoo. If Abigail were a little less concerned about her social standing, the whole thing could have gone horribly wrong.

As it was, things worked out pretty well. Not that we just sat down together, made a quilt block, and all was suddenly forgiven. Not even close. It took a lot of time, pain, misjudgments, and misunderstandings on both our parts before Abigail and I were able to mend our broken relationship. It's a process, one we're still working through, but it started on that day when Abigail and I first walked into Cobbled Court Quilts.

"It's a long story," I said, waving off the questions I could see formulating in Professor Williams's mind, "and way too complicated to explain but, well . . . let's just say that my aunt Abigail and I share a few of the less admirable Burgess family traits, like a tendency toward stubbornness and a deep-seated certainty that we are always right."

The professor smiled. "You know, I've got an aunt Abigail, a great-aunt, on my father's side, and she's just the same. Maybe there's something about the name. But, Liza, you don't *seem* like that sort of person at all. Not to me."

"Thanks. I don't think I'm as bad as I used to be. At least I hope not. I was a pretty angry kid."

"And now?"

"Not as much. There are still moments. I miss my mom. It makes me mad that she's not here. Sometimes, when my roommates gripe about their mothers, I just want to smack 'em. They don't realize what it's like to have to go through life without one."

As always happens when I talk about my mother, I felt a catch in my throat. I changed the subject, not wanting to tear up in front of the professor. Why was I telling her all this stuff, anyway? I didn't want her feeling sorry for me.

"But I'm lucky in lots of ways," I said breezily. "There are a few advantages to being an orphan. I mean, my girlfriends are stuck with their families, but I got to pick mine."

"Your quilt circle, yes?" the professor asked, reaching down and flicking on her turn signal a good mile before we had to take the exit to I-84. Unfortunately, her blinker was signaling in the wrong direction.

Glancing up in the mirror again, I saw that there were five cars piled up behind us. The nearest one had pulled so close I could see the outgrowth of gray roots in the female driver's brown dye job and the infuriated movement of her lips as she told Professor Williams exactly what she thought about her driving skills.

"I find that fascinating," she continued, ignoring the cacophony of honking horns. "Tell me more about—"

"Um. Professor? The drivers behind us seem a little frustrated. I think they think you're going to move over to the left. You've got the wrong signal on."

"Do I? Is *that* what all that noise is about?" she asked, making no move to correct her mistake. "People shouldn't get so worked up about driving. It's not the *destination* that matters, it's the *journey*. I know it's a cliché to say people should stop and smell the roses, but they *should*. Life is *short,* Liza."

She tapped the brake, decreasing her speed to twenty-six miles per hour as she slowly navigated the exit ramp, smelling every rose along the way. The lady behind us started gesticulating wildly.

I looked away from the mirror and slunk down in my seat.

"Now. Tell me more about your quilt circle. Your aunt Abigail and the others. Do you have much in common? Are there other women near your age?"

"I'm the youngest. Ivy is a few years older than me. Margot is in her late thirties. Evelyn is around fifty. Aunt Abigail is sixty-five, but she looks ten years younger." I smiled, thinking about what an unlikely group we made. "We're all women and we all like to quilt. Other than that, we're about as different as we could possibly be. All you have to do is take one look at our quilts to know that."

"Really?"

"Really. For example, usually, we each work on our own individual projects, but once, just for fun, we all decided to make a sampler quilt. We picked out nine blocks, the same nine for everyone, but when the quilts were done, they all looked completely different. We chose different colors, fabrics, and bindings, and we set them differently and quilted them differently. The same nine blocks, but they resulted in five totally unique quilts."

"*Fascinating.*"

I looked over at the professor. Her eyes were glittering and her expression was interested, *deeply* interested. I knew that look.

"Professor, are you sitting there thinking up a topic for a new research paper?"

"Well, why not? Quilting *is* an art form, one of the first that was considered acceptable for women. And I find the communal nature of it just fascinating. I can't think of another studio art form that fosters such community participation in the creative process. Most artists create in solitude. For many, that solitude is an absolute requirement. So what makes quilting *different?* How and why did it evolve to become a communal art?

"But," she said, "you're right. I can't even *think* of tackling new research until I've finished this paper. However, I really am interested in knowing more about your relationships with the other women in your quilt circle. You truly think of them as family?"

"I do. They care about me. Watch out for me. Put up with me. And when I need advice, they are the people I ask. Of course," I laughed, "I usually get four different opinions, but somewhere in there I can usually find something that helps. That's one of the reasons I wanted to come home this weekend."

"You need advice?" The professor turned her head to look at me.

I hesitated before answering. Professor Williams was my favorite teacher, but we didn't know each other well. I wasn't sure it was smart to tell her the truth about Garrett's proposal. On the other hand, I wasn't sure it was a smart idea to tell the quilt circle the truth, either. The last thing I wanted was to tip Abigail off about any potential engagement, and I didn't want Evelyn to know either.

Abigail is family, but when I need good, solid, unbiased advice, Evelyn is the one I turn to. Everybody in the Cobbled Court Quilt Circle is . . . well, a little frayed at the edges. I mean, nobody's perfect. But Evelyn is a little more put together than the rest of us. Wiser, I guess. If she weren't Garrett's mother, she'd be the first person I'd ask for advice. But she *is* Garrett's mother. And though we've never exactly spelled it out, there are some things Evelyn and I don't talk about. No. Make that *one* thing. Garrett. We don't talk about my relationship with Garrett. It would be pretty awkward if we did. There are just some things you don't discuss with a guy's mother. You know?

So somehow I had to figure out how to ask Evelyn, Abigail, and the others if I should marry Garrett without *actually* asking if I should marry Garrett. My encounter with Zoe had shown me the hazards of a direct approach. Though I couldn't imagine the others would be quite so rabid in their responses as Zoe had been.

Maybe if I took a sort of poll of the opinions and experiences of a bunch of different women, I could find some nugget of truth that would tell me for sure if I should marry Garrett or not. But to get accurate, honest opinions I needed to take the emotion out of the equation. Which meant I had to take me out of the equation, look at this thing from a purely logical standpoint.

"Yes," I said, finally answering her question. "I need advice about a quilt. I've been thinking about making a new one, a studio piece, entirely from wrapping materials: tin foil, waxed paper, parchment, cellophane. That kind of thing. I need their advice about the actual sewing. It'll be tricky."

This wasn't a lie. I'd been experimenting, unsuccessfully, with substituting different kinds of papers for fabrics in my art quilts. I hoped Evelyn and the others might be able to give me some tips on how to do so. The professor didn't have to know that wasn't the only sort of guidance I was seeking.

"Professor Williams . . . are you married?"

Her eyebrows arched in surprise as her head swiveled toward me and her frizzy curls jumped, as if they, too, were startled by the question. "Me? No! Why would I want to do that? And why do you ask?"

"Well . . . I, um . . . It's for a painting I'm working on. A mural. Just in the planning stages now. Just an idea I'm exploring. A mural about the evolution of marriage. I mean, is marriage even relevant for women today? Seems to me that opinions about marriage are completely different from how they were a hundred years ago."

"Oh, more recently than *that*. For my mother, marriage wasn't a question to be considered. It was just what you *did*. What *everybody* did." She turned her eyes back toward the road and was quiet for a moment before going on in a softer, more introspective tone, oddly unitalicized.

"I was asked once, when I was an undergrad at Penn State. There was a boy, Drake. He was an engineering major." She laughed quietly and shook her head. "Imagine. Me being proposed to by an engineer. We met at a peace rally. This was back during the Vietnam War, you know. He was a sweet man. Loved Vivaldi. I'd never thought an engineer would be such a music fan. He was surprising in so many ways. . . .

"Anyway, he asked me out for coffee after the rally, and the next thing I knew, we were dating. I never thought he'd propose. When he asked, I actually thought it was some kind of joke. But after a minute I realized he wasn't kidding. It was such a shock. I said no right off, almost before he'd finished asking. He got angry, hurt. Understandable, I suppose." She shrugged. "I never saw him again after. I don't know what happened to him. Probably he married someone else. He was the marrying kind."

"And you're not?"

How could she know that? At twenty, twenty-one, or twenty-two, is it possible that she absolutely knew that she wasn't the sort to marry? And the way she'd said no to Drake's proposal, even before he finished proposing, without even stopping to think about it—did that make her enlightened or narrow-minded? Was Professor Williams's refusal to consider the possibility of marriage any better than her mother's refusal to consider the possibility of not marrying?

"I never wanted to have to answer to someone else," she said. "As a single woman, my time, my life, my opinions are my own. My mother, on the other hand . . . After my father died, she couldn't even decide what to have for breakfast. Seriously. When we'd go out to eat, she couldn't make a choice, so she'd just hand the menu to me and let me order for her, just the way Dad had for all those years. My mother never had an opinion that my father didn't give her. Except perhaps about my refusing Drake's proposal. She was furious with me!

"'What were you thinking!'" the professor said in a nasally imitation of her mother. "'You're not a beautiful girl, Selena, and you've got too many ideas, too much education. That kind of thing scares men off. He might have been your only chance! You'll be alone, Selena, and lonely. For the rest of your life.'"

Professor Williams pressed her lips together. "My mother was a stupid woman. And cruel."

She'd get no argument from me on that. What an awful thing to say to your own daughter. And not just awful, but wrong. Professor Williams was beautiful. With her big brown eyes and riot of curls, she was actually kind of exotic looking. I bet lots of men found her very attractive. Not every guy is looking for a Barbie clone. If they were, Garrett would never have given me a second look. But still . . .

It was such a personal question to ask. If I hadn't needed to know so badly and she hadn't already revealed so much, I'm sure I'd never have found the guts to ask. But I did and she had.

"And . . . were you? Are you?"

"Lonely?" She puffed in disgust. "Of course I am. But so was my mother. She spent her whole life catering to my father, but he didn't have the slightest *idea* who she was. And what's worse, neither did she. I *know* who I am, Liza. At least I know *that*."

She tightened her grip on the steering wheel and stepped on the gas, taking the New Bern exit at fifty. "Yes, I'm lonely. Hell, yes, I am. Isn't everybody? Aren't you?"

6

Evelyn Dixon

"But why do you want to come?" she asked warily. "Why now?"

I paused for a moment, reminding myself to be patient, but really . . . What kind of mother greets the announcement of her child's upcoming visit with suspicion? The kind who is smart enough to realize that the visit has an agenda, that's who. Well, there was some comfort in that. Mentally, Mom was obviously as sharp as ever.

"Because I haven't seen you in a long time, that's why. And I miss you. Can't a daughter want to come visit her mother for a few days without getting the third degree? I just thought it would be nice to see you now that I have some time. It's been over a year."

"Oh. Well, in that case. It'd be nice to see you, Evie," she said, calling me by my childhood nickname. "I just wanted to make sure you weren't coming out here to check up on me. I was afraid that Mary Flynn had called you and started blabbing."

Mary Flynn has been Mother's next-door neighbor for thirty years. She moved in right after I graduated. She used to have a golden retriever, Rufus, that she let run loose. One day, Rufus ruined Mother's prize roses, dug up the whole bed. Mother was livid.

The dog died four years later and Mary had never gotten another, but that didn't make any difference to Mom. My mother, Virginia Wade, is known far and wide for her kind and charitable nature. She's one of the sweetest, most forgiving women you'd ever hope to meet, but in Mom's book there are certain infractions that simply cannot be pardoned. Letting your dog dig up her prize-winning roses just a week before she was due to defend her title at the county fair was one of them.

"Why would Mary be blabbing? What happened?"

"Nothing. Nothing at all. Mary doesn't need a reason to blab. She just does it. The woman's a terrible gossip. So if she called and told you about me falling, you can just tell her . . ."

"Falling? Mom, you fell? When? Where? Are you all right?"

"Well, of course, I'm all right!" she snapped. "I'm talking to you on the telephone, aren't I?"

"Okay. All right. Good," I said, purposely adopting a calm tone. "But tell me what happened. How did you fall?"

"It was nothing. I was going out to get the paper and slipped on a patch of ice, that's all. Mary saw me and came running, yelling for Tom Pearson to leave off shoveling his sidewalk and help me up. Lot of fuss over nothing," she groused. "It's not like I've never fallen before. It's January, the walks are icy. This is Wisconsin, for heaven's sake! In January, in Wisconsin, people fall! There's no need to go calling a person's daughter about it! Mary Flynn should just mind her own darned business. And you can tell her I said so!"

"Mom, calm down. Mary didn't call me. Really."

"Sorry, Evie. I didn't mean to snap. I'm just annoyed with myself for falling, especially in front of Mary and Tom. It's hard getting old, Evie. Having people think you can't manage things on your own. People fall all the time, but if you fall and you're eighty, everybody thinks it's because you're losing your marbles. I am not losing my marbles. I was just too lazy to go to the basement and bring up the rock salt. Stupid. I *know* the ice always collects in that one spot. I should have tossed out the salt before going to get the paper."

"But you're feeling fine now?" I asked.

"Yes. I am. And if you'd like to come out for a visit, I'll feel even better. It would be nice to see you, sweetheart. Saturday, did you say? Shall I pick you up at the airport?"

"Yes, Saturday. About six o'clock. Don't worry about picking me up. I'll get a cab to the house. I'm looking forward to it."

"Me too, Evie. I've missed you."

7

Evelyn Dixon

I come from what my dad called "good, hardworking Midwestern stock," and it's true. I've always worked.

My first job was in my mother's garden, ten weeds for a penny, then babysitting for the neighbors, fifty cents an hour, and, once I was old enough to get a work permit, waitressing at Gino's Pizzeria, minimum wage and all the pizza I could eat, which was my idea of heaven.

For the first two weeks I worked at Gino's I single-handedly ate an entire pepperoni pizza every single day—this was back in those wonderful bygone days when I could eat anything and never gain an ounce. At fifteen, I had the metabolism of a wolverine. But by the third week, I was down to a couple of slices a day, and by the end of the summer, you couldn't have paid me to eat a piece of pizza.

That experience led me to formulate Gino's Law, which states that overexposure to objects once considered desirable will eventually lead you to regard them with disgust and loathing. Gino's Law applies to almost everything—pizza, pistachio ice cream, certain men—but it does *not* apply to quilting. At least, not for me.

After spending my days ordering fabric, racking fabric, cutting fabric, and selling fabric, and spending my nights sewing quilt samples for the shop and teaching quilting classes, Gino's Law would dictate that the last way I'd want to spend my none-too-plentiful free time is quilting and fussing with fabric, but it's not.

Friday night, quilt circle night, is my favorite night of the week. As soon as I turn the Closed sign face out, I can't wait to climb the stairs to the big, open workshop where we hold our weekly meeting of the Cobbled Court Quilt Circle. This is the time when I get to kick back and relax in the way that seems most natural to me: with a number ten needle pinched between the thumb and index finger of my right hand, a pair of thread snips looped on a ribbon around my neck, and a glass of good red wine sitting close at hand, surrounded by a pleasant buzz of female voices as my best friends talk about whatever's on their minds at the moment. The questions under discussion on any given night can range from the inconsequential (Does drinking diet soda actually make you gain weight?) to the profound (Is there any real hope for a lasting Middle East peace?) and everything in between.

This Friday night, my questions are unspoken and all about Mom.

How did she fall? Why didn't she tell me about it? What else hasn't she been telling me? Should she be living on her own anymore? If not, what am I going to do about it?

I won't get any answers until I get to Wisconsin tomorrow, but that doesn't stop the questions from spinning around in my mind, which is probably why I didn't hear Liza's voice at first.

"Evelyn, what do you think? Evelyn?"

"Hmm?" I looked up from my stitching to see four pairs of eyes on me, obviously waiting for some kind of response. "What?"

Abigail was standing at the ironing board, pressing the seams of a table runner. "Haven't you been listening?" She pressed her lips together to signal her disapproval. "We've been discussing this for the last twenty minutes."

"I'm sorry. Guess I was concentrating on my quilting," I said and then casually moved my hand, trying to cover the section of the quilt I'd been working on.

One look at my uncharacteristically long and uneven stitches and they'd realize that I'd been a million miles away. Not that I have any compunctions about discussing my problems with the others, but I wasn't ready for their advice just yet. Not until I had a chance to spend some time with Mom and see how she was doing.

Abigail craned her neck, peering at my stitches, and then raised an eyebrow. "Concentrating on your quilting? Hmm. More like thinking about your vacation. I highly approve of you taking some time off, Evelyn, but really . . ."

Her second eyebrow lifted to join its partner. "Wisconsin in January? Why not Miami? Or Bermuda? Somewhere you can thaw out a little, take Charlie along, lie on a beach and drink cocktails out of coconuts with little paper umbrellas sticking out of them. You could use my condo at Hilton Head if you wanted to. Why don't you call Charlie, tell him there's been a change of plans, and book two tickets? I can call my travel agent."

"That's very generous of you, Abigail. Maybe another time. Now, what were we talking about?"

"Liza is planning a new painting, a mural, about how attitudes toward marriage have changed in the last century. Terribly interesting theme. An issue of profound societal importance," she said, clearly proud that Liza's artistic expression has evolved from self-portraits in rusty bottle caps to actual paintings utilizing actual paint on subjects of profound societal importance.

Abigail's eyes were gleaming. I could practically see the wheels turning in her brain as she made a mental list of everyone she knew who sat on the board of major modern art museums and tried to calculate which of them owed her the most favors and might be open to the idea of hanging Liza's mural in their gallery. Abigail has more connections than LaGuardia Airport, and she loves using them on behalf of people she cares about, especially Liza.

"Liza's taking a poll," Abigail continued. "She wants to know what you think about marriage. Is it necessary or relevant to women today?"

Liza rolled her eyes a little, pushed aside the pile of dangling shell paillettes she was sorting through—flat, buttonlike discs that she was going to use as pearly scales on the tail of a mermaid quilt she was getting ready to embellish—and got up to refill her wineglass.

"You don't need to make it quite so clinical sounding, Abigail. I'm not gathering data so much as impressions. I just want to know what everybody thinks about marriage. Abigail is all for it"—she smiled—"but what would you expect from a newlywed? So, I'm not sure her opinion is exactly reliable. And she completely glossed over her failed first marriage to Woolley Wynne. Now she's twittering about the joys of matrimony."

"I was *not* twittering," Abigail declared. "I've never twittered in my life. And I wasn't glossing over my marriage to Woolley because, quite honestly, I don't consider it a marriage, not really. Woolley and I were friends, but what we had was more like a business arrangement than a marriage. And, as a business arrangement, it was more or less successful. I never loved Woolley and he knew that. But I do love Franklin. We're very happy. My only regret is that I didn't marry him sooner."

"Like I was saying"—Liza smirked—"Abigail's viewpoint is tainted by those rose-colored glasses she's wearing. Ivy, on the other hand, thinks all men are untrustworthy and has vowed never to marry again."

"Hold on, hold on," Ivy protested. "I didn't exactly say that. Probably some men are trustworthy. Franklin and Charlie are good guys. Garrett and Arnie too. But my track record speaks for itself. I seem to be lacking the kind of internal radar that helps separate the good guys from the bums. Given my history, I think it's best to leave them all alone."

"All right, I stand corrected. Ivy concedes the point that there may be one or two decent men in the world. . . ."

"Which, for me, is a big concession," she said with a laugh.

"And Margot," Liza said, "agrees with Abigail that marriage is a wonderful institution."

"One which I will probably never experience personally." Margot sighed.

"What's the matter?" I asked. "Things aren't going well between you and Arnie?"

Arnie is one of the associates at Franklin's law firm. He and Margot have been dating for quite a while now.

"Oh, no," Margot answered. "We're fine. Arnie takes me out to dinner every Saturday night. We've gotten to be such regulars at the Grill that we don't even need a reservation. Charlie just holds a table for us. On Sundays we go to church together and then he comes over to the house. I fix breakfast. It's all very nice. But it doesn't seem to be going anywhere. Last weekend, while we were watching TV, *Four Weddings and a Funeral* came on. Arnie practically dove under the sofa cushions hunting for the remote so he could change the channel. He's obviously terrified of commitment." Margot shook her head regretfully.

"Maybe he just needs a little more time," I said.

"Maybe. But forty is getting closer and closer in my rearview mirror. More time is something I don't have a lot more of."

"Oh, don't be ridiculous," Abigail scoffed. "You've got plenty of time. I didn't marry Franklin until I was almost sixty-five."

"But you said yourself that you wished you'd done it sooner. What if Arnie never proposes? I don't dare bring up the subject. It might send him running for the door. But how long am I supposed to sit around and wait?" Margot swallowed hard, the way she did when she was trying to keep her emotions in check.

Liza wisely steered the conversation in a different direction. She carried the wine bottle around the room, making sure that everyone's glass was topped off.

"So, here's where we stand. On the question of marriage, we've got two votes for and one against. But let's face it," she said, tilting her head toward the others, "these three aren't exactly in a position to give a valid opinion. Guess it's up to you, Evelyn. After all, you're the only one in this room who's ever had any real experience with this. You were married for . . . how long was it?"

"Twenty-four years. By the time the divorce came through, it was almost twenty-five."

Liza shook her head as she topped off my glass. "Wow," she deadpanned. "That's longer than I've been alive!"

"Yeah, yeah," I said. "Don't rub it in."

"No, I mean, that's just a really long time. And then it was over." She moved her head slowly from side to side, as if she couldn't believe that so long a union had broken apart. Well, that was a fair enough response. At the time, I hadn't been able to believe it, either.

"So, was it worth it? If you had it to do all over again, would you?"

It was a good question, one I'd pondered myself from time to time. And over time, my answer had changed.

"Right after Rob left, I'd have said no. But now . . ." I paused to take a sip from my wineglass and give myself time to think.

"Garrett was a product of our marriage. There is nothing on earth, not even the quilt shop, that I value more than my son, or that has brought as much joy and meaning into my life. If I'd never married Rob, then I wouldn't have had Garrett."

"But if you'd wanted, you could have had a son without being married," Liza said. "Lots of women do now."

Margot, who was ripping apart the seams of a star block whose points hadn't met tightly enough to satisfy her, looked up and said, "If I could, I'd adopt a baby and raise it by myself, but I don't think that's the ideal situation. It's really best to raise a child in a two-parent home."

"Wait a minute!" Ivy put down the rotary cutter she'd been using and raised her hand. "I think that really depends on what two parents you're talking about. Bethany and Bobby are way better off living with me alone than they ever were living with me and Hodge."

Ivy's ex-husband, Hodge, an abuser as well as an embezzler, was in prison for his crimes and would likely remain there for many years to come.

Abigail, who was nodding her agreement, started to say something else, but Liza held up both hands and interrupted her.

"Okay, okay. We're getting off track. I want to talk about marriage. Children can be an important part of marriage, I know, but I want to get back to the original question." She turned and looked at me. "Knowing what you know now, would you have married Rob?"

"Hold on. That's not what you asked the first time. Knowing what I know now? You mean, knowing that we'd end up divorced, would I do it again? That's a silly question. When you're making that decision, you don't get to know how it will turn out. You make that decision because you're sure that it *will* work, that you and your groom will go through life together from that day forward ‘until death do us part.’ If you don’t believe that, why get married in the first place?”

Liza frowned, a little crease of doubt indenting the space between her eyebrows. “So when you got married, you truly believed that you were going to stay married to Rob forever?”

“Yes.”

“But it didn’t happen that way.”

“No”—I shrugged—“it didn’t. Lots of things in life don’t turn out the way we plan. If it had been up to me alone, I’m sure I’d still be married to Rob. When I walked down the aisle and said, ‘I do,’ I had every intention of spending the rest of my life married to Rob Dixon. The possibility of divorce never crossed my mind. Maybe that seems naïve, but that’s the way I was brought up. My mother married my dad when he was twenty-two and she was eighteen, and they were very happy for the entire fifty-one years of their marriage. It never occurred to me that it wouldn’t be exactly the same for Rob and me.”

“So, maybe you didn’t really think your marriage through as much as you should have?”

“Maybe not,” I said. “I was nineteen and in love and, in my mind, love was enough. I didn’t realize that it takes more than love to make a marriage work. A lot more. And I never figured on Rob becoming, well, someone so drastically different from the person I married.

“If you’d asked me about Rob, even up until the day before he said he wanted a divorce, I’d have said he was solid, steady, a good husband, and the last guy in the world to run off with the receptionist at his gym. I mean, he hadn’t dyed his hair, bought a sports car, nothing. I had no idea he’d fallen face first into a midlife crisis until he was going down for the third time.”

Abigail, who had long since finished pressing her seam, was standing at the ironing board, listening intently. “Is that why you won’t marry Charlie? Because you’re afraid he’ll change and end up breaking your heart? That’s the only reason I can think of for you putting him off for so long. Charlie is a wonderful man. You’re perfect for each other. When are you going to say yes to that poor, lovesick Irishman?"

"Abbie," I said pointedly, which is really the only way to deal with Abigail, "butt out. I am not going to discuss my love life with you tonight. We're supposed to be talking about Liza's painting, aren't we? If this whole discussion was cooked up with some ulterior motive . . ."

"Oh, no. Nothing like that," Liza answered immediately, and that made me suspicious. When she wasn't being truthful, Liza had a tendency to respond to questions rapidly, as if she'd prepared her answers in advance.

"Charlie didn't have anything to do with this. I'm really just interested in knowing more about people's opinions on marriage."

"Mmm," I murmured, not entirely convinced.

Liza wasn't acting like herself this evening. She was working on a third glass of cabernet, but the wine hadn't mellowed her in the least. She seemed nervous. We'd been working for nearly an hour, but she had yet to stitch a single "scale" onto the tail of her quilted mermaid. Instead she just kept sorting and re-sorting the pile of pearl-colored paillettes, moving them around like a picky toddler pushing peas around a dinner plate. Something was bothering her. On a night when I was less preoccupied with my own concerns, I might have tried to dig deeper.

"This isn't the kind of thing I can give a simple yes or no answer to, Liza. It's not that easy. I spent more than half my life with Rob. We were happy. Not all of the time, but much of it. Even now, I wouldn't want to give back a single one of those happy memories.

"But yes, when Rob told me he didn't love me anymore, that our marriage was over, I felt like my world had come to an end. In a way, it had. The end of our marriage marked the end of my life as a couple. What I didn't know at the time was that it also marked the beginning of my new life as an individual.

"It's been hard. But in many ways, I find life richer and more satisfying now than it's ever been. I've only been in New Bern a couple of years, but I actually feel more at home here than I did after twenty years in Texas. This is my home. Where I've got wonderful friends,"

I said and lifted my glass a hair to acknowledge them, "the best ever. And, if it doesn't sound too conceited to say so, I'm really proud of this shop. When I stumbled down the alley, spotted this awful, broken-down building, and decided to open a quilt shop in it, maybe one person in a hundred would have given odds on it surviving the first year."

"Oh, I don't think the odds were nearly that good," Abigail said with a smile. "More like one in a thousand."

"You're probably right. But," I said, "they were wrong! All of them. I *did* survive that first year and the next and the next one after that. I didn't do it alone, of course. Without all of you, I'd have closed in six months. But I did have all of you, and Cobbled Court Quilts became what I always hoped it could be: a real community, a place where people make friends, and are friends, and slog their way through life arm in arm.

"Look at it now," I said, spreading my hands out to encompass every foot of this wonderful, formerly ramshackle old ruin of a building, the embodiment of my dream come true. "The oddsmakers were betting against us a thousand to one, but here we all are. Maybe that's my point. When it comes to making the big choices, the ones that really matter—falling in love, following your dreams, taking a chance—you can't just sit down and tally up the odds. If you try to make important choices based on the odds of winning and losing, you'll never make any choices at all.

"A person can think this out all they want, and they should. Carefully. *If* I ever decide to marry again," I said, giving Abigail a pointed glance, "you can bet I'll sit down and give it a lot of serious, practical thought beforehand. Much more than I did the first time. But even so, even after calculating all the pros and cons, compatibilities and differences, in the end it would involve a huge leap of faith on my part. It does for everybody. Liza, there's not a marriage in the world that comes with a gilt-edged guarantee. There never has been."

8

Liza Burgess

Garrett and I had breakfast at the Blue Bean on Saturday morning.

We drank coffee and ate bagels spread thick with cream cheese and raspberry jam, talked about how my research for Professor Williams was coming along, and the classes I would be taking next semester, and the website design business Garrett was starting on the side.

We talked about everything under the sun except the elephant in the room: Garrett's proposal and my answer.

After breakfast, we walked down Commerce Street, looking into the shop windows with the signs offering twenty percent off merchandise that hadn't sold over the holidays. This time of year the temperature in New Bern rarely rises much above twenty, but when the sun is shining, glinting a mirage of diamond dust off the snow, it feels warmer, especially if you're walking next to someone you love with his arm around your shoulders and your hand tucked into his jacket pocket because you lost one of your gloves.

For a little while, I forgot all about the elephant, the unanswered questions of life, everything except the fact that when Garrett looks at me with his huge brown eyes, I feel beautiful, and when he laughs, my heart laughs along with him. Sweet.

We strolled toward Hidden Treasures, a shop that sells old silver, china, and estate jewelry. The display window was filled with a dazzling array of diamond, emerald, ruby, and sapphire jewelry. But it was a less ostentatious piece that caught Garrett's eye, an art deco bracelet with alternating rectangles of green chalcedony and black onyx in a simple silver setting. Exactly the piece I'd have chosen if Garrett had asked me which I liked best. But he didn't have to ask. He knew me.

"I'll get it for you," he said. "Let's go in."

"Oh. No, you don't have to do that. You already got me a Christmas present and—" I stopped, suddenly aware of the silver chain around my neck and the weight of the ring that hung from it, hidden beneath the bulk of my wool sweater. "Anyway, it's probably too expensive."

"It can't hurt to ask. Besides, I can afford it. I never spend any money. New jeans twice a year, a couple of sweaters, and I'm all set. My paychecks just sit in the bank and collect dust. I should be doing more to support the local economy."

"Oh, yeah? What about your addiction to all things technogeek? Your obsessive need to own the absolutely newest model of every electronic and computer gadget on the face of the earth? Not to mention your ever-growing collection of jazz recordings from the twenties and thirties, three-dimensional puzzles, and antique baseball cards. You're a man of many hobbies. All of them expensive. Didn't you just tell me that you started storing your towels in the oven because you needed more room in the linen closet to store the puzzles?"

Garrett grinned and shrugged. "Okay. So your boyfriend's a big nerd. So what? But fortunately I'm a computer nerd, and that's the best kind—very profitable. Didn't I just tell you? I've got three new web design clients. I'm rolling in dough. Come on. Let's go inside." He lowered his arm from my shoulder to my waist and urged me toward the door of the shop.

"No, Garrett. Really. I don't need it."

"I know you don't need it, but you want it, don't you? It's perfect for you."

"No! I don't want anything else. Not right now."

My voice was emphatic, maybe a little more emphatic than I'd intended. I pulled my arm out of his grasp. The light went out of his eyes. Standing so far apart, I could suddenly feel how cold the day was.

Garrett looked at me. He didn't say anything else about the bracelet. "Do you want to have dinner tonight?"

"Can't. I really should get back to the city. I've got to finish cataloging those articles for Professor Williams. I really just came up for the quilt circle meeting. If I catch the one forty-five train out of Waterbury, I'll be back in New York by four."

Garrett nodded. "You need a ride to the station?"

"Thanks. That'd be great." My feet were cold, the chill of the snow coming up through the soles of my boots. I looked at my watch. "I'd better go back and get my stuff, say good-bye to Abigail."

"Yeah. Okay."

We turned away from the store window, crossed the street and then the Green, leaving two trails of footprints in the snow, walking side by side with a shaft of sunlight beaming through the space between us, my hands in my pockets, balled up into fists, trying to generate their own warmth.

Back in New York, I continued my survey.

I posed my questions on marriage to a woman I sat next to on the train, my landlady, the lady who runs the cash register at the mini-mart on the corner, and two reference librarians. They all said pretty much the same thing that Evelyn had said, but less eloquently: It's a big decision, love is crucial, but love isn't always enough, and, no matter what, there are no guarantees.

But I want a guarantee. I *need* a guarantee.

I lost my father before I knew I had one. And I lost my mother, the only person I was ever sure I could count on, before I was even out of high school. Unless it's happened to you, too, you can't know what it was like. I sat by her bed in that white, sterile hospital, surrounded by monitors blinking green, numbers descending as the minutes passed, watching my mother's chest rise and fall, rise and fall, rise and fall, until it didn't anymore and she was gone.

And I was still here. Abandoned, orphaned, alone, and in pain, the kind of pain that rings in your ears and seeps out your eyelids and rakes your throat and heart and insides raw. The kind of pain I never want to feel again.

I want a guarantee. Please, someone give me a guarantee.

If I ask enough people, surely I will find someone, just one person who will tell me the secret to love that never ends. I want more time. And no matter how unrealistic it may be, I want a guarantee.

But reality is Monday night and a knock on my door and Garrett standing in the hallway with his eyes that see inside me, asking if he can come in. Reality is that you can question a million people and never find the answer you want to hear.

Reality is that I love Garrett and he loves me and he doesn't want to wait any longer for an answer. Reality is that I'm afraid to put him off again, afraid that I'll lose him now because I am so afraid of losing him someday. Reality is Professor Williams's words echoing in my mind.

Of course I'm lonely. Aren't you? Isn't everybody?

And so I push down my fears, take a step back, open the door a little wider, and tell him to come inside.

9

Evelyn Dixon

"Mom, why do you keep tapping the brakes?"

"Because I want to make sure the other cars see me," she answered indignantly. "I took a defensive driving class at the community center, and the instructor said you should tap your brakes every now and then to make sure you're visible to other drivers."

"Oh," I said.

I wondered if Mom and the instructor had the same definition of "every now and then." To Mom, it seemed to mean about every twenty feet, which meant a fifteen-minute drive to the grocery store took about twice as long as it should. She's cautious. So cautious that she's a little bit dangerous.

Other drivers were impatient with her pace and following too close, probably thinking this would urge her to increase her speed, but it only made her nervous, and that made her drive even slower. A teenager following us in a green Mustang honked his horn. It rattled her so much that she didn't see the stop sign and went straight through the intersection. Fortunately, there were no other cars waiting at the four-way stop.

"Mom," I said, trying to sound casual. "Do you want me to drive?"

"No!" she snapped. "I do not. I'm perfectly capable of doing it myself. I've been driving for sixty years and I've never had an accident. . . ."

Not yet.

She shouldn't be driving, not anymore, but living alone with her only daughter hundreds of miles away, what other choice does she have?

I only arrived yesterday, so it's hard for me to know for sure exactly how things are with Mom, but I was relieved to see that she looks about the same as she did last time I came home. A little thinner, though. Her gait seemed as steady as ever. Perhaps her fall on the ice was exactly what she said, just one of those things, the hazards of living in a cold climate. It could happen to anyone at any age, right?

To celebrate my arrival, Mom made my favorite meal from childhood: T-bone steaks, a layered salad with iceberg lettuce, tomatoes, peas, bacon bits, cheddar cheese, and a thick layer of mayonnaise, plus her famous twice-baked potatoes stuffed with sour cream, more cheddar cheese, and a sprinkling of chives to make them look pretty. Dessert was homemade caramel pecan bars and vanilla ice cream.

The total cholesterol count for that meal was enough to make a cardiologist break into a cold sweat, but these were the dinners I, and everyone I knew, grew up eating. How it is possible that we ate this stuff and didn't grow up to be as fat and round as a flock of Butterball turkeys, I can't tell you, but we did. I suppose only getting three TV channels—the fuzzy picture beamed in via a set of rabbit-ear antennae—may have had something to do with it. Lacking the endless choice of electronic enticements that kids have today, my friends and I spent a good part of our time playing outside—red light, green light and kick the can in the summer, snowball fights and ice skating in the winter.

Mom and I sat at the table after supper, laughing and talking and remembering those times. She remembers so much. She told me about buying this house soon after she and Dad were married, how she was sure they'd never be able to make the payments and how, trying to think of every way she could save money, she'd served variations of cheese or tuna and noodle casseroles every night for almost two weeks until one evening Dad came home from work in a huff, slapped a paper-wrapped packet containing a five-pound rump roast on the counter, and said, "Virginia, I don't want to see another noodle on my dinner plate until the spring thaw."

He didn't, and they managed to make the mortgage payments just the same.

Mom told me all about those happy, early days in this house she was sure they couldn't afford. She told me how Snowball, the first in a series of rescue cats, just walked in the back door one day, settled herself into the sunny kitchen window, looked at Mom as if to say, "Well? Are you going to just stand there or get me a saucer of cream?" and never left. Mom was a firm believer that cats adopted their people, not the other way around. Mom's current feline resident was a very regal, very fluffy, and very spoiled tortoiseshell tomcat. Apparently, when Mom brought Petunia home from the rescue shelter, the paperwork listing gender had been in error. By the time the vet pointed this out, it was too late to change; Petunia was already used to his name. At least that's what Mom says.

With Petunia sitting on her lap, sleeping, Mom told me how she'd gone about making the old place into a home and how, in the days before strippable wallpaper, she'd spent hours and hours steaming and scraping dark, flocked papers off the walls, then repainting them herself.

"Oh, there was miles of that stuff," Mom said, shuddering at the memory. "Once I got it off, I vowed I'd never have another inch of wallpaper in my house. And I didn't, until you were born. I saw that Bo Peep paper at the hardware store and just couldn't resist."

"That's right! I'd almost forgotten about that!" I exclaimed, pouring a stream of honest-to-heaven cream into my coffee and stirring it. "The sheep were all hiding behind fences or under bushes, and there was poor Bo Peep standing there in her big pink skirt and looking confused."

Mom smiled. "You loved that paper—right until the day you turned nine and decided you were too big to have animals on your walls. So I pulled out the steamer again and took it all off."

"You spoiled me."

"A little," she said, and patted my hand affectionately. "But you turned out all right."

We sat up reminiscing for hours. When I finally climbed into bed in my now sheepless and Peepless childhood bedroom, I slept well, sure that I'd been worrying over nothing and that Mom was as capable as she'd ever been.

But when I got up the next day I started to notice things, little things, that concerned me.

Mom has always been a meticulous housekeeper. The house was still clean; there wasn't the least sign of clutter anywhere. Her collection of Hummel figurines was lined up neatly in the china hutch in exactly the same order it'd stood in since I was a girl. But there was a layer of dust on the glass shelf of the hutch. In the bathroom, I noticed that the grout between the bathroom tiles was chipping. That kind of thing would have never escaped her notice in the past. The lenses of her glasses were a little thicker than they'd been when I last saw her. I wondered if she could still see the dusty corners and neglected repairs in the old house. And, in spite of the sumptuous repast she'd cooked for me the night before, when I opened the refrigerator in the morning, the pickings inside were surprisingly thin.

The freezer held a half-eaten pint of vanilla ice cream, left over from the previous night, two microwavable chicken and rice entrees, and a package of English muffins. I pulled out two of the muffins to toast for breakfast, spreading them with homemade raspberry jam because I couldn't find any butter. After that, I checked out the cupboards. They weren't much better stocked than the refrigerator, containing only a box of wheat crackers, a half dozen cans of condensed soup, and some tomato paste.

What had she been eating?

"Oh, I just haven't been to the market," she said when I asked her later. "I wasn't sure what you'd want to eat, so I decided to hold off until we could go together."

And I guess that could be true, but when I took another look and saw how loose her pants were around the waist, I wondered.

It took a good half hour to locate the car keys. Mom finally found them in the pocket of her other coat. When we were halfway to the store she remembered that she'd left the shopping list on the kitchen counter. She wanted to go back home and get it, but I assured her that we'd be fine without it and so, like a pair of speeding turtles, we continued on our journey. We finally pulled into the parking lot of Aldi's grocery a good hour and a half after we'd decided to make the trip.

Inside the store, I was pleased to see that so many people knew Mom and were happy to see her—and me. Mr. Segers, the butcher, stood behind the meat counter in his spotless white apron and cap, just as he had when I was a teenager.

"Evelyn! Haven't seen you in a long time! How are you? How's your boy?"

"Garrett's fine. He lives in Connecticut now. Does all the computer work for my quilt shop."

"Does he? Well, isn't that something. Time sure flies, doesn't it? Last time I saw him he was just so high." He held his hand flat at a spot a little above his waist. "That was back when you and your husband came out to visit your folks in the summer. I gave him a slice of braunschweiger to try. He didn't like that at all."

The old man laughed, remembering the look on Garrett's face when he took a bite of the unknown delicacy and realized that braunschweiger had liver in it.

"It's good to see you, Evelyn. You, too, Mrs. Wade. Where've you been lately?"

"Oh, I came in just a couple of days ago," Mom said airily. "Picked up two nice T-bones. You must have been on a break."

"Must have been," he said with a nod and then clapped his hands together. "Now, what can I get for you today? We've got some nice, thick pork chops on special."

We took two pork chops, two chicken breasts, and a half pound of sliced turkey for sandwiches before heading over to the produce and dairy departments, where the various clerks expressed delight over seeing Mom, echoing the butcher's comment about how long it had been. Mom had answers for them all, explanations as to how they might have missed her, but I wasn't buying it. She obviously wasn't getting to the store as often as she used to. Maybe because the driving had become too hard for her, or maybe because cooking for one seemed like a lot of bother for nothing, but whatever the reason, she clearly wasn't eating as well as she should.

By the time we got home and unpacked the groceries, with Petunia winding hopefully around our legs until Mom opened the packet of deli meat and fed him some turkey, it was almost noon. I told Mom I wanted to take her out for lunch.

"Well, that's silly. We just bought some perfectly good lunch meat. It won't take me two shakes to make sandwiches. Why spend money going out to eat?"

"Because your only daughter's in town and she wants to spoil you a little, that's why. Come on. Get your purse. We'll make sandwiches tomorrow."

"Well, I don't know," she said, reaching up to pat her hair. "I'm not dressed to go out to lunch. I look just awful."

"What are you talking about? You look great. You always look great."

"Oh, don't give me that," she said, shooing the compliment away with her hand. "My face looks like fifty miles of bad road. Well"—she shrugged—"if you're set on going out. . . . But at least let me go fix myself up a little first. I'm not going anywhere without lipstick and earrings."

A new restaurant had opened near the college. Mom said she'd heard it was good, so that's where we went. After a little resistance, she let me drive. I ordered a bowl of butternut apple soup and a green salad. Mom got the Southwestern chicken salad.

"What's this?" she asked suspiciously, poking at a white sliver of vegetable with her fork.

"Jicama. It's from Mexico—tastes kind of like a potato, but sweeter. Try it."

She took a tentative nibble. "Mmm. It's good. Crunchy."

I tasted my soup, which was delicious, and made a mental note to ask the waitress for the recipe. Some men want a present when their girlfriend goes on a trip, but Charlie is just as happy with a new soup recipe.

"It's so nice to see you, Mom. I wish you lived closer so we could get together more often. You know, now that you're living alone, the house must be an awful—"

Mom put down her salad fork. "Evelyn, don't say another word. I knew you'd come out here with ulterior motives. But you listen to me, young lady, and listen well. I was born in Wisconsin and I will die in Wisconsin! I am not moving and that is all there is to it!"

I held up my hands, warding off this verbal attack. "Okay! All right. I'm just concerned about you. I hate being so far away from you."

"Well, who says you have to be? If somebody has to move, then why not you? Go right ahead. But I'm not pulling up stakes and leaving behind eighty years of memories just because you're a worrywart. Honestly, I don't know what you've got to be concerned about. I'm perfectly fine."

The time had come to lay my cards on the table.

"Mom, that's not entirely true and you know it. You're nervous about driving. Admit it," I said, stopping her before she could contradict me. "Driving is getting to be hard for you. So hard that you don't even want to go to the store anymore. Other than the incredible meal you made for me last night, the ingredients of which I'm pretty sure you asked a neighbor to pick up for you . . ."

She didn't say anything to this, just pressed her lips into a thin line of irritation.

". . . I bet you haven't been to the market in weeks, have you? There is hardly any food in the house. Everybody at the store was so surprised to see you."

"That's ridiculous. I get to the store as often as I ever have. I can't help it if people are too busy to notice me when I am there. Who notices an old lady, anyway? The only reason they were so friendly this morning is because you were with me."

I decided to let this pass. I love my mother. I didn't want to accuse her of lying to me, even though I knew she was.

"But you *have* lost weight, Mom. Those pants are hanging off you."

"Oh, they are not," she said dismissively. "Yes, I've lost a little weight. Big deal. Two or three pounds, but what's wrong with that? I just started getting some exercise is all. The doctor's been after me to do more walking, so I finally listened to him. Last month I started taking a walk every afternoon before supper—three times around the block."

She started a walking regimen? In Wisconsin? In January, when the average temperature is sixteen degrees and the snow is three feet deep? I didn't think so.

"What about your fall? You could have really gotten hurt, broken a hip or something."

"For goodness' sakes, Evelyn, it was just a fall! I slipped on the ice. Could have happened to anyone. Haven't you ever fallen on ice?"

"Sure, of course—"

"Well, there you go," she interrupted. "One little fall doesn't mean I'm doddering. Not yet anyway." She bent her head over her salad and stabbed a chunk of chicken with her fork.

This was hard for me, but it was ten times harder for Mom, I could tell. She knew exactly what I was talking about. She simply wasn't able to do things the way she had once, but she couldn't bring herself to admit it for fear that, if she did, she'd have to give up her independence.

But what could I do? I couldn't just fly blithely back to New Bern and hope that everything would magically turn out for the best, that the next time she fell she'd be as lucky as she had been this time. She was my mother. When I was little, she'd taken care of me. Now it was my turn to do the same for her, but she wasn't making it easy.

"Mom, what if we looked into getting you some help? Some kind of companion who could help with cooking and driving? Might be good company for you."

Mom's head snapped up like it was on a spring. "I am not lacking for company, Evelyn! No! I mean it. I am not going to have some stranger in my house. And I am not moving to Connecticut and that is that."

Her eyes were blazing. If she still could, she'd probably have docked my allowance or sent me to my room. But she can't do that anymore. She can't do a lot of things anymore. The balance of power between us is beginning to shift. Our roles are starting to reverse and we both know it. I don't like it any more than she does, but there it is.

I had to do something. The direct approach had failed miserably, so I took another tack.

"Well, what if you just came out to visit me for a while? Just for a couple of weeks? New Bern is so nice. You'd love it. I know you would."

Mom made a face. "Oh, don't be silly. What would I do with myself? You've got a business to run. The last thing you need is some useless old woman getting in your way."

"Don't talk like that. You're not useless. In fact, you'd probably be a big help to me."

"How?"

"You could teach some of my classes." I'd blurted this out almost without thinking, but as soon as I spoke, I realized it was true. Mom is a wonderful quilter. Machine piecing, hand piecing, needle turn appliqué—you name it and she can do it.

Mom gave me my first quilting lessons back when I was a little girl, and even after all my years of study, practice, and teaching, I still think she is the better quilter.

If I have any skill with a needle, it's because of her. Or, as Charlie might say, "You don't just lick it up off the rocks." Meaning that a lot of the talents we think of as belonging to us alone are actually inherited from those who've come before.

Charlie made his first banoffee pie in the warmth of his mother's kitchen. I stitched together my first nine-patch block in Virginia's sewing room. And so it goes and the torch is passed.

No, indeed, you don't lick it up off the rocks.

"Yes!" I said enthusiastically, realizing that it really was a good idea. "Why not? I don't have another skilled teacher in the shop. If you could come visit for a few weeks and take over a couple of my classes, it would be a huge help to me."

Mom looked at me carefully, gauging my sincerity. I could see the idea intrigued her, so I plunged ahead, a little too quickly.

"And if you liked it, you might want to stay. New Bern is *such* a nice little town—"

"Stop, Evelyn! Stop right there! I know what you're up to and I'm not having any of it. I told you before." She pointed her fork at me like an admonishing finger. "And if you bring it up again, I am going to get up from this table and leave the restaurant and I don't care if I have to walk home. Do you hear me?"

I took another bite of soup and changed the subject.

No matter what Mom said, we weren't done with this. I realized that. But round one went to Virginia Wade.

10

Evelyn Dixon

Charlie phoned me on Monday night and, as usual, he got straight to the point.

"When are you coming home? I miss you."

I smiled. Charlie sounded cranky. I had no problem envisioning the scowl on his face, but it was nice to be missed. Hearing his voice, I realized I missed him, too, and for some reason, this pleased me.

"I know. I want to come home but I can't. Not yet."

"Things not going well with Virginia? Is she all right?"

"Yes. More or less. She's not ill or anything. For her age, she's actually pretty healthy. Certainly as feisty as ever," I said, recalling the imperious tone she'd used with me in the restaurant. "But she really shouldn't be driving. And she won't admit it, but I think she's lonely. In the three days since I've been here, the phone hasn't rung once and no one has stopped by. So many of her friends have passed or retired and moved. I don't think she has many contacts left in town. And she needs to eat better. She's losing weight. I don't know how much, but more than she should."

"She's not eating?" Charlie was horrified. "That's terrible! She should come out here for a while. Bring her to the restaurant. I'll work up a few special dishes for her. A week at my table, maybe two, and we'll have her back at fighting weight."

I laughed. "Fighting weight isn't a problem, my love. Mom can still spar with the best of them, at least verbally. Seems we've done nothing but fight since I arrived. We're either arguing or trying to bite our tongues and *not* argue, which makes for a lot of uncomfortable silences. She just refuses to admit she shouldn't be living alone. At this point in her life, she needs a little support. It wouldn't take much. She's as sharp as ever. But she refuses to let me find someone to come in and help her and she refuses to come to Connecticut, even just for a visit."

I sighed. "The bottom line is, she doesn't want anything to change. But things have changed. Deep down, she knows it."

"You must feel like you're banging your head against a wall."

One of the things I love about Charlie is his ability to speak plainly. He didn't tell me everything would be fine, or offer me advice, or, like so many men, grab a toolbox and sledgehammer and try to fix things. Not that the urge to play Mr. Fixit is necessarily a bad one, but there is a time to jump in and take charge and a time to listen. Charlie Donnelly knows the difference.

"Yes. I just keep putting forth the same arguments and getting nowhere. Thank heaven for quilting! That's the one thing we can talk about without it blowing up into a fight. I suggested we go on our own little shop hop. We visited all the quilt shops in Green Bay and we had a great time. I've been a quilt shop owner for so long that I'd almost forgotten how nice it is just to be a customer."

"But I bet that didn't stop you from taking notice of what those other owners were doing right and wrong, did it?"

I laughed. Charlie knew me so well.

"No, it didn't. I was jotting down some notes when you called. And I took a few pictures of some displays I liked. But mostly I just enjoyed Mom's company. Charlie, she has such an eye. Her color sense is flawless. She picked out some fabrics for a wall hanging with birds and birdhouses. . . . Did I tell you how she loves birds?"

"No."

"She must have six feeders in her yard. I bet she's feeding half the birds in De Pere. They eat better than she does. Anyway, you should see the fabrics she chose—gorgeous combinations. And there was no hemming and hawing about it. She just walked down the aisle of the shop eyeing the bolts, grabbed the ones she wanted, eight fabrics in all, and was right on the money the first time. She didn't have to fuss and fret and lay out the fabrics to see what worked and what didn't. She just *knew*. She's got such a gift."

"Are you surprised? You got it from her and she probably got it from her mother. You don't just lick it up off the rocks, my girl."

"So I've heard. I wish she'd come to New Bern. Even for a visit. She'd have a wonderful time hanging out with me at the shop. Everyone would just love her. And she really could be a help to me. She doesn't believe it; she thinks I'm just saying that to flatter her, but it's true!"

Charlie clucked his tongue sympathetically. "Poor darling. You sound exasperated. You should come back home and let old Uncle Charlie feed you a good dinner, pour you a nice glass of wine. Then we could build a fire in the fireplace and I could rub your feet. Or anything else you'd like me to rub."

"Listen to you," I teased. "Turning a woman's distress to your own nefarious advantage. Cad."

"Not so! I was just suggesting a way for you to forget your troubles."

"Uh-huh. Sure you were."

"Seriously, I miss you. Come home."

"I will. I want to. But I can't until I get things settled with Mom, make her see reason. Speaking of which, I'd better hang up. She's in the sewing room cutting out her wall hanging. I said I'd help."

"Give Virginia my best. I'll talk to you later. I miss you. I love you."

"I love you, too, Charlie. A bunch."

When I went into the sewing room, Mom was standing at her cutting table, rotary cutter in hand, humming to herself as she deftly sliced fabric into quarter-square triangles.

"How is Charlie?"

"Fine. He said to tell you hello."

Mom nodded. "I like that man. At least, I like the way he sounds, that Irish accent of his. Does he look as good in person as he sounds on the telephone?"

"Better."

"Really? Well, that's nice. And he cooks too. And he's so funny." Mom shook her head. "Why don't you marry him, Evie? If I were you and had a handsome, funny Irishman who can cook chasing me, I wouldn't be running quite so fast."

I unfolded a fat quarter of cardinal red fabric prior to cutting it into two-and-a-half-inch strips. "Thank you, Mother. But you're not me."

"I'm just saying . . ."

"Mom," I said in a warning tone.

"All right. All right. It's none of my business."

She went back to her cutting, slicing squares on the diagonal, but not for long.

"It's just that you're not getting any younger, Evie. After fifty, most of the best fish in the sea have already been hooked. Charlie sounds like a catch."

"I'm sure he'll be happy to know you think so. And I agree with you. If Charlie were a tuna, he'd be sushi grade." I smiled to myself, thinking how Charlie would have appreciated the culinary reference. "But, at the moment, I'm perfectly happy with things as they are. For the first time in a long time, my life is going along exactly as I want it to. I'm not anxious to make any big changes."

"Well, that's fine for you, but what about Charlie? How long do you think he's going to be willing to wait for you, Evie? Charlie seems like a good man, but he's still a man, and if there's one thing I know about men—" Her lecture was interrupted by the ringing of the telephone.

Saved by the bell.

"Are you going to get that?" I asked.

"Why?" Mom continued her cutting. "It's probably for you. Nobody would be calling me after eight o'clock on a Monday night."

Thinking it might be Charlie again, I jogged to answer the phone, the same old wall-mounted, dial-up model that had hung in Mom's kitchen for as long as I could remember.

"Hello?"

"Hi, Mom."

It was Garrett. I was surprised. He'd called earlier in the day to let me know that things were going fine at the shop and that he planned on going into the city to see Liza in the evening. I hadn't expected to hear from him again so soon.

My heart immediately switched into mother mode, pumping a little faster, worried that he might have been in an accident, or that Liza had broken up with him, or that while he was walking down the street, a team of careless Acme movers had dropped a piano on him. When it comes to her children, a mother's heart can conjure up an infinite number of calamities to contemplate.

"Honey, is everything okay? Did something happen?"

Probably sensing my concern from the other side of the house—after all, she's a mother, too—Mom padded into the kitchen. "Is that Garrett?" she whispered. "Is everything all right?"

I shrugged silently.

Garrett laughed. He knows how my mind works. "No, Mom. Nothing happened. Well, nothing bad. Everything is fine. In fact, everything is just great."

I blew out a relieved breath of air, unaware that I'd been holding it in, and relaxed my tensed shoulders, at least for a moment.

"Liza and I are engaged!"

What?

"Mom? Did you hear me? I asked Liza to marry me and she said yes. We're engaged!"

Engaged? My son, my baby was engaged? Without thinking, I blurted out the exactly wrong thing.

"Oh, Garrett . . . I . . . Garrett . . . Are you sure?"

He was quiet for a moment before speaking very carefully and evenly, making me realize that Liza was standing right next to him.

"Yeah. It just happened and I wanted you to be the first to know. No, we haven't set a date yet. Probably in the summer."

The tone in his voice told me he was absolutely serious about this. I could be happy for him, or not, but either way, he was getting married.

I closed my eyes and bit my lip, hoping that Liza had been standing far enough away from the phone that she hadn't heard my first response.

"That's wonderful, Garrett. I'm so happy for you." I backtracked as best I could.

"Thanks. Do you want to talk to Liza?" This wasn't really a question and I knew it.

"Sure. Put her on."

"Hi, Evelyn," she said cautiously. "Big news, huh?"

She had heard me, I could tell by the sound of her voice, and she was hurt. That was the last thing I wanted.

I love Liza, truly love her. But I also know her, perhaps a little better than a prospective mother-in-law should. Liza wasn't the same angry, embittered nineteen-year-old who had walked into my quilt shop three years before, bent on punishing the world for all the pain she'd known in her young life. She had grown up so much since then. But she was still nursing a whole collection of scars and half-healed hurts.

Liza is a wonderful young woman and I was sure that, someday, she would be a wonderful wife and life partner to someone. When the time was right and if she still loved him, I had no doubts that Garrett and Liza could be very happy together, but today? Now? I wasn't so sure.

Still, the decision had been made. Garrett is a grown man. He wasn't asking for my opinion, only my support.

"Very big news. The biggest. Congratulations, Liza. I wish you every happiness," I said, which was true. "Have you told Abigail yet?"

"We're calling her next. Do you want to say good-bye to Garrett?"

I said I did, told her congratulations again. Before Garrett could get on the line, Mom interrupted.

"Wait a minute. Let me talk to her."

"Liza? Hold on. Mom wants to talk to you."

Mom took the phone and grinned, bowing her mouth into a smile that beamed excitement and approval right through the receiver.

"Liza? It's Grandma Virginia. I just wanted to tell you how happy

I am for you and Garrett, dear. This is wonderful news! Evelyn has told me so many, many good things about you. I'm sure you and Garrett are going to be very happy together. I can't wait to meet you. When I get out there, maybe I can throw a bridal shower for you."

When she gets out there?

"That is, if I can get Evelyn to yield her prerogative as mother-in-law elect. I'm sure she won't want to, but maybe I can arm wrestle her for the privilege." She laughed. "Well, I just wanted to tell you how thrilled we are, dear."

She paused, nodding and listening, before Liza said good night and handed the phone off to Garrett. Mom repeated her enthusiastic congratulations to Garrett, then gave me the phone so I could do the same.

I hung up the phone and turned around to see Mom standing with her hands on her hips.

"Evelyn, what in the world was that about? Your only son and his bride-to-be called to share their happiness, and you just burst their bubble. What were you thinking?"

"I know. I know. I didn't mean to, but . . . I'm not sure this is a good idea, for Garrett or for Liza. Liza's a wonderful girl, but she's so young. And she's carrying around a lot of baggage from the past. Dating is one thing, but marriage? I'm not sure she's ready for that. And I bet I'm not the only one who thinks so," I said, remembering the supposed "marital research" she'd been conducting at our last quilt circle meeting.

Suddenly, it was obvious to me that Garrett had proposed before our meeting and that Liza, uncertain in her response, had been trying to ask our advice on the subject without doing so directly. Liza and I were pretty close, and when she was facing a difficult decision she often used me as her sounding board. But since the decision involved Garrett, maybe she hadn't felt she could come to me directly.

"I'm sure Liza has doubts. I could hear it in her voice. Couldn't you?"

"Well, how would you expect her to sound? She has to know you're something less than thrilled by the news. You didn't exactly mask your misgivings, did you?"

I rubbed my forehead, trying to massage out the headache I felt forming behind my eyes. "I know. I'm sorry. It just caught me by surprise. I can't help myself. I'm just not sure this marriage is a good idea. If they'd just wait a few years . . ."

"That's not your decision, Evelyn. Garrett and Liza are adults. They have to make their own decisions. And you have to make the best of it," she said, lowering her chin and peering at me over the tops of her glasses before walking over to the stove to turn on the gas burner.

"Did I ever tell you about what happened when your father and I got engaged?" she asked as she filled the teakettle with water.

"No." I sat down at the old wooden dinette.

Mom turned on the back burner and set the kettle on the flame. "I met your father at a church picnic. His people were pillars of that church, literally. His grandfather dug and poured the foundation with his own two hands. The Wades were farmers, like everybody else, my family included. But their farm was big, a lot more productive and profitable than our place. Of course, that wasn't just because they had more land than we did. My father was a drinker, a drunkard actually. That's what they called it back then. Daddy wasn't a bad man. He was always good to me and my sisters, but he just had this weakness. He tried to quit the bottle"—she paused and squinted, trying to remember a number—"oh, more than a few times, but he never could."

"Is that why you never drink?"

Mom nodded. "That's right. I worried that I'd be like Daddy, that if I started I wouldn't be able to stop, so I never took a drop. Didn't seem worth the risk.

"Anyway, Daddy would go on these binges, right when there was the most work to be done around the farm, or so it seemed. So the fields didn't get planted or harrowed or harvested like they should have. We were always owing money. When Dad would go off on a tear, my mother would try to pick up the slack and work the fields herself, but she had three daughters to raise and a house to run. When we girls got bigger, we helped out with the farm work, but we were in school, so we weren't able to do as much as was needed."

The teapot started whistling. Mom took it off the fire, poured hot water into two mugs, put a tea bag in each, carried them to the table, and sat down across from me.

"Everybody in town knew about Daddy. People were always polite to our faces but behind our backs, they talked. Nothing malicious, mind you. Just clucking and looking at my mother and sisters with this 'poor thing' expression. They didn't mean any harm, but when people are feeling sorry for you, it gets under your skin, makes you feel ashamed." Mom blew on her tea to cool it, then took a sip.

"I never knew about this. Why didn't you tell me before?"

Mom smiled and shook her head. "When you grew up and started drinking wine, I almost did. But I kept an eye on you. It didn't seem to be a problem, so I kept my mouth shut. Even though he died before you were born, I didn't want you thinking badly of your grandfather. Like I said, he was a good man at heart. He just couldn't seem to help himself."

Holding the mug in my hands, I propped my elbows on the table and leaned in. This revelation regarding my family history was fascinating, but I couldn't quite see what it had to do with my mother and father's engagement, or with Garrett and Liza's.

"Anyway," she went on, "things being the way they were, I didn't like going to town much. Never went to church at all. But there was a woman, Hazel Miles, whose farm wasn't too far from ours. Hazel would come by and have coffee and visit with my mother. No one else ever did. And it wasn't like she came out of pity or trying to do her good deed for the day. She was just nice to us.

"One day she dropped by the house on her way to the church picnic and asked if I wanted to go. I was nervous but for some reason I said yes, probably because I didn't want to disappoint Hazel. Your dad was there, home from college. I'd seen him around town before, of course, but he was a few years ahead of me in school, so we'd never really talked. I was sitting at a picnic table and he walked up with two big slices of watermelon, one for me and one for himself, and started chattering like a magpie." Mom grinned and shook her head.

"Dad was always a talker," I said.

"Oh, wasn't he just?" She laughed. "He could charm the birds out of the trees. He sure charmed me. I started showing up at church every Sunday. Hazel would give me a ride into town and your dad would give me a ride home. Next thing I knew, I was in love. And not just with your dad. I fell in love with God too. Every time the minister opened his mouth, it seemed he was talking directly to me, speaking to all the hurt and shame I'd been shoring up for so many years, showing me the better way. I came to faith in that little church. Not too long after, just before he had to go back to college, your dad proposed. I said yes, that quick." She snapped her fingers.

"Well, why not?" I said, recalling Liza's approach toward marriage and mentally juxtaposing it with my mother's. "You didn't have to think about it long because you knew it was the right decision. You were sure."

Mom lifted her tea mug, nodding as she took a drink. "I was sure, but your grandmother Wade wasn't."

"Grandma Bennie?" My grandmother's given name was Bernice, but everybody always called her Bennie. "She said she didn't want you and Dad to get married?"

Mom tipped her head to one side. "Not in so many words. But when we told her about the wedding, she wasn't exactly jumping for joy. She smiled and hugged me, but awkwardly. Then she said, 'I've been praying for Bud's bride since the day he was born.' "

Mom sighed heavily. "I should have just let that go, but something in her voice got under my skin. I so wanted her approval. 'And am I everything you prayed for?' I asked."

Hearing the words, picturing my dear mother, young and vulnerable, wanting so much to be loved and accepted by her new family, I winced inwardly, afraid of what came next but compelled to ask, "What did she say?"

"Oh, I don't remember now. Something nice, I'm sure. But she hesitated before she answered and her eyes flickered away from mine, as if she was embarrassed to look at me. That told me everything I needed to know. She was ashamed of me. She didn't want your dad to marry me, didn't think I was good enough for him, and I knew it."

I didn't know Grandma Bennie very well. She lived way on the other side of the state, far from us but not that far. Not so far that we couldn't have seen her more than the two or three times a year that we did. Suddenly, the infrequency of our visits to Grandma Bennie made a lot of sense.

"It didn't change our plans," Mom continued. "But it did affect my relationship with Bennie. Dad's too. Eventually, I was able to get past it, but by the time I did, so much water had passed under the bridge. . . . It was too bad."

Mom got up from her chair and took our empty mugs to the sink. I grabbed a sponge and began wiping down the table.

"That's why I told you this, Evelyn," she said as she rinsed out the mugs. "I don't want history to repeat itself. Garrett and Liza have made up their minds, so you'd better get with the program. You can't take back what you said tonight, but I don't think it's too late to make up for it. Not if you start right away. The first thing we should do, when we get to New Bern—"

I nearly dropped the sponge when I heard that.

"When *we* get to New Bern? But you've spent the better part of the last three days telling me, in pretty clear language, that you have no intention of going to New Bern now or ever. The phrase 'over my dead body' comes to mind."

"Well, that was different. That's when we were talking about me. Now we're talking about you. And Garrett. And the woman who will likely be the mother of my great-grandchildren. I don't want to fly off to Connecticut now any more than I did this morning, but when your family needs you, sacrifices must be made. You're a mother, you should know that."

I am and I do.

"When do you want to leave?"

"The sooner the better," she said, drying the last mug and putting it back in the cupboard. "Tomorrow, I think. Can you get my suitcase down from the top shelf of the closet? And Petunia's carrier. We need to start packing."

11

Liza Burgess

Already deep into the semester, my final semester before graduation, the last thing I had time to do was meet Aunt Abigail for lunch, so why do it?

Because once Abigail has made up her mind that she wants you to do something, even something as seemingly innocuous as lunch, she can be a bit insistent. Insistent in the way a hurricane insists on blowing or a volcano insists on erupting. Basically, she's a force of nature. Resistance is pointless. Not that I'm exactly a shrinking violet myself. I've thwarted Abigail's plans on plenty of occasions, sometimes just to prove I could.

But finally, after her twenty-second phone call insisting that we *must* get together to discuss wedding plans, I decided it would be easier to bow to the inevitable than to keep wasting time arguing about it. Besides, lunching on gulf shrimp and hand-crafted fettuccini with Abigail at '21' beats eating microwaved ramen noodles in my apartment any day of the week.

It's still winter, still freezing cold, still months away from June, the date Garrett and I set for the wedding, but as I tromped in my black snow boots down the icy stairwell to the subway, I couldn't help but think about the wedding, and that made me nervous.

I know there are girls who start planning their weddings while they're still in grade school, but I was never one of them. Everything about this feels new to me—and not in a good way. New in the way that new leather shoes feel, stiff and uncomfortable, maybe even a little painful.

Hearing myself say yes to Garrett's repeated proposal was a shock. It didn't turn out like I'd planned.

When I opened the door to my apartment, it was a surprise to see him standing there. I think he'd decided that I was going to say no and, that being the case, it would be better to get it over with than endure more days of waiting, only to be refused in the end.

He looked miserable. I couldn't bear to see him so sad.

And so I said yes. The second I did, Garrett's face just lit up. He was so happy. Beyond happy. Elated. Enraptured. Ecstatic. It was amazing, even a little daunting, to see the effect my answer had on him. Maybe that sounds strange, but the idea that someone's happiness or unhappiness could rest upon one little word from me was scary.

I mean, why should he be so happy to marry me? There's nothing so very special about me. Sooner or later, he's bound to figure that out.

Garrett's face went from miserable to exultant in less time than it takes to change your mind, and all because I said yes. I am happy that I made him happy, but in a month or a year or ten years, when he knows me better, couldn't he change his mind just as quickly as he did his expression? The idea of being responsible for someone else's happiness isn't any more comfortable than the idea of being responsible for someone else's misery.

Maybe, if I'd had a little more time to get used to the idea, to mull it around in my mind, to practice wearing my engagement ring in secret, sneaking into the closet or the bathroom a few minutes a day, to accustom myself to the feel of this weight on my hand, maybe I could get used to the idea. But I hadn't had time.

Garrett looked miserable and I couldn't bear it, so I said yes.

Then there was a kiss and that frightening look of joy on Garrett's face. And with the word still hanging in the air, surprising and too near, Garrett grabbed his phone, hit number two on his list of contacts (mine occupying position number one), and called Evelyn to tell her the happy news.

Except Evelyn wasn't happy. I knew it. Garrett keeps the volume on his phone turned up pretty loud. And though the comment wasn't directed to me and the sound quality was tinny, I could hear the doubt in her voice.

Well, Evelyn knows me. More than anyone else, maybe even more than Garrett, she knows my past and my fears, the grudges I hold on to, the ones I've let go, and the ones I wish I could let go. So I'm not really surprised by her reaction. Evelyn may be like a mother to me, but her first loyalty is to Garrett. It has to be. And knowing me like she does, of course she has doubts about this engagement. How could she not?

But that doesn't mean it doesn't hurt.

She's called me—or tried to call me—a bunch of times. I haven't picked up when I've seen her number on the caller ID and I haven't returned any of her messages. I'm not trying to be mean. I know I should call her, but I just can't.

I already knew what she'd say. She'd say she was sorry, and that she didn't mean what she said. And that's why I can't bring myself to talk to her, because I don't want to hear things that aren't true. Not from Evelyn. She did mean what she said that night. She wasn't trying to be cruel; she was just being honest. Evelyn has never been anything less than honest with me. That's one of the things I love about her. No matter what she said to Garrett that night, no matter how much it hurt, it'd hurt twenty times more to hear her say that she didn't mean what she said and know it was a lie. I can't face that. Not right now.

Eventually, I'll have to call her. I've meant to do it before now. A couple of times I've even picked up the phone, but . . . Every day that passes, every message she leaves just makes me feel worse and more awkward and awful. I'll call her. Soon.

Once we told Evelyn about our engagement, we had to tell Abigail too. Her reaction was one hundred eighty degrees the opposite of Evelyn's. She was beyond thrilled, and in a way, her delighted response to our announcement was more upsetting than Evelyn's cautious one.

She immediately started pushing the way she does, demanding clarification on our nonexistent plans. Garrett had said something about June to his mom. So when Abigail asked me for a date I said, "June, I guess," because Garrett had said so first. With classes, and paintings, and graduation to worry about, June was about as far in the future as I could project, a date that seemed distant enough to give me some space to breathe.

After calling the families, Garrett took me out to dinner at Roma's, a little Italian place near my apartment. We've gone there a few times before, so it felt familiar and normal. After a couple of glasses of Chianti I didn't feel as nervous about the whole wedding thing.

I knew my roommates would be home by ten, so after dinner, Garrett and I stood in the foyer and kissed good night for a long time, until I remembered my eight o'clock class in the morning.

I said good night and walked up the stairs slowly, feeling good, feeling the wine, feeling the memory of Garrett's lips on mine, feeling like maybe everything would be all right after all. But when I got to the top of the stairs I twisted the diamond of my ring around to the palm side of my hand where Zoe and the others wouldn't be able to see it. I didn't want to have to talk to them about it. Not yet.

When the alarm rang at seven twenty the next day, the metallic buzz alerting me to the fact that I'd drunk too much wine the night before, I left the diamond where it was, hidden on the interior of my hand. That's where it's been ever since.

June is so far off. I don't need any distractions right now, especially since I'm still working with Dr. Williams on the article. I want to make sure it's letter perfect.

I'm also taking her graduate art history seminar. I had to get special permission to sign up. I want to make sure I do a really good job with the two papers Professor Williams has assigned. I don't want her to think she made a mistake letting me in the class. I'm also working on my senior project, my last painting as a student and my entry into the senior art show.

This year, the show will be a juried exhibition and the judges will be a mix of faculty, museum curators, and some of the most prominent art critics in New York. The best piece will be purchased for the school gallery's permanent collection. Everybody is buzzing about that. That kind of thing can really jump-start an artist's career. The competition will be fierce. I'm definitely a long shot to win but, hey, somebody's got to. Why not me?

I've had plenty to think about besides getting married. In fact, other than occasional, sweet phone calls from Garrett, who knows how hard I'm working and doesn't want to distract me, or the frequent, pestering ones from Abigail, who knows how hard I'm working and could give a rip if she's distracting me, I've hardly thought about the wedding.

A couple of times, while I've been sketching, I've looked down to see my left hand holding the paper, caught a glimpse of the diamond peeking out from underneath my fingers, and thought, "Oh! That's right! I'm engaged!" It's still kind of hard to believe.

But I suppose Abigail is right. I've got to make a few decisions about the wedding. If I do, then maybe she'll get off my back and let me get back to work.

The subway ride from the college to the restaurant takes about twenty minutes. I was so lost in my thoughts that I almost missed my stop and had to jump from the train to the platform just as the doors were closing. I was supposed to meet Abigail at noon, but it was a few minutes past when I arrived at the restaurant.

I've eaten at '21' a few times, always with Abigail. The food is great, but it's too expensive for college students. Abigail has been coming here for years, so they know her. That's why I wasn't surprised when the maître d' greeted me by name and said that my aunt was waiting.

What did surprise me was that he didn't lead me to Abigail's usual table. Instead, I followed him down a corridor to a private dining room hung with a series of huge pen-and-ink drawings of orchids in silver frames, starkly elegant against black silk wallpaper and painted white woodwork. There were more orchids, dozens of them, placed on the side tables and on the white-clothed dining table set with sterling and crystal. Abigail was waiting for me, and she wasn't alone.

With her were four incredibly attractive and stylish-looking people, all dressed in shades of black, gray, and white, as though they came with the dining room, a package deal. They got to their feet when I entered the room and began applauding, beaming at me as if I'd just won some sort of prize.

"Liza! There you are, darling!" Abigail, smiling even wider than the others, got up from the table. "You're late. But that's all right. You're here now."

"Sorry," I said and then whispered in her ear as she hugged me, "Who are all these people?"

"Oh," Abigail said, as if surprised by the question, "didn't I tell you? This is your bridal design team: Byron, Leslie, Camille, and Karin. Collectively they are known as Best Laid Planners, the finest wedding-planning firm on the eastern seaboard."

Best Laid Planners? What was she talking about?

I may not have given much thought to what kind of wedding I wanted, but it definitely didn't involve hiring a four-person "bridal design team"—whatever that meant.

"Abigail, I don't need . . . I mean . . . you really shouldn't have . . ."

"Oh, you don't need to thank me, darling! It's my pleasure. After all, you're my only niece and you'll only be married once," she said, raising an eyebrow and turning her head slightly, so she was addressing Byron, Leslie, Camille, and Karin, "so we want to get it right the first time, don't we? Because the first time will be the *only* time, do you hear me, Liza?"

Abigail chuckled. The team, bright-eyed and still beaming, joined in on cue.

The beautiful blonde wearing a simple black suit and cream-colored silk blouse, the one Abigail introduced as Leslie, stepped forward. "Don't worry, Mrs. Spaulding, we're going to make sure that Liza's special day is absolutely perfect in every detail. With such a short engagement, it won't be easy. For most society weddings we have at least a year's lead time, often closer to two."

Society wedding?

I turned to see if there was someone else standing behind me, because I was sure she couldn't be talking about me. I'm nobody's idea of society.

"However"—Leslie smiled and tossed her head, causing a silken hank of hair to fall neatly over one shoulder—"if this were easy, then you wouldn't need us, would you?" She laughed a low, musical laugh, soothing, like a tune played on an oboe.

Byron, a tall, slim man in his mid-forties wearing an expensive and expensively tailored charcoal gray pinstripe suit with a snowy white shirt and a light gray silk tie that was an almost perfect match to his thick head of prematurely gray hair, stepped forward. He was quite possibly the best-dressed man I have ever seen in my life.

"Liza," he said in a kind voice that sounded faintly British but wasn't, "you're looking a little shell-shocked. Don't worry about a thing, my dear. Normally, of course, we'd have our initial meeting at our offices, but in the interest of saving you travel time, we decided to meet here. We've brought everything we need," he said with a sweep of his arm, gesturing toward a large pile of black and gray boxes, portfolios, and files that were stacked in the corner.

"Your aunt has explained how busy you are with your studies and that you don't have time to deal with the endless details involved in coordinating a wedding. That's why we're here, to handle all those details for you.

"I'll be in charge of clothing—your dress, going-away outfit, bridal lingerie, and honeymoon wardrobe—as well as invitation design and all the floral and lighting design at the church and the reception. Of course, the final selection will be up to you and Garrett, but I'll be consulting on your choice of wedding bands. Leslie will be in charge of catering, music, the photographic and video team, as well as transportation coordination and hotel accommodations. Camille will be in charge of hair, makeup, and spa treatments for the entire bridal party. And Karin will handle whatever is left over: contracts, reservations, invitation printing and mailing, choosing and coordinating rentals, helping with the bachelor and bachelorette parties and any bridal showers. Karin is the best bridesmaid wrangler in the industry," he said proudly.

Bridesmaid wrangler? That's a job? Is he serious?

I stared at Abigail and then at Byron, waiting for someone to break into laughter and tell me it was all a joke, but everyone just kept smiling and nodding as if there was nothing unusual about this conversation. There have been very few times in my life when I was completely at a loss for words, but this was one of them.

"So, as you can see, everything is under control. We do need some input from you, but after today, other than showing up for a few fittings, all you'll have to do is focus on your studies until the big day." He smiled brightly and then pulled out an upholstered chair and nodded to indicate I should sit.

I did, too stunned to do anything else. The others did the same. Abigail took the chair next to mine, squeezing my hand affectionately as if everything was just too wonderful for words.

Byron pulled an enormous black portfolio off the pile in the corner, unzipped it, and started laying eight-by-ten photographs of bridal gowns on the table, convening a meeting whose agenda seemed clear to everybody but me. Byron glanced at his watch, a shining, sculptural timepiece I'd seen advertised in the pages of *Gentlemen's Quarterly*. "Let's get started. We've got a lot of decisions to make today. If we stay on task, we should be able to finish in five or six hours."

Five or six hours? Spent doing what?

"Now, Liza, there are any number of places we can begin when planning a wedding, but I've found that the selection of the gown often dictates the tone of the event, gives everyone a clearer picture of what we should be reaching for. Obviously, we could waste time traipsing around to every bridal shop in town, but we have personal relationships with all the important designers in New York. What we'll do this afternoon is look at these photographs and choose a designer, and then I'll have Karin call the showroom and they'll send over a rack of actual gowns for you to try on after lunch." Byron smiled at me. "Does that sound all right to you?"

Finally! Someone was actually asking what I thought of all this, and what I thought was that this whole thing was crazy.

Abigail meant well. During one of our twenty-two phone conversations, I'd told her I didn't have time to fool around with a big wedding and that she should just go ahead and deal with it. Obviously, she'd taken me at my word, but this . . . ? This was nuts!

I was sure Garrett would feel the same way. We both had pretty simple taste, neither of us the glamorous type. We were just as happy eating spaghetti and drinking the house Chianti at Roma Bistro as we were eating lobster and sipping champagne at the Carlyle Club, maybe happier, as recent events had proven. I was sure that Garrett didn't want a "society" wedding any more than I did, even if it was designed by the most prominent wedding planners on the eastern seaboard.

I looked at Abigail, then at Byron, and held up my hand. "Well, actually, it doesn't sound all right to me. Not at all. I appreciate what you're trying to do, Abbie, but, I'm just not sure . . ." I stumbled over my words, trying to find a way to put a stop to this without upsetting Abigail. "It's just that . . . I don't think that Garrett would . . ."

Byron nodded sympathetically. "I know, my dear. He should have been here by now, but I really don't think we should wait any longer, do you, Abigail?"

"No," Abigail said and patted my hand. "We really must get started, Liza. I'm sure Garrett will get here any moment. We can catch him up when he does. Besides, darling, we're just choosing the dress right now." She frowned, then reached up and pushed a stray lock of hair off my face.

"But," I protested, "Garrett—"

"Is so, so sorry for being late! It started snowing again and I couldn't find a cab from Grand Central."

And suddenly there he was, bounding past the bowing maître d' and into the elegant room, wearing his favorite faded blue jeans, an old cable-knit sweater, and a grin. Byron's eyes flitted up and down Garrett's frame, as if mentally measuring him for a tuxedo.

After Garrett said hello to Abigail and kissed her on the cheek, Leslie, Camille, and Karin got up from the table and surrounded him, introducing themselves and congratulating him on being fortunate enough to have found such a lovely bride.

"You don't have to tell me," Garrett said, walking up behind my chair and placing his hands on my shoulders.

"It took some time to talk her into it, but when she finally said yes . . ." He bent down and kissed the top of my head. "Well, all I can say is, it was worth the wait. I'm the luckiest man on earth."

Byron stepped forward to shake Garrett's hand. "You make a very handsome couple. Garrett, I'm Byron, the head of Best Laid Planners. I'll be producing your wedding."

Still smiling, Garrett nodded as if this seemed a completely reasonable thing to say, as if people had weddings that required "producing" every day of the week.

"Nice to meet you, Byron."

The introductions completed, Byron clasped his hands together and said, "Now that everyone is here, I think we should get to work, yes? Karin, would you run out and find a waiter? Let him know that he can begin serving. There's no reason we can't plan and eat at the same time."

Karin hustled off. Everyone else shuffled around, shifting seats to make room for Garrett, who took the chair next to mine, then leaned over to kiss me on the cheek before whispering in my ear, "Isn't this great! Now you can concentrate on your papers and your painting and not worry about the wedding. Me too. I got two new clients this week. I'm working sixteen-hour days just trying to keep up. It's great that Abigail is taking over. All we have to do is show up, get married, eat some cake, drink some champagne, and then sail off on our honeymoon and into our future. What could be better? It's a dream, don't you think?"

I nodded. That's exactly what I thought. This room filled with orchids, the stone-faced waiters who were carrying in plates covered with silver domes, the smiling and oblivious faces surrounding me, the panoply of pictures Byron was pointing to, the succession of brides dressed in yards and yards and yards of silk and satin and lace—it couldn't be real.

12

Evelyn Dixon

I sat on one side of the booth with Mom and Charlie opposite me. He dipped his spoon into the dark, dense chocolate and urged Mom to take a bite.

"This is my mother's secret recipe for chocolate mousse. There are chefs who would commit a crime to get this recipe, Virginia. They would! Have a taste and see if I'm not right."

Mom rolled her eyes, thoroughly charmed. "Oh, you. Isn't that what you said about the apple crisp yesterday? And the banoffee pie the day before that?"

"Could be," Charlie said with a wink. "My mother is a woman of many secret recipes, all well worth stealing."

"Charlie," she said, "why is it that whenever you talk, the word 'blarney' comes to mind?"

"I can't imagine, Virginia. You're the first to mention it. Now, go on. Give it a try. You won't be sorry."

"I can't," she groaned, patting her stomach. "Really, Charlie. I'm stuffed like a Christmas turkey already. Those short ribs were heavenly, but so filling! I don't have room for dessert."

"A bite," he urged. "One."

Mom sighed, resigned to the inevitable, and took the spoon from Charlie's hand. One bite and her resistance melted away like a chocolate bar left in a sunny window. Mom's face was an expression of pure rapture.

"Oh, my. That is either heaven or real close to it. Here, Evelyn," Mom said, pushing the spoon toward me, "have a bite. You've just got to try this."

I shook my head. "No, thanks. I already have, on many, many occasions. Charlie's chocolate mousse is the reason I had to get a gym membership. But," I said to Charlie, "I wouldn't mind a nice cappuccino."

Charlie jumped up from the booth. He'd just bought a new espresso machine for the restaurant and was still having fun fooling with it. "Skim milk, extra foam?"

"Perfect."

He leaned over to kiss me on the cheek before heading off to play with his new toy, but I called him back to the table.

"Charlie, come here a minute. I want to tell you something." He leaned down. I grabbed the collar of his sweater, pulled him close, and kissed him on the lips. "I love you."

"Me too."

I rested my chin in my hand and watched him walk away, whistling a tune as he did.

Mom swallowed another bite of chocolate mousse and clucked. "Why you don't marry that man is just beyond me."

I changed the subject. "I changed my mind. Can I have a bite of your dessert?" She fed me a spoonful of the mousse. "Mmm. That is so good."

"Too good," Mom said. "I've only been here three weeks and I've gained two pounds."

I nodded in mock sympathy and made a mental note to report this information to Charlie later. He would be so pleased. I certainly was.

So far, Mom's visit to New Bern had been an unqualified success. She was eating well, gaining weight, and as I had predicted, everyone in the shop was just crazy about her. I'd set her up in her own little quilting corner with a comfortable chair, sewing machine, and floor hoop right near the big bow front window of the shop, the one that faced the cobbled courtyard from which Cobbled Court Quilts had taken its name.

I'd chosen that spot because the light was good and I thought she would enjoy looking out the window to see the comings and goings of people passing through the courtyard. At Mom's suggestion, I put a bird feeder in the courtyard planter. It didn't take two days for the New Bern bird population to realize that a new all-you-can-eat buffet had opened up in Cobbled Court. Now, in addition to people watching, Mom could watch the succession of wrens, robins, and scarlet-winged cardinals that stopped by for a quick lunch.

The second the birds arrived, Petunia, who had spent the previous days skulking in dark corners, obviously unhappy in his new surroundings, jumped up onto the wide ledge of the window and made that his permanent hangout. Now everyone was happy, Mom and Petunia. And though that hadn't been my motivation, having Mom and Petunia sitting in the front window turned out to be good for business.

People passing through the courtyard on their way to other businesses were charmed by this live display: the fluffy tortoise-colored cat eyeing the avian visitors and the older woman working at her quilting hoop. Many of those passersby came into the shop, often for the first time, to pet Petunia, who tolerated their caresses with royal disregard, then stayed to get a closer look at Mom's work and chat with her about how difficult it must be to make those tiny, perfectly even stitches. Mom always said it was much easier than it looked, often sitting the person down to let them try a few stitches for themselves (which she quietly removed later).

Next thing you knew, Mom was talking them into buying a few yards of fabric, or a kit for a wall hanging, or signing up for a beginner's class. I'd always known she was a good quilter, but I'd never realized she was also a good saleswoman. She'd brought in five new students the previous week, completely filling the beginner's class and forcing me to start a waiting list. I knew I should offer a second class, but I just didn't have time.

"Mom," I said as I watched her scraping the last ribbons of mousse from the sides of the glass dessert dish, "would you consider teaching a class for me? Hand quilting for beginners?"

"Oh, I don't know, Evelyn. I've never really taught before, not in a real quilt shop."

"Well, you never sold fabric in a real quilt shop before, and look how well you're doing. Do you realize that your customers added eight hundred dollars to my coffers last week? I should start paying you a commission."

"Really? My! I didn't realize it added up to so much. I don't want a commission, though, but," she said cautiously, "I was wondering if I could have a little fabric. . . ."

"Well, sure, Mom. You don't even have to ask. Anything you want."

Her eyes lit up. "Good! I'm just about done with my wall hanging. I'd like to start something new. But," she continued doubtfully, "I'm not sure about teaching. I don't like staying up late."

It was true. Mom was active during the day, full of energy, rising before the sun was up to make breakfast for both of us. It was nice to wake up to the smell of hot coffee and fresh muffins. But by eight o'clock her head started to nod and she was generally asleep by nine, tonight being an exception. Dining with Charlie meant dining late, after the dinner rush.

"There's no reason we couldn't schedule a class during the day. The only reason I teach at night is because I'm too busy to do so during business hours. I bet lots of people would love a daytime class."

Mom bit her lip, thinking. "I did meet a couple of young mothers who said they wished they could take a class while their children were in school."

"Well, there you go!"

"There she goes what?" asked Charlie, who was back with my cappuccino.

"I'm trying to talk Mom into teaching a beginner's class during the day—hand piecing and quilting. I don't have time to do it. Besides, Mom is better at handwork than I am."

Mom waved her hand. "Oh, pshaw. I am not. I've just had more practice is all."

"Sounds like a great idea, Virginia. What's she paying you?" He leaned closer to Mom. "Whatever she's offering, tell her to double it," he advised.

"Mom prefers to take her salary out in trade. All the fabric she wants."

Charlie nodded. "Very sensible, Virginia. It'll keep you from bumping up into a higher tax bracket. So, what do you say? Are you going to do it?"

Mom blinked a couple of times, mentally tallying up the pros and cons of my proposal.

"Well . . . let me think about it. I'd need at least four sessions to teach a proper class and I hadn't planned on staying here for another month, only long enough to meet Liza and welcome her into the family properly. When is she coming out here, anyway? I've been here three weeks and still haven't laid eyes on the girl."

"Maybe on Friday, but I don't know for sure," I said. "She usually makes it out here for a quilt circle meeting every couple of weeks, but Garrett said she's busy working on a big project for school, so who knows?"

"Project or no, you'd think she'd manage to come see her fiancé more often, wouldn't you?" Mom frowned.

I agreed but I didn't want to say so. To most people, Liza can come off as hard-edged, but I know her better than most people. She's tough on the outside, but inside, she's tender and easily wounded. She's also not one for confronting her feelings head-on. And overhearing my doubtful reaction to the engagement had clearly hurt her feelings. I knew she was busy at school. Even so, I couldn't help but wonder if the desire to avoid me was the real problem. But I didn't say that to Mom.

"Oh, I don't know," I said casually. "Young people are more career-oriented than they used to be. And Garrett is just as preoccupied as Liza. This whole web design business started as a sideline, just something to do for fun in his spare time, but it's exploded so much that he doesn't have any spare time left."

Mom shook her head. "That's not right. He and Liza should be spending more time together."

"I wouldn't worry about it too much, Virginia," Charlie said.

"They've got the rest of their lives to spend together. Garrett is just trying to get his business up and running before the wedding."

"That's right," I agreed. "He wants to buy a house, so he's trying to put some more money in the bank. For his age, he's actually done well, but most of his money is invested in the quilt shop. We're partners, you know. Wish I could buy him out now so he'd have that money for a down payment, but I can't afford to just yet. Maybe in a couple of years."

"Well," Mom replied, "nothing wrong with a young man wanting to take care of his family, but I still think he and Liza should be spending more time together. They've got their whole lives to be weighed down by responsibilities. Right now they should just relax and enjoy their engagement."

"They are," I reassured her. "Garrett was in New York all afternoon, remember? I told you all about it. Abigail hired some sort of wedding planner to help—"

The door of the restaurant opened. Garrett came in, his coat collar turned up against the cold. He spotted us and walked over to our booth.

"Hi, sweetheart," I said, scooting over to make room for him next to me.

"Hi, everybody." He laid his coat across the back of the booth before sitting down.

"So? How did it go?" I asked. "Did you get everything decided? Was the wedding planner nice?"

Garrett rubbed his eyes and then pinched the bridge of his nose between his thumb and forefinger, the way he does when he's tired. "Wedding planners—plural, as in a whole team of wedding planners, make that a 'bridal design team'—Byron, Leslie, Camille, and Karin. I swear you could plan the military invasion of a medium-sized country with fewer people than it'll take to plan this wedding."

Charlie's eyebrows shot up and he leaned in. "Byron? Byron Dennehey?"

Garrett nodded.

Charlie let out a low whistle, obviously impressed. "Until he left to form his own wedding planning firm, Byron Dennehey was the editor of *Mode* magazine and one of the most influential style arbiters in New York."

I stared at Charlie and shook my head slowly from side to side. "How do you know these things? You're starting to scare me."

"I read," Charlie said, a little defensively. "The worlds of food and fashion are closely related. To stay in business I've got to keep up with the trends. I've got subscriptions to all the big style magazines."

I bit my lip to keep from smiling. Charlie was wearing his favorite threadbare blue wool sweater, a pair of baggy black corduroys, faded from many washings, and brown moccasins, very scuffed at the toe. Not quite the wardrobe you'd expect from a man who has subscriptions to all the big style magazines.

"Must have cost Abigail a pretty penny to hire Byron Dennehey," Charlie continued. "I heard he won't take on a job unless the client has a budget of at least sixty grand."

"Well, nobody has mentioned any figures," Garrett said. "Abigail's taking care of all that. But if you ask me, sixty seems like the lower end of the ballpark. There was talk of horse-drawn carriages, butterfly releases, magnums of specially imported champagne from France, and the Boston Symphony. Abigail wants to hire them to play at the reception."

I choked, nearly spitting a mouthful of cappuccino onto the tablecloth. "You're joking," I sputtered. "Tell me you're joking."

Garrett shook his head. "Nope. She is dead serious. Abigail is determined to give Liza the most spectacular wedding in Connecticut history. The absolute best of everything."

"What about the catering?" Charlie asked, drawing his brows together. "Who's going to do the food?"

"Byron suggested the Walden Inn."

The Walden Inn was a very elegant, very expensive lakeside hotel about ten miles away from New Bern, popular with the type of elegant, style-conscious New Yorkers who like to spend weekends in the country in a place they'll be seen by other stylish New Yorkers who like to spend weekends in the country. The Inn has a beautiful dining room with excellent service, and an astronomically priced menu that only adds to their reputation for exclusivity. But the management can't seem to hold on to a chef for more than three or four months at a stretch. Consequently, the food can be very hit-or-miss. Even so, the Walden attracts a lot of attention. It was rare that a major newspaper or magazine did a piece on weekend getaways to New England without declaring that dinner at the Walden is a must. This drives Charlie crazy.

"The Walden! Is he mad? The kitchen at the Walden is a revolving door for culinary school dropouts and has-been celebrity chefs recently released from rehab! The Walden!"

Garrett held up his hands. "Calm down, Charlie. Abigail told Byron that the catering would be done by the best restaurant in the county, the Grill on the Green. Byron or one of his minions will call tomorrow to begin discussing the details."

Charlie crossed his arms over his chest and gave a quick, self-satisfied nod. "Good for Abigail! She's smart enough to know that it takes more than a big bill and a big PR department to make a good restaurant. I'll cater your wedding for half the price the Walden would and the food will be four times as good." He shook a finger in Garrett's direction. "You tell Abigail that!"

"I don't think Abigail is very much concerned about the size of the bill, Charlie. I'm not what you'd call up to speed on the prices of Manhattan's finer restaurants, but I bet you could buy a pretty good used car for what it cost Abigail to host our lunch meeting today."

Charlie leaned in, his eyes bright. "Where did you go?"

" '21.' The orchid room."

"The orchid room!" Charlie exclaimed. "That's their newest private dining space! Gorgeous. *Mode* did a huge spread on it. What was for lunch? Did you bring a menu?"

Garrett pulled a crumpled-up menu from his pocket and handed it to Charlie. By now we were all well trained in the art of culinary espionage. Garrett and I never eat at a new restaurant without bringing home a menu for Charlie to study.

Charlie squinted as he looked over the menu. "What did you have? The beef tenderloin with red wine and shallot sauce, or the grilled snapper with blood orange nectar?"

"The tenderloin. Liza had the snapper. And before you ask, they were both delicious. Listen, gang. I don't mean to be rude, but I'm going home. I just wanted to stop by and say hello."

Mom reached across the table and patted his hand sympathetically. "Poor baby. You've had a long day. Go home and get some sleep."

"Wish I could, Grandma," Garrett said as he heaved himself up from his seat. "But I've got a couple of hours of work to do first. I told Mr. Kaplan I'd have his design finished by Tuesday. I'm way behind."

I was worried. Garrett has always been a night owl, working on his computer until the wee hours of the morning, but he looked truly exhausted. I couldn't help but wonder if long hours were the only reason for his haggard condition.

In the family drama that is the modern American wedding, the mother of the groom is definitely a bit player. My job was to wear beige, and keep my mouth shut, and until now, I'd done so. But I couldn't keep my concerns to myself any longer.

"Garrett, this wedding, with the butterflies and the symphony and the magnums of champagne. Is this what you want? Because it just doesn't seem like you."

He picked up his coat, wearily put his arms in one sleeve and then the other. "What I want is to be married to Liza. I don't care if we dance our first dance as husband and wife to the stylings of the Boston Symphony or two guys playing kazoos. If this is what Liza wants, then it's what I want."

"But . . . *is* this what Liza wants?"

"Sure," he said with a shrug. "Liza wants a nice wedding, right? Personally, I think this one is going to be a little over the top, but she agreed to everything. If this wasn't what she wanted, I'm sure she'd say so. She's never had any trouble speaking her mind before," he said with a proud little smile.

That was true. When it came to deeper, personal issues, Liza wasn't much for confronting things head-on. But when it came to questions of style or self-expression, she had never been shy about voicing her opinions—especially if those opinions ran counter to her aunt Abigail's.

"I guess you're right."

Garrett shrugged. "It's all a little crazy, but if it makes Liza happy, then I'm all for it. I think she's grateful to Abigail. Not only is she willing to pay for all this, she's taking over the planning. Liza's schedule is as bad as mine. Neither of us has the time to deal with this. So if Abigail wants to take the ball and run with it, I say let her."

He smiled as he zipped up his jacket. "I talked to Scott Fineman the other day. My old roommate from college."

"Oh, I remember Scott," I said. "How is he?"

"Engaged. His wedding is more than a year off, but he's already going nuts with the arrangements. He and his fiancée, Alisha, have visited eight reception halls so far. Eight! And they still haven't been able to find one they like. When I told him about our wedding and how Abigail is taking care of everything, Scott was so jealous he could hardly stand it.

"'Dude!'" Garrett exclaimed in a perfect imitation of Scott's beach bum accent. "'You mean all you gotta do is show up wearing the tux? I'd kill to be in your shoes, man!'"

Garrett grinned before continuing in his usual tone of voice. "So believe me, I'm not complaining. Things could be a lot worse. And Liza is happy. That's all I care about."

I nodded. Perhaps my worries were misplaced. If Liza was happy and Garrett was happy, that was what mattered. That and figuring out a way to patch things up with my future daughter-in-law.

"Garrett, when you talk to Liza, tell her I miss her, will you? I know she's busy, but if she can get away for a weekend we'd love to see her at the quilt circle."

"And," Mom said, wagging her finger, "you tell her that Grandma Virginia flew halfway across the country to meet her. If she doesn't come out here soon, I'll just have to take the train into New York and hunt her down."

Garrett grinned and headed for the door. "I'll tell her."

13

Liza Burgess

Before today, if somebody had told me that trying on clothes could be more tiring than running a race, I'd never have believed it. But after trying on twenty-three different wedding gowns, I felt exhausted. The good news is, I finally found a dress I love.

Staring at dozens of pictures of wedding gowns was overwhelming. I had no idea what I wanted, so when Abigail pointed to a couple she liked, I just nodded and went along with it. Two hours later, after nodding in agreement to Abigail's suggestions on everything from the typeface on the invitations (Bickham 3) to the flowers for the bridal bouquet (pink mini calla lilies, white cymbidium orchids, green dendrobium orchids, and seeded eucalyptus—all to be shipped in from Hawaii), a rack of bridal gowns and a full-length mirror were delivered to the restaurant.

Byron hustled Garrett off to another room to try on tuxedos while Abigail, Leslie, Camille, and Karin stayed to help me with the dresses. They were all big and white and fluffy and lacy and, I'm sure, somebody's idea of the fairy-princess gown she'd always dreamed of, but I wasn't that somebody.

Twenty dresses into the process, Byron knocked at the door.

"How are we doing in here?" He peered over the tops of his glasses, looking me up and down before crossing his left arm over his waist and resting two fingers of his right hand on his cheek.

"Doesn't she look beautiful!" Abigail exclaimed.

Byron's eyes shifted from the dress to my face, to Abigail's, and back. The room was silent. Everyone awaited his verdict.

After a long moment, he clapped his hands together twice and said, "All right! Everybody out! You too, Abigail. Why don't you all go next door and see how fabulous Garrett looks in his tuxedo?"

After they left, Byron walked over to the bar where the waiters had left a bottle of champagne chilling in a bucket. He poured a glass and handed it to me. "Don't spill it on the dress. If you do, the designer won't take it back and," he said, pulling up a chair so I could sit down, "*that* dress is definitely going back."

What a relief! I sank into the chair and took a drink of the champagne. "Isn't this just the worst dress you've ever seen?"

"Well, that depends. If you were Scarlett O'Hara descending the staircase at Twelve Oaks, then I'd say it was perfect. But if you're a bright young art student with a modern style sense? Not so much."

Byron crossed back to the bar and poured a glass of champagne for himself, albeit a smaller one, less than half full.

"Liza, dear, why in the world did you choose this designer? Stephanie Gallante makes nothing but fluffy, frilly gowns. Every one a meringue. When Abigail said Gallante, and you agreed, I wondered. Your look is so modern, a little edgy. Gallante didn't seem like your cup of tea, but who am I to interfere?

"I deal with all kinds of brides, and for some, a meringue is exactly what they want. So that's what we give them because, in the end, it isn't any one particular gown that makes a bride beautiful, but the fact that she *feels* beautiful in whatever gown she's wearing. But you don't feel beautiful in that dress. In any of these dresses," he said, sweeping his hand to encompass the rack of white that stood by the wall. "If I'd come in here about two minutes later than I did, I think I might have found a bride in tears. Am I right?"

I sniffled. Byron pulled a crisp, white handkerchief out of his pocket and handed it to me.

"Here. Use this. It wouldn't do to have you wiping your nose on the sleeve of the dress. Then Stephanie *really* wouldn't take it back."

He smiled and I laughed through my tears.

"I'm sorry," I said, dabbing my eyes with the handkerchief. "I'm just feeling . . ."

"Overwhelmed?"

"Yes! None of this seems quite real. I had no idea there would be so much to do, so many decisions to make." My eyes started to tear up again. "I'm sorry."

"Don't be." Byron raised his eyebrows and took a sip of champagne before going on. "I've planned over two hundred weddings in my career, nearly all of them for lovely, wonderful women who had every reason to feel overjoyed about their good fortune, and do you know something? Every single one of those wonderful, lovely brides had at least one good cry between the engagement and 'I do.' It's perfectly normal."

The hard knot of tension in my stomach loosened just a little. I wasn't as crazy as I thought I was. I was normal. Everything would be all right. It would be. Byron said so, and he'd been through this two hundred times.

"Once we get through today it will be easier, I promise. You're having everything thrown at you at once! If I were you, I'd have grabbed that bottle of champagne, locked myself in the closet, and told Abigail and me and everybody else to go away and never come back." He winked at me.

I sniffled and wiped my nose with Byron's handkerchief. "Not everybody. I'd let Garrett stay," I said.

"Good call," he said. "Garrett is a wonderful young man. The two of you are going to be very happy together."

The knot loosened a little more. "Do you think so?"

"Think? I know! All my brides are happy. I absolutely insist on it."

He was teasing, I knew, but his words were reassuring.

"Ah, there we go. A smile at last. The crying jag is over." He got up from his chair, took our empty glasses, and put them back on the bar. "Now, take off that awful rag of a dress and hang it up. I'm going to have another rack sent over."

My shoulders drooped. Another rack of dresses?

"Don't look at me like that," Byron said. "Not another rack of meringues. A rack of chic, gorgeous gowns you will absolutely love. Trust me."

"Karin!" Byron shouted. The door opened immediately and Karin peeked in the room.

"Call Velma Wong's studio. Tell them to send over whatever they have in a size six."

Forty-five minutes later, the gowns arrived. Even before trying them on, I could tell these dresses were much more to my taste than the others. The first was pretty. The second was lovely. And the third—a gown of ivory silk-taffeta, with tiers of pleats that draped irregularly on a skirt that was full but not overly so and tied at the waist with a wide, taupe silk-taffeta bow—took my breath away.

Byron stood back to look me over, a self-satisfied smile on his face. He turned to Leslie. "I think we have a winner. Am I right, Liza?"

It was modern and chic and, dare I say it? Glamorous. And with those tiers of pleats, feminine. I'd have never thought I could feel so feminine or so beautiful. I loved it. I couldn't say anything for fear I'd start to cry again.

There was a knock on the door and, without waiting for anyone to give him the all clear, Garrett walked in. "Are you decent?"

I turned around. Garrett stopped short in the doorway, open-mouthed. Abigail started fussing at him, but he paid no attention to her.

"Liza . . ." he breathed. "You look amazing. Beautiful. Just . . . you're just amazingly beautiful."

I bit my lips to keep back a smile. His words weren't exactly eloquent, but that was all right. The look on his face told me everything I needed to know.

"Thank you."

"You're just . . . so amazingly beautiful," he repeated. "Is that the dress? I hope so. You just look so . . . so . . ."

"Amazingly beautiful?" Byron offered.

"Yeah." Garrett nodded.

"Well, Liza?" Byron asked. "Is this the dress? You can try on the rest if you'd like, but I don't think there is one that could make you look any lovelier than you do right now. And, if there was, I'm not sure that would be a good thing. Garrett wouldn't be able to take it."

"No," I said, my eyes glued to Garrett's face. "I don't need to try on any others. This is the one I want."

After I changed, we sat down to discuss the rest of the items on what was still a very, very long "to do" list.

"There's not that much left here," Abigail said, scanning the list, which had at least twenty items left on it. "Liza, you've got classes tomorrow and Garrett has to work. Why don't you two go home. I can stay and finish this up. I'm staying in the city tonight anyway."

"But," Byron said hesitantly, "there are a few things here that are really a matter of Liza's personal taste."

"Oh, Liza and I have very similar taste," Abigail assured him. "I can work out these last few details, just to get things rolling, and Liza and Garrett can go on their merry way. Doesn't that seem like a good idea, darling?"

At the moment it did. Unless I wanted to pull an all-nighter to finish my homework, handing off the rest of the list to Abigail was the only solution.

"Yes. That'd be great. Thanks, Abigail."

Byron pushed his glasses up a little higher on his nose. "All right. As long as everyone is comfortable with that. . . . But before you go, we haven't discussed bridesmaids. How many?"

"Oh." I thought for a moment. "Two, I guess. Margot and Ivy. Margot can be the maid of honor."

Abigail was shocked. "Only two?"

I looked at Byron. He tilted his head to one side and said, "Of course, it is up to you, Liza. But for a wedding of this magnitude, having only two attendants would be highly unusual. A larger bridal party does give more visual impact."

"Surely you want more than two," Abigail said.

Did I? Abigail seemed so certain about this, and Byron too. They were probably right. After all, what do I know about weddings? But still . . .

I wish I had someone to talk to about all this. Someone whose opinions I trusted. Someone who understood me. Someone like Evelyn. Aside from Garrett, she knew me better than anyone and, knowing me so well, she had concluded that I wasn't good enough for her son.

Oh, Garrett. Are you sure?

I could still hear what she'd said. And it hurt. That's why I couldn't talk to her anymore. That's why I stayed away from New Bern.

The thought of going back there—of climbing those familiar steep wooden stairs at the back of the shop, walking into the big workroom with the exposed brick walls and the tall windows, sitting around the table where I've spent so many hours talking and laughing and stitching—only to find that the old familiarity has been replaced by uneasy silences and words unspoken as Evelyn and I try to pretend that she hadn't said it and I hadn't heard it, was more than I could stand.

I wish my mom were alive.

I'd give anything to be able to talk to her for even five minutes. She would know if two bridesmaids is enough. She would know what I should do about that—about everything.

But I can't. Not for five minutes. Not even for one. I can't talk to Mom. I can't talk to Evelyn. Abigail is the only one left in my corner. Without her, I'd have no one.

Two bridesmaids or twenty—I don't care. But she does. So why not let Abigail have her way? What could it hurt?

"I . . . I guess I could ask my roommates. That would make five. Would five be enough?"

Abigail beamed. "Five would be perfect!"

Garrett and I shared a cab. It made more sense to go to the train station first and then have the cabbie take me to my apartment, but Garrett insisted. "I know you need to get back to work ASAP. Besides, this way I get to spend more time with you." He draped his arm around my shoulders and I snuggled up close for a kiss. The cab driver could see us in his rearview mirror, but I didn't care. Let him look.

"Mmm," Garrett murmured, pulling back a little so he could look in my eyes. "Nice. Did I ever tell you that you're delicious?"

"Thanks." I laughed. "I try."

He pulled me closer. "I can't wait to be married to you, Liza. I want to wake up next to you every day for the rest of my life. What do you say we just bag the whole wedding deal and run away—to Aruba, or Hawaii, or Trenton, anywhere. I don't care, as long as we're together."

"Okay," I teased. "As soon as I graduate, we'll elope to Trenton."

"We have to wait that long?"

"Afraid so. I haven't worked this hard only to drop out in the last semester."

"But you wouldn't have to quit school just because we were getting married."

Garrett's tone was perfectly even, and I realized he wasn't kidding. He was seriously suggesting we elope. My shoulders twitched involuntarily. Everything was moving so fast. I could barely wrap my mind around the idea of a June wedding. I certainly wasn't ready to advance the date.

"Wouldn't work," I said airily, purposely trying to keep things light. "You're much too distracting. Besides, if we eloped to Trenton, we'd better be prepared to stay there forever. If we run out on this wedding, Abigail will send the dogs out to track us down and drag us back to New Bern. We'd have to enter the witness protection program or something."

"Yeah. Guess you're right." Garrett sighed his resignation. Inwardly, I sighed with relief, glad that he'd abandoned the idea. "And I really wouldn't want to miss seeing you walk down the aisle. You look like an angel in that dress."

"Thank you."

He shook his head. "No. Thank *you.*"

"For what?"

"For saying you'll marry me."

We kissed again. The cab pulled up to my apartment building. Garrett told the driver to keep the meter running while he walked me to the door. It was cold out. Garrett shoved his hands in his pockets while I fumbled around in my purse, looking for my keys.

"Oh, I almost forgot," he said. "Mom and Grandma want to know when you're coming out to New Bern. Margot and Ivy too. They want to throw you a bridal shower."

My fingers brushed the jagged edge of my keys. I pulled them out of my bag. "Oh. Um . . . I don't know. Soon. I just have so much work right now, you know?"

"I know," he said. "That's what I told them, but they keep bugging me about it. Everybody misses you. I miss you too," he said. "I was thinking about coming back to the city on Saturday. How about lunch? Or dinner? I don't care which."

"Yeah, sure. That'd be nice. There's a new exhibit I want to see at the Whitney. Want to go? We could have dinner after."

Garrett smiled wide. "I'll call you and we can figure out a time."

Still smiling, Garrett moved closer and kissed me again. The cab driver tapped on his horn a couple of times.

"You'll miss your train."

In my room, I lay sprawled on my bed, with my hand shielding my eyes. The girls were watching some new reality show on TV. They'd wanted me to come join them, but I said I had too much homework. It was true. I knew I should get up and get to work, but I was so worn out. Maybe, if I just took a twenty-minute catnap, I'd have enough energy to start.

I was just dozing off when I heard a collective whoop coming from the living room and the sound of footsteps in the hallway.

Zoe called out, "Liza! You've got to see this! They've just announced that they're bringing back all the guys who've gotten kicked off the show and that *they* will decide who makes it through to the next round. Skanky Jared is finally going to get what's coming to him."

I heard the door open and Zoe's voice inside the bedroom. "Come on, Liza. Just for a little while. You've got to—"

She stopped in mid-sentence. I opened one eye, wondering what had interrupted her. She was standing in the doorway, openmouthed, and staring—at my hand.

"Holy . . . You did it, didn't you?" She shook her head, her voice hushed and disapproving. "You told Garrett you'd marry him."

14

Evelyn Dixon

With a few minutes left until closing time and not a customer in sight, I decided to count up the cash drawer. Margot is better with figures than I am, so this is usually her job, but she was already upstairs with Ivy and Mom, cleaning up before our quilt circle meeting, which would begin as soon as I locked the shop door and turned out the lights downstairs.

February is generally a slow month for us, but the till looked good today. I knew why.

This had been the first day of the "Baby Quilts for Mothers and Mothers-to-Be" class. We'd had a full house. All eight spots were filled by young mothers, some expecting their first child, others their second or third, and some with a toddler or two in tow. That was why the upstairs workroom needed tidying up. Mom suggested that, for a small fee, we should offer child care to those taking the class. I wasn't sure about the idea at first, but Margot had been highly enthusiastic about the proposal. Since the project was to be hand quilted, the students wouldn't need machines and could meet around a big table in the shop. Margot volunteered to watch the little ones upstairs in the workroom while their mothers enjoyed two uninterrupted hours of quilting instruction.

It had been a grand success for the mothers, the children, and for Margot. Margot loves children and they love her. One of the kiddos, Harry, a shy four-year-old whose mother seemed hesitant about leaving him in Margot's care, was a testament to her magic touch with the diaper-and-tricycle set.

"Mommy will be right downstairs, okay, Harry?" Harry's mother said hopefully. "You stay up here and have fun with the other kids."

But Harry was having none of it. He was fixed to his mother's leg like Velcro. Harry's mother sighed.

"I'm sorry," she said to Margot. "He's like this with everybody. I shouldn't have signed up for the class, but I was really hoping it would work out. I've always wanted to learn to quilt," she said wistfully. "Oh, well, maybe another time."

Without looking at Harry, who had two fingers in his mouth and was peeking out from behind his mother's legs, Margot said, "Oh, that's too bad. I'm so sorry Harry won't be joining us today. Well, it's probably just as well," she said casually, "because today is Dinosaur Day. We're going to make our own stuffed dinosaurs to take home. But, like I said, it's just as well. Harry probably doesn't like dinosaurs."

Harry pulled his fingers from his mouth and tugged on his mother's pant leg. She leaned down and Harry whispered in her ear.

"Actually," she said with a smile, "dinosaurs are his favorite."

"Really?" said Margot, shifting her surprised gaze to Harry, who nodded vigorously.

"Do you have any T. rex dinosaurs?" Harry asked.

"Why, yes! Two! I have a green T. rex and a blue one all cut out and sewn and ready for someone to stuff, decorate, and take home. Which would you like?"

"Blue," said Harry before taking Margot's hand and heading over to the craft area without so much as a backward glance.

While Margot was upstairs with the little ones, the mothers learned the basics of fabric selection, cutting, and stitching under the patient and grandmotherly eye of Virginia Wade, arguably the best hand quilter in the state of Wisconsin, and now Connecticut. While the women sat around the table working on the quilts that were destined to become some of the earliest and most tangible evidence of a mother's love for these babies still unborn, the ladies in waiting were inducted into that other and equally important aspect of the long tradition of our craft: the camaraderie of quilters.

Some of the women knew each other; most didn't. As they sat together, piecing their simple four-patch blocks under Virginia's watchful gaze, they talked and laughed, comparing notes on everything from the alleviation of stretch marks and swollen ankles to keeping the flame of marital romance burning after children arrive.

One woman, the mother of seven-year-old twins with a two-year-old upstairs and a baby due in April, looked doubtfully at her swollen belly. "Are you kidding? Fanning the flame is the least of my problems. Somebody tell me how to douse it."

The group broke into giggles.

Somebody else jumped in. "Or just how to quit falling asleep before my husband. He keeps sneaking up on me. That's how I got Timmy *and* Molly."

I smiled as I counted up the day's receipts. Besides their class supplies and fees, many students had purchased fat quarters of fabric, the first in what would become their "stash," the quilter's addiction and most prized possession, that collection of impulsively purchased fabrics we have no specific plans for but simply *must* have, our hoarded cache of inspiration. These apprentice quilters' purchases helped my bottom line today, not a lot but a little, and those eight women were well on their way to becoming full-fledged quilters and, in all likelihood, good customers for years to come. That was good, but it wasn't why I was smiling.

Cobbled Court Quilts is more than a business to me, more than a way to eke out a living. It is a community of quilters, a place where people with completely different backgrounds, ideals, and experiences enter as strangers and leave as friends. As the class came to an end and Mom distributed hugs and homework assignments, I could hear the moms making plans for play dates. Every woman in that class left with at least one new friend. That's what made me smile. Those are the kinds of treasures that don't show up on a balance sheet but, for me, add up to the best sort of payday.

My quilting friends, my sisters in stitches, have been my companions on the road of life. Without Margot, Abigail, and Liza, the original members of my quilt circle, and my old quilting friend from Texas, Mary Dell, I can't imagine how I would have gotten through my mastectomy. They have supported me in good times and bad, and I've tried to do the same for them.

Haven't I?

I think so. In the past, I have, certainly. But it's been weeks since Liza came to a quilt circle meeting and, in spite of Garrett's assurances to the contrary, I can't believe that a busy schedule is the only reason for her lengthy absence.

I am the cause. In my heart, I know this and it makes me feel awful. I wish I knew what to do. If she'd just come back to the circle, if we could just spend an evening side by side, quietly cutting out scraps of cloth and stitching and patching them into quilts, I feel sure that we'd be able to patch up the tears in our friendship too. But in spite of the messages I've sent through Garrett, the unanswered phone calls, and the voice-mail messages I've left saying how much we all miss her, she has stayed away.

I do miss Liza. Her absence leaves a hole in our group and in my life. Surely she feels it too, doesn't she? I didn't think she'd be able to stay away for so long. If she'd just come home, I could fix this. I'm sure I could.

I should have been more careful.

I keep thinking about my grandma Bennie, how her attitude toward Mom caused a rift between them and, by extension, between Grandma and my father, and later, though I was unaware of it, between Grandma and myself, that never completely healed.

A thoughtless word, an unkind attitude, and three generations of what could and should have been a loving family were wounded forever. I didn't want that to happen to me and Liza and Garrett, or to the children that might come from their union. I wish I could take back my words, but it's too late. Barring the immediate invention of some Wellsian time machine, I'm going to have to figure out a way to repair this rip before it grows into an ungulfable chasm. But if Liza won't come home or respond to my multiple messages, how can I?

I closed the cash drawer and headed toward the front door to turn the Closed sign face out. Looking out the window, I saw Abigail scurrying across the courtyard with Franklin in tow.

"Hellooo!" Abigail called out merrily as she entered.

Franklin lifted his hand in greeting while stomping the snow off his boots. Abigail did likewise, though much less vigorously.

"Franklin," I teased, "you joining us for quilt circle night? Finally decided to give up poker in favor of some real fun?"

Shortly after their wedding, knowing that Abigail would be busy at the quilt circle every Friday night, Franklin had recruited a few of the local attorneys—including Arnie Kinsella, Margot's boyfriend—to form a Friday night poker club.

"Would that I could, Evelyn. Would that I could. It'd probably save me some money."

"Oh, I don't know about that," I said. "Collecting a good fabric stash can run into more money than a few hands of Texas Hold'em, but at least you have something to show for it."

"Which is definitely more than you can say about poker," Abigail said affectionately as she brushed snow off Franklin's coat. "He's been on a losing streak. Judge Bruegger is one of the regulars. Franklin's lost so much money to him that I've started to think he's doing it on purpose so the judge will be more inclined to give him favorable rulings."

"Dishonest as that would be," Franklin said, "I almost wish it were true. It might salve my bruised ego. The truth is I'm just a bad poker player. But maybe tonight will change that. Sometimes taking a break is the best way to end a losing streak."

"There's no game tonight?"

"There is," Abigail said, answering for him, "but Franklin won't be going. And I'm afraid I won't be at the quilt circle tonight either. I just wanted to run in and tell you."

"Where are you off to?"

Abigail's face lit up and she clapped her hands together. "The Walden Inn! Byron called from New York. He was at a party last night and heard that—wait for it!—Emiliano Vargas is spending the weekend at the Inn! So Byron made a few calls and got Emiliano to agree to have dinner with us!"

Abigail let out a short, excited little yelp. "Isn't that the most fabulous news?"

I looked from Abigail to Franklin, trying to fathom the reason for her excitement. "Yes. Of course." I nodded. "It must be. Who is Emiliano Vargas?"

Abigail stuck out her chin and widened her eyes in a look that made it clear she was wondering what sort of rock I lived under. "You've never heard of Emiliano Vargas?"

"Afraid not."

Abigail rolled her eyes. "He's only the most exclusive hair stylist in the country. He's done the hair for cover models in all the big fashion magazines—*Vogue, Elle, Cosmopolitan.* His clients are all celebrities. If you're not a model or a movie star, it's nearly impossible to get an appointment with him, not for any price. And he *never* does weddings. But he and Byron are old friends, so when Byron called, he agreed to meet with us and to at least *consider* doing Liza's hair for the wedding. Byron's driving up from New York to meet us at the Inn."

Abigail laid her hand on her chest as if trying to calm her racing heart. "I hope we make a good impression. I'm so nervous!" And then she giggled. Actually giggled!

Nervous? Abigail Burgess Wynne Spaulding, the sixth-wealthiest woman in the state, the woman whose surname graced the wings, laboratories, or libraries of every prominent charitable organization on the East Coast, the woman who ate snotty Manhattan headwaiters for breakfast, slicing them to ribbons with just one imperious glance from her steel blue eyes, was nervous about meeting a hairdresser? I didn't get it.

I looked questioningly at Franklin, but he just shrugged.

"I thought you said someone from Byron's firm was in charge of hair and makeup."

"Yes, but that was before this came along. Camille may still end up doing it. Emiliano hasn't actually agreed to take the job. But wouldn't it be something if he did? If he does, I think we can guarantee an article in *Society Bride* magazine!"

Hearing this, I frowned, not because I doubted Abigail but because I suspected that she was absolutely right. *Society Bride*? How would Liza and Garrett feel about that?

What was Abigail thinking? She'd always lived life more than a little bit larger than the rest of us, but it seemed to me that she'd lost focus about the whole meaning and purpose of this wedding.

When Abigail married Franklin, it had been a quick, charmless affair, a rushed ceremony performed by a hospital chaplain at Franklin's bedside. Abigail had believed he was dying. But once the vows were spoken, Franklin made a rapid and somewhat miraculous recovery. Abigail loved Franklin but had made no secret of the fact that she felt cheated out of the wedding she'd wanted, the one she'd obviously spent considerable effort planning out in her own mind. I couldn't help but wonder if she was living out her own fantasy wedding with Liza as a stand-in.

Though there was no one in the shop besides the three of us, Abigail glanced left and right, as if afraid someone might overhear her, before leaning toward me and whispering, "You know, Emiliano is not only the most exclusive stylist in the country, he's also the most expensive. Ten thousand a day, plus expenses. And that doesn't even include the fee for his assistants. Emiliano works with at least two assistants."

Now I truly was worried, and not just about Liza. Something was seriously out of whack here. For as long as I'd known her, Abigail had always had lots of money and spent lots of money, but never foolishly. In fact, she and Franklin had recently downsized. Abigail sold her enormous Proctor Street mansion, donated the proceeds to the Stanton Center to help victims of domestic violence, and built a "cottage" for herself and Franklin to live in.

When I say "cottage," think cottage like the ones in Newport, Rhode Island, where, in the late nineteenth and early twentieth centuries, New York's uber-rich built enormous homes overlooking the sea. So while Abigail and Franklin's "honeymoon cottage," with only five bedrooms, a library, and a living room that can host eighty at a cocktail party, is rather modest by Abigail's standards, most people would call it a mansion. Even so, it's a much smaller mansion than the one she lived in before, and it was incredible of her to donate the proceeds from the sale of her home to help others.

But that's Abigail. She's one of the most generous people I know, donating enormous sums to any number of good causes, often anonymously and always intelligently. Abigail keeps a close eye on where her donations go, making sure the money is used for its intended purpose. In spite of her millions, at her core Abigail is a true Yankee, intensely private, tradition-bound, and subtly elegant, spending wisely and abhorring the freewheeling, headline-chasing flash and panache of those she derisively dubs the "new rich." That's the Abigail I know.

But this woman who is willing to throw tens of thousands of dollars away in the hopes that hiring a celebrity hairdresser might garner her niece a magazine spread is someone I don't recognize.

"Doesn't ten thousand seem like a lot to spend just for a cut and blow-dry?"

"I know," she said a little defensively, clearly displeased that I wasn't as enthused as she about the fabulous Emiliano. "But Liza *is* my niece. My only living blood relative and my sister Susan's only child. I want to do what's right to make sure that Liza's wedding is perfect in every detail. If it costs me a little, then so be it. I owe this to Liza and to the memory of my sister."

"But," I said slowly, "do you think that this is really the kind of wedding Liza wants? It just doesn't seem like her style."

Abigail straightened her shoulders and gave me a look that made her doubts about my opinions on style of any kind obvious. "Well, I think I know a little about Liza's likes and dislikes. After all, *we're family,*" she said in a pointed tone. "Liza hasn't voiced the least objection to any of the wedding plans. In fact, she's thrilled. What bride wouldn't be?"

Off the top of my head, I could have named a few but didn't. I had my doubts about Liza being "thrilled" by this upcoming three-ring circus of a wedding, but both Abigail and Garrett said she was going along with it. Who was I to question them? I hadn't spoken to Liza in weeks. Maybe I didn't know her as well as I thought I did.

Abigail's unanswered question hung awkwardly between us. Franklin cleared his throat.

"Abbie, we'd better head out if you want to get there on time."

"Yes. All right," Abigail said and pulled her coat closer around her. "Good night, Evelyn."

"Good night, you two. Have fun. Drive carefully. The roads are icy."

"Oh, Evelyn, one more thing. I need your guest list by the end of the month. That's when we have to put the invitation order in to the printer. You should see them!" she said, brightening. "Each invitation will come in an individual lidded keepsake box, upholstered with ivory watered silk and topped with Liza and Garrett's monogram in sterling silver. The post office won't deliver them, so we're having each invitation sent via messenger."

Invitations in upholstered silk boxes? Individually messengered? I couldn't even begin to imagine what a thing like that must cost. I swallowed hard. "They sound beautiful, Abigail."

"They are! So please, do get your list to me as soon as possible, and try to be judicious in making it. June is such a busy month for weddings. People book their rentals years in advance and we had gotten a late start. Byron's people have called simply everywhere, but the largest tent they could locate for the reception only holds five hundred. Well, really seven hundred, but we had to leave room for the orchestra and dance floor. Did I tell you about the orchestra?"

I nodded. "Boston Symphony."

Abigail beamed. "Can you believe it!"

"Not really."

"I know! Such a coup! Anyway, it does mean cutting back the guest list. You don't mind, do you?"

Only five hundred?

"That's fine. Won't be a problem."

"Oh, good! I was hoping you'd feel that way."

"Abigail," Franklin said, tapping his watch.

"You're right! Must run, Evelyn! Tell the girls I'm sorry about missing tonight. I'll call you and let you know how it went with Emiliano. Wish me luck!"

I stood in the doorway and waved while Abigail and Franklin hurried across the courtyard and down the alley.

"Good luck."

15

Evelyn Dixon

Mom was sitting in a chair, appliquéing leaves on her birdhouse project. Ivy, who had always been nervous about trying appliqué, was watching while Mom explained the process, assuring her that it was easier than it looked.

Ivy is strong. If not, she'd never have found the courage to pack up her two children, flee her abusive marriage, and start a new life in New Bern. That's why, when I decided that Cobbled Court Quilts should become involved with New Beginnings, the Stanton Center's program to help mentor victims of domestic violence and make them ready for life in the workplace, I chose Ivy to be our shop liaison. Ivy works full-time at Cobbled Court, but ten hours of her week are spent working with women from New Beginnings. They all look up to Ivy. She's a great role model.

But Ivy is still uncertain about so many things, and she often doubts her own abilities. Even something as simple as trying a more advanced quilting technique can bring up her old fears and insecurities. Ivy hates to fail.

She often says "I've perfected failure and don't need any more practice, thank you very much." It's supposed to be a joke, but deep down she means it. Sometimes, rather than risk trying and failing, Ivy doesn't try at all. She's come a long way but still has a long way to go. Well, don't we all?

But watching her lean closer to Mom, her gaze fixed intently on the deft movement of Virginia's needle, I could almost see the wheels turning inside her head as the better voices of her nature shouted down her doubts. I've got a feeling that Ivy's next quilt is going to be graced with any number of appliquéd flowers and leaves. One more step down the road—a baby step, but a step just the same. Way to go, Ivy.

And way to go, Mom! There's just something about the loving assurance of a wise older woman that gives a younger woman faith in herself. Cobbled Court Quilts should have had a Grandma-in-Residence from day one.

The workroom was all tidied up. Margot was sweeping the last few green spangles, leftover dinosaur scales, off the floor. She looked up as I came in carrying bolts of green and blue fabric I was thinking of using to make a set of quilted place mats for Liza's bridal shower, assuming she comes home long enough for us to throw her one.

"Where's Abigail?" Margot asked. "I thought I heard her."

"You did. She just dropped by to say she couldn't come tonight. She and Franklin are going to the Walden Inn to meet Emiliano Vargas—hair banger to the stars. Abigail wants him to do Liza's hair for the wedding."

Margot's eyebrows rose. "Wow. That's got to run into some money. Huh."

"What?"

"I'm just surprised, that's all," she said, tipping the glittering contents of the dustpan into a nearby wastebasket. "I didn't think Liza went in for that kind of thing. But, on the other hand, why not? You only get married once."

"If you're lucky."

I dumped the bolts on the cutting table, rolled out a couple of lengths of fabric, and stood looking at the combination. In this light, I could see that the blue was leaning toward turquoise. Pretty, but not quite right.

Mom got up from her chair. "Ivy and I are going downstairs to pick out some appliqué fabric. She's going to try adding a vine border to her quilt."

"It'll probably end up looking more like a weed border, but what the heck." Ivy shrugged. "I'll give it a try. If it doesn't work, I can take it out."

Mom shook her head. "You are not going to need to, I promise. For goodness' sake, Ivy! Have a little faith in yourself."

"Yes, ma'am," Ivy said with a grin.

Mom glanced at the bolts of fabric I had laid out and frowned. "That's a nice turquoise. Doesn't look quite right with the others, though."

"That's what I was thinking." I sighed.

"What's it for?"

"Place mats for Liza."

"Place mats? For a wedding gift? Why not a quilt?"

"Well, I was thinking the place mats could be a shower gift. I'd like to do a quilt, but it'd need to be a big one. I'm not sure I've got time to finish it before June." That was the truth, if not the whole truth. With things so unsettled between Liza and myself, I wasn't sure she'd want a quilt from me.

Mom shot me a look that bored right through me, the expression on her face exactly the same as it had been when I was five years old and had accidentally broken one of her Hummel figurines and blamed it on Snowball. It always was impossible to get anything past her.

"There are four of us here," she said in a voice that made it clear she wasn't buying my story, not for one minute. "Place mats are fine for the shower, but for the wedding, you should make Liza a quilt. If everybody pitches in, I'm sure we can get it finished in plenty of time."

"Oh, let's!" Margot squealed. "Let's make Liza a quilt, from all of us! A double wedding ring!"

The double wedding ring pattern is very pretty and, as the name implies, the traditional choice for a bridal quilt. But somehow, it just seemed a little too traditional for Liza's taste. On the other hand, what did I know about Liza's taste anymore?

"I don't know," Mom said, narrowing her eyes. "Do you think that's the right pattern for Liza? I realize I've never met her, but from everything you and Garrett have told me about her, she doesn't go in much for the traditional patterns."

Ivy nodded. "Virginia's right. Remember the Dream House quilt?"

She turned to Virginia and explained. "It was a present for me. Everybody made a block of their dream house, but it wasn't so much about the actual house as what it represented, the life we wanted for ourselves. Liza's house was modern and sparse with tall ceilings and plenty of room to hang her paintings. Basically, it was an art gallery with a couple of sofas thrown in—not like anybody else's," Ivy said with a grin.

"Liza's an original," she said. "Think about the quilts she's made for herself. I don't think she's ever used a traditional pattern without altering it or updating it. And her fabric choices are just as unique. Bold colors and fabric combinations I'd never be able to come up with, but somehow, in Liza's quilts, they always seem to work. The double wedding ring is a nice quilt, but I can't see her actually using it. And if we're going to go to the trouble of making Liza a quilt, I'd just as soon it be one she'd be happy to put on her bed."

"Well, I guess you're right." Margot sighed, reluctant to let go of the quilt she'd pieced together in her imagination. "But if *I* ever get married—not that there's ever a chance of that happening," she said with a derisive snort, "I want a double wedding ring."

Virginia patted Margot's arm. "All right. And I'll pick out the fabrics myself. Pink and white, with a touch of spring green, right?"

Margot nodded.

"But I think Ivy is right," Mom continued. "A traditional quilt won't do for Liza. You know, Garrett is taking me into New York with him tomorrow to meet her."

"He is?"

This was news to me. Garrett gets to see Liza so infrequently these days that I couldn't help but think he'd be anxious to have Mom tag along.

"That was nice of him."

Mom's eyes twinkled. "It was, not that he really had much choice. I insisted he bring me along. After all, I've been here for weeks in hopes of meeting Liza! I can't wait around forever, not at my age. Anyway, after I meet Liza for myself, get to know her a little, maybe I'll have some ideas for a wedding quilt she'd like."

"Good plan," I said.

When making a quilt for someone else, Mom has an uncanny knack for choosing exactly the right pattern and style for that person. Over her lifetime, Mom has made hundreds of quilts, most of them intended as gifts, and I've yet to see a recipient open one of Virginia's quilts without going on and on about how it was the absolutely perfect quilt for them.

"I still want to make these place mats," I said, "but why don't we hold off deciding about a wedding quilt for Liza until Mom comes back and gives us a report?"

The others agreed.

"Good!" Mom beamed, pleased to be entrusted with so important a task. "I'm so looking forward to meeting Liza—and to seeing New York City! I've never been. I wish it wasn't so cold. I'd love to go to Ellis Island and see the Statue of Liberty."

"It'll warm up soon, Mom. I'll take you myself in the spring."

"Oh no," she said dismissively. "I won't be here that long. I really should be getting back to Wisconsin as soon as I finish teaching this class. I should never have let you talk me into it, Evelyn. It'll hold me up another three weeks at least."

"I know, but think what it means to those moms to have you here. They're already crazy about you. Natalie told me she thinks you're a fabulous teacher and that she can't wait until next week's class."

"Oh, pshaw! She just said that because it's her first quilting class and she doesn't have anyone to compare me to. Quit trying to flatter me, Evelyn." She frowned and made her tone scolding, but I could tell she was pleased.

"Anyway, enough gabbing," Mom said. "It's coming up on seven o'clock and so far, other than myself, no one has sewn a stitch. Ivy, let's go pick out fabric for your appliqué. Evelyn, I think I saw some coffee- and mocha-colored batiks, kind of an art deco pattern, that would look nice with that turquoise. I'll bring them back up for you."

"Thanks, Mom."

Mom and Ivy went downstairs. As they did, I heard Ivy say, "You know, Virginia, I've been thinking. Would you consider teaching a class at New Beginnings? We've got so many moms with children in the program, and I was thinking that a Mommy and Me hand quilting class might be . . ."

Ivy's voice faded away as she descended the stairs. Margot sat down and started pinning fabric triangles, readying them for the sewing machine.

"Come spring," she said, "I've got a feeling Virginia will still be here."

"I hope so," I said as I shoved a green print to one side and rearranged the remaining fabrics into different combinations. "She keeps talking about going back to Wisconsin, but I don't know why. She loves it here. She's more active, physically and intellectually. I can see a big difference in her already. She seems sharper and remembers things more easily than before. Mom needs to be needed. With Dad gone and so many of her friends passing on or moving to warmer climates, not to mention the trouble she's had with driving, her world was getting smaller and smaller. Here, she's got friends again."

Margot raised her eyebrows knowingly. "I'll say she does. I saw her chatting with Gibb Rainey in the post office lobby the other day."

I looked up from my work and chuckled. "So what? Everybody chats with Gibb. He sits smack in the middle of the lobby. It's kind of hard not to."

"Maybe, but they seemed awfully friendly. And haven't you noticed how Virginia volunteers to go to the post office at the drop of a hat? I think she's got an itch for old Gibb."

An itch? At the age of eighty my mother had an itch? It didn't seem likely.

"Margot, you're imagining things. I'm sure she just enjoys talking to Gibb. They must be pretty close to the same age. And that's my point. Here in New Bern, she's got connections, people who listen to her and respect her. More importantly, she's got purpose again. Her students just love her. She's much happier here than she was back home. You can tell just by looking at her. She looks ten years younger."

"Hmm. Wish I could say the same of you."

"Hey! That's not very nice," I said, offended and a little surprised. Usually Margot is sweet to a fault.

"Sorry, Evelyn," she replied and blushed a little. "I hate to be the one to say it, but you look tired. Have you been having trouble sleeping? And you're distracted too. I was looking over the vendor invoices today. Do you know that you ordered three bolts of the same red paisley?"

"I did?"

"Uh-huh. You've got something on your mind. What is it?"

"Liza," I admitted.

Margot bobbed her head as if she'd expected as much. "You're upset that Liza and Abigail aren't including you in the wedding plans."

"No," I said. "Of course not. I've got questions about a wedding that's going to make the union of Prince Charles to Princess Diana look like a backyard barbecue, but that's none of my business. I'm keeping my opinions to myself. But I do have some other reservations, or rather, I did. I should have kept those to myself too."

I told Margot all about Garrett's phone call to Wisconsin, my foolishly unfiltered response, and the radio silence that had existed between Liza and me ever since.

"Oh, Evelyn," Margot said in a disappointed voice.

"I know. I know. It was stupid. But the engagement came as a complete shock. Garrett hadn't given the least hint that he was going to propose. Before I stopped to think, out it came."

My eyes felt tired. I rubbed them. "I wish I could take it back," I said, "but I can't. And the thing is, I'm still worried about this wedding. Not the ceremony so much, but what happens after. They're so young! And Liza is . . ." I paused for a moment, wanting to choose my words carefully, but I was talking to Margot, and Margot understood.

"Bruised?" she offered.

"Yes! I love Liza. She is caring and creative and intelligent, but she's also been through a lot. Her father abandoned her before she was even born, and then, with her mother's death . . ." I shook my head and pushed another bolt of blue to the side, rejecting it. "The poor girl has a lot of scars, and I'm just afraid she's going to carry them with her into this marriage."

"Sure she will," Margot said. "Doesn't everybody? Didn't you?"

"Yeah. And look how that turned out."

"So you think you're going to be able to find a bride without baggage for your son?" Margot said with a laugh. "If you want Garrett to wait for that girl to cross his path, then I think you can kiss any visions of you bouncing a grandbaby on your knee good-bye forever."

"You're right. I know." I started rolling up the rejected bolts of fabric, letting them thump hard against the table as I did, taking out a few of my frustrations. "But marriage is such a big step and, quite honestly, it's a big risk. I never thought my marriage to Rob would end in divorce, especially not after twenty-four years. When it did—well, there's no pain like it. Even losing my breasts to cancer wasn't as painful as losing my husband to another woman. That's the kind of hurt there just aren't words for. I don't want Garret to know that kind of pain. Or Liza, either."

"And you think that their marriage could end in divorce?"

"Well, heck, Margot. *Any* marriage could end in divorce! Did you hear about Wendy Perkins's daughter, Sheila?

"After ten years and three kids, she and her husband are getting divorced. They were here in the shop just last summer. Sheila was picking out fabric for a quilt and Bill was with her. They looked so happy together. He opened the door for her when they came in, was completely patient while she was picking out her fabric, even carried the bolts over to the counter for her. He was so sweet! They seemed to have everything in common. They loved golfing and swing dancing. They were both active in their church. And now they're getting a divorce."

Margot nodded knowingly. "And did you hear about my cousin Louise? She's eight years older than Ted. When they got married, everybody said it would never work, that it was one thing to have the husband be that much older than the wife, but that the second

Louise started getting a few miles on her, Ted would drop her like a hot potato."

"And?"

"And, after five kids, six grandkids, and almost forty years of marriage, this summer they renewed their vows prior to sailing off for a honeymoon cruise around the world."

Margot crossed her arms and tilted her chin down and her eyes up in a perfect "so there" pose.

"All right. Good point. You can't predict which marriages will fail and which will succeed just by measuring the odds. But," I puffed as I carried the unwanted bolts to a table near the staircase so I'd remember to take them back downstairs later, "you'd be stupid not to at least consider the odds. And with a girl like Liza, a girl who's carrying around so much baggage, I can't help but think the odds aren't so good."

"Not to mention a boy like Garrett, coming from a broken home and all."

Ouch. That one stung.

"Fair enough. Garrett's got issues of his own. He was out of the house by the time Rob filed for divorce, but he still had to endure his share of the fallout. I hear there are people who manage to get 'amicable' divorces, whatever that means"—I shrugged—"but Rob and I sure weren't among them.

"Margot, I know I'm being unfair, but I can't help it. I know too much! About Liza. About marriage. About how uncertain life can be! I just wish I had a crystal ball to see into their future, some kind of guarantee that they won't get hurt."

Margot opened her mouth to speak, but I lifted up my hand to stop her.

"There are no guarantees. Believe me, I know that. But you can't blame me for wishing. If I just knew . . ."

Margot put her hands on her hips. "Your problem is that you know too much. Evelyn, let's think this out. What if Garrett had never moved out here? What if he'd stayed at his old job in Seattle and then one day, out of the blue, he'd called you and said, 'Mom,

I've got some news. I'm in love with a wonderful girl and we're getting married'? What would you have said then?"

"Congratulations?"

"Right! Because even though you didn't know the girl, you'd trust that Garrett is a good man and a good judge of character. But," Margot said, tipping her head to the side, "what's to say that that girl wouldn't have had just as much baggage as Liza does?"

"She could," I admitted. "It's just that I wouldn't know about it. You know what they say, 'ignorance is bliss.' "

"They also say, 'better the devil you know than the devil you don't.' As long as we're trading proverbs, how about this one? This train is about to leave the station, Evelyn. Garrett and Liza are getting married, and you really don't have any say in the matter. If you don't get on board, you'll be left standing all alone on the platform, chasing after the caboose and—"

"Margot? Enough with the train analogies. I get it."

"Sorry."

I did get it. I had for a while. Garrett and Liza were adults. They were engaged and soon they'd be married. If I didn't patch up my relationship with Liza, I could end up being shut out of her life and Garrett's forever. I understood the progression of thought here; it was all very logical.

What wasn't logical was the cold lump of anxiety that had formed in the pit of my stomach when Garrett called to announce the engagement and that had been there ever since. Probably I did know too much about Liza, and that helped fuel my anxiety. But if he'd called up from Seattle and told me he was engaged to some faceless Becka, or Jackie, or Charlotte, would I have congratulated him? I wasn't so sure.

Maybe I did know too much about Liza, but the bigger truth was that I knew too much about life, about the gaping wounds that are left open when that which God hath joined together was torn asunder.

I never want to feel that kind of pain again. And I don't want Garrett to feel it, either. Or Liza. But I know it could happen. Life is risky. And I suddenly know, as I pull out my emotions one by one, untying that knot of anxiety within myself and examining every kink and twist in the cord, that I've made this about me and it isn't.

More than three years after my divorce, after pulling up stakes and my socks and resurrecting my forgotten dreams, after getting knocked off my feet by breast cancer and pulling myself back up by reaching out to grasp the outstretched hands of my friends, after opening my heart to Charlie and the possibility of love, and even after refusing Rob's tearful plea to take him back, why am I still nursing this hurt?

I thought I was over this. I thought I'd left my fears behind me, but the truth is they're still tied to my bumper, trailing along in my wake, weighing me down like a renegade rudder, threatening to steer me back into my old fears and resentments, ground I've already paid for.

I have to put a stop to this.

Margot looked sheepish after I'd cut her off, but because she's a good friend and a good friend tells what you need to hear even when you're in no mood to hear it, she went on. "Evelyn, you've just got to figure out a way to patch things up with Liza."

"I know. I've tried. But she won't answer the phone and she won't respond to my messages. I've tried making Garrett my mule, sending messages through him, but that hasn't worked, either."

"Well, what if you went to New York? Just showed up on her doorstep? Virginia is going into the city with Garrett tomorrow. Why don't you tag along?"

I shook my head. "Uh-uh. I know Liza. She's like a turtle. If I sneak up on her uninvited, she'll just draw back into her shell."

"Then what are you going to do?"

I reached out and ran my hand over the bolt of beautiful turquoise fabric, smooth and slippery, the thin threads so tightly woven they felt like silk under my fingers.

"I don't know. Something."

16

Liza Burgess

I was in the bathroom, putting on lip gloss, when the doorbell rang. I ran to open it, expecting to see Garrett.

What I saw instead was a tiny, elderly woman with hair so white and shiny it looked like that fiberglass stuff I used as snow in the window display I'd made for the quilt shop last Christmas. She had a huge black patent leather purse looped over her arm, and eyes that sparkled like bright blue pebbles at the bottom of a stream, eyes like Evelyn's.

"Disappointed?" the old woman asked with a grin. "Don't be. Garrett's downstairs looking for a parking space. He dropped me off first so I wouldn't have too far to walk. He'll be up in a minute."

"Grandma Virginia?"

"I know you weren't expecting me. Don't worry, I won't hang around all day and spoil your date. At my age, a few hours in the big city is probably all I can handle. And at my age," she said, peering up at me through the thick lenses of wire-rimmed glasses that made her big blue eyes look even bigger, "I also can't afford to waste time sitting around waiting for my future granddaughter-in-law to find a spare moment to come out to New Bern and meet me. I could kick the bucket at any moment. Why, when I was born, people still got around by horse and buggy!"

Obviously Grandma Virginia shared more with her grandson than the Dixon good looks. She had his goofy sense of humor too.

"Really?" I said. "Ford started making Model Ts in about 1908, didn't they? Wow! You look pretty good, considering you're over one hundred."

She laughed. "Well, maybe I'm not quite *that* old, but at my age every morning you wake up on the top side of the dirt is a gift. I didn't want to die before meeting you, so here I am. Aren't you going to ask me in?"

I opened the door and Grandma Virginia came in, looking around the apartment as I hung up her coat.

"Garrett said you have roommates. Where are they?"

"Out. At the gym, running errands, getting a manicure."

She poked her head into our tiny living room and even tinier galley kitchen. "Is this all there is to it?"

"That and a bathroom and the two bedrooms."

She clucked her tongue, amazed that four women could share this matchbox-sized apartment. "How much is your rent?"

"Twenty-four hundred a month," I said.

She gasped. "Dollars!"

"Well, it's not yen." I laughed.

She made a tsking sound with her tongue. "Twenty-four hundred dollars a month for an apartment too small to change your mind in. Back in Wisconsin, you could get yourself a nice three- or four-bedroom home on a big lot for that kind of money."

"You think this is bad, wait until you see the bedrooms. They're about the size of my closet back in New Bern, but with worse ventilation. Would you like to see?"

She followed me down the narrow hallway to my room. "It's tiny, all right," she said. "Good thing you're so organized."

"We kind of have to be. But the light is good," I said, nodding toward the easel I had set up in the corner.

Grandma Virginia approached the easel slowly, looking my painting up and down. "You painted this? It's very good. Not that I know much about modern art, but I like the colors. It's got a real energetic feeling to it. Seems like it reminds me of something."

"Chagall." I sighed. "Marc Chagall. That's the problem with it. And with me. I love art, and now that I'm studying it more, it turns out I love art history too. But I'm not a fabulous painter. . . ."

"What are you talking about?" Grandma Virginia protested. "This is a beautiful painting! You're a wonderful artist."

"Mmm. It's nice of you to say so, but trust me, compared to a lot of painters, I'm not that good." I stood next to her in front of the canvas and crossed my arms over my chest. "I mean, the technique is good. Very good, in fact, but it's not very original. Lately, when it comes to painting, I'm like tofu. I tend to absorb the flavors of whatever is nearby. For my art history seminar, I just finished a paper on Chagall. So guess what the painting I've been working on for the last month, the one I'd planned on using as my senior project, comes out looking like?"

"Chagall?"

"Yeah," I said and sat down on my bed. "Chagall. And if I'd written my paper on Pollock, or Matisse, or Hopper, or Lam, it probably would have turned out looking like one of them. The way things are going, the only way I'll be able to make a living as an artist is by painting copies of other people's work—those horrible, mass-produced knockoffs that they sell at cheesy auctions in the ballrooms of crummy hotels that smell like stale cigarettes and swimming-pool chlorine."

Grandma Virginia sat down next to me on the edge of the bed and patted my shoulder. "There, there. It can't be as bad as all that. I'm sure that lots of young artists are influenced by the work of other artists."

"Yes, but it's usually the kind of thing that happens early on, when you first begin studying. And it was never a problem for me until now. I always had plenty of ideas, but lately . . ." I threw up my hands. "Nothing. I haven't come within two hundred miles of an original thought all semester. And the thing is, I didn't even see it until my oils instructor pointed it out to me.

"It was so embarrassing. He pulled out my portfolio, laid out my paintings and, one after another, ticked off the names of the artists who had influenced my work—all artists whose work I'd been studying in my art history seminar. The instructor wasn't mean about it or anything. This is the second course I've taken from him, so he knows I'm capable of producing original work. He just wanted me to realize what I'd been doing. It was so awful. I just wanted the floor to open and swallow me up."

"Poor Liza." Virginia pulled her big black purse onto her lap, snapped it open, reached into its depths, and pulled out a piece of candy wrapped in shiny yellow cellophane—a butterscotch.

"Here," she said. "This will help."

And strangely, it did. A little.

"The worst part is that even though it will be completely humiliating and absolutely everyone will think I'm copying Chagall, I'm going to have to enter this in the senior exhibition. I don't have time to paint something else. Even if I did, I still don't have any ideas. No original ones."

"Don't give up yet," Grandma Virginia said. "Something may come to you."

"Doubtful."

"Oh, don't be so negative. Here. Have another butterscotch." She handed me the candy and then squinted, looking at the quilt that hung over my bed.

"That's very interesting, Liza. Is that one of your designs?"

"Yes. Just something I was playing around with, but it turned out all right."

"Well, it's a lot more than all right," she said. "I love your color combinations, and those big bold stars scattered around in different sizes really draw your eye across the piece. Such an unusual arrangement, almost like a stream of stars . . ."

"I like stars," I said, pleased and a little surprised that she seemed to genuinely like my wall hanging. I wouldn't have figured that someone her age, who has been quilting for about three times my lifetime, would have liked the design.

She leaned closer and laughed. "Are those fish?"

I nodded. "Yeah. I was walking outside one night and the sky was so cold and clear, and the stars were just scattered across the sky like diamonds. I like to use bright colors against dark backgrounds.

It gives the colors such deeper dimension. Anyway, looking up at the sky, I kept thinking it looked like a midnight ocean. So"—I shrugged, thinking how silly this must sound to her—"I came home and added some fish."

"And what did you make them out of? Is that plastic wrap?"

"Not quite. I actually tried that at first, but it didn't work. Too flimsy. So I used designer cellophane, the stuff that quilters draw stitching patterns on and lay over their quilt tops to see how the different patterns will look."

"That's very ingenious. I'd never have thought of something like that."

"Thanks, but it's just something I was fooling around with."

The doorbell rang.

"Garrett must have found his parking spot," Grandma Virginia said, following me to the door.

Garrett was holding a pale blue envelope in his hand. "Hi, babe," he said before giving me a kiss on the cheek.

"You brought me a card?" I reached for the envelope.

"Nope. It's a note from Mom. She made me promise to deliver it to you personally. Want to read it now?"

"Um. Later," I said with a pang of guilt. I laid the envelope on our tiny hall table, the place where everybody dumps everything from mail to books to the flyers that pizza places and Chinese restaurants shove under the front door. With any luck, it would be buried under a pile of paper before I returned. Or maybe someone would accidentally throw it out with the junk mail. I couldn't bring myself to read it any more than I could bring myself to answer Evelyn's calls. Not yet. I knew I should, but . . .

"We'd better get to the museum."

"Okay," Garrett said. "Sorry I took so long. I almost had to park in the Bronx."

"That's all right. I've had fun getting to know Grandma Virginia. She gave me some butterscotch."

"She did? Let me have some." And, mindless of the fact that his grandmother was watching, he pulled my body tight to his and gave me a long, lingering kiss.

"Mmm." He grinned, pleased with himself.

"Garrett!" I scolded after he released his grip on me. "Your grandma is standing right here!"

"Oh, I don't mind," Virginia said. "But if you two are done smooching, let's get to this museum Garrett was telling me about. What was it again?"

"One of Liza's favorites," Garrett said. "The Whitney Museum of American Art."

"Huh." Virginia nodded, but looked less than sure about what we were getting her into. "And you say they have quilts there?"

"They do today," I said. "The Quilts of Gee's Bend. Trust me. You'll love it."

Normally, I prefer not to go to museums on weekends because of the crowds, but today, even with a press of people around us, I didn't mind. The voices, the faces, the sounds of footsteps just melted away as I lingered first in front of one quilt, then another, then another, with my hand clutching my throat because there were simply no words to describe what I was seeing.

No. That's not true. There was one word.

Honest.

Those quilts were just so honest, so unabashedly true. The bravery of them left me speechless.

I only started quilting a couple of years ago, so I'm certainly no expert on the subject, but it seems to me that a lot of modern quilts and quilters have kind of wandered away from the point of it all.

Quilting is an art form: a means of expressing yourself, of communicating feelings and hopes and observations and beliefs without resorting to anything as pedestrian and inexact as words. Or it should be. But a lot of quilters get so wrapped up in precision and technique that they reduce quilting to something that has about as much to do with individual expression as filling in the spaces on a paint-by-number kit—or laboring for weeks over a canvas that you'd thought was an original only to stand back and realize that you'd just regurgitated something somebody else, say Chagall, had said a long time ago and a whole lot better.

If you don't produce something honest, something that stands boldly on the mountaintop and shouts, "This is who I am and I won't apologize for it!", then what's the point? Of quilting? Of painting? Of anything?

These quilters didn't have much in the way of fancy tools: no rulers that mark quarter-inch seam lines with carefully calibrated precision, no computerized sewing machines that can backstitch or appliqué or sew trails of leafy vines and hundreds of other stitches with the touch of a button. They labored over their seams, squinting by the dim light of a silent midnight, cherishing the few quiet moments at the end of a day spent tending to everyone's needs but their own.

They didn't have access to thousands upon thousands of bolts of perfectly milled cottons with fifty different shades and nuances of lemon yellow or peachy pink or jade green. Instead they borrowed scraps from each other, or salvaged fabric from worn work shirts with the elbows out, or skirts too short to cover the scabby knees of a growing child, making do, piecing the bits together into odd and arresting patches when there wasn't enough to go around.

They didn't have the chance to take classes or workshops from world-famous instructors with twenty pattern books in publication and an interactive website. Instead they learned from each other, lessons that were never printed in books but were handed down, woman to woman, written clearly in their quilts and in their memories.

And so their quilts are raw and real. They are art. And their honesty! Oh! Their unvarnished, unapologetic honesty brings tears to my eyes. They are so brave.

Could I ever dare to be so brave?

17

Evelyn Dixon

"Stars? Are you sure?" I asked as I unlocked the shop door on Monday morning.

If there is one thing quilters love to make, it's stars. The sheer geometry of star patterns, combined with the nearly endless variations possible when piecing them, make stars one of the most popular and traditional pattern choices for quilters, including myself. Over the years, I've made dozens of star quilts. But when we sent Mom off on her mission to figure out what sort of unique, bold, avant-garde quilt we should make for Liza's wedding, I was thinking she'd come up with something a little less traditional than stars.

"Liza likes stars."

"So do I. So does everybody. But you're not exactly breaking new ground here. I was thinking you'd suggest something a little more unusual."

"Well, I'm not talking about just any old stars, Evelyn," Mom huffed. "Give me a little credit for good sense. But Liza does like stars, she told me so herself. I was thinking about it all day yesterday. Remember the Broken Hearts Mending quilt the circle made for you?"

I nodded. It was Liza's first original quilt design and a pretty remarkable accomplishment for someone who had been quilting such a short time. More importantly, it was an expressive quilt, made with love, showing a series of bright pink, strip-pieced whole and half hearts scattered haphazardly over a field of brilliant green, as if the broken pieces were moving back toward their sundered halves in the process of becoming whole again, representing the thing we all had in common: broken hearts that were still mending.

Liza thought up the design all on her own and, with Abigail and Margot, she had sewn it and given it to me in the hospital, right after my mastectomies. It was one of my most cherished quilts and was lying on the foot of my bed at that moment.

"Yes, of course I remember it."

"Well," Mom said, with a definitive nod, "that just goes to show you."

"Goes to show you what?" I grabbed a stack of fabric bolts from behind the counter and started walking around the shop, putting them back in their proper spots.

Mom trailed behind me as I worked and let out a sigh, disappointed to realize that she'd raised so dense a daughter.

"Don't you understand? Liza has nothing against traditional themes in quilting. In fact, when we were at the museum . . . Oh, Evelyn! I wish you'd have come too! Those quilts were just remarkable, real works of art. And to think that a museum—a museum in New York City—recognized that! Isn't that something? And did I tell you? After the museum, we went to this little Italian place. Did I tell you that we had pizza with no sauce on it? A white pie, Garrett called it. I didn't think I'd care for it, but it was delicious!"

I shelved a bolt of red paisley, one of the three I'd ordered, only half listening as I tried to come up with ideas for a class project that could incorporate as many yards of red paisley fabric as possible. "Yes, East Coast pizza is completely different from the kind they make in Wisconsin. What does that have to do with Liza's quilt?"

"Nothing. I just thought it was interesting. Anyway, the point is that Liza was in the museum, looking at these beautiful, old-timey, folk art quilts, and she was so moved she was actually crying! You see? Liza appreciates the old patterns, the history and traditions that go with them, but she likes to interpret them in new ways. That's what she did with the quilt she designed for you. After stars, hearts are probably the most traditional theme in quilts, but she found a way to take that old theme and bring it into the present day, to give it meaning and a message. I think that's what we should do with Liza's star quilt!"

"Okay," I said as I squatted down to slide a bolt of blue batik into an opening on a bottom shelf. "But how? You said you didn't want to use just any old star, so what kind of stars were you thinking of?"

"Hunter's."

I left the pile of fabric bolts on the floor, got to my feet, and looked at Mom. "Do you think we have time?"

Hunter's star blocks, sometimes called Indian arrowheads, make beautiful quilts, but you don't see too many of them, and there's a reason for that. They're a little more complicated than other star designs. It's a little hard to explain, but the basic idea involves appliquéing an elongated diamond onto the points of a triangle and then joining the two triangles together to create a block. A series of these blocks, when joined, end up making very pretty eight-pointed stars.

"I'd really like to give the quilt to Liza at the bridal shower. That's only a few weeks away, during her spring break. That way she won't have to skip classes to come. I don't want her to have any excuses for not attending. By the way, did Garrett give her the invitation and note from me?"

Mom nodded. "He did. As soon as he came in the door."

"Good." I stooped down to pick up the remaining bolts of fabric. "Well, if you think we can get it done in time for the shower . . ."

Mom had stopped following me and was standing in front of the batiks section, looking at fabrics with sparkling eyes and toting up color values in her head. "Oh, we can. I'm sure of it."

"All right, then. When do we start?"

"Soon. As soon as I figure out a design." She placed a finger on top of a bolt of burnt orange batik and tipped it forward to see how it looked in the light.

"Evelyn, can I have some drafting paper and a pencil? I've got an idea."

18

Evelyn Dixon

Along with the invitation to her own bridal shower, I'd sent Liza a long, handwritten letter of apology, trying to explain why I'd been so stupid, how my careless words erupted from my old resurfaced hurts and fears rather than from any doubts about Liza. I told her how much I cared about her and how I hoped she could forgive my thoughtlessness so we could renew our old friendship. I said I was sorry in every way I could think of.

I know Garrett gave her the note; Mom saw him do it. To make sure, I even asked him about it myself, but he said exactly what Mom did, that he'd given it to Liza as soon as he saw her. But that was two weeks ago and I still haven't heard a word from her. Just as before, my calls and phone messages have gone unanswered.

Margot suggested I talk to Garrett and enlist his help in getting Liza to respond, but I don't want to do that. Rob's mother used to do that—send me messages, usually critical ones, through him—and I always resented it. Things are rocky enough without involving Garrett in this.

Weddings are supposed to be such happy things. So why had this one gotten to be so complicated? And this rift between Liza and me wasn't the only thing. Abigail is driving me insane.

I know that I'm just the mother of the groom and that my primary function is to stay silent, especially since I'm not paying for this. So far, I have, but I'm about this close to throwing Abigail to the ground, rolling her up in a bolt of high-loft quilt batting, and stuffing her into a closet!

It's one thing for her to turn this wedding into one great big, glitzy circus, but when she starts trying to meddle in the only two things that are really my responsibility—the bridal shower and the rehearsal dinner—we've got a problem. Well, as maid of honor, the shower is really Margot's show, but we're working on it together.

When we threw Abigail a surprise bridal shower, it was very hurried. Because Franklin was still recovering from his heart attack, we held the shower in a conference room at the hospital. We didn't have much time to plan, so we kept things simple, but we still managed to put on a nice little party with cake and champagne, flowers, and a few gifts. Everyone had a wonderful time, Abigail included. It was only last year, so you'd think Abbie would still remember that and have a little faith in us.

Now we've got more time, so while we're not going overboard, we are planning a very special shower for Liza. We're going to have it in the shop. By moving a couple of display units out of the way, we'll have plenty of room for the tables. Charlie is making the food, lots and lots of appetizers. Liza is more of a grazer than an eater, I've noticed. She likes to take a couple of bites of something and then move on, so we thought an all hors d'oeuvres menu would please her.

Margot and I are making cupcakes, daisy cupcakes. I'm baking the cupcakes and Margot will do the decorating. When she was in high school she had a job in a bakery, so she's had a little experience with that. We'll have a few silly games, just for fun. And the flowers will be simple: big bowls of daisies, Liza's favorite. I was a little surprised when Abigail told me she hadn't chosen them for her bridal bouquet.

During the party, Margot is going to take pictures of Liza with all her friends, and Ivy will quickly download them on the computer and print them out on special photo fabric. Then all the guests can sign them and later we'll sew them up into a little wall quilt as a keepsake for Liza.

All in all, I think it will be a lovely party, just a fun, relaxed get-together with the girls. With all the pressures of school and the wedding, I think that's exactly what Liza could use, but Abigail disagrees. Strongly.

She thinks we should have the shower at the Walden Inn, or the country club, or just about anywhere besides the shop, never mind that this is the place where we first met Liza and that some of our best memories took place right here. Abigail thinks that shower games are silly, that we should hire a professional photographer and florist, that we should have sterling silver party favors for all the guests engraved with Liza's initials and the date, and, most of all, that we should turn the whole thing over to Byron Dennehey, that wedding planner.

Abigail has always breathed rarified air. I've gotten used to it because, for all her eccentricities, she is a good woman and a good friend and unfailingly polite, even to people she doesn't much care about. But right now, she's acting like a complete witch. She was so dismissive of our plans that she made poor Margot cry. I'll admit, that isn't that hard to do. Margot is very tenderhearted. But Abigail knows that. She should have been a little more sensitive. When I told her so, she stormed out of the shop in a huff. She's missed two quilt circle meetings since then.

"I don't understand it," I told Charlie over coffee at the Blue Bean. "Abigail is being completely unreasonable."

"I understand it," he said through a mouth full of muffin. "You're all bonkers."

"Charlie!"

"Well, you are! Mad as hatters, every one of you. And by 'every one of you,' understand that I don't mean you, Abigail, Margot, Liza, and Ivy, specifically. I mean the female population as a whole."

"Is that right? Huh. You know, Charlie, it's hard to believe you didn't have a really serious girlfriend until I came along."

"Isn't it?" Charlie said and then washed down the muffin with a slurp of coffee. "Seriously, Evelyn. You're daft, the whole lot of you. Women are always going on and on about the need for honest communication and meaningful relationships. But the second there's a difficult issue, the moment there's a disagreement or difference of opinion among you, you all run off to your separate corners, terrified to talk about it. Well, that's not quite true. You do talk about it, to each other, but somehow those conversations never involve the person who's actually causing the problem.

"You'd never see a man do that. If men have a disagreement, they just take it outside, give each other a good pounding, then buy each other a beer, and that's that. Simple.

"See this?" he said, pointing to a silvery white thread of a scar that extended from the left corner of his lower lip. "Brendan Cohan gave me that. I was nineteen. He fancied Mary Kate McAfree and so did I. There was a dance coming up. We both wanted to take her, so we decided to fight it out. Oh, Brendan had a tremendous right," Charlie said with admiration. "He split my lip and I blacked his eye. Afterward, we went into the pub, shared a pint, and were the best of friends ever after."

"And who got the girl?"

"Bill O'Shaughnessy. Brendan and I were so banged up from the fight that Mary Kate said she wouldn't be seen with either of us. So, O'Shaughnessy snuck in under the fence and stole our girl. The scoundrel." Charlie frowned as he took two pats of butter out of a dish and smeared them on the other half of his muffin.

I rested my chin on my folded hands and stared at him.

"What?" he asked.

"That's it? You and a guy disfigure each other over a girl who dumps you for someone else, someone without a split lip or black eye? That was your big morality tale on the superiority of the male style of communication?"

Charlie reared back his head, offended. "Well, at least it was up front and honest! At least we didn't pussyfoot around the problem, hoping that if we didn't deal with it, the whole thing would just go away. No! We had an issue and we faced it, head-on. That's what men do. But women? Women are pussyfooters, every last one of you. And you're the worst of them all."

Now it was my turn to be offended. "I am not! I do *not* pussyfoot, Charlie. What a rotten thing to say."

"It's the truth, Evelyn, and you know it." He narrowed his eyes and pointed a finger at me. "You are a pussyfooter through and through. Don't believe me? I'll prove it to you. Let's start with Abigail. You've been sitting here all morning, griping about Abigail, telling me that she's driving you insane, so insane that you'd like to lock her in a closet!"

I waved off this accusation. "Oh, well, I was just venting. Makes me feel better to talk about it. That's how women keep from getting into fistfights with our friends. We vent."

"Yes!" Charlie took his finger out of my chest and raised it into the air, triumphant. "But never to each other! You never confront the issue, you just nibble around the edges of it, like mice circling cheese in a mousetrap, trying to get your little bite in without triggering the trap!"

"Well, isn't that better than setting it off deliberately? Who wants to get caught in a trap?"

"Nobody. But eventually, you always do. You talk *about* each other but not *to* each other. And eventually, inevitably, the word gets back to the one you were talking about, and *zing!* There goes the trap! You get caught with your foot in your mouth, and a perfectly good friendship is destroyed."

"Oh, Charlie, you're exaggerating. Abigail and I have been friends for too long to let something like this come between us. After the wedding is over, we'll patch things up."

"Maybe," he said between slurps of coffee, "but relationships have never been easy for Abigail. Until you and Margot came along, I don't think Abigail ever had a real friend. You let this fester too long and she might just convince herself that she was right all along, that friendships aren't worth the price you have to pay for them. She'll cut herself off from you and go back to being an island unto herself. You know how she is, Evelyn," he said, raising his eyebrows.

"You're right to be worried about her," he continued. "She's not acting like herself. Heaven knows, if a client wants to spend a pile on a catering job, I'm happy to oblige, but even I think Abigail is going overboard. It wasn't enough that she's ordered a two-pound lobster for every guest, now she's got me putting white Alba truffles on everything! Do you know how much they cost? Sixteen hundred a pound, that's how much! And that's *my* cost. The thing is, it's completely unnecessary; the menu was fabulous before, fit for the Queen of Sheba. Next thing, she'll have me sprinkling gold leaf on the salad course."

Charlie put down his coffee cup. "I've known Abigail for going on twenty years. She's always been able to afford the best of everything, but until now, I've never known her to waste money, and that's all this is. Pure waste. Something's not right with her, Evelyn. I'm serious. All this excess has gotten, well . . . excessive. Almost frantic. Franklin's worried about her too. He pays her bills, you know. Even before they were married he managed her business affairs. He sat down to talk to her about the costs of the wedding. It didn't go well. She said some pretty awful things to him, the kindest of which was that he should take care to remember that her money was still hers, and she could spend it any way she wanted. Words were exchanged." He paused a moment before deciding to spell it out for me.

"Franklin is sleeping in the guest room."

"Seriously? Whose idea was that?"

"Mutual agreement," Charlie said. "Seems it was the only thing they could agree upon."

"Oh, no. That is bad. Really bad. That doesn't sound like Abigail."

Abigail had told me that her first marriage, to the wealthy and long-deceased Woolley Wynne, had been far from passionate, and their years together did nothing to change that. Given that, it wasn't surprising that, when it came to the pleasures of marital intimacy after her wedding, Abigail's expectations had been low.

I don't know all the details and Abigail doesn't feel the need to share them, but all you have to do is spend five minutes with Abbie and Franklin to know that their marriage has been a success in every area. They're always holding hands and their conversations are sprinkled with endearments. And I know they think it's a big secret, but everybody has figured out that they have this secret signal going.

Whenever they're at a party or dinner or even a luncheon and Franklin pulls on his nose, as if it was tickling him, and then sniffs,

Abigail's cheeks suddenly flush red and she makes some excuse about having a headache or being tired. Then Franklin gets her coat and they scamper back home, Franklin grinning and Abigail blushing, looking awfully bright-eyed for a woman with a headache. Of course, Abigail would be mortified if she knew that I knew this, but I think it's sweet. After enduring so many years in a loveless marriage, followed by many more as a widow, Abigail deserves this. She and Franklin are very much in love. She adores Franklin. So, if what Charlie said was true, then Abigail really did have a problem.

"Poor Abigail. Something is really bothering her."

"It certainly is," Charlie said. "And you're probably Abigail's best friend in the world, but are you helping her? Have you talked to her? No. Instead, you're pussyfooting."

"Now, wait a minute, Charlie."

He held up his hand. "No. Hear me out. Abigail's not the only one you're too chickenhearted to confront. There's Liza too. She's not just your friend, she's going to be your daughter-in-law. Someday she may be the mother of your grandchildren, yet you've done nothing to mend the broken fences between you. Why? Because you're afraid of confronting her, that's why. Pussyfooter."

I was used to Charlie's brusque manner and teasing by now. Normally, I enjoy it, but this was hitting a little too close to home. He was starting to make me mad.

"Hang on, Charlie. That's not fair," I protested as I ticked my objections off on my fingers. "I have called Liza countless times. I've left scores of messages. I wrote her a letter that was basically three pages of groveling. And for all my effort, I haven't received even a hint of a response! Nothing! At the moment, I'm helping organize a bridal shower for Liza that I've got serious doubts she'll even bother showing up for! The way things are going, I'm beginning to wonder if she'll even show up for the wedding. So don't you sit there and call me a chicken, Charlie Donnelly! I've done absolutely everything possible to patch things up with Liza!"

Charlie pressed his lips together and crossed his arms over his chest. "Not everything. You haven't gone to see her, to confront her face-to-face."

I shook my head. "Why should I? After the way she's rebuffed me, why should I?"

"Because she's not only about to be your daughter-in-law, she's been like a daughter to you. And because she's your friend."

"Well," I harrumphed, "friendship is a two-way street."

"Sometimes. Not always. When a friend's in trouble, sometimes friendship is a blind alley, a climb down a rope into a dark hole you're trying to pull somebody out of, a rescue mission. Of course, it's nice if the one you're trying to save cooperates, but sometimes they don't. Sometimes they don't even know they're in trouble. And you, of all people, know that." His words were chiding, but his voice took on a gentler tone.

"After your mastectomies, you were so down and depressed. Remember? We all wanted to help, but you wouldn't talk to anyone. Wouldn't even get out of bed. If Mary Dell hadn't flown up here from Texas and lovingly kicked you in the butt, you might be there still."

It was true. I hadn't invited Mary Dell to visit. If she'd asked for my opinion, I'd have told her to stay in Texas and leave me alone. Instead, she blew into town like a tornado and literally dragged me from my bed of self-pity.

"Mary Dell is a good friend," I said.

"I didn't know you well enough then or I'd have done the same thing myself. Of course, now," he said, looking me in the eye as he reached across the table to grab both my hands in his, "things are different. Chickenhearted pussyfooter that you are, I love you, Evelyn Dixon. And if you needed it, my love, I'd fly around the globe to give you a good kick in the arse."

"Sweet talker."

He grinned and bent his head over my hands, kissing one and then the other before looking up and saying, "Your friend's in trouble, Evelyn. If she won't come to you, you're going to have to grab a rope, climb down the hole, and go after her. That's what friends do."

Charlie was right. Pushy and opinionated, but absolutely right.

And so, on Thursday night, without telling anyone but Mom about my plans, I took a train to Grand Central Station and then a cab to the college art gallery where Liza and her classmates, along with assorted friends, family, and faculty, were gathered for a reception celebrating the opening of the senior class art exhibition.

I arrived at seven on the dot. I'd heard through the grapevine that Abigail and Franklin were going to the opening, but first they had to make an appearance at a cocktail benefit on the other side of the city.

Hopefully, that would buy me time. I wanted to see Liza alone. Of course, there was still the matter of Garrett. It was a big night for Liza and naturally he was planning on being there to support her. He was driving. If he'd gotten caught in traffic, that might give me the time I needed to speak to Liza, but if not? I'd just have to cross that bridge when I came to it.

I asked the cab driver to drop me off a block away from the college and walked the rest of the way. The gallery faced the street. The front wall was all glass, exposing a big, brightly lit room with tall ceilings and white walls covered by paintings. There were a few dozen people milling around, holding glasses of wine, some looking at artwork, others chatting with friends.

When I spotted Liza standing in a far corner, I did a double take. She was so thin! Perhaps she'd decided to lose a few pounds before the wedding, but if that was the case, she'd gone overboard. Liza has always been slim. Now she looked gaunt and tired. Her makeup couldn't completely conceal the dark shadows under her eyes. Garrett told me she'd been working so hard this last semester that she barely had time to eat or sleep. I'd thought he was exaggerating, trying to come up with excuses to explain her long absence from New Bern. Maybe he'd been telling the truth after all.

She was talking to a curly haired woman about my age, probably one of her teachers. Thankfully, Garrett was nowhere in sight. The coast was clear, but I knew I didn't have much time.

Liza's back was turned to the door. She didn't see me come in. As I approached, I heard a snippet of their conversation.

"I mean it," the woman said with a warm smile. "You'd be my absolutely first choice."

I couldn't see Liza's face, but I could tell by her voice that the woman's words pleased her and caught her by surprise.

"Seriously? That's . . . Well. I don't even know what to say."

"You don't have to say anything right now. No rush. It's still *very* up in the air, but I want you to think about it. Okay?"

"Okay."

"Good," she said and then looked over Liza's shoulder and saw me waiting. "In the meantime, I'm going to go look at the rest of the exhibit and leave you to your adoring public. W*onderful* piece, Liza. You should be proud."

"Thanks, Professor."

The woman walked away. I tapped Liza on the shoulder. She turned, smiling, probably expecting Garret, or Abigail, or a classmate. When she saw it was me, her smile faded. That was no more than I expected, but it still hurt.

Garrett could come in at any moment, and I wanted to be gone before he did. There were many things I wanted to say, questions I wanted to ask, but I couldn't, not then. Instead, I cut to the chase.

"I'm sorry."

Her eyes shifted from mine to a spot a little to the left of my nose. She didn't say anything, just nodded ever so slightly, which might mean anything. I couldn't tell.

"I am, Liza. I am so terribly sorry. Please believe me when I say that I didn't mean to hurt you. My divorce from Rob has left me a little gun-shy on the whole subject of marriage. If you don't believe me, just ask Charlie.

"Of course," I said with a little smile, then reached out to take her hand, lifting it so I could see how her diamond sparkled in the light, "if he'd have offered me a ring as nice as this, I might have said yes by now."

My attempt to inject a little levity into the situation fell flat. "I didn't mean what I said, Liza. I love you, you know that. Don't be mad at me forever."

Her gaze shifted up to meet mine. "I wasn't mad. I was . . ." She blinked a couple of times. "I was afraid. Afraid that you might be right. Afraid that Garrett was making a mistake in wanting to marry me."

Now I was the one who had to blink back tears. "No! Liza, no!

Don't ever think that! You're bright and beautiful and strong. Garrett loves you and so do I. Garrett is so happy. He's never been so happy—and you're the reason. He goes around the shop whistling all day. I don't have the heart to tell him he's off-key."

A tiny smile tugged at the corner of her mouth. "He's not very musical, is he?"

"No." I smiled. "He can't carry a tune in a bucket, but that's all right. He has other qualities. He's funny, smart, loyal, kind, and has a finely tuned appreciation for art. And artists."

The light returned to Liza's eyes. I felt a surge of relief. Things were still awkward between us, tentative, but we were talking, beginning again.

"Speaking of art," I said, "where is your painting? Garrett says it's a masterpiece."

"He did? Then his taste in art isn't as good as you think. I trashed it."

"But you slaved over it for weeks! Garrett told me so!"

She nodded. "Spent hours and hours working on it, only to realize I'd spent all those hours trying to pretend I was someone I'm not. It was no use."

I looked around the room, trying to decide which piece might belong to Liza, but none of them looked quite right. "Did you paint something else?"

Liza shook her head. "Not painted. Quilted. Come see."

I followed her to the opposite side of the staircase and into a corner near the back of the gallery.

"This is mine."

The woman on the quilt was tall, a slender and faintly cartoonish silhouette like a nineteen sixties paper doll, but looked even taller because her arms were extended over her head, reaching, her body stretched like a bowstring, with long locks of patchwork hair in every shade that might grow from a human head and some that didn't—brown, black, blonde, gray, red, and blue—flowing behind, lifted by an invisible wind.

She was a collage woman, a contradiction, a puzzle, one leg clad in a shapely bell-bottomed blue jean, the curve of which mirrored the elegant sweep of the white spangled gown worn on the other leg. There was a belt around her waist, black and thin and studded with a collection of objects—a bottle cap, a cast-off pearl earring, a bright yellow button shaped like a rubber duck. Above the blue jean leg, the left side of the torso wore a suit jacket, inky black and severely cut. The right side was dressed in a bright pink tank top with a spaghetti strap that looped over the exposed flesh of the shoulder and led the eye upward, past the gentle crook of the elbow, toward the smooth curve of the forearms, and finally to the open hands, reaching up with long, slim fingers.

It was an astonishing quilt, an arresting and disturbing image, especially the hands.

The black sleeve of the jacket and the pink flesh of the wrist were joined to hands that were only suggestions of hands, constructed from thick, transparent plastic, empty and insubstantial, almost ghostly, outlined against a royal blue skyline, fingertips stretched with longing toward a host of doves in flight, passing overhead with slender silver cords, like loosened tethers, clutched tight in their beaks and trailing after them, just out of reach of the hands too illusory to catch hold of a thread so thin.

I stood there for a long moment, looking at the quilt, saying nothing. I glanced down and saw a small white card that said, SELF-PORTRAIT IN PATCHWORK. LIZA BURGESS.

"What do you think?" Liza asked.

I turned to look at her. "I think that you are an astounding talent. And very brave." Liza shrugged and started to say something self-effacing, but I wouldn't let her.

"No. I mean it. Self-examination takes guts. And to stitch it out and put it up on a wall where everyone can see it? That requires a special kind of courage."

Liza looked at me, trying to weigh my sincerity.

"Thanks."

"I have to go, but before I do, there's something I want to give you." I reached into my coat pocket, pulled out a small package wrapped in layers of white tissue paper, and placed it in Liza's hand.

She pulled back the tissue and looked at the brooch, a Victorian silver bow set with four small diamonds on each side and a large single sapphire in the middle.

"It's beautiful."

"It's mine. Before that, it belonged to my mother, and before that, to my grandmother. I wore it on my wedding day, just like they did. Now it's yours."

Silent, she ran a fingertip around the silver loops of the bow. "I don't know what to say," she whispered.

"How about that you're coming to your shower next month? Won't be much of a bridal shower without a bride. And Margot would be heartbroken if you said no. Not to mention me."

She nodded quickly, a little embarrassed. "Yes. Yes. Of course I'll be there. I'm so sorry, Evelyn. I should have . . . I wanted to . . . but I didn't know how to . . ." She hung her head. "You must think I'm so selfish. I just didn't know what to say."

I lifted my hand to stop her apology. "It's all right. We're past all that now, okay?"

She looked up, her dark eyes questioning, wondering if I meant it. She bit her lower lip nervously. "Okay," she whispered.

"Good."

"How is Margot? And Ivy? And everybody?"

"They're good. Everyone is great. Margot is still seeing Arnie. And even though he turns a sickly shade of green anytime the words 'wedding' or 'marriage' are mentioned in his presence, I wouldn't be surprised if, one of these days, they tie the knot. Ivy is doing some great things over at the Stanton Center. Virginia keeps making noises about needing to get back to Wisconsin, but I'm trying to keep her in New Bern as long as I can."

Liza smiled. "Virginia is something, all right. Hope I'm like her when I'm eighty. And what about Charlie? How are things at the Grill?"

"Sweetie," I said, looking at my watch, "I wish I could stay and talk, but I've got to run. My coming here tonight is sort of an undercover operation. I didn't tell Garrett or Abigail anything about it, so I'd just as soon be gone before they arrive. And please don't mention it to anybody, especially Abigail."

"Why? What's wrong with Abigail?"

"Nothing. We just had a bit of a falling-out. Don't worry about it. It'll blow over. She's just been a little on edge recently."

"Yeah," Liza huffed. "Tell me about it. She phones me about fifty times a day, hysterical over some detail that, frankly, I couldn't care less about. This week it was truffles. White or black? How would I know? It's her wedding," Liza said and then, realizing her gaffe, corrected herself. "I mean, she's paying for it. She can have whatever color truffles she wants."

Her words confirmed my suspicions. Liza didn't want this enormous, over-the-top ceremony but, for some reason, she was putting up with Abigail's machinations. That really didn't seem like the Liza I knew. I wanted to know more but there wasn't time, not then.

"Well, when you come to New Bern for the shower, we'll have to find time to sit down and have a good long talk, okay? Make sure you leave room for me on your dance card."

"I've missed you."

"Me too." I gave her a hug. After a moment, she shifted her weight, trying to pull back, but I wouldn't let her. I held her tight, wrapping my arms around her and holding tight until I finally felt her relax in my embrace. Only then did I let go.

"I'll see you soon, okay?"

"Okay."

Outside, it had started to rain. I hailed a passing taxi and got inside quickly, trying to dodge the raindrops.

As the driver pulled away, I turned to look through the window of the cab, to the window of the gallery and beyond, to Liza, who stood with her back to the glass, looking up to the tall portrait in patchwork and the woman with the see-through hands.

19

Liza Burgess

"Liza! Liza, wait!"

I stopped and turned around. Professor Williams, not quite jogging in her scuffed blue pumps, was coming toward me, waving a magazine over her head.

"It's here! Just came in!" She laid her hand on her chest when she caught up to me, pausing to catch her breath before shoving the magazine into my hand.

"Page twenty-six," she gasped.

I flipped through the pages. There it was, right next to a black-and-white picture of Jackson Pollock's studio on Long Island. The title, *Pollock in Black and White: The Post-Drip Period,* was printed in bold sans serif typeface and under it, in smaller letters, "by Dr. Selena Williams and Liza Burgess."

I looked up, shocked. "It's . . . it's got my name on it. You listed me as a coauthor?"

Still a little out of breath, she nodded. "You worked very hard on this piece, Liza, and your work made it better. Your name *deserves* to be there."

A surprising surge of happiness coursed through me. "That's my name! I . . . I can't believe it! That's my name!" I put my hand over my mouth to keep from giggling.

"It is," Professor Williams confirmed with a grin. "Your first credit in a professional journal. And I've got a feeling it won't be your last. Not after the phone call I got this morning."

My hand fell away from my open mouth. Was she saying what I thought she was saying?

"Chicago? They called?"

She nodded emphatically, making her frowzy curls bounce with excitement. "They *called!* You're looking at the next executive director of the Pinkham Museum of Modern and Decorative Arts. I start in August, right after I finish my summer seminar."

"Professor! That's wonderful!"

"Isn't it!" Tossing aside all veneer of academic reserve, she splayed her fingers and let out a squeal of pure unadulterated enthusiasm.

I didn't blame her. The Pinkham is arguably the most prestigious modern art museum outside of Manhattan. There wasn't a professor in the college who wouldn't have traded places with her in a heartbeat.

"And, Liza," she said, beaming as she pointed to the magazine, "this article? Obviously it wasn't the whole reason they decided to hire me, but it sure didn't hurt. The Pinkham is tired of playing second fiddle to the Manhattan museums. The board was dead set on hiring someone with solid academic credentials whose name is well known and respected in the New York art world. Having our piece as the lead article in *Manhattan Art Monthly* definitely helped tip the scales in my direction."

I looked down at the magazine still clutched in my hands. The professor was right. Her article—our article—was the first one listed on the cover. I'd been so excited before that I hadn't even stopped to notice.

"This is amazing! Ours is the lead story! I can't believe it!"

"Believe it," she said, still grinning. "And I meant what I said at the exhibition opening. I told you if I got the job, I want you to come with me. Well, I got the job."

She opened her palms, as if balancing an invisible tray of treats on her hands and offering it to me, waiting to see which one I would choose.

"There's an opening for an assistant curator in the decorative arts division. You wouldn't be working directly for me, but the curator is an older man. He's good but he'll probably retire in a few years. If you play your cards right, you could be curator for that whole department in five or six years. It's a fabulous opportunity, Liza."

"But . . . why would they want someone like me?" The professor had told me about her potential career move that night at the opening of the senior art show, and said that she'd like to take me with her. At the time, I'd been flattered, but I couldn't believe she was serious. I still couldn't. "I don't have any museum experience. I don't even have an advanced degree."

She inclined her head, conceding the point. "That's so, but the board of the Pinkham is very forward thinking. They're looking to build a deep field of talent, to find and cultivate the next generation of important voices in the art world. Who better than a young woman who, even before completing her undergraduate work, has already coauthored an article in a major art journal? You're an artistic wunderkind, Liza. Didn't you know?" She laughed.

"Of course," she said, narrowing her eyes and pinching her fingers together, "it might have helped a *little* that I said I wouldn't come unless I could bring in my own team. Just a little. You're not the only one who'll be joining me in Chicago. I'm hoping I can lure Randall Tobin to leave his job here and become my new director of development. As well as a few other people.

"*But* you'd be the youngest of my hires, and the only one without an advanced degree. Which reminds me—this offer comes with one condition. You've *got* to begin work toward your master's degree as soon as possible. But don't worry, your tuition will be paid for by the museum, and the schedule won't be arduous, just a couple of classes a semester. You can go at night. So? What do you say? Are you on board?"

She rubbed her hands together, certain she knew my answer. A person would be crazy to turn down an offer like this. Wouldn't she?

"Wow. This is . . . I'm just . . . well . . . I'm overwhelmed. After graduation I figured I'd be joining the rest of the starving artists, running a cash register during the day and painting at night. This is such an incredible surprise. I don't quite know what to say."

The professor's smile faded.

"I'm not saying no," I rushed to assure her. "I just want to think it over a little bit. With the wedding coming up, I feel like I ought to . . ."

"Oh! The *wedding!* Oh, *of course,*" she said, smiling again, as if everything suddenly made sense.

"I'd forgotten about the wedding," she said. "Garrett. That's his name, isn't it? I always forget that other people aren't as untethered as I am. That's fine. Talk it over with Garrett. He works with computers, doesn't he? He can do that anywhere, I'm sure. And he'll *love* Chicago. You both will. So much going on. *Vibrant* city. Much cheaper than New York. With both of you working, you'll be able to buy an apartment right away. There's a great neighborhood right near the museum where they're rehabbing a lot of wonderful old buildings. You'd be able to walk to work."

She laughed again. "Listen to me! I'm getting ahead of myself. You talk it over with Garrett. Take your time. I know you've got a lot on your plate with the wedding coming up. I don't have to know until June anyway," she said carelessly. "Possibly even later. You'll have plenty of time to get married, go on your honeymoon, and then move to Chicago by August. And if you did suddenly lose your *mind* and turn me down, it wouldn't take me five minutes to find fifty people who'd love to take your place."

Her voice dropped to a lower register and her eyes became serious, cautionary. "This is a once-in-a-lifetime chance, Liza. Once in a lifetime."

"I realize that, Professor. And I'm so grateful for the opportunity."

"Good." Her face brightened, confident I'd make the right choice. "By the way, congratulations! I heard your piece took second place in the senior exhibit."

"Thanks. I was pretty surprised."

"*Were* you? Why? It was an extraordinary piece. *Very* original. If

I'd been judging, you'd have taken first." She smiled and changed the subject. "After all these weeks of work, I bet you're ready for spring break. I know I am. You're going up to New Bern, aren't you? For your bridal shower, right?"

"I'm headed out in the morning, along with my roommates. They're just staying for the shower, though. They've got a flight to Acapulco the next morning."

She raised her eyebrows. "You're not going with them? It's your last chance for an undergraduate fling."

I shrugged. "I'm not really the fling type. How about you, Professor? Are you going out of town during the break?"

"I'd planned on visiting my sister in Tampa, enjoy a little warm weather, but now I'm going to Chicago instead. Must spend some time getting to know the staff, look for an apartment, that sort of thing."

Behind me, I heard a door open and the sound of footsteps. Professor Williams raised her eyes, focusing on a spot past my shoulder.

"Pardon me, Liza. There's Randall Tobin. I've *got* to talk to him."

She started jogging down the hall after Mr. Tobin, her curls bouncing in time with her steps, the sound of her stacked heels echoing through the corridor.

"Oh, Randall! Randall, wait a minute!"

"Professor? Thanks."

She looked quickly over her shoulder as she tottered away. "You're welcome!"

And then, as if already convinced of my decision, she called out, "Congratulations!"

It should have been an easy decision. For anyone but me, it probably would be. Going back to New Bern didn't make it any easier.

Even though I told her the train would be fine, Abigail insisted on sending a car to take me and my roommates/bridesmaids from New York to New Bern.

When you hear the words "send a car," what picture appears in your mind? I'd envisioned a basic black sedan—something subtle and serviceable that'll get you from point A to point B. What Abigail sent instead was a bright yellow stretch Hummer, the kind of ridiculous vehicle gangs of high school juniors pool their money to rent on prom night and then pack into like sardines in a can, which, to my mind, kind of defeats the point of having a car that big.

It was huge and hideous and blindingly yellow and when I came out the door with my suitcase in hand on Saturday morning, it was parked right in front of my apartment building.

"You've got to be kidding," I moaned as the driver climbed out to open the door for us.

Zoe looked at me with eyebrows raised. "Is this it?"

"Yeah. Sorry."

"But what if somebody I know sees me?"

"Zoe, it's eight o'clock in the morning on a Saturday. Everyone you know is still asleep. Just get in, all right?"

Just to be sure, she looked left and right before handing her suitcase to the driver and climbing into the cavernous vehicle.

Kerry, who was active in the college chapter of Greenpeace, was horrified. "I can't ride in that! Do you know how many gallons of gas we'll use getting from New York to New Bern in that?"

Janelle giggled. "Oh, come on. It'll be fun."

"Do you have any idea the effect this will have on the environment?" Kerry scolded. "We might as well just mow down the rain forest with a bulldozer."

"Well"—Janelle shrugged—"later we'll load it up with old newspapers and cans and drop by the recycling center. That should even things out. Oh, come on. Just get in."

It was a long ride to New Bern, and the girls, unaccustomed to rising so early on a Saturday, fell asleep before we even crossed the bridge out of Manhattan. I wished I could do the same.

I haven't been sleeping. And when I do sleep, I keep having all these crazy dreams. There's one where I go to try on the wedding dress only to find it's become too big, so big that even when I stand on my tiptoes I can't get my head to come out through the neck and so I'm shrouded in this cocoon of white fabric. I can hear people calling me, Abigail and Garrett and Professor Williams, saying, "Liza? Liza? Are you in there? Liza? Where have you gone?"

And then there's the one where that enormous flock of beautiful birds is flying overhead through a bright blue sky, their bodies casting shadows on my face as I look up. Each of the birds is holding a silver thread in its beak, so thin but strong, strong enough to hold my weight . . . possibly. I hope so. I can't be sure. I reach up as high as I can, trying to grab on to one of the silver threads, but the minute I feel the strand, pinch it between my fingertips, I see another thread nearby that looks like it might be stronger, more dependable, or another that looks somehow shinier and more appealing than the one I am holding. And so I let go and reach for one, or two, or ten of the other threads, but now my hands feel suddenly weak, unable to take hold of anything. When I look more closely I see that they're fading away, from fingertips to wrists, fading like a morning mist.

Weird, huh? I bet a shrink could make a mint of money off me. But, hey, it's not all bad. The bird dream inspired my entry for the senior art show, the quilt that not only rescued me from the shame of having to enter my pathetic Chagall knockoff, but it took second place, which isn't the same as winning but it's pretty darned good. Especially considering the competition and that I pulled the whole thing together in less than a week. See? There are some advantages to sleeplessness.

Still, I wish I could just pass out like my roommates, let the sound of rubber on asphalt lull me into a deep and dreamless sleep, but it's no good. They're out cold and I'm left alone with two empty hours ahead of me and nothing to do but think—something I've been trying to avoid for some time.

In the last three months, my entire world has turned upside down. Before then, I was sure I knew exactly what my post-college future looked like. I'd graduate, move to New Bern, into Abigail and Franklin's new house, into the suite of rooms—bedroom, bath, and art studio with the wide windows and great sunlight—that Abigail had built just for me.

I'd paint in the morning, when the light was good, work afternoons at the quilt shop, and at night or on the weekends, except on my Friday quilt circle nights, I'd go out to dinner, or a movie, or on a hike, or whatever with Garrett until, on some distant day in the far-off shadowy future that I didn't need to worry about for years to come, Garrett and I would get married. After that I'd open a little art gallery on Commerce Street and, in no particular order, Garrett and I would acquire two children, an Irish setter—or maybe a pug, I hadn't been able to decide—and a house of our own. That was my plan, such as it was.

I know, I know. It sounds pretty lame to finish college and then move into your old bedroom, but it seemed crazy not to. Even though Abigail's "downsized" house was less than half the size of her old Proctor Street mansion, it was still big enough to house a small army. And the truth is, I liked the idea of moving back in with Abigail, back to New Bern, to home and a simple, predictable life, a life that doesn't require too much in the way of commitment on my part—easy, uncomplicated, untethered, as Professor Williams would say.

Until January, I had my future all worked out. Then Garrett asked me to marry him and complicated everything.

If I didn't love him so much I could hate him for that.

But I do love him. And I don't want to lose him, so I convinced myself that it'd be all right, that marrying Garrett doesn't mean changing my plan, just accelerating it a little. I've told myself that after the wedding, everything would be fine and life would go on almost like I'd envisioned it.

But then Abigail got all revved up about the wedding and started turning it into something that was looking more and more like this stretched-out, bright yellow monstrosity I was riding in—enormous and vulgar and more than a little ridiculous. And then Evelyn made me doubt my decision and myself and our friendship and if I could ever be accepted into Garrett's family. Then Grandma Virginia showed up unannounced, all wrinkles and warm smiles, and Evelyn right behind her, with her family heirlooms and her selfless apologies that made me feel simultaneously loved and unworthy to be loved.

I don't understand how this whole family thing is supposed to work. I'm not sure it can, not for long, anyway.

My father, who doesn't really deserve that title, gave me my first lesson in the fragility of family units.

Lesson number two came from my mother. She didn't want to die of breast cancer but the bottom line is, she did, and that left me completely alone. Well, except for Abigail. But Abigail seems like the kind of family somebody like me would have, you know? Odd. And difficult. And just as damaged as I am, though in different ways.

She's mercurial: compassionate and self-effacing one minute, demanding and proud the next. Even so, I love Abigail. She's the only piece of my mother that I've got left. But the thing about Abigail is that you can't always count on her, so I never have. Do you see what I mean? I can count on *not* being able to count on her, and I find that comforting because it fits in with everything I've always known.

But these Dixons? They do family differently—like they mean it. They get in your face with their love, they give and forgive as though they expect love to last, and it scares me. Because it can't last, can it?

Do you want to hear something crazy? When Evelyn expressed her doubts about me to Garrett, it hurt—I won't say it didn't—but at the same time a tiny part of me was relieved. I thought, "Well, at least she knows. And if Evelyn has figured out what a mess I am, then maybe Garrett will, too, before it's too late."

But it's already too late. I am in love with Garrett.

Sooner or later, it's bound to blow up in my face. Part of me would rather it be sooner than later. Except, of course, for that other part, that tiny atom of my being that wants, against all evidence to the contrary, to believe that love can last—even for me. That's the part of me that, every day, fights down the compulsion to call up Garrett and tell him that I can't marry him.

This job offer from Professor Williams would be the perfect excuse.

I could sit down with Garrett and tell him that I can't pass this up, that I'm calling off the wedding because this is the chance of a lifetime and I've decided I want to move to Chicago and try to become "the wunderkind of the artistic world."

And it wouldn't be an excuse, not entirely, because I *would* like that. At least, a part of me would.

After a lifetime of being nobody very special, nobody that anybody cared so very much about, nobody that anybody else had to pay much attention to, I'd like to be . . . somebody. Somebody who matters.

I'd like to love and be loved and have it last forever.

And I'd like to live alone in Abigail's upstairs rooms and never need anyone.

And I'd like to wake up every morning for the rest of my life with Garrett lying beside me.

And I'd like to have children and be their whole world and have them be mine.

And I'd like to live life free of the weight of anyone's expectations.

And I'd like to run away to Paris and never come back.

And I'd like to come home to New Bern and never leave again.

And I'd like to move to Chicago and become the youngest curator in the history of the Pinkham Museum and mount exhibitions that will wow the art world.

And I'd like to be the youngest artist in history to have her own show at the Pinkham and let some other bright young wunderkind mount *my* exhibition so *I* can wow the art world.

But most of all, I'd like to know for sure what I should do. And to know if *any* of these dreams could ever really come true for somebody like me—somebody who, at the core of her being, knows she really is nobody and is waiting in fear and trembling for the day when everyone else, including Garrett, realizes it too.

20

Liza Burgess

The driver dropped us at Abigail's front door.

Franklin, trailed by Tina, the faithful, aging black Labrador, came out to greet us. Franklin hugged me and shook hands with the girls. Tina sniffed the newcomers' pant legs and then, tail wagging, walked over and leaned against me, urging me to pet her. I patted her on the side, hard, the way she likes it. She thumped her tail against my legs in appreciation.

"Hey, Tina's looking very svelte these days." Tina was a lovable and well-loved dog, as evidenced by the size of her waistline. Franklin adored her and just couldn't resist giving her a treat whenever she turned her big brown eyes in his direction. But now she was looking decidedly thinner. "Did you put her on a diet or something?"

"Abigail did. After my heart attack, Abbie said no more pepperoni pizza for me—or Tina. Instead she's got me eating salad and Tina eating canned green beans, no salt. Tina just loves them. I'd have never believed it, but she does. The second she sees the can, she practically stands on her back legs and dances a jig."

Franklin reached out his hand and patted Tina affectionately on the head. "Don'tcha, girl?"

"Where is Abigail?" I asked. "She called me about ten times yesterday, reminding me to be here by ten. We're here. So where did she run off to?"

"Don't know," Franklin said. "She was up before the sun, making lists and mumbling to herself, and she left right after breakfast. She said she had to get things ready before the bridal shower."

"What kind of things? Margot and Evelyn are hosting the shower. What would Abigail have to do with it?"

Franklin held up his hands and heaved a sigh. "I don't know, Liza, and these days, I've found it's better not to ask. Say the least little thing to her and she flies off the handle. Nothing personal, Liza, but I'll be very glad when this wedding is over."

That makes two of us.

"Anyway"—he smiled, remembering his duties as host—"you're all here and that's what matters. Come on upstairs, ladies. I'll show you to your rooms. Come on, Tina. Let's show the girls where they'll be staying."

After everyone was settled in, Franklin gave the girls a tour of the house, including a peek into Abigail's dressing room, which is about half the size of our apartment. Needless to say, they were impressed and more than a little jealous.

After that, we still had some time to kill. It was chilly outside, but when Franklin informed us that the hot tub was heated to a delicious one hundred and two degrees, the girls ran upstairs to change into the swimsuits they hadn't thought they'd be able to use before they got to Acapulco.

The bluestone patio was cold on our bare feet as we ran outside, but the hot water felt great. Franklin brought out a tray with a bottle of champagne and four glasses, which he filled and handed to each of us.

"Thanks!" Zoe said, sipping her champagne and grinning at Franklin. "Sure you don't want to join us? There's plenty of room."

"Thank you, but no. I've got work to do. But if you girls need anything, just yell. I'll be upstairs in my office, going over some contracts for my most important client."

"And that would be?" I said, feigning concentration. "Wait, don't tell me . . . Aunt Abigail?"

Franklin smiled and turned to leave with Tina following close on his heels. "You girls have fun. I'll see you later."

"Oh, he's a doll!" Zoe said after Franklin left.

"Yeah," I said. "Franklin's great. He's the best lawyer in the county. That's how he met Aunt Abigail. He's been her lawyer since way before I was born, but they didn't realize they were in love until a couple of years ago. Then Franklin had a heart attack. Abigail was with him every minute, never left his side. One night, when he was feeling really bad and they both thought it was the end, he asked Abigail to marry him and she said yes. They called for the hospital chaplain to perform the ceremony and that was that. But the second it was over, Franklin suddenly felt much better." I laughed.

"You should have seen Abigail! When she realized that Franklin was fine and that she'd missed her chance at having a big wedding, she was ticked! She was sure the whole thing had been a ruse, that Franklin had faked his symptoms just to get her to marry him!"

Zoe made a wry face. "Well, yeah. Of course she did, especially since he did."

"Zoe!" Janelle exclaimed, splashing a little water in her direction.

Zoe rolled her eyes and took a swig of champagne. "Sorry if the truth bothers you, but get real. I mean, look at this place!"

Holding her empty champagne glass, Zoe swept her arm through the air, taking in the pool, pool house, and manicured English gardens, as well as the back wall of Abigail and Franklin's beautiful new home, before reaching over to grab the open champagne bottle that Franklin had left on the side of the tub and refilling her glass.

"You can't blame poor old Franklin. If I could get myself lifelong membership to this little country club, I'd fake a heart attack too."

"Franklin did not fake a heart attack," I snapped. "Don't be so stupid, Zoe. You can't fake a heart attack. The hospital has machines that can tell that."

"Oh? Well then, how do you explain why old Franklin felt so much better as soon as your aunt Abigail said, 'I do'? Hmm?"

"Because," I said testily, "Franklin had terrible indigestion, but he didn't realize it. He thought he was having another attack. As soon as the ceremony was over he had this enormous gas attack and felt much better."

Janelle giggled.

"It's true," I said. "Abigail told me all about it. Right after the minister pronounced them man and wife, Franklin just let one rip! Pretty much cleared the room. The minister suddenly remembered he had an appointment, shook hands with them, and ran out holding his breath." I laughed. "But Franklin felt much better."

Kerry shook her head, smiling. "Wasn't exactly a dream wedding, was it?"

"No, but Abigail got over it. They're just as married as if they'd held the ceremony in St. Paul's Cathedral. That's what counts. That's what they both wanted."

"Yeah," Zoe said. "It's just too bad that poor old Franklin is so unhappy now."

She shook her head before lifting her glass to her lips and draining it to the halfway mark.

"Oh, knock it off, Zoe. Franklin is *not* unhappy. They might be going through a rough spot. Abigail is acting a little whacked right now, but once the wedding is over, everything will be fine. Franklin loves Abigail."

"Oh, I'm sure he does," she said mockingly. "Or at least he did. Look at him, Liza. The man is completely miserable. And henpecked. He might be the best lawyer in the county, but at the end of the day he's still your aunt's employee. I'm sure he makes a pretty good living, but it can't be enough to pay for all this, can it? And what money he does make is all because of her. You said it yourself, Liza. Your aunt Abigail is poor old Franklin's biggest client."

"So what? So what if she is? What difference does that make? And quit calling him 'poor old Franklin.' You make him sound like some sort of charity case."

"I'm just saying that he's probably feeling a little emasculated, that's all. Before, he was an important man, the best lawyer in the county. Probably everybody looked up to him. Now he's just your aunt Abigail's husband, playing second fiddle to a rich and powerful woman. I mean, look at him today. Your aunt flies off in a huff. . . ."

"He didn't say she left in a huff," I protested.

"Maybe not, but I bet she did. Anyway, off she goes, doesn't tell him where she's going or when she'll be back, and leaves him behind to play bellhop and waiter to a bunch of college girls. The man's unhappy. Why wouldn't he be? He used to be *somebody*. Then he got married and became your aunt Abigail's boy toy. And the way things are looking, he's about to be demoted to houseboy." Zoe belched and then gave me a triumphant, challenging look.

"Shut up, Zoe. You don't know what you're talking about."

Janelle, who was usually the last one to give her opinion, eyed me nervously. "Zoe does have a point, Liza. A lot of men, older men especially, don't like it if their wives are more powerful than they are."

Kerry nodded. "Not just older men. My sister Cheryl married her high school sweetheart, James. He was a machinist and made pretty good money, but they wanted to be able to buy a house, so Cheryl got a job selling real estate. She turned out to be really good at it. Before too long she was making twice as much as James. Next thing you know, he filed for divorce. He said it was because she was working so many nights and weekends, and that she never had time for him. But Cheryl said it was because he didn't like it that she made more money than he did. And he *really* didn't like it when she suggested that he start doing the laundry since she was working more hours than he was."

"My point 'zactly," Zoe said, slurring her words a little. "Men are all a bunch of knuckle-dragging Neanderthals who want to go out and bring home the bacon while the little woman stays at home, waiting to cook it. Men," she said emphatically, "are jerks."

Zoe put her glass to her lips and lifted it high, finishing the last of her champagne.

"By the way, have you told Garrett about your new job offer? Wonder how he's going to feel about having to give up his business to follow you to Chicago so he can sit alone in an empty apartment with his computer for company while you're going to work all day and school all night. Don't think he'll be too wild about that idea, do you?"

"Zoe!" Janelle exclaimed, reaching over to take Zoe's glass before she could refill it.

Kerry looked at me sympathetically. "Don't listen to her, Liza. She's just had too much to drink."

"That's right," Zoe said with a wave of her hand. "Don't listen to me. Nobody should ever listen to me."

I'd had enough. I stood up in the water and reached for a towel.

"Liza, don't go!" Janelle urged. "Sit back down. Don't be mad."

"Come on," Kerry said. "Stay. We're supposed to be celebrating. Zoe didn't mean anything by it. Did you, Zoe?"

Zoe didn't say anything, just shook her head and then sank under the water, blowing bubbles as she went.

"It's too hot in here," I said, wrapping the towel around my wet shoulders and resting my behind on the edge of the tub. "I'm going to get dressed and run over to the quilt shop a little early, see if Evelyn needs any help. You remember where it is, right? Just two blocks up the street, then take a left."

They nodded.

"I'll meet you there. Don't be late. And don't let Zoe have any more champagne." I looked down at the fountain of bubbles as they broke the surface of the water. "A drunken bridesmaid. Just what I need."

"Don't be mad at her," Janelle whispered, apparently afraid that, even underwater, Zoe might be able to hear. "She's pretty upset. Her mother sent an e-mail last night. Apparently the latest stepfather is having an affair, but that's all right because her mom has already met potential husband number five, the next in the series of men Zoe's mom is prepared to wed until death do them part."

Kerry reached down into the water and pulled up a sputtering Zoe. "Come on. You can't stay down there forever."

Zoe wiped her hand across her face, pushed her mop of wet hair from her eyes, and looked at me, blinking away tears and chlorine.

"I'm sorry, Liza," she mumbled. "I shouldn't have said that. It's just that I . . ."

"It's okay," I said. "Don't worry about it."

I swung my legs over the edge of the hot tub and jogged across the patio and into the house, the cold from the bluestones penetrating my bare feet and making me shiver.

21

Liza Burgess

March in New England is pretty ugly.

The snow has mostly melted, exposing muddy swatches of soggy earth and streets littered with gray, gritty sand. As I walked down the street from Aunt Abigail's house to the quilt shop, the whole landscape was sober and sodden and tired, as if Mother Nature was suffering from a painful hangover. The scene matched my mood perfectly.

I thought about Zoe and Zoe's mother and her four husbands—soon to be five. Five husbands? How does a thing like that happen? How does a woman *let* that happen?

If I get married—I mean, *when* I get married—to Garrett, I'm doing it once. And making it last. Forever. If I can. If I have anything to say about it.

Will I have anything to say about it?

I've been away from New Bern for too long, and I'm so worn out. It'll be good to spend a whole week at home, just relaxing and hanging out with Garrett. It's crazy, but we've probably seen each other less since we got engaged than we did when we were dating. Maybe, by the time I go back to school, I'll be feeling calmer about everything.

I turned the corner into Cobbled Court, so named because of the cobblestones paving the wide courtyard and the narrow alleys that lead to it. It's a funny little corner, and because of its tucked-away location, it's not exactly the greatest place to put a retail business. But I can see why Evelyn fell in love with it. There's just something magical about this little courtyard with its old-fashioned cobbles. It's like a secret walled garden, hidden away from the worries of the world. At least, that's the way it seems to me. The minute I enter it, problems wither and drop away like leaves in autumn, spent and weightless, ready to be swept away by a passing gust of wind.

And today, the sensation was even stronger. The moment I turned the corner, I started to laugh.

Each of the four corners of the courtyard was "planted" with enormous daisies—bright green stems constructed from columns of twisted balloons, each topped by a daisy blossom made from six big white balloon "petals" surrounding a yellow balloon center. But that wasn't all. The painted front door of Cobbled Court Quilts was topped by an enormous balloon arch with more daisies evenly spaced along an expanse of long, lighter green balloons, twisted into crazy shapes to simulate leaves and vines.

The whole effect was whimsical, lighthearted, and absolutely perfect. It must have taken hours for Evelyn and Margot to create this balloon garden entrance to my bridal shower. I couldn't believe that they'd gone to so much trouble for me.

As I approached the door, I saw a sign saying . . .

> *Dear Quilters,*
>
> *The Cobbled Court Quilt Shop will be closed today as we celebrate the upcoming nuptials of our own Liza Burgess. If you're here for the bridal shower, come on in! If you're here to purchase fabric, notions, or browse, please know that we'll resume our regular operating schedule tomorrow. Thank you!*

I went inside.

Someone had pushed back the center shelving units to make room for tables covered with hot pink tablecloths and spring green napkins with handmade napkin rings—daisies, of course, to match the clear vases brimming with fresh-cut daisies sitting in the middle of each table. I smiled, knowing that Margot had chosen the palette—pink and green are her favorite colors.

The daisy theme had been carried in from the courtyard to the shop, where more giant balloon daisies sat in the corners of the room, these with stems slightly bent, as if they were leaning down to hear some interesting gossip. Once the guests arrived there would probably be plenty of gossip worth hearing.

How many people were they expecting? I'd have figured maybe twenty people would want to come to my shower—twenty-five, tops. But the tables were set for twice that number. Speaking of guests, where was everybody?

I called for Evelyn and Margot. No one answered. I heard footsteps overhead and decided to go upstairs.

Walking toward the stairs, I passed the refreshment table. An empty crystal punch bowl sat in the middle of the table, waiting to be filled with whatever fizzy concoction had been chosen for the guests. If Margot had anything to say about it, I was sure it wasn't just fizzy but pink and fizzy. Crystal tiered trays flanked the punch bowl. They were loaded with dozens of individually decorated daisy cupcakes, with white icing petals and green icing leaves radiating from the yellow sugar center of each cupcake.

Seeing them, each one carefully and painstakingly decorated, stopped me in my tracks. I hadn't had cupcakes since before Mom died.

Since it was just the two of us and since we couldn't afford big parties, every year my mom baked a batch of special cupcakes on my birthday. We'd eat two ourselves, mine with a candle on the top for me to blow out after Mom finished singing "Happy Birthday, Dear Liza"—always way off-key—and the next day I'd take the leftover cupcakes to school to share with my classmates.

Mom would decorate the cupcakes herself, according to whatever I was "into" at the time. I remembered the blue Cookie Monster cupcakes during my *Sesame Street* phase, which was followed by smiling blondes with long, flowing tresses during my Barbie phase, and black stallions with long, flowing manes during my horse-crazy phase.

Later, when I got older and angrier, it became harder for Mom to find themes for my cupcakes, but she never gave up. The last cupcakes she made for my birthday, before she got sick, were decorated with red frosting topped by the Metallica logo, my band of the moment, in black lightning-bolt lettering. At sixteen I was embarrassed to have anyone know that my mom still made me cupcakes on my birthday, so I'd tossed them in the Dumpster on my way to school.

I wish I'd known those would be the last cupcakes she'd ever make for me. If I had, I'd have crawled back into that Dumpster, pulled out every cupcake, and carried them through the front door of my high school shouting, "My mother, Susan Burgess, the best mother on the face of the planet, baked these for me!"

But it's too late for that. You only get do-overs in games of schoolyard dodgeball or hopscotch. They don't count in real life. Real life you've got to get right the first time because you never know—the first time could be the only time, or the last time. Real life doesn't leave room for mistakes.

With that in mind, I climbed the stairs, hoping to find Evelyn and Margot and tell them—before the guests arrived and we were surrounded by noise and confusion—how much I appreciated everything they'd done. Not just for the shower, and the decorations, and the cupcakes, but everything—for putting up with me and my moods, for making me feel wanted and loved, for being my friends. I don't deserve them.

When I pushed on the door to the workroom, I was surprised to catch a glimpse of not only Margot and Evelyn—the official hostesses—but Ivy, Grandma Virginia, and Garrett. And all of them, Garrett included, were sitting in a circle with sewing needles pinched between their fingers and holding the edge of a quilt, hurriedly stitching on the binding. It was a big quilt, queen-sized at least, with some beautiful colors and black in the border to make them pop, but I couldn't see the rest of it because Garrett's and Evelyn's backs were to me, blocking my view.

An hour before the shower and they were working on a quilt? What were they up to? I stood back quietly and listened.

Evelyn, who always wore reading glasses when she did hand sewing, peered over the tops of them to look at Garrett's work and frowned.

"Honey, try to keep your stitches a little smaller. And space them evenly. Make sure you're taking just a tiny bite of the fabric, and run the thread up under the edge so you can't see it."

"Mom," Garrett said with half a grin, "I told you I wouldn't be any good at this. I only agreed to help because you were so desperate to get it done in time. You can always take my stitches out and redo them later."

Virginia leaned over and examined her grandson's handiwork. "We may have to."

"Everybody's a critic," Garrett said. "Personally, I think this is all a plot you cooked up. You didn't ask me to help just because Abigail didn't show up at the quilt circle. . . ."

"Again," Evelyn said, stabbing the binding with her needle. "Leaving us shorthanded . . . again. We'd have had this quilt finished days ago if she'd helped us like she said she would."

"Evelyn," Virginia said evenly, "let it go. We're going to finish on time and that's what matters. Thanks to Garrett. And his big, uneven stitches." She winked at him. "Hurry up, dear. We've got to finish this up and go downstairs to put out the rest of the food. Just a few more inches to go now."

"Yeah, yeah. Just heap more abuse on me," Garrett said good-naturedly. "Enjoy yourselves at my expense. But don't think I buy that Abigail excuse for one minute. You planned this whole thing, didn't you, Mom? You've always been sorry you didn't have a girl. Now you're trying to turn me into one."

Margot giggled. "Oh, Garrett, don't be silly. Lots of men quilt. Some of our best customers are men. You know that."

"Okay. But I'm not one of them, got it? You're all sworn to secrecy. If word of this gets out, I'll have to take up bear hunting or bungee jumping or cave diving or some other stupidly dangerous hobby to regain my lost sense of masculinity," he said, pointing the end of his needle at the women. "If I'm eaten while wrestling alligators in the Amazon, it will be on your heads. I mean it. And whatever you do, do not tell my bride that you roped me into sewing a quilt."

"Why not?" I asked. "You look so cute doing it."

"Liza!" everyone exclaimed at once.

Garrett jumped to his feet, dropped his needle, and came over to give me a kiss.

"What are you doing here? The shower doesn't start for another hour."

I glanced at my watch. "Make that fifty-four minutes. What are *you* doing here? And all of you? Some hostesses you are. Shouldn't you be downstairs pouring almonds into nut cups or something?"

Ivy looked at Margot, her eyes twinkling. "Well, you're the head bridesmaid, this is your show. Should we tell her?"

"Tell me what?"

Margot's face lit up. She clenched her fists and held them in front of her mouth, as if the effort of keeping whatever secret she was trying to keep left her in danger of exploding. Finally she exclaimed, "It's for you! It's your present! From all of us! We wanted to wrap it before the shower, but since you've already seen it. . . ."

Her hands fluttered, beating the air like birds in flight. "Isn't it beautiful!" She turned to face the table where the beautiful quilt lay, waiting for a final few stitches to its binding.

"Beautiful" is such a puny little word, at least in comparison to that quilt, flat and pedestrian and faded, like the difference between a photograph of a quilt and seeing the quilt itself. I've never, ever seen a picture of a quilt that did justice to an actual quilt, and probably my words will be just as inadequate, but I'll try.

The colors in my quilt . . . Oh, the colors! Pulsating patches of color! Vermillion and emerald and cobalt and fuchsia and jade. Orange and cherry red and lime green and bright banana yellow. Amethyst and azure and aubergine. Garnet and sapphire and amber and lapis. Colors! Dozens of colors, diamonds of colors joined into perfect eight-pointed jewel-stars, multicolored and multifaceted, like rainbow flashes of light blinking from the glass planes of a crystal bead set in a sunny window. Colors and colors and colors! Star diamonds of color and light set into and surrounded by larger triangles of more colors, eight of them, each of the eight triangles a different shade so that no two stars and no two blocks were the same. The star blocks were bordered in black, making the colors even deeper, richer, and more alive. And that first border was surrounded by a second border made from rectangle patches of still more brilliant jewel-toned patches, like gemstone baguettes in a jeweler's window, and the whole thing was surrounded by a final, wider band of inky, velvety black to complete the picture.

It was a quilt that took your breath away, a quilt that could bring tears to your eyes. It was beautiful.

"Do you like it?" Virginia asked, smiling because the look on my face had already answered her question.

"Virginia designed it," Margot added. "I was all for doing a double wedding pattern, but Virginia convinced us that stars would be better for you. It's called Star-Crossed Love."

"I love stars," I whispered.

Margot nodded. "Virginia knew that. So she sat down and sketched out the design. She picked out all the fabrics too."

"All my favorite colors. All the colors there are."

"And we all worked together on the cutting, piecing, and quilting. Did you see? It's hand quilted—the whole thing!"

I leaned forward and traced my finger carefully along a serpentine vine of leaves and flowers, the most intricate quilting I'd ever seen. How had they ever done it?

"We've been stitching on it every spare moment we had for the last month. I was afraid we wouldn't be able to finish in time. Come to think of it, we didn't," Margot said with a giggle.

"It's beautiful," I said inadequately. "Simply beautiful. Thank you all so much. And I want you to know how much . . . I want you to know . . ." I stopped. I just couldn't find the words to say what I meant.

I'd never dreamed of having friends—and family, a husband, and mother, and grandmother—who would mean so much to me. Suddenly, I was deeply aware of how little I deserved them and how much I needed them and how frightening it was to know that.

I wanted to tell them all that and a million things more. I wanted to tell them the truth, about me and them and everything, and to say it all before it was too late, before the moment passed, but I couldn't. I didn't know the words.

And so I cried. Not a pretty, silent stream of tears, not a soft and sentimental ladylike weeping suited to a bride, but a floodgate-bursting bawl, open-mouthed, keening sobs, complete with the running nose and mascara to match.

It wasn't pretty.

I don't blame Garrett for standing there helplessly, not knowing what to do or say, not picking up on the look on Evelyn's face, the not-so-subtle shift of her head as she silently prodded him to put his arms around me. Garrett has worked around women for a long time now, but he's never been comfortable with tears or big emotional displays. Garrett is the most even-tempered guy in the world. I have never seen him furious, or flustered, or depressed, or wildly elated. In other words, he's exactly the opposite of me.

Mom once said I started my teenage mood swings at the age of five and never stopped. And that's not that far from the truth. Sometimes I feel like an emotional blender set on puree. But I don't like to show that emotion, just laying it out there for everyone to examine or comment upon. Too much emotion makes people uncomfortable. And why not? It makes me uncomfortable too.

Maybe that's why I paint. A painting is a safe place to store all those feelings I have too many of. I lay them out on the canvas and then walk away.

And if people ignore them, or like them, or don't like them, or don't like me, it doesn't matter. I've got my out all prepared. "Art is a matter of taste."

And so Garrett hasn't seen me cry, not often, and never like this.

I don't blame him for not knowing what to do, for letting Evelyn get to me first. I don't blame him for shoving his hands in his pockets, swallowing hard, and mumbling something about how he should probably get out of the way before the guests all arrive, then scuttling downstairs while my sisters encircled me, holding on tight, wiping my tears.

I don't blame him. I'd have done the same thing.

22

Evelyn Dixon

It takes a lot to make me mad.

It's not like I'm a robot. I do have feelings. I get miffed, irked, annoyed, and ticked off as much as the next person, but mad, angry, furious, livid? Those are not emotions that I experience often. In fact, until today I could number on one hand the times I've been well and truly furious.

One—St. Patrick's Day, when I was nine years old and Denny Miles, our "Dennis the Menace" next door, snuck into my bedroom, stole all my dolls, and dyed their hair green.

Two: When my father informed me that I had to be home from my high school prom by eleven. Fortunately, Mom talked him down from that particular position.

Three: When Rob informed me that he'd fallen in love with the receptionist at his gym and wanted a divorce.

Four: When, at my husband's behest, a guy from a moving company showed up unannounced to inform me that I had to vacate my home.

Five: When Ivy's abusive ex-husband tracked her down and, after lying in wait for her in the quilt shop parking lot, attacked her.

And that sixth time? That would be today when, after weeks of planning and work to make Liza's shower special—and staying up half the night to finish her quilt, only to have her burst into a worrying episode of sobbing, then finally calming her down and helping wash her face and reapply her smeared mascara right before the shower guests arrived—Abigail walked in the door.

Make that, Abigail made her entrance. And quite an entrance it was. It wasn't just Abigail, but Abigail and a phalanx of pink-smocked strangers carting an assortment of bags, boxes, and tables.

"Afternoon, all!" she chirped, her eyes darting around the room, taking in everything. "How is everyone? Liza, how are you, darling? You look lovely. Have you lost a little weight?"

"A little," Liza said.

Abigail nodded approvingly. "It looks well on you."

It was more than a little weight. Liza has always been slim, but now she looked skinny. There were dark circles under her eyes, too, and not from any vestiges of tear-streaked mascara. Liza *didn't* look well, and I was concerned. But Abigail didn't seem to notice.

"How are things coming along? Everything ready? Everyone well?" she asked and then, without waiting for answers, she turned to one of the women in the pink smocks and started issuing orders.

"Simone, set up the manicure stations along that wall and the massage chairs in the opposite corner. There should be plenty of room, but if there's not we can just scoot the dining tables into the center a bit. Hurry! We haven't much time before the guests arrive."

"Yes, Mrs. Spaulding. Right away."

Simone nodded to her troop of pink-smocked partners, who began unloading their gear and setting it up per Abigail's instructions.

Abigail frowned as she scanned the room. "The tables are set for fifty? Hmm. That's a few more than I'd expected. Well, I suppose we can reduce the chair massage time from twenty minutes to fifteen. That should help speed things along. But that won't help with the manicures. I don't want the guests standing in line waiting for a treatment. Simone, can you call the spa and get some more help over here quickly?"

"I'm sorry, Mrs. Spaulding, but I've brought my entire staff. The only one left is Ann Marie, but it's her day off."

"Call her, please, would you? Tell her I'll pay her overtime. I'll pay you all overtime."

"Thank you, Mrs. Spaulding. I'll call her right away." Simone reached into her purse and pulled out a cell phone.

I didn't quite believe this was happening, that Abigail was marching in at the last moment and taking over a bridal shower that Margot and I had been planning for weeks. Liza, Ivy, and Mom looked confused, and poor Margot looked like she was about to burst into tears. But I was mad.

"Abigail, what are you doing? We've got everything set up already and there isn't—"

"Yes," Abigail replied without looking at me, her eyes fixed on the front door as she walked over to the punch table and began shifting everything on it—punch bowl, cupcake trays, and flower arrangements—into slightly different positions, "and it's all very nice. Though I must say I'm surprised about the daisy theme. Daisies are perfectly nice flowers, of course. Serviceable. But they aren't terribly elegant, are they? If I'd known, I'd have ordered in some orchids for you. Or gardenias.

"Though," she mused, "gardenias have such a strong scent. Perhaps a bit overpowering in so small a space. You really should have rented a room at the country club. Well. Too late now. It's done. I suppose we'll have to make do with the daisies. But I do like the cupcakes. Very sweet. Where did you get them?"

"We made them. I baked them and Margot decorated them."

"Really?" She sounded surprised. "Well, *they* turned out very nicely," she said.

"I'm so relieved that you approve."

Abigail didn't notice my sarcasm. She picked up a bright green plate, pinching the edge between her thumb and forefinger and making a tsk noise with her tongue. She looked at me with raised eyebrows. "Paper? You can't be serious." She looked at her watch. "I wonder if there's time to call Hilda and ask her to bring over my Limoges."

"Listen, Abbie. Margot is in charge of this shower. It's supposed to be casual, relaxed. You don't need to call your housekeeper and have her scurry over with your china. Everything is fine as it is. Lovely, in fact," I declared, glancing at Margot.

"Abigail, the wedding is your baby and I understand that. I've kept my mouth shut on that score. But the shower is the responsibility of the maid of honor. Margot was kind enough to let me help. You could have, too, if you'd bothered to ask. Or if you'd bothered to show up at any of the quilt circle meetings for the last month. But you didn't! And now, at the last moment, you can't just expect to traipse in here and—"

Just as I was winding up to tell my dear friend Abigail exactly what I thought about her rude, manipulative behavior for the last few months, I felt a hand on my arm and looked to see my mother standing close by my side.

"Evelyn," she whispered through the side of her mouth, jerking her head in Liza's direction.

I glanced across the room to where Liza was standing. Her eyes were glistening.

"This isn't the time, Evelyn."

Mom was right. With the party set to begin in fifteen minutes and the bride teetering on the brink of another crying jag, now was not the time to confront Abigail.

I bit my tongue. Hard.

Abigail barely noticed. Truly, I don't think she had the least clue that I was mad at her or that I had any reason to be mad at her. I'm not sure she was aware of anyone or anything besides her single-minded vision of what she wanted this shower to be.

"Where in the world is Greg? He called three hours ago saying they were leaving the city. They should have been here by now." Scowling, Abigail strode past me to the front door and opened it.

"There you are!" Abigail said to the short, dark-haired man wearing a tuxedo and carrying a violin case. He was followed by three other similarly clad men, all of them with instrument cases.

Oh, dear Lord. Why did I have the feeling that some tearoom maître d' in New York had recently learned that his entire string quartet had called in sick?

"Sorry," the man puffed. He was winded. "We couldn't find a

place to park that was close. And then, we all had to help Mark carry the cello. It's pretty heavy."

"Yes, yes," Abigail said impatiently. "Fine. Go ahead and set up there in the corner. And, Greg, remember what we talked about. I want you to play *quietly*. This isn't a concert. You're here to provide background music. And do not *move* from your corner. No strolling. There's nothing more irritating than trying to carry on a conversation while someone is standing next to you playing a tango in your ear."

Greg looked a bit annoyed but didn't say anything. Abigail was clearly paying too much to be argued with. He picked up his case and skulked off to his corner with his fellow musicians following behind.

The door to the shop opened yet again.

I thought it might be an early guest, but it was Charlie. He was carrying an enormous, foil-covered tray and beaming. Gina and Jason, two of the servers from the Grill, were right behind him, also toting trays.

"Hello, everyone! Hello, Liza! You look wonderful. Big day, right?" He walked to a nearby table and set down the tray, then came over to give me a kiss.

"Hi, sweetheart. How are you? Everything ready for the party? Sorry I'm late. It was hard finding that exact brand of caviar on short notice. I really had to jump through some hoops to find a supplier." He smiled. "Worth it, though, twice over. This is one caviar that's actually worth the exorbitant price you pay for it. Do you want to try some?"

"Charlie! What is all this?"

Charlie looked confused. "It's the hors d'oeuvres you wanted for the bridal shower—beluga caviar, grilled scallops on mini brioche with red pepper coulis, and marinated Kobe beef skewers. Abigail called late last night and said you wanted a few more appetizers, more *better* appetizers, and that you were too busy with the party arrangements to call yourself. The restaurant was already closed, Maurice had gone home for the night, so I was up until two baking mini brioche. I woke up half a dozen restaurant suppliers in the middle of the night, trying to find that caviar. But Abigail said my girl needed brioche and caviar, so my girl gets brioche and caviar." Charlie ended this speech with a proud little smile and paused a moment, waiting for the adulation his Herculean efforts surely deserved.

I crossed my arms over my chest and glared at Abigail, who, oblivious to my ire, was going around to each individual place setting and moving the napkin rings up one inch from where I had placed them, then standing back to make sure each ring was precisely even to the one next to it.

The room was silent. I turned to look at Charlie.

He spread out his hands. "What?"

23

Evelyn Dixon

For Liza's sake, I followed Mom's advice and didn't confront Abigail about her high-handed hijacking of the bridal shower.

I would have as soon as the party was over but for the fact that after the musicians, masseuses, nail technicians, and all the guests with the exception of Liza's three roommates had departed, Abigail turned to Liza and said, "Well, darling. I suppose we'd better be off too."

"Off to where?" Liza asked.

"To the city, of course," Abigail said with a little laugh. "We've got to work on the wedding plans. I've booked us a suite at the Algonquin for the week."

"But," Liza sputtered, "I just got here. I was looking forward to spending my spring break at home. You said you'd taken care of all the wedding stuff. You said that after that marathon planning session at the restaurant, it was all done."

"Well, the *plans,* yes," Abigail replied impatiently. "That's all in place, but there's still a lot to do. You've got final fittings for the gown and your going-away outfit. And we haven't even talked about your trousseau or lingerie. The florist has made up test bouquets for approval and we need to visit the printer to see the proofs of the invitations. Plus I've scheduled appointments with Emiliano

Vargas's assistant to do a test run for your makeup and hair. We certainly can't leave that until the last minute. And tonight, the wine importer has scheduled a special tasting, just for the two of us, so we can make certain that the vintages we ordered are all they should be.

"In fact," Abigail said, glancing at her watch, "we're due there in three hours, Liza. So we'd really better get moving. I've got a car waiting outside. Don't worry about luggage. I had Hilda repack your things and give them to the driver."

Liza closed her eyes for a moment and shook her head, as if she couldn't quite understand what her aunt was saying.

"But . . . now? Right now? Shouldn't we stay to help clean up? And what about Zoe, Janelle, and Kerry? They're supposed to be staying overnight, then I'm driving them to the airport in Hartford tomorrow so they can catch their flight to Acapulco."

"I know. Very regrettable that you can't stay to entertain your friends, but you understand, don't you, girls?" Abigail glanced quickly at Liza's three roommates but didn't pause long enough to give them the opportunity to answer.

The short one, Zoe, had an irritated look on her face, as if she wanted to say something, but she didn't. Probably, like me, she didn't want to make a fuss in front of everyone and risk upsetting Liza.

"And it isn't like you don't see each other every day." Abigail chuckled. "After all, you do all live in the same apartment. Don't worry about your friends, Liza. I've arranged everything. I made a seven o'clock dinner reservation for them at the Grill. My treat."

She tossed a beneficent smile in their direction.

"And I've booked a car to take you to the airport in the morning. The driver will be there promptly at seven, so don't stay up too late, girls." Abigail picked up her purse and looped it over her arm, preparing to leave.

"Thank you so much for coming so far out of your way to attend Liza's shower. I hope you enjoyed yourselves. Have a wonderful vacation. I'm sure you will."

"Wait a minute! What about *my* vacation?" Liza asked.

There was an edge to her voice and she put her hands on her

hips. The old Liza—the stubborn, pigheaded girl who could go fifteen rounds with her equally stubborn and pigheaded aunt without even breaking a sweat—was back, and that Liza can be a serious pain in the behind. In the past I've often wished she would grow up and learn to be a little more accommodating. But recently, Liza has become too accommodating, letting herself be steamrolled by Abigail at every turn. Mom was right: I couldn't confront Abigail during Liza's party. But Liza could. And it seemed, at last, she was ready to do so. It was everything I could do to keep from standing up and leading a cheer.

"I've been working like a dog for months! Between classes, and the art show, and helping research that article for Professor Williams, and the wedding, I'm exhausted! And I've really been looking forward to having some time, just one week, where I didn't have to be someplace or do something for somebody else."

That's it! You tell her, Liza!

Abigail lifted her chin, took her purse off her arm, set it back on the table, and stared at Liza, unblinking.

"I see," she said in a voice as cold and even as an ice floe. "I can certainly understand that. I'm pretty exhausted myself. For the last three months I have devoted myself to nothing but this wedding, working myself to a frazzle, not to mention spending a small fortune, because I want your special day to be perfect in every detail. It's been an enormous task, but I haven't minded. You're my niece, after all. And I want to give you the wedding your mother would have, if she'd been able." Abigail sighed.

"But if that's not what you want . . ." She shrugged. "If, after all the trouble everyone has gone to on your behalf, you're not willing to make a few sacrifices to make sure that everything goes smoothly, I certainly can't force you. But I'm disappointed, terribly disappointed. On many levels.

"After so many months of us passing like ships in the night and you hardly ever coming home for weekends, I was looking forward to spending this week with you, just the two of us. Besides our appointments, I'd planned all sorts of little treats for you: an afternoon at a wonderful new spa, theater tickets, opera tickets, dinner at Jean

Georges and Le Bernardin, and a private tour at the Museum of Modern Art . . ."

Abigail raised a fluttering hand, indicating that there were other delights on her list, delights that had taken her a great deal of time and effort to arrange, but if Liza wasn't interested, then there was no point in going on.

Liza was standing next to me. I waited for her to say something sharp and cutting, but she was silent. Her shoulders drooped. I could feel her deflate under the weight of guilt Abigail was so obviously trying to heap upon her.

What was going on?

Six months ago, Liza would have seen right through Abigail's manipulative machinations and wouldn't have had the least compunction about saying so. What had happened? The sassy, hard-edged, smart-mouthed Liza I knew suddenly had no more spine than a limp dishrag.

"No matter how important this trip is," Abigail said, "I can't *make* you go to New York with me, Liza. If you want, I'll cancel everything. We'll stay here all week, and I'll just have to keep shouldering all the responsibilities of the wedding myself and hope that after all the time and money I've invested, everything turns out all right."

Abigail paused, her hand suspended in the air. She looked Liza in the eye.

"Is that what you want?"

Liza bit her lip. Her eyes darted around the room, avoiding Abigail's piercing gaze. After a long pause she mumbled, "I don't know."

"Well, it's your wedding, Liza, your day. You're in charge. I'm just here to do your bidding. So? What is your bidding? What shall we do? Go to New York, put the finishing touches on your wedding while we enjoy a wonderful week of treats and adventures? Or stay here, while away the days doing nothing, and hope against hope that the invitations are free of mistakes, the wines haven't corked, and the gown fits? Which will it be?"

Abigail waited. We all did.

"I don't know," Liza whispered. "I can't decide."

"No?" Abigail said.

"No."

Abigail smiled sweetly. "Well, in that case, why don't you just trust me on this? Come to New York with me. It's the right decision. Later you'll thank me for it."

Liza nodded but said nothing, her silence denoting her consent.

Abigail smiled. "Good girl. Very wise."

Abigail breezed out of the shop with Liza in tow, barely waiting long enough for Liza to give good-bye hugs all around and to thank everyone for everything (whispering in my ear that she liked daisies better than orchids any day) including the quilt, which she said was absolutely the most wonderful gift she'd ever received.

Liza's roommates offered to stay and help clean up, but I said we had it covered, so they left with Abigail and Liza.

I kept my game face on until the last moment, standing at the door, waving good-bye until Liza, who kept turning around to call out her thanks, crossed the courtyard and disappeared into the alleyway. Then I closed the front door of the shop and screamed at the top of my lungs, letting out all the pent-up fury and frustration I'd been swallowing back for the previous four hours.

"Better now?" my mother asked.

"No!"

"Evelyn, calm down," Mom clucked as she started stacking empty punch cups onto a tray.

"Did you see the way she just barged in here and took over like she owned the place?"

Margot, in a feeble attempt to defuse the situation, said, "Well, technically, she does. I mean, Abigail does own this building."

"Yeah," Ivy said sarcastically, "along with every other building in town."

"That may be, but she doesn't own this business. Or me. And she doesn't own Liza! Did you see how she bulldozed her into going back to New York?"

Ivy, who had begun helping Mom clean up the refreshment

table, frowned and shook her head. "Or the way Liza caved in and went with her? What was that about?"

"I don't know." I shrugged, my ire tempering a bit as I thought about Liza's baffling behavior. "She's been under so much stress lately. Maybe she was just too exhausted to put up a fight."

"Weddings have gotten to be such a hullabaloo," Mom muttered. "In my day, you either eloped and went off for a quickie honeymoon to Door County or, if you had a little money, you had a nice church wedding with fifty or sixty guests, just family and very close friends, and afterward everybody trooped down to the church basement for cake and punch. Weddings today are too stressful. Poor Liza."

Bells jingled as the shop door opened and Garrett walked in, flanked by Charlie, Franklin, Arnie, and, much to my surprise, Gibb Rainey, wearing his Huskies cap and grinning at Mom. Even more surprising, Mom was grinning back.

"Cleanup crew is here," Garrett said. "I heard you needed a few big, muscular guys to help cart away these tables and chairs. Unfortunately, the temp agency was fresh out of big, muscular guys, so they sent us instead."

Margot giggled. "Thanks for coming, fellas." She walked over to Arnie and planted a kiss on his lips. "It was nice of you to give up your Saturday to help."

"Wouldn't have dreamed of missing it," Arnie said, kissing her back. "You want us to start taking down those tables?"

Margot nodded and returned to work while the guys started breaking down tables and stacking chairs in a corner.

Gibb looked pretty fit for his age, whatever age that was. Even so, I wasn't sure I wanted him hefting heavy tables and chairs in my shop, and I was pretty sure my insurance agent would feel the same way.

"Um, Gibb, could you do me a favor?"

"Sure!" he said affably while I racked my brain to think of some mission to send him on.

"Could you . . . Could you run upstairs to the workroom and get me a few empty boxes? I need some to store things in—the punch bowl, leftover cups, and . . . things."

He beamed, happy to be singled out for an important task. "Sure! Shouldn't take me a minute. Be back in a jiffy," he said and winked at Mom, which kind of threw me.

"Um. Actually, it might take you a little longer. The boxes are all broken down, flattened, and ready for recycling. I'll need you to put them back together. There's a big stapler on the worktable upstairs."

Gibb's smile faded a little. Clearly he didn't relish the idea of going off into another room, away from Mom, for more than a few moments.

"Oh," Gibb said hesitantly. "Well, if you really need me to . . ."

"I do," I said earnestly. "You're a lifesaver."

Gibb smiled weakly, tipped his Huskies hat, and headed for the stairs. Mom glared at me, but I pretended not to notice.

"Thanks, Gibb!"

"You're welcome."

"So, how was the shower?" Garrett said, clapping his hands together. "Did the guests bring useful gifts? Lingerie, perhaps?" He raised and lowered his eyebrows before walking toward the break room. "Liza! Come out here and model some of your presents for me!"

"She's not here," I said, trying to keep my voice neutral. "Abigail took her back to New York."

Garrett frowned as he placed another chair on the pile. "She did? Why? When will they be back?"

"Wedding planning. They'll be there all week." I should have stopped right there but, angry as I still was, I couldn't resist adding one more detail. "Liza didn't want to go, but Abigail insisted."

Even with my eyes fixed on my son, I could feel my mother's disapproving gaze beaming into me from the other side of the room. Don't ask me how, but I could. Some childhood memories are indelibly branded into our psyches, such as the heat that can be generated from eyes of a miffed mother giving her offspring "the look."

"What?" Garrett said, his face beginning to flush. "Where does Abigail get off dragging Liza back to New York for the week?"

Garrett was ticked. And I was happy he was. If there's one emotion that loves company more than misery, it's anger. I was still angry and glad to have Garrett as a member of my club. And it wasn't just Garrett. It turned out there were any number of people who were irritated with Abigail—a fact that, at that moment, pleased me more than I now care to admit.

"We're supposed to spend the whole week together! I've got plans! Concert tickets! Dinner reservations! How much planning can one wedding take, anyway? We're supposed to be planning for our future, not just the ceremony. Liza's my fiancée, but for the last three months, I've barely had a chance to see her!"

"And I've barely had a chance to see my wife," Franklin added, no more pleased than Garrett about this turn of events. "When I do, the conversation breaks down into some sort of argument about this wedding. It seems like we argue all the time now. I don't understand what's gotten into her. Abigail enjoys a little friendly banter, the occasional intellectual sparring session, but she's never liked arguing for the sake of it."

Ivy smirked as she swept crumbs off the table. "Could be worse, Franklin. Poor Liza's been seeing—and hearing—too much of Abigail. Way too much."

The closest in age, Ivy and Liza share a special bond. I'd seen them sitting in a corner during the shower, heads together, their whispers punctuated by occasional laughter and furtive glances thrown in Abigail's direction.

"Abigail has been calling her twenty times a day, bothering her about some detail or other. Liza wants a nice wedding, but this is way more than she bargained for."

"Did she tell you that?" Arnie asked. The consummate lawyer, Arnie is always looking for proof. Assumptions will not do.

"Not in so many words. I don't think she wants to seem ungrateful, but come on! We know Liza. White truffles and caviar and music by the Boston Symphony?"

"Those are *very* good truffles," Charlie groused.

"I'm sure they are, Charlie. The caviar was good too," Ivy said.

"I didn't think I'd like it, but I tried some. If you close your eyes and don't think about what you're eating, it's really pretty tasty."

Charlie rolled his eyes, impatient with Ivy's lack of culinary sophistication, but was somewhat mollified. At least she'd tried it and had the good sense to enjoy it.

"But," Ivy continued, "my point is, it isn't really Liza, is it? I mean, if Abigail had gone out and hired Nirvana to play at the reception, at least that would have made some sense. But a symphony orchestra?" Ivy made a face and shook her head.

"The bottom line is, Abigail is orchestrating the wedding she wanted but didn't get. It's all about her. Liza's been left totally out of the picture. Abigail's not letting her have her own way on anything. And this business of dragging her back to New York . . . Liza's exhausted. She told me that the thought of this vacation is the only thing that's gotten her through the last three weeks. Now Abigail has taken that away from her too," Ivy huffed. "I've always known Abigail was pushy, but I never thought of her as manipulative. Well, not *this* manipulative."

Even Margot, who always has something nice to say about absolutely everybody, was mad at Abigail. "I couldn't believe the way she barged in here, criticizing our decorations. Calling our daisy theme ordinary. Do you have any idea how much time we put into those decorations?"

No one ventured a guess, but the answer was hours upon hours. Margot and I got here at dawn to start filling the balloons. And filling them was just the beginning. If Ivy, Mom, and Garrett hadn't helped us before we all turned our attention to finishing the binding on Liza's quilt, we'd never have been ready in time.

"I thought they were really cute," Margot said in a wounded tone. "And very original. More original than a bunch of orchids would have been. Anybody can have orchids. All you have to do is buy them."

Arnie put an arm around Margot's shoulders. "They're fabulous," he said. "Next time I need a balloon sculpture, I'm calling on you. No one else."

"Thanks a lot," Margot said with a pout.

"Oh, come on," Arnie continued. "Cheer up. They're great. I mean it. I bet Liza loved them."

"Arnie's right," Mom said. "Liza must have told you how much she loved the decorations and the cupcakes a dozen times. That's what counts. Liza's opinion, not Abigail's."

Margot sighed. "I guess you're right, but still. Abigail was so nasty and superior. I've always known she has very particular tastes, but I've never known her to be so critical."

"Well, at least she didn't lie to you, getting you in trouble with your girlfriend in the process," Charlie grumbled, giving me a sideways glance so I'd know that the whole caviar and beef skewer thing truly had been Abigail's plan and that he was just an innocent dupe in Abigail's nefarious scheme.

"I cannot *believe* that she lied about that, passing off her instructions as coming from Evelyn," he railed. "Abigail is always bent on having her own way, but I've never known her to resort to deceit to get it. I'd never have thought she was capable of something like that. Not in a million years."

That comment pulled me up short. Charlie was right. Everyone was.

Franklin said that Abigail enjoyed intellectual banter, but she'd never been outright argumentative, not before. And Ivy was right; Abigail could be pushy at times, but she wasn't manipulative. Margot's comment that Abigail, while exacting, had never been known to be purposely critical was equally true. And while Abigail was more than willing to use every ounce of her intellect, influence, and connections in pursuit of whatever cause she was currently working on, generally a worthy one, neither Charlie nor anyone else had ever known her to employ means that were deceitful. Or rude.

Abigail was particular and occasionally prickly, but hers were the sort of prickles you found on a rose, so overshadowed by the beauty of the bloom that they were quickly forgiven and forgotten. Abigail knew what she wanted and knew how to get it, for herself and for those people and causes she cared about, which were legion. In spite of her faults, Abigail had a large and sincerely generous heart. She was bright, beautiful, witty, charitable, well read, well traveled, and well bred and, because of that, well liked. Arguably, she was the best-liked woman in New Bern.

Abigail would never hurt someone else, not purposely, and we all knew it.

It took my mother, the person who knew Abigail the least well, to sum up what all of us were thinking.

"It sounds like Abigail isn't herself these days."

"It's true," Franklin said quietly. "Every mother of the bride goes a little crazy, but Abigail's behavior has been beyond the pale. Especially considering the fact that this is far from the first big event she's planned. In any given year, Abigail organizes half the charity fund-raisers in this town, and all without so much as breaking a sweat or raising her voice. Not this year, though. She turned them all down, saying she was too busy with the wedding."

"He's right," said Ivy. "Donna Walsh told me that Abigail called last week to say she couldn't help with the Stanton Center charity auction because of the wedding. In fact, she even said she'd have to take a leave of absence from the board until it's over. I couldn't believe it. I know that Abigail supports a lot of different community organizations and causes, but I'd never have thought she'd leave the Stanton Center or New Beginnings in a lurch. I thought it was her favorite charity."

"It is," Franklin said. "Or was. Until this wedding came along. That's what I'm talking about. This whole thing seems to have gone far beyond the boundaries of the usual mother-of-the-bride meddling. Abigail is almost manic about this wedding. Bent on making sure every little detail is perfect, whatever that means. I'm not even sure Abigail knows anymore. No matter how much she does or spends, none of it seems to satisfy her."

Thinking about Abigail and the way she'd gone around the tables, adjusting each and every napkin ring to the exact same position as its neighbor's, made me think Franklin's choice of words seemed accurate. Since the moment Liza and Garrett had announced their engagement, Abigail had been seized by an outsized and uncontrollable mania.

"I keep telling her that it's already enough and more than

enough, but she doesn't seem to hear me. I don't like saying anything against my wife, even among friends, but I'm at my wits' end with her. I don't know what to do."

"You don't think that this is just her trying to live out her own fantasies through Liza?" Margot asked. "Making up for the wedding she never had?"

"No," Franklin said. "Sure, Abigail would have liked a big wedding. But this isn't the sort of thing Abbie would want for herself. I mean, there's big and then there's *big.* This wedding has gone over the top, way over. In fact, it's bordering on vulgar."

Suddenly remembering he was in the room, Franklin took a quick look at Garrett and cleared his throat. "Sorry about that, Garrett. No offense intended."

"None taken," Garrett replied. "I agree with you. If I had my way, we'd have a nice little ceremony in the church or the park, just invite family and close friends. Afterward, we'd take everybody to dinner at the Grill. . . ."

Charlie nodded approvingly.

". . . And then Liza and I'd sail off on a trip around the world, or a grand tour of Europe, or a month on a deserted island. Anything. I don't care. Whatever makes Liza happy." He sighed heavily. "I never imagined that getting married would be so complicated."

"It doesn't have to be," I said darkly.

Charlie rubbed his chin. "Evelyn, why don't you do what I suggested a month ago? Talk to her. Sit her down and tell her how you feel. Abigail can be difficult. We all know that. But," he said with a little smile, "we difficult people are worth the effort. Just talk to her. You're her closest friend. She'll listen to you. Abigail may be difficult, but she's not unreasonable. She's never been that."

"Not until now," Ivy muttered.

"It's true," I said. "The Abigail we saw here today—argumentative, manipulative, critical, self-absorbed, and even deceitful—isn't the Abigail we all know and love. But I've already tried to talk to her, Charlie, a couple of times. It didn't do any good. She completely ignored me. It was almost like she didn't hear me."

Franklin was nodding as I spoke, as if he understood completely.

"I've tried to talk to her as well. It hasn't helped. If anything, it's made things worse. Something is wrong with her, really wrong. Something beyond the wedding. She won't discuss the problem. She won't even acknowledge its existence. And if she won't admit that there's a problem . . ." Franklin's weary voice trailed off. "I just don't know what to do."

Margot, who had been listening for some time with an intense expression without saying anything, put in her two cents.

"I do," she said earnestly. "The eighteenth chapter of Matthew explains exactly how to deal with something like this. It says that if your brother has sinned against you, you should go and show him his fault, just between the two of you."

"They already did that," Ivy said. "And it didn't work."

"But there's more that comes after that," Margot said. "If the first attempt doesn't work, it says you should try again, but the next time, you should take along two or three others as witnesses. If a few of us go together and lovingly confront Abigail about this, I'm sure she'll listen. She'll have to!"

"Maybe Margot is on to something," I said. "It might work."

"So," Garrett said slowly, narrowing his eyes as if trying to imagine how this would all play out, "it's an intervention? We all go as a group, confront Abigail, and tell her she's been acting nuts? Like on those reality TV shows?"

"Well, probably not *all* of us," I said.

Franklin agreed with me. "I don't think that would go over well. She might feel like she's being ambushed. A few would be better. Two or three, like Margot suggested. Those who know her best. Don't worry, Garrett. You're not on the list."

Garrett let out a sigh. "That's a relief! I wasn't too excited about the prospect of telling my future in-law she's whacked."

"Well, if that's how you were going to put it," Mom said, "I'm sure everyone else is relieved that you won't be going along too."

Franklin smiled. "Immensely. I think it would be better if we limited the 'interveners' to myself and, if you don't mind, perhaps Evelyn and Margot? You're her closest friends. If she'll listen to anyone, she'll listen to you."

"Okay."

Margot echoed her agreement, then said with a laugh, "Isn't it funny? Here people are talking about interventions as if they're the latest, newest thing in human relations, but the disciples already had it figured out about two thousand years ago."

"Well," I said, laying my hand on Margot's arm, "let's just pray it works."

"Oh, I will," Margot said. "Count on it."

24

Evelyn Dixon

Since Abigail was going to be in New York for at least a week, we couldn't put our "intervention" plan into action until her return, but at least we had a plan. That was a start.

In the meantime, the shop was an enormous mess. Everyone pitched in to clean up. Ivy and Mom threw the paper plates into a big garbage bag, then Ivy carted the heavy trays filled with dirty cups into the break room, where Mom began washing them. After the men finished breaking down the chairs and tables, they loaded them into Charlie's catering van. Charlie volunteered to return them to the rental company for me. Margot and I shifted the fabric shelving back into the middle of the room and then started taking down the decorations.

Margot stood with her hands on her hips, examining one of the balloon daisies. "Seems a shame to have to take them down after all that work."

"Well then, let's not. The helium should be good for a couple of days. Let's just leave them up for a while. The customers will get a charge out of it. The ones in the courtyard are fine, but we'll need to move these out of this corner. They're blocking the fabric."

"What if we put a few up by the register?"

I nodded. "And the others on one end of the cutting table? That'd be adorable. Let's do it!"

Margot grinned, pleased that our daisies would live to bloom another day or two. Just as we were about to begin transplanting the flowers to new locations, Garrett came up behind me and tapped me on the shoulder.

"Mom? Can I talk to you?"

"Sure, sweetheart. What is it?"

Garrett glanced quickly at Margot. "I meant, can I talk to you alone? Just for a couple of minutes. Sorry to steal her away from you, Margot."

Margot waved her hand. "No problem. I've got this under control anyway."

Mom and Ivy were still in the break room, so we went upstairs to Garrett's apartment and met Gibb coming down the stairs, carrying a stack of reassembled cardboard boxes.

"Thanks, Gibb! That should be plenty. Could you take those in to Mom? She's in the break room."

"Will do!" he said with a grin as he bounded down the stairs.

"Looks like Grandma has an admirer," Garret said.

"You might be right."

Garrett lives above the shop, in the apartment I occupied when I first came to New Bern, before I rented my little house on Marsh Lane.

"After Liza moves in, I'm thinking that Grateful Dead poster might have to go," I said with a smile as I settled myself onto Garrett's lumpy brown sofa, pushing a pile of computer and gaming magazines aside. "Probably the Seahawks poster too."

After college, Garrett had taken a job with one of those big computer companies in Seattle, Claremont Solutions. He wasn't a huge football fan, but he'd gone to a few games while in Seattle and had picked up the poster as a souvenir.

"That's all right," Garrett said, moving his laptop off a chair and sitting down. "I just put them up there so the walls wouldn't be bare. Liza's paintings will look much better."

Garrett turned his head left and right, taking a good look at the apartment.

"It does kind of look like the proverbial post-college bachelor pad, though, doesn't it? Guess once we're married I'll have to do a little decorating. Get some lampshades, towels that match, that kind of thing."

I smiled. "By the time the wedding is over and the presents are opened, I've got a feeling you'll have enough matching towels to open a linen store."

"Yeah," Garrett chuckled, but his eyes were flat. "Once we're married. Feels funny to say that."

"I bet. You nervous?"

Garrett took in a deep breath and let it out. "Mom, today, when Liza started to cry? I . . . I just . . . I didn't know what to do. Or say. She was so upset, and I couldn't think of one thing to say that would make her feel better. I felt like an idiot."

He rested his elbows on his legs, clutched his hands together, intertwining his fingers, and dropped his head down, looking at the floor—the exact same position that his father always sat in when something was bothering him and he was having trouble putting it into words.

"And then, all of you were there, hugging her and patting her, and I felt even more like an idiot. I mean, why didn't I do that? Why didn't I go over and hug her and tell her it was going to be all right?"

Hands still clutched together, Garrett lifted his head and looked me in the eye. "Do you think I'm going to be a good husband?"

My heart melted inside me. Garret was a man, and a good man, but at that moment, he was my little boy again.

"You will. The fact that you're even willing to ask that question tells me you will. Maybe not from the very first moment and probably not during every single day of your marriage, but you'll get the hang of it. You know what I mean?"

He nodded, but his questioning expression made me realize that he really didn't know, but he wanted to.

"The thing is, Garrett, love is more than a feeling. It's something you do. Every day. Love, love that lasts. is . . ." I rolled my eyes heavenward as if the explanation that I was searching for, an outline of the concept that had taken me almost fifty years to understand and, even then, incompletely, might be plastered up on the ceiling, a clear, simple definition of love, complete with appropriate diagrams and pronunciations. No such luck.

"Oh, Garrett." I sighed. "Love is just really weird."

Garrett raised his eyebrows skeptically. "That's it? That's the great insight about love you want to pass on to your only child as he prepares to marry? Gotta tell you, Mom, I was hoping for a little more."

"Yeah, that wasn't too helpful, was it? Let me see if I can't do better. What I'm trying to say, honey, is that love is just completely contrary to our natural human inclinations."

He tipped his head to one side and frowned, skepticism lining his brow. "What do you mean? Falling in love with Liza was the most natural inclination I've ever had in my life. The second I met her, in your hospital room after your mastectomy"—he chuckled softly at the memory—"not exactly the most romantic place in the world."

"No, I'd say not."

"But the second I met her," he said earnestly, "that was it! I was signed, sealed, delivered, and cooked to a golden brown—done! From that moment on, there was no other girl in the world for me. Nothing could have been more natural than that, Mom. I couldn't have stopped myself from falling in love with Liza if I'd tried."

It was true. I'd seen it. Even through my own emotional turmoil and the haze of postoperative drugs that made my brain function at around fifty percent, I'd seen the spark that passed between Garrett and Liza.

"Yes, but that's *falling* in love, Gar. Staying in love, creating a love that lasts, is the tough part—the part that runs counter to our humanity."

Garrett still looked confused. I tried another tack.

"Why do you love Liza? I know she's beautiful and talented and bright and funny, but so are a lot of girls. Why Liza in particular?"

"Well," he said slowly, formulating his answer, "I guess it's the way I feel when I'm around her. She makes me happy, makes me laugh. I feel like she understands me, you know? And accepts me. She doesn't think it's weird that I go to a Magic tournament every year with my old college buddies and a bunch of other computer geeks, or that a guy my age has a ratty Grateful Dead poster on his wall and a collection of original cartoon cells from the Roger Rabbit movie hung in his bedroom. Including a particularly sexy one of Jessica Rabbit, the only woman who has ever rivaled Liza in my affection."

Garrett grinned at this and I couldn't help but do the same. My son. He really was a nerd. A handsome one, but a nerd just the same.

When he was a little boy, I'd taken him to see *Who Framed Roger Rabbit,* and he had loved that movie, absolutely loved it. Made me take him to see it over and over again, collected all the movie merchandise, that kind of thing. I thought it would wear off in time, the way childhood fads do, but it never did.

When he was out of college, he started working for Claremont Solutions and making money. What was his first major purchase? A new car? A plasma screen TV? A cool new computer game system? No. He bought a production cell from the Roger Rabbit movie. Later he bought another and another, a whole collection of them, now hanging in his bedroom. Besides his posters, these were the only pieces of art he owned.

"And not only does she not mind," he went on, "she's all for leaving them up after she moves in. I said that maybe we should move them to someplace less prominent, the bathroom or something. But she said no because she knows how much I like them. So that's another thing I love about her. She cares about me, wants the things that I want, wants me to be happy.

"And I want her to put her artwork up in the living room, not just because it's beautiful but because I know how important that is to *her*. Because I want her to be happy too."

I was nodding as Garrett spoke, and smiling, especially at the last words, because he'd summed it all up so well.

"That's it, Garrett. See? Love is a progression. It starts with attraction, falling in love, the spark you feel when you touch for the first time, that irresistible connection. Then comes romance, being in love, that part where you're getting to know the person better. You like what you see and, even more, how they make you feel—understood, accepted, appreciated, valued, loved. That's a wonderful time in a couple's life, so exciting. But the thing is, that being in love stage is still really all about *you*. How that person makes *you* feel, meets *your* needs."

Garrett frowned and opened his mouth, wanting to dispute me, but I held up my hand to stop him.

"Let me finish. I know that what you feel for Liza isn't just about you—not anymore. Your love has matured. You're not just in this for yourself, you're in it for her now. You want to care for *her,* put *her* first, meet *her* needs. Love that lasts isn't about you, it's about her.

"Mature love means you turn your natural human inclinations upside down, putting the happiness of your beloved before your own. That's why you'll be a good husband, Garrett. Not because you get it right all the time, not because you always know exactly what to do, or say, or how to care for Liza, but because you *want* to know those things. You've turned your love for yourself on its head, and now you're redirecting it to Liza. That's your new desire, your instinct, even, to try and make Liza happy."

"Well, I didn't do a very good job of that today," he said glumly. "She fell apart and I just stood there. And then I ran out on her, left the rest of you to pick up the pieces."

"That's true," I admitted. "That was not one of your finest moments. But you'll do better next time."

"You think so? I hate it when she cries. I have no idea what to do, how to make it better."

I nodded. Garrett was one hundred percent guy. Uncomfortable with tears, uncomfortable with any situation he couldn't fix.

"Honey, you don't *have* to make it better. That's not your job. Most of the time that's not what women are looking for, anyway."

"No?"

I shook my head. "Women are all about relationships, communicating, just being there for each other. Next time she cries, don't run away from her. Run *to* her. Put your arms around her. Comfort her. Listen to her. Tell her that you're there and always will be, and that everything will be all right. Later, when she's calmed down, you can help her work out the details of exactly how to make that happen—if that's what she wants. Most of the time, she'll just need to know you're there."

Garrett was listening carefully, taking it all in, but he wasn't entirely ready to let himself off the hook.

"But I still don't think I'm very good about putting Liza first. When I came in here today and found out that she'd gone to New York, I was really mad. It upset all my plans for the whole week. That was all about me."

"Not entirely. You want to spend time with her and naturally, when you found out that wasn't going to happen, you were upset. But I also think you were concerned about Liza. You know how tired she's been and how much she needed a break."

"Yeah," he said in a voice that was almost a growl. "If I saw Abigail right now, I might smack her. What's the deal with her? Doesn't she see how much stress Liza is under? I'm worried about her, Mom. She isn't sleeping."

Or eating, I thought, mentally conjuring the image of Liza's too-thin frame. Garrett wasn't the only one who was worried about her.

"Well, Liza is young, Garrett. This is a lot of pressure for her."

He hesitated for a moment, then looked at me with those big brown eyes and said, "Too young, do you think?"

That caught me by surprise. Was he having second thoughts? And what *did* I think? Was she too young? Was he? Maybe. But Liza was about the same age I'd been when I'd married and probably no more mature than I'd been then—though at the time, I'd thought I was extremely mature. On the other hand, my marriage hadn't worked out. But that hadn't been because I was too young.

Until Rob dove headfirst into a midlife crisis by having an affair with a woman only a little more than half his age, we'd been fairly happy. So, had Rob been too young? He was three years older than I was when we married. If he'd waited, sown a few wild oats, would that have made any difference? In my heart, I didn't think so, but there was really no way of knowing for sure.

"You are young, Garrett. Both of you. But that doesn't necessarily mean you're too young. That's one of those questions only you can answer. Learning to be a good husband or a good wife is like learning to play a musical instrument. No matter how old you are when you begin, it takes practice. And the more you practice, the more you determine to put her needs ahead of your own, even when you don't feel like it, the better and easier it will be. It won't happen overnight. You'll make plenty of mistakes, but if you keep at it, in time your marriage will reflect that.

"But," I cautioned, "a good marriage is also a duet. It takes both spouses, both putting their partner first, to make it work. You've both got to be on board. Love is a verb, Garrett. Something you do, even if you don't feel like doing it. That's what 'for better or worse' means."

"We're supposed to start our premarital counseling pretty soon."

"Good! Take it seriously. A lot of couples rush through that, and they shouldn't. If every engaged couple spent half as much time preparing for marriage as they do preparing for the wedding, I think we'd have about half as many divorces."

Garrett scratched his temple with one finger. "In our case that would mean we'd have to spend about three years solid in premarital counseling. I swear, the collective man-hours involved in putting on this wedding must be running up close to a decade's worth of work by now."

"You might be exaggerating a little there." I laughed. "But not by much."

He looked at me, waiting to see what else I might have for him. I wished I did have more, some special gnosis, some secret nugget of truth that I could pass on to my son about love and marriage that would ensure its endurance, some warranty against nicks, dings, breakdowns, and catastrophe. But I could offer him no such guarantee. Life just isn't like that. Who would know better than I?

Garrett clasped his hands together, dropped his head, and looked at the floor again, mulling things over, trying to sort everything out and arrive at some definite conclusion, something he could hang his hat on.

That's Garrett, through and through. He's a computer guy. He's not afraid of complex problems. In fact, he relishes them. But Garrett's world is made up of numbers and codes and formulas, things that can be theorized with reasonable certainty, tested, and ultimately proven. In Garrett's world there is always one optimal solution. It might take a while to reach it, but there is great comfort in knowing it's out there, somewhere.

These were uncertain waters and they scared him, I could tell. Frankly, they scared me too. They had from the first moment Garrett had called me and said he was getting married.

After a long time, he raised his head. When he did, the searching little boy look was gone.

"Mom, would you mind if I took off a little time this week? I'd like to go into the city and see Liza. Maybe just for a cup of coffee or something. I don't want to put any more pressure on her. But I think I should see her, let her know I'm thinking about her."

His gaze was steady and full of resolve. He had made up his mind. Never again would Garrett stand distantly, helplessly by when the woman he loved needed him. Next time, he would do something. Maybe not the right something, but something.

I smiled. I was right. My son was a good man, and he would be a good husband. One way or another, he would be okay. They both would.

25

Evelyn Dixon

There was a sound of tires crunching gravel. A pair of headlights beamed two columns of light through the living room window. A moment later, I heard the slam of a car door, a 1968 Chevy Corvair.

"Finally!" I said to the empty room. I stopped pacing midway between the kitchen and breakfast room and marched to the front door, ready to fling it open and shout, "Where have you been? Do you have any idea what time it is?"

But as my fingers wrapped around the glass knob, I had a mental image of my mother and Gibb Rainey standing on my front porch lip to lip, and it stopped me in my tracks.

What if they were out there doing just that? Was that something I wanted to see? Definitely not. The thought of seeing my mother locked in the embrace of a man besides my father, especially if that man was Gibb Rainey, was a scene I didn't want to witness, now or ever. Not that I had anything against Gibb personally—he was a nice enough guy, but he was short and monosyllabic and spent his days sitting in a lawn chair in front of the post office, for heaven's sake! While my father, my darling father, had been a college professor—tall and handsome and respected in his field! So respected that when Dad died, the alumni had endowed a full-ride scholarship in his name. After living fifty-one years with my father, what could Mom possibly see in Gibb Rainey? What?

And if I opened that door and saw Mom and Gibb together, there was no doubt in my mind that I would ask Mom exactly that, undoubtedly with my voice raised. I wouldn't be able to stop myself.

"Don't go there, Evelyn," Charlie had said when I told him about my suspicions regarding Mom and Gibb. "I'm telling you, *do not go there.* It's none of your business. And even if it's true, why do you care? So what if Virginia and Gibb have a little romantic fling? They're both of age."

Ha! They certainly were! I'd done a little sleuthing and found out that Gibb was even older than I'd thought. Come October, he'd be eighty-eight. Eighty-eight! What business did Gibb have going around luring innocent little old widows into romantic flings at his age? At Gibb's age, a romantic fling could be fatal. I told Charlie that.

"Oh, stop it," Charlie said with a roll of his eyes. "Virginia is healthy and Gibb looks pretty fit as well. I'd sure never have pegged him as eighty-eight. And we've all got to go sometime. Can you think of a better way?"

Yes, I could. Pretty much any way that involved lifetime fidelity to the memory of my deceased father would be a much better way. Charlie had a good laugh over that one. Easy for him to be so glib. How would he feel if Margaret, the legendary matriarch of the Donnelly family, inventor of the many secret family recipes and, since Charlie's father's death, the sole proprietor of the county's only three-star restaurant, suddenly took up with a busboy at the local diner? Huh? Answer me that?

"There are no diners in Ireland." Charlie made a sucking noise with his teeth. "Evelyn, your father was a great man, I've no doubt about that. But he's been gone for ten years. Even if this were any of your business—which, I repeat, it is not—is it possible that you're being just a wee bit irrational?"

Well. Maybe.

I backed away from the door and went back to pacing. After

what seemed like an age, the door opened. Before she came in, Mom turned around and waved. "Thanks again, Gibb."

"My pleasure," Gibb replied.

"Go, Huskies!" She laughed.

"Go, Huskies!" Gibb called back, raising his fist over his head as he made his way down the sidewalk and got into his car.

Not noticing me at first, Mom chuckled to herself as she closed the door and took off her coat.

"How was the game?"

Mom looked up and jumped a little. "Oh! Evelyn, I didn't see you there. What are you doing up so late? The game was fine. We won!"

"I know," I said. "Almost three hours ago. I listened to the radio broadcast."

Mom frowned as she hung up her coat on one of the wall pegs near the door. "Evelyn, is something wrong?"

"No," I mumbled, feeling suddenly ridiculous. Charlie was right. It was none of my business. I should have left it alone. If Mom had, I would have. But she didn't.

Mom narrowed her eyes. "Evelyn Dixon," she said, "don't stand there looking at me like that!"

"Like what?"

"Like I am some sort of delinquent teenager who's been caught sneaking in after curfew, that's how. Take your hands off your hips and quit glowering at me. If you've got something to say, then say it!"

I shoved my hands in my pockets. "All right, I will. Do you have any idea what time it is?" I asked before answering my own question. "Nearly one o'clock in the morning! Where have you been?"

"That is none of your business, Evelyn."

So I'd been told, twice, by Charlie.

Mom's lips flattened into an indignant line. "Quit looking at me like that!" she demanded.

"Like what?" I said, throwing up my hands in frustration. This wasn't fair. My expression was a blank canvas, as neutral as Switzerland. I was sure of it. "I'm not looking at you like anything. I just asked you a simple question. I've been pacing around here for hours, worried to death that something might have happened to you. I mean, you might have at least called or something. Just to let me know everything was all right and you were going to be late. After all, I am responsible for you, and I think . . ."

"Responsible for me?" Mom barked. "Responsible for *me?* Oh no. I don't think so. I am a mature, experienced, and capable adult. Only *I* am responsible for me. That's the way it's been and that's the way it will be until I die!"

She was mad, and rightly so. What was wrong with me? Why was I behaving like a jealous daddy's girl? Maybe because I still was. I was also out of line.

"Mom," I said, deliberately lowering my voice. "I'm sorry. I didn't mean it like that. It's just—"

"You don't have to tell me what you meant. I've known for a long time. Ever since you showed up in De Pere to spy on me."

"Spy on you! Mom, I wasn't spying on you."

"Oh, yes, you were," she said, pointing her finger at me accusingly. "Poking around my refrigerator and my cupboards. Not letting me drive. Insinuating that I couldn't take care of myself anymore, that I needed some kind of babysitter."

"Mom, be fair. I never said you couldn't take care of yourself."

"You didn't have to say it!" she scoffed. "Don't think I don't know what you've been up to, Evelyn. Ever since I came to New Bern, you've been trying to convince me to stay, to give up my home. Well, I'm not going to do it! Your father and I lived in that house for our entire married lives. All my memories are tied up in that house. I'm not going to sell it. Not ever!"

Mom was clenching her jaw so tight that I could see the muscles twitch in her neck. I took a step toward her. "Mom, I'm sorry. I didn't mean to upset you. Let's sit down and talk about this."

She turned her head away and held up her hands to ward off my approach. "No," she said in a voice that was calmer but no less resolved. "There is nothing to talk about. I'm tired and I'm going to bed. And in the morning, I'm going to call up a travel agent and book a ticket back to Wisconsin."

"But," I protested, "what about the wedding?"

"I'll stay until the wedding to help you and to help Garrett and Liza. But after that, I'm going home."

I tried to speak but she wouldn't let me.

"No! Don't start. I've made up my mind. There's no use trying to talk me out of it. If you do, if you bring it up again, then wedding or no wedding, I'll be on the next plane back to Wisconsin. Don't test me on this, Evelyn. I am dead serious. I won't hear another word about it, not one."

26

Liza Burgess

I glanced up and looked at the clock that hung on the red brick wall, right next to the poster announcing the new "Summer Can't Come Fast Enough!" line of citrus-flavored Frappuccinos.

"I wish I had more time. I feel guilty that you drove all the way into the city again just to have a cup of coffee with me." I paused and looked up at him from under my lashes. "But I'm glad you did."

"I'm glad I did, too. It isn't that far."

I raised my brows. "Two hours?"

"Okay, so it is that far. So what? I wanted to see you, even if it was for only twenty minutes."

"I'm sorry," I said for the third time since we'd sat down.

"Liza, forget about it. Besides, later we'll actually get to spend some time together. We're still on for tonight, right?"

I nodded. "I've got to meet Abigail at Byron's office at ten sharp. I'll call you as soon as I'm done. That's my last obligation in this very long week. Unless, of course, Abigail thinks up some other obligations for me—which seems like a good bet."

"It's all right," Garrett said patiently. "We're in the home stretch. Things will be better after the wedding, you'll see."

I nodded, hoping he was right. Hadn't I been telling myself the same thing for weeks now?

He reached out to adjust my engagement ring, turning it so the diamond sat square on the center of my finger. "This is really loose. Didn't I get the right size?"

It used to be the right size. When Garrett gave it to me it fit perfectly. But I'd lost seventeen pounds since then, and my fingers were as bony as the rest of me. I wasn't dieting; I just wasn't hungry. When I did eat, the result was an instantaneous stomachache.

"It's fine," I said, pulling back my hand, picking up my Frappuccino and pretending to take a sip. "I've just lost a couple of pounds."

"Just a couple? Looks like more than a couple. Are you feeling all right?"

"Oh yeah. Really. I'm fine," I assured him and then took a big slurp, a real one this time, to prove it. "Just busy. Byron says that most brides lose a few pounds before the wedding. It's perfectly normal. Like you said, things will be better after the wedding."

With his brows still drawn together, he slowly nodded, agreeing with me, wanting it to be true as much as I did. We were quiet for a moment, each thinking our private thoughts. What Garrett's were I didn't know, but mine, as they had been for much of the week, were all about Professor Williams's job offer in Chicago.

Should I accept? I didn't know. It was the chance of a lifetime. Professor Williams said it was, and in my heart I knew she was right—but did that mean it was right for me? I'd never been to Chicago, not even to change planes. Truth was, I'd never been much of anywhere outside of New England. Mom and I went to Florida once and Philadelphia another time, but that was pretty much the extent of our travels. Of course, I'd been away to school in Rhode Island. That had been a complete disaster.

I didn't have any friends at school there. Not surprising. My mother's death had been so recent that the pain of it nearly paralyzed me. I held myself together, but only just. Without realizing it, I kept crying out in my sleep, apparently pretty loudly. By Halloween my roommate asked to be moved. I roomed alone for the rest of the year.

Once, I heard a girl in the library who was on her cell phone, loudly arguing with her mom about something stupid. I don't remember exactly what it was about now, but she was just going off on her mom. I walked up, grabbed the phone out of her hand, hit the End button, and told her to shut up because people were trying to study. The girl yelled at me and I yelled back and we both got tossed out of the library. I was so mad!

At the time, I really believed I was angry because she was being loud, but now I realize it was all about my mom. I was mad at everyone whose mother was still living, which amounted to basically everyone.

By the middle of the third semester I was on the verge of flunking out, so I decided to drop out of school and beat the administration to the punch. I was miserable, anyway. After that experience, the idea of going off to some strange place made me very nervous. And, especially after this weekend, after getting to go to New Bern and spend a little time (thanks to Abigail, only a very little) with family and friends in the only place I think of as home, the thought of accepting a job halfway across the country is scary.

Of course, I'll only go if Garrett wants to go too. But what if he doesn't? What if I talk to him about it and he says he won't go? Will I resent him forever? Or what if I talk to him about it and he says he will go and we do, but then it turns out like Kerry's sister and her husband, and Garrett ends up resenting *me* forever? What then?

This job offer in Chicago is the chance of a lifetime. At least, I think it is. That's what everybody says. But Garrett's the chance of a lifetime, too, isn't he? You don't get two chances of a lifetime in one lifetime, so what do I do? How do I choose? And what if I choose wrong?

I can't decide—about anything.

Last night, Abigail handed me the room service menu, the kind you hang on the doorknob of your hotel room at night so they know what you want for breakfast the next morning, and I just couldn't make up my mind. Should I have pancakes? Or oatmeal? Or the fruit plate? I don't like poached eggs but, finally, I just put another checkmark next to what Abigail had ordered.

It's never been easy for me to talk about my feelings. I know I should talk to Garrett about Chicago. I have to. This is the first moment we've had alone in weeks. Maybe now would be a good time. The way things have been going, maybe it will be our only time. Maybe. But maybe not. Professor Williams said she didn't have to have an answer for a while yet. Would it be better to wait until we're somewhere more private than a noisy coffee bar? Some time when we'd have more time? I'm not sure. And I want to be sure. I want to get this right. I want to get *everything* right.

Four months ago I was just a student. I went to class. I painted. I went out with my friends. On weekends I either went home to New Bern or I didn't. That was it. There was plenty of room in my life for screwups. Now, practically overnight, everything is for keeps. Every choice I make matters, every door I walk through means there are ten other doors I walk past, doors that may stay closed to me for life. How can I know which is the right one?

I should talk to Garrett about all this; I know I should. But I can't. Not today.

After taking a long drink from his coffee cup, Garrett said, "So where do you want to go for our honeymoon?"

"Abigail says we should go to Bermuda. She's booking a suite for us at a hotel on Elbow Beach. She says it's the perfect honeymoon spot."

Garrett put down his drink with a soft thump and pushed back from the table. His smile was gone.

"Then Abigail should go there—on *her* honeymoon. I'm only interested in our honeymoon, yours and mine, which *I* will be booking, by the way. The groom pays for the honeymoon, Liza, and I'm paying for ours. So where do *you* want to go? Not Abigail. You."

"I . . . I don't know. Where do you want to go?"

Garrett's shoulders drooped. He tucked his chin closer to his chest and just looked at me, not saying a word.

"What?" I said. "I don't know. I really don't. Why don't you decide?"

"Because this is my gift to you and I want this to be special," he said, trying to keep the exasperated edge from his voice. "Look, I want the first days of our married life to be exactly what you want them to be. I don't care if we go to the Caribbean, or on a cruise, or camping. Anywhere you are is fine with me. That's where I'm happy."

"Well, I feel the same way, so why do I have to be the one to decide? Why not you? If you'll be happy anyplace, then why not Bermuda? Why *not* let Abigail decide? If she says Bermuda will be perfect, then I'm sure it will be."

"Because it seems to me that Abigail has been pushing you around plenty these days," he grumbled, shifting in his chair. "I guess, since she's paying for the wedding, there isn't a whole lot we can do about it. But the second we leave the reception, we're in the driver's seat—you and me. After all this time, I'd think you'd be happy to get out from under her thumb, have things your own way."

"I am," I lied.

Initially, Abigail's bulldozer approach to wedding planning had gotten on my nerves. Now I was happy that she was in charge and that all I had to do for this wedding was show up. It was too much for me to deal with.

"Let me think about it, okay?"

"Okay. Anywhere you want." Garrett's mouth bowed into his customary smile. "Anywhere but Bermuda."

I smiled back at him. He was so sweet. There wasn't much in my life that I was sure of right now, except that I loved Garrett. No matter how bad things were, I felt better when Garrett was around.

I pushed away the plastic cup with my barely touched drink and wiped my lips with my napkin. "I've got to go."

Garrett's smile disappeared. "Already?"

"Yeah," I said, taking my purse off the back of my chair and putting it on my shoulder. "I've got a fitting. Well, not a fitting, really. They finished the alterations to the dress a month ago. This is for accessories. Abigail and Byron want to see what shoes, veil, and jewelry look best with the dress."

"What about that necklace? The one you made, the one you wore on New Year's Eve? You looked beautiful that night."

He was talking about the night I'd refused him, or rather, the night I'd pushed him off, telling him I needed time to think. It hadn't been a good night for him, but he didn't remember that now. He only remembered the good things. Maybe, someday, I'd be more like him.

"I think Abigail is talking diamonds."

"Who cares what Abigail is talking? She's not going to be waiting for you at the end of the aisle, I will. And I like the necklace you made. It's beautiful, just like you, and there's only one in the whole world, also just like you."

I laughed. "You just want me to wear it because Abigail doesn't."

His eyes became serious. "No, I don't. I want you to wear it because, in this whole insane circus performance that has become our wedding day, I'd like there to be one thing, just one, that is about you and me. Something that reflects our history, our love, and the things that matter to us. At least think about it, okay?"

"Okay." I got up and kissed him on the top of his head. "I've got to go."

"Don't."

I smiled. "I have to. But I'll see you tonight. It'll just be a little while."

He sighed and got up from the table. "Come here." He put his arms around me, pulled me close, bent his head down, and kissed me like there was no time, no appointments, nowhere else we had to be, no people in a crowded coffee bar watching, wishing they were us.

When he finally lifted his lips from mine it was all I could do not to pull him to me again.

"Do you have any idea how much I want to get you alone?" he breathed.

I dropped my head forward, resting it against his chest, blushing, not with embarrassment but from the heat of my own desire.

"Me too."

"Honeymoon," he reminded me. "Think about where you want to go. Don't forget."

I nodded. I wouldn't forget. I couldn't.

He bent down toward me, ready to kiss me again, but I turned my head and offered him a cheek, knowing that if I let him kiss me again I wouldn't be able to leave.

"I have to go."

"I love you."

"I love you more."

His eyes followed me to the door. I turned to get one more look at him before I walked out onto the busy Manhattan sidewalk and disappeared into the throng of people hurrying on their way to work and appointments and a million mundane meetings, the tyrannically urgent nothings that drive us through our days but pale in the light of love.

27

Liza Burgess

Abigail's arms were crossed over her chest. She scowled as I walked into the thickly carpeted waiting area of Best Laid Planners.

"You're late. You've kept everyone waiting."

Nice to see you, too.

"Sorry," I said, which wasn't true. I was late because I preferred Garrett's company and kisses to Abigail's orders and harangues. But I didn't say that. Easier to go with the flow than start an argument.

A few months ago, starting arguments with Abigail, striking a match against the grit of her easily ignited temper, had been one of my favorite pastimes. It was entertaining and oh so easy to do. One quick jab, one sharp, well-placed bit of sarcasm touched to the fuse of Abigail's ire, was all it took to set off a satisfyingly showy but ultimately harmless shower of sparks. But now, those formerly inert sparks had the power to sting, and I avoided them whenever possible.

Abigail started to say something just as Byron entered the waiting room carrying my dress. He chirped a cheery good morning before giving each of us a quick air kiss and asking us to follow him back to the dressing area. Abigail scurried after him and I followed, not having time to take off my coat.

"Sorry I'm late, Byron."

"No worries, Liza. It gave us a little time to steam the dress again."

We turned a corner and entered a large, brightly lit room furnished with a series of white upholstered slipper chairs sitting around a beveled glass coffee table set with an ornate sterling silver coffee service. At one end of the room and half circled by mirrors stood a small platform, the spot where the bride-to-be stood clad in her elaborate white gown, turning slowly like a plastic ballerina on a little girl's music box, while the audience sat apart, drinking tea and deciding if she would do.

"Abigail, why don't you have a seat? Or help yourself to some coffee. It's a new Ethiopian organic that you're going to love. Liza, darling, follow me.

"Here we go," Byron said as he hung the dress up on a hook in a curtained changing area. "I've got to go and check on your accessories, see if everything came in. Shall I send back one of the girls to help zip you up?"

"That's okay. I can do it myself."

Eight minutes later, after much stalling in the changing room, I nervously pushed aside the curtain and emerged.

Abigail looked up and stared at me as I came into the room, her coffee cup frozen midway between the saucer and her lips.

Hearing the rustling of my skirts, Byron, who was standing at a side table arranging a collection of white slippers, pumps, and sandals, turned.

"Liza? What?" His jaw dropped onto his chest and for a moment, he just stood there, speechless and disbelieving.

"What . . . what happened? The seamstress just altered that dress. Last month it fit perfectly and now . . . It's just hanging on you!"

Byron rolled his head back dramatically and let out a loud, frustrated, must-I-do-everything-myself sort of sigh, stomped toward a half-open door and called out, "Someone get Olga on the phone. Now! She must have sent over another customer's gown by mistake. This one can't belong to Liza. The poor girl is drowning in it!"

Leslie came scurrying in, looked at me in the dress, and gasped. "Oh my! I'll call Olga and see what happened."

"I don't care what happened," Byron said with an uncharacteristically impatient edge to his voice. "Just tell her to get the right dress over here. Now."

"Right away." Leslie left the room and went back to her office to make the call.

Byron turned back to me. "I'm sorry. I can't imagine how this happened. What are the chances of the seamstress having two clients with the exact same dress? Especially a gown from such an exclusive designer? Velma Wong only made six of those dresses."

"Well, I certainly hope so," Abigail said impatiently, finding her voice again. "I don't want to open my copy of *Society Bride* the week after the wedding only to see a picture of Liza and another girl, both in the same dress!"

"No, no." Byron rushed to assure her. "That's not going to happen. I promise you. We'll get this straightened out and have Liza's gown sent over immediately. Don't worry. In the meantime, we can start trying on shoes and jewelry. We'll have it narrowed down by the time your dress arrives. All right? Or we can put off choosing accessories until this afternoon and start working on the trousseau now. The racks are all ready to go. If you'd like, I can have them brought in. I'm so sorry about all this."

I swallowed hard, reluctant to speak. "Byron, wait a minute. I . . . I don't think there was a mistake. I'm pretty sure this is my dress."

He yelped out a half-laugh. "No, it's not. It couldn't be, darling. It's enormous on you!"

"I know. I . . . but I've lost weight."

Abigail put her coffee cup down on the glass table and stood up. "No, Liza. Byron's right. This can't be your dress. There's been some kind of mix-up.

"She has lost weight," Abigail confirmed to Byron, "but it can't have been that much, surely no more than a couple of pounds. Otherwise, I'd have noticed, wouldn't I?"

She was right to sound incredulous. Frankly, spending almost a week together in the same suite, I'd been amazed that she hadn't said anything about my weight, or about the sound of my retching in the bathroom. But it was a big suite and Abigail's bathroom was far from mine. Plus, she'd been pretty wrapped up in the wedding.

Too wrapped up to actually notice me, inconsequential as I was, among the distracting collage of floral arrangements, to-do lists, and white tulle.

Byron had a sharper eye. If I hadn't been wearing my thick winter coat to ward off the cold of an unseasonably chilly April morning, I bet he'd have noticed right off.

"I'm actually down quite a bit. Seventeen pounds," I said, but then quickly added, "but that's total. It's only another twelve since the last fitting."

This didn't sound as bad in my mind, but when I looked in the mirror I could see that the numbers didn't make any difference. Twelve pounds or twenty, the bottom line was that my beautiful dress didn't fit anymore.

Byron put his hand on my arm. "Liza, what's going on? You don't need to diet, darling. You're a beautiful girl, and the gown looked lovely on you as it was. You were already a size six to begin with. What made you think you needed to be thinner?"

"I don't. I didn't. I . . . I wasn't dieting. I just can't eat, that's all. Nerves, I guess. Nothing to worry about. All brides get pre-wedding jitters. You said so yourself."

"Seventeen pounds is more than a case of jitters, Liza. Just look at yourself."

He took me by the hand and led me to the mirror-encircled platform. He was right. The dress was drowning me. It was as if my nightmare, the one where I kept shrinking to the point where the gown swallowed me completely, was coming true.

Abigail came up and stood behind me, peering over my right shoulder into the mirror, flattening her mouth into an appraising line. "Can it be altered? Or would we be better off to order a whole new dress in a smaller size?"

Byron raised his eyebrows curiously, as if he didn't quite grasp her meaning. "Well, yes, we can alter it, but don't you think we ought to take Liza to a doctor? Just to see if there is a physical or"—the word "psychological" hung in the air, but Byron didn't say it aloud—"some other sort of problem. A seventeen-pound weight loss on a girl as slender as Liza is worrisome."

Abigail nodded. "Yes, I'm sure you're right. Liza, I'll call the doctor and make an appointment for you next time you're in New Bern. You need to see a gynecologist before the wedding, anyway."

I blushed, wishing she wouldn't feel quite so free to talk about the intimate details of my personal life in front of Byron, but she didn't seem to notice.

"That way we'll be able to kill two birds with one stone." Abigail smiled, the matter now settled in her mind.

"But," Byron said cautiously, "don't you think she ought to see someone right away?"

Abigail waved her hand dismissively. "Oh, I'm sure everything is all right. Liza's schedule this spring was just insane. She barely had time to eat, that's all. I'll keep a better eye on her from here on out, make sure she eats properly. I'm sure she'll be able to gain back at least a few extra pounds before the wedding.

"In fact," she said slowly, her eyes narrowing as she reached down to my waist and pinched a good two inches of white satin between her fingers, "perhaps Olga should leave a little extra room when she does the alterations. Better to have the gown a little too big than too small. Don't you agree? That would be a disaster."

Looking at my reflection, Byron's gaze flickered from Abigail, fussing with the waistline of my dress, to my face and then back to Abigail before circling in front of me to discuss the possible use of a more heavily padded bra as a means of filling the gown's suddenly-too-big bosom without the use of deeper darts.

I stood still on the platform with my eyes to the front and my arms out, saying nothing, waiting for them to finish, feeling like that little music box ballerina, turning and turning but never going anywhere, molded from plastic, feeling nothing.

Hours later, after Olga, the redoubtable Russian seamstress, had been called over to Byron's offices to re-measure and re-pin the gown she'd already altered once, we were finally able to move on to the business of choosing accessories.

I'm tall, so it was quickly decided that the white satin slingbacks with a two-inch kitten heel would be the best choice. This meant that the dress had to be shortened another inch and a half.

Grumbling in Russian through a mouthful of straight pins, Olga got on her knees next to the platform and started marking the hem.

In the meantime, Byron brought out a series of black velvet trays loaded with a virtual mine of sparkling diamond and pearl chokers, necklaces, and earrings that had been sent over from jewelers. Byron chose a piece from one tray, a breathtaking necklace of alternating oval- and emerald-cut diamonds, and looped it around my neck, coming around behind me to fasten the platinum clasp and adjusting it so the necklace rested evenly below the jut of my collarbones.

"Liza," he said with a smile as he stepped back to admire his handiwork, "you have an exquisite neck. And this piece only enhances it. And the dress." He turned to look at Abigail, who was standing to one side with her hand resting lightly near her own throat, looking very pleased.

"I love the emerald-cut stones," she said. "So elegant."

Byron nodded. "Of course, we can try on the others if you'd like but, for my money, this is the way to go."

"I agree," said Abigail. "It's perfect."

"Good. Now I'm sure you've rented jewels for special occasions before, Abigail, but just to remind you, we'll need to call to make arrangements with the insurance—"

Abigail held up her hand. "No, no. That won't be necessary. I'm not renting it. I'm buying it. For Liza."

Abigail's mouth stretched into a wide, beatific smile. For the first time that day, she looked me in the eye.

"It's your wedding present." She paused, waiting for me to gasp, or cry, or launch into some appropriately emotional expression of surprise and gratitude.

"I don't want it."

Abigail's sunny smile shriveled. I was glad.

"What do you mean? If you're concerned about the cost, don't be. It's expensive, yes, but this *is* your wedding and you are my niece, Susan's only child, and my only living relative. I want your wedding to be entirely perfect, completely memorable. You mustn't worry about the expense. I can afford it."

I shook my head. "You're not listening. I don't *want* it. I don't want you to buy it for me. I don't even want you to rent it for me. I don't like it, and I don't want to wear it at my wedding."

Abigail's brow furrowed. She looked to Byron, searching for an explanation for my inexplicable behavior, but he looked as perplexed as she did.

"Perhaps . . . perhaps you saw another piece you prefer?" Byron hopped off the platform, walked over to the jewelry trays, and stood in front of them, his finger to his lips, considering the options. "The sunflower vine choker is pretty. A bit ornate, perhaps, but the neckline of the dress is so simple that I think it would—"

"No. I don't want that. I don't want any of those."

Sidestepping Olga, who spat out a pin and cursed me in Russian, I climbed down from the platform, walked to the coatrack, picked up my purse, reached inside, and pulled out a plastic storage bag. "I'm going to wear this."

Giving Abigail a quick glance, Byron crossed the room and took the plastic bag from my hand. He pulled out the necklace with its five strands of silver beading twisted together and held it up to the light.

"You know," he said, his voice a bit surprised, "this is really quite lovely. Where did you get it?"

"I made it. I was wearing it when Garrett proposed." I didn't bother to add that I hadn't accepted that initial proposal. "He wants me to wear it at the wedding. That's what I want too."

Byron cast a tentative glance in Abigail's direction. "It's really very pretty. Not diamonds, but it does catch the light nicely and is the perfect shape for the neckline. I think it's sweet, especially because it carries such a romantic history with it."

Abigail erupted. "No!"

Ah, there it was—the old shower of sparks. I fought to keep myself from smiling.

"Certainly not!" Abigail stormed across the room and snatched the necklace out of Byron's hand. "It simply won't do!"

I put my hands on my hips. One of Olga's straight pins jabbed into my flesh, but I didn't care. "Well, it's going to have to do, because this is my wedding and this is what I want to wear to it!"

"Liza! Be reasonable!" She took in a deep breath and let it out slowly. I could practically see her counting to ten in her mind.

"It is a pretty piece," she admitted grudgingly. "And I'm sure it's very special to you and to Garrett, but it isn't appropriate for the wedding. It's not formal enough, not for the ceremony.

"I've got an idea," she said, brightening. "Why don't you wear it with your going-away ensemble. Hmm?"

I said nothing.

"Or," she went on, taking another tack, "perhaps you could even change into it for the reception. Yes! That would be lovely. So much more appropriate, don't you think?"

She looked to Byron for support. He smiled a diplomatic, peacekeeping sort of smile.

"No, I *don't* think!" I shouted and stomped my foot. "You keep telling me that this is my special day, that you want everything to be perfect for me. Well, this *is* perfect for me! For *me!*" I grabbed the necklace away from Abigail and held it up high.

"Up till now, I have gone along with everything you wanted, everything. But this is *my* wedding, and I think I should get to have at least one thing exactly as *I* want it! More importantly, I should get to have one thing exactly the way Garrett wants it. This is supposed to be about me and Garrett—not you!"

Abigail's expression was implacable and cold. The louder I shouted, the colder it became until, by the time I finished speaking, her face seemed to have been chiseled from marble, smooth and flat, incapable of feeling. When she spoke, her voice was low.

"Is that what you think? That I'm doing this for myself?"

I nodded.

She closed her eyes, as if the effort to keep them open was suddenly too much to bear. The tendons under the flesh of her neck twitched ever so slightly and she winced as if some secret pain had pierced the marble mask.

Abigail lifted her chin and opened her eyes, revealing a sheen of unshed tears, something I had seen there only once before, on that day when she told me about herself and my mother and the lover's betrayal that had torn them apart, forever separating sisters who once had been inseparable.

"Is that what you really think?" she repeated and then turned her head away, looking up toward a far corner of the room, her gaze focused on some distant point in the beyond.

"I just want to make it perfect for you, to make it up to you. But if that's what you think . . . that I'm doing this for myself . . ." She lifted her hand, blocking my face from view, weakly warding off the possibility of any backpedaling on my part.

"Then there isn't much point, is there, Susan? It will never be enough, will it?" She closed her eyes for a moment. "It's just as well, then. Do as you like. I don't care anymore."

Without looking at anyone or stopping to reclaim her coat from the rack in the corner, she walked out, ignoring Byron, who trailed behind her, pleading with her to come back. Olga sat on the edge of the platform, hunched and frowning. I stood dumbstruck in my bare feet, dressed in my too-big wedding gown with the half-pinned hem, my mother's name a question in my mind.

28

Liza Burgess

I shivered and Garrett put his arm around my shoulders.

As we walked down Fifth Avenue past the store window displays filled with faceless mannequins dressed in spring skirts and short-sleeved cotton cardigans, ignorant of the chilly April wind, I indulged in a little fantasy. What would it be like to live in that window world? Inhabiting a climate-controlled paradise, peopled by cheerily clad dressmaker's dummies where, accessories excepting, everyone was pretty much alike, had nothing much to think about, and all the time in the world not to think about it?

"A terrarium for human beings," I said.

"Didn't somebody already invent that?" Garrett asked. "I think they did. I think it's called Miami."

"Ha." I tipped my head, gently butting his shoulder.

"Do you want to get some dinner?"

I shook my head. "Not hungry."

I pulled my cell phone out of my coat pocket, checking to see if Abigail had answered one of my calls. The ringer was turned up as high as it would go, but with all the noise from the traffic—the honking horns, and the rush-hour hum of engines—you never knew.

Garrett tightened his grip on my shoulder and stopped on the sidewalk, turning my body toward him. "Liza, she'll call when she calls. Stop punishing yourself. Let her stew for a while. After all, you didn't do anything wrong. All you wanted was the right to wear the jewelry you wanted at your wedding. What's the big deal? It's about time you stood up to Abigail. I'm proud that you finally did."

I pressed my lips together. I hadn't told him what happened next, that after Abigail stormed off I told Byron that I'd changed my mind. I would wear the diamonds after all.

"Abigail is my only family. I don't want to . . ."

Garrett frowned. "To what?"

"I don't want to lose her!" I covered my mouth with my hand, a dam against tears. I didn't want to cry. Not again.

"Liza," Garrett whispered. "Liza, baby." The frown disappeared, the line of misunderstanding between his brows flattened out, smooth again, and it annoyed me. He didn't understand, he couldn't. He'd never been alone, not like I was. Not like Abigail had been. We knew what it was like, she and I. And we knew it could happen again.

Garrett took a step toward me, but I pulled back, wrenching my arm from his grasp.

"I know what Abigail is! And how she is. But she's all I have, my only family. I don't want her to be mad at me, to cut me out of her life, like she did my mom."

Garrett's mouth opened incredulously. "Is that what you think? That she'll get mad and never speak to you again?"

I curled my hand into a fist, pressed it against my lips. My heart was pounding in my chest and suddenly, instead of the cold April wind, I felt a flush of heat and fear. There was a knife-sharp pain between my eyes. I couldn't answer him. I couldn't say anything. I was afraid to speak, to think, knowing some unnamable awful something could happen if I acknowledged, even in thought, the fears that washed over me.

But Abigail's voice, the way it sounded when she said my mother's name, breached my refusal to think, filled my brain, crowded out everything else, even Garrett's face and the last light of the day, until I couldn't see anything or hear anything but the sound of my mother's name and far in the distance, Garrett's voice, calling to me, in words that sounded like fear feels.

29

Evelyn Dixon

When people fantasize about opening their own business, part of the dream is often a vision of being their own boss, which generally translates into some wholly misguided notion of longer vacations, shorter workweeks, and setting their own hours.

As just about any small business owner can tell you, it almost never works out that way. In point of fact, most people who exchange salaried jobs for the joys of being their own boss quickly discover that while business ownership does mean setting your own hours, those hours are basically twenty-four/seven. And vacations? Those are a thing of the past.

When two small business owners fall in love, carving out time for togetherness can be a real challenge. Early on, Charlie and I established a habit of meeting every morning for coffee at the Blue Bean. We don't manage to keep those appointments every day—business does interfere—but we try. And whenever one of us has a window of opportunity, maybe on a day when business is a little slow, we'll call to see if the other can sneak away for a quick bite, or a walk, or whatever.

Today "whatever" constituted a late lunch/early dinner, not at the Grill because whenever we eat there Charlie is forever getting up and down to answer the phone, or seat a customer, or settle some dispute in the kitchen. Instead, we snuck away to our favorite pizza joint, Di Luca's, to split a salad and a large basil and buffalo mozzarella pie.

Understand that splitting a pizza means I eat two slices and Charlie, who at fifty-plus years of age still has the metabolism of a teenager, eats the other six, crusts and all.

"Good?" I asked as I watched Charlie attack slice number five with no less relish than he'd displayed for slice number one.

"I'd give my right arm to know how Tony makes this crust, but he won't share the recipe with anybody, not even his staff. He told me that when he takes the family on vacation, they have to stay within a couple of hours of the restaurant. That way he can drive back twice a week to mix up the pizza dough."

Charlie took another bite and then nodded toward the last slice of pizza on the tray. "Sure you don't want another piece?"

"You go ahead. I'm stuffed."

I rested my chin on my hand, watching Charlie eat and thinking what a good man he was. Charlie is very serious about food in general and Di Luca's pizza in particular, but if I'd wanted that last slice of pizza, he'd have happily given it up, pleased to see me enjoy something that he enjoyed so much himself.

It's a little thing, but in my book it's the little things, like giving up the last slice of pizza, or offering to return the chairs and tables to the rental company, or showing up unannounced on a Saturday morning with a tire iron in hand to change out my snow tires, that count. My ex-husband, Rob, was all about grand gestures. He liked sending floral tributes that would have done the winning horse at the Kentucky Derby proud, presenting me with beribboned boxes from the jeweler every birthday or anniversary, that kind of thing. But when it came to things like helping with the dishes after we'd had a crowd over for dinner, or dropping off the dry cleaning, or taking a turn at the baby's midnight feeding, Rob was nowhere to be seen.

Please understand, I'm not bitter about Rob. He was generous and we shared some happy years, but since I've met Charlie, I've come to realize that small, daily acts of love matter more than all the grand gestures in the world. At least to me.

Charlie stopped chewing. "What are you grinning at? Have I got marinara on my nose or something?"

"No." I laughed. "I'm just thinking how lucky I am and how much I love you."

Charlie's eyes twinkled, the way they do when he's thinking up a witty retort, but instead of launching into a bit of banter about his irresistible Irish charm, he just smiled and said, "Me too. And twice again as much."

We were quiet for a moment, just enjoying each other's company, before returning to an earlier topic of discussion.

"So," Charlie said after swallowing his last bite of pizza, "it's on for tomorrow then? The Intervention?"

I rolled my eyes. Every time we talked about this, Charlie insisted on calling our upcoming discussion with Abigail "The Intervention," highlighting it with hand-signaled air quotes and an ominous tone of voice.

"Stop that."

"Stop what?" he asked, feigning innocence.

"You know what. Stop calling it 'The Intervention.' And quit using that creepy voice. I'm nervous enough about this as it is."

"Fine. How shall I refer to 'The Intervention'?"

"I don't know, but not like that. Why do we have to refer to it as anything? We're going over to Abigail's to have a quiet little talk with her, that's all."

"Uh-huh," Charlie said skeptically. "A quiet little talk. A nice in-your-face confrontation would be more like it."

I shot him a look.

"All right," he said, raising his hands. "You don't have to give me the eye. I'm just expressing my opinion. So when does this quiet talk take place?"

"Tomorrow afternoon. After Abigail and Liza wrap up their trip to New York. Franklin thought it would be best to speak to her right away. No point in putting it off."

"Good idea. Grab the bull by the horns, I always say. And in that spirit . . ." Charlie shifted in his chair, squared his shoulders, and cleared his throat.

"Evelyn, marry me."

"Oh, Charlie." I looked away.

"I've asked you to marry me at least a dozen times. When are you finally going to say yes? You say you love me, so why not marry me?"

I took a long drink from my water glass, buying myself time to collect my thoughts, but Charlie was not in a waiting mood.

"Why not, Evelyn? Unless you've just been saying you love me and don't mean it? Or maybe you mean a different kind of love?"

He drew his brows together, his frown clouding his previously sunny smile. There was a sliver of sneering in his voice. "Maybe your love is the platonic sort—the kind you feel for an old school chum or a faithful spaniel? Because if that's the deal, Evelyn, tell me now and I'll quit making a fool of myself. Is that all I am to you? Your faithful spaniel?"

I reached across the table and grabbed Charlie's hands. "Of course not, Charlie. You know that. When I say I love you, I mean I *love* you. I do. I love everything about you. Well, everything besides your tendency to be pushy," I teased, smiling.

Charlie was not going to be jollied out of his mood. He wanted answers.

"Is there someone else, then?"

"Someone else? How can you even ask that? I love you and only you. You know that. But, Charlie, it's not as easy as you make it sound. Once upon a time, I only loved Rob Dixon. And he only loved me. And then one day, after twenty-four years of marriage, he decided to love someone else. That broke my heart." I pulled my hands away from his and stared down at the leftover pizza crusts littering my plate.

Charlie crossed his arms over his chest and jutted out his chin. "So because Rob Dixon turned out to be a faithless, heartbreaking adulterer, that means you're afraid to marry me? After all this time and all we've been to each other, are you saying that deep down you think I'm just like Rob?"

Of course I didn't. Charlie is nothing like Rob. In fact, Charlie is nothing like anyone I've ever met.

I do think about marriage sometimes. On those days when I'm tired of eating yet another meal alone, standing over the sink because it seems pointless to set the table for one, I dream of how nice my table would look with two white plates and a little vase of flowers in the middle. I dream of small talk about the news and weather, of private jokes and easy silences. I dream of arguing fearlessly with my beloved because I know that, in the end, we always make up. I dream of a man coming up behind me as I rinse dishes, twining his arms around my waist, of lips brushing the curve of my neck, telling me how delicious everything was, and then smiling that private, knowing smile, reaching for my hand, and leading the way up the stairs. I dream of cool white sheets, and the press of a masculine hand on the swell of my hip, of an outline of suntanned fingers spread fanlike against white skin. I dream of lips and fingers and secret sighs, of two heavy breaths sharing one rhythm, of bodies arcing toward one another, urgent and impatient. I dream of longings fulfilled, of release, of the comfortable weight of a torso resting on mine, covering me like a blanket, of falling asleep and waking to find that it wasn't a dream at all, that he is with me still, husky-voiced after endearments murmured in a room lit by moonlight.

And when I dream this, when I dream of caresses and kisses and quiet talk, of being there for someone I love and him being there for me, and our being together lasting until we draw our last breath, the only hands or lips or voice I imagine is Charlie's.

There is no one besides him.

When I do imagine marrying again, I can't imagine being married to anyone but Charlie. But my imaginings are just that: flights of imagination, dreams that feel far removed in some distant someday, a thing too lovely, too perfect to ever really happen.

I have been alive a long time now, five decades and more, long enough to know that when dreams come true, they never come true in quite the same way you dreamed them. I also know that dreams don't last forever, not always. And I guess that's what I want. I guess that's what is holding me back. I want forever. I want always. I want a guarantee. And I've lived long enough to know there aren't any.

Why is Charlie pushing? Why risk spoiling a perfectly perfect dream by dragging it away from the soft-focus, pastel world of the imagined into the cold light of reality? I do want to marry Charlie. Someday. But now isn't a good time and I tell him so.

"Why not?" he growls. "Now seems as good a time as any to me. In fact, now seems like the perfect time."

I shook my head. "There's too much going on, too many things up in the air, especially this wedding. I can only deal with one at a time, and right now the wedding I'm dealing with is Garrett's to Liza. That's drama enough for the moment."

"Who says there has to be any drama? We could keep it simple. You. Me. A minister. Done. If we need witnesses, we can ask Garrett and Virginia. Keep the folderol and frippery to a bare minimum."

"Gee," I said. "You make it sound so romantic. Speaking of Virginia, there's another problem. What am I going to do about Mom? She's still upset with me. I've tried and tried to patch things up with her, but she's so stubborn.

"She loves New Bern, I know she does. Everyone at the shop is crazy about her, staff and customers alike. Did I tell you? One of the women from her Mothers-to-Be quilting class had a little girl and named her after Mom. All her students just love her, and not just the ones in the shop," I said, thinking of Mom's Stanton Center students. Ivy had finally talked Mom into teaching a Mommy and Me beginner's quilting class at the shelter. All those new quilters, from ages seven to thirty-seven, had already fallen in love with Mom and had dubbed her Grammie Ginny. To them she was more than just a patient teacher; she was a wise friend and, for some, a substitute grandmother.

"Between the wedding and the situation with Mom, I just don't think it's a good time to take such a big step."

Charlie gave his chin a jerk. He thought I was inventing excuses to put him off, but I did have some legitimate concerns about the possibilities of a successful union between Charlie and me, now or ever.

"And it's not just Garrett and Mom I'm worried about," I said.

"Charlie, when is the last time we were able to get away like this? Just take the afternoon or evening off for a real date?"

His gaze shifted from mine. He knew what I was getting at. "A week ago."

I shook my head. "Nope. Nine days. Not counting quickie coffee dates before we dash off to work, you and I haven't been able to find a spare moment to spend with each other in the last nine days. Nine. And this is the slow season! Come summer, we'll be lucky to see each other every nine days, and you know it. I love you, Charlie, and I know you love me. But we both know that making a marriage work takes more than love. It takes time. And that is something you and I have very little of."

"Well . . ." He scowled, thinking. "We could try harder to carve out time for each other. Maybe we could bring in some more help—hire managers or assistants or something."

"Charlie," I said softly. "You've tried that before. It never works. Every manager you've hired you've ended up firing within three weeks, sometimes within three days. The Grill is the love of your life, your baby. You're no more able to hand over the running of the restaurant to a stranger than you'd be able to hand over your child to someone else to raise." He opened his mouth to argue with me, but I raised my hand. "You know I'm right. And as far as me hiring a manager, I can't afford to hire any more help. Not right now. The shop is doing much better financially, but I've got a lot of debt to pay off. I've only just been able to give Margot a long-overdue raise."

"Well, what about Margot?" he asked. "Why couldn't you promote her to manager? She's a smart businesswoman."

"She is," I agreed. "I'd be lost without her. When it comes to marketing, accounting, and general organization, I couldn't ask for a better partner. But she just isn't the quilter that I am. Maybe she will be someday, but not now. She wouldn't know what fabrics to order or how much, which patterns will be in demand next season, and, most importantly, she doesn't teach. Half my job is teaching classes. The rest is divided up between ordering and keeping an eye on the inventory, helping customers choose fabrics or answering their questions about techniques, and sewing up class samples. Actually, sewing samples is about half a job all by itself. When you add it all up, I'm doing the work of at least a body and a half. Who could I find who's crazy enough to take a job like that at a salary I could afford to pay?"

Charlie balled up his fist and tapped it on the point of his chin, as if trying to jar loose some brilliant solution to our problem, but it didn't seem to help. He offered no answer to my question.

"Face it, Charlie. You're too much of a control freak to leave the care and feeding of your customers to a hired gun. And at the risk of sounding egotistical, I'm the only one around here who is quilter enough to actually run a quilt shop."

I stopped, waiting for him to concede the rightness of my observations, but he just kept tapping his fist against his chin in a rhythm as slow and steady as the beat of a resting heart.

I was getting frustrated with his silence. Finally, I laid my whole hand out on the table, speaking the truth as it was.

"And there's something else, Charlie, something more than just the difficulty of trying to find someone to do what I do. I love my work, Charlie. I really do. And I'm good at it! Do you know how long I've had to wait to be able to say that? Oh, I was a good wife and a good mother, but this is different. Maybe it sounds self-centered, and maybe it is, but after a lifetime of measuring my worth in terms of other people's achievements, of how many promotions my husband got or how high my child's grade point was, it feels good to be accomplishing something that is just about me." I leaned in, urgent to make myself understood.

"I know I don't do this alone. Margot, Garrett, and Ivy make my life a lot easier. But at the end of the day, this whole thing hinges on me—my ideas, my decisions, my hard work and, ultimately, my success. And I'm really proud of that success, Charlie. For the first time in my life, I'm proud of me! And I don't want to give that up. Not right now."

The unspoken end of that sentence, *not even for you,* hung in the air. I was quiet, waiting for him to say something.

"Charlie?"

Finally, he lowered his fist and rested it, still clenched, on the table. "All right, then."

"All right what?"

"All right, then." He took in a breath and let it out. "I'll sell the Grill."

"What!" I gasped. For a moment, I thought I'd heard him wrong. "Charlie, you can't do that. You'd be miserable without the restaurant to run. You love the Grill!"

Charlie moved his head slowly from side to side. "You're wrong. I do love the Grill, but it isn't the love of my life, Evelyn. You are. And even if you are right and it turns out I'm miserable without a restaurant to run, I know I'll be twice as miserable if, after waiting more than half my lifetime to find the love of my life, I let love slip away.

"I love you, Evelyn. I want to spend the rest of my life with you, and if selling the restaurant is what it takes to make that happen, then so be it. I'll sell the restaurant."

He was serious. Clear-eyed and calm and waiting to see what I would say next.

But I didn't know what to say. It was a gesture of astounding proportions, but it was more than a gesture. I could tell by looking in his eyes. He meant it.

I wasn't prepared for this, not now. And honestly, was it a good idea?

If we were to marry and have a hope of making our marriage work, we would have to find a way to spend more time together, but was Charlie giving up the restaurant the only option? Wouldn't he come to regret it later? Resent it? Resent me?

"Charlie, this is a lot to think about. And with everything that's going on right now . . . I just need some time to process this."

"How much time?" His voice was flat, almost without emotion, as if he were negotiating a business deal.

"Well . . . I don't know."

"What about after the wedding?"

"The wedding? But, Charlie, that's only a few weeks away. I need time to think. So do you. You may wake up tomorrow morning and decide you spoke too soon. You've poured your whole life into the Grill and now, just like that, you want to—"

"Six months," he said in the even, definitive tone that game-show contestants use for declaring their final answers. "In six months' time I want your answer. Will you marry me or won't you? If you don't know by then, you never will. That's the deal. I won't mention it again. Won't bother you or pressure you or propose for the next six months. But then, one way or another, I want an answer. Okay?"

He extended his hand, his expression serious and solemn, as if we were about to seal some very important bargain. Which I guess we were. I took a deep breath and stretched my hand toward his.

"Okay." I grasped his hand in mine just as my cell phone ringer went off. Margot was calling.

30

Evelyn Dixon

When I got back to the shop, Margot was standing by the door, waiting for me.

"I'm sorry to bother you, but when Franklin called looking for you, he sounded so upset. I thought you'd want to know."

"What did he want? You said Abigail came home early. Is everything all right?"

I was worried about Franklin. After his heart attack, his doctor had told him to lose weight, get regular exercise, and avoid stress. The first two goals had been relatively easy to achieve, but the third was much tougher. Franklin was a successful and very dedicated attorney. It hadn't been easy for him to reduce his hours and hand off some of his more demanding clients, Abigail excepted, to Arnie Kinsella. But at Abigail's urging, Franklin had done so, and his cardiologist was pleased with the results. Within a few months, Franklin's blood pressure had been reduced to near-normal levels.

However, that was before. There was no prescription the doctor could give him to help temper Franklin's primary source of stress at the moment: Abigail.

On the other hand, I thought, *maybe there is. A few tranquilizers might do Abigail a world of good. Or, if she won't take them, maybe the rest of us should.*

"He wants us to come over," Margot reported.

"Now? But we're already set for tomorrow."

"I know, but apparently Abigail and Liza had some sort of argument or . . ." Margot shrugged. "Well, I don't know what happened, but whatever it was, it has Abigail pretty upset. As soon as she got home she went up to her bedroom and locked the door. She won't come out and she won't let Franklin in."

Margot clucked her tongue sympathetically. "Poor Franklin. He didn't know what to do, so he called us."

I blew out a long, weary breath. This day already had more than its share of drama; I wasn't relishing the thought of getting involved in more. But I knew Franklin. He was capable and clearheaded, exactly the sort of fellow you'd want on your side in any dispute or emergency, which was why he was such a terrific attorney. If Franklin Spaulding was calling for help, then something was really wrong.

"If she won't open the door for Franklin, I can't imagine she will for us. But"—I sighed—"I guess we have to try."

I ran upstairs to the workroom where Ivy, Mom, and Dana, our first New Beginnings intern, were cutting bolts of turquoise, green, and purple fabrics into fat quarters to be packaged up and sent to our mail-order customers. Ivy and Mom were slicing through their fabrics with quick and practiced ease. Dana was more cautious, carefully positioning her ruler on the fabric before slowly cutting across the width of the cloth, pressing on her rotary cutter a little harder than she needed to.

Ivy looked up and smiled as I came in. "Hi, Evelyn. I'm just showing Dana how to use a rotary cutter. She's doing really well too," Ivy said encouragingly.

Dana smiled at the praise, just barely. Still, that was progress. Donna Walsh had told me a little bit of Dana's history of abuse, and it was particularly gruesome. When I first met Dana, she wouldn't even look at me. She was so timid. After all she'd been through, I wasn't surprised, but I had wondered if we'd really be able to help her.

"You might not," Donna had admitted. "Dana's emotional scars are very deep. Let's give her a couple of weeks and see what happens. If anyone can help bring her out of her shell, it's Ivy."

Obviously, Donna was right. Dana had a long way to go, but that shadow of a smile was a good sign. With time and Ivy's patient encouragement, Dana just might make it.

"That's great! Thanks, Dana. We're sure glad to have your help. We've had a run on those block-of-the-month kits." I looked at Dana and smiled and she did the same—just for a moment, but she did it, a real smile. Yes, indeed. Progress.

I turned to Ivy. "Hey, I hate to break up your little party, but Margot and I have to go over to Franklin and Abigail's. Could you come downstairs and watch the shop? Maybe you could start teaching Dana how to help customers and run the register."

Dana's shy little smile fled. She looked absolutely terrified.

Ivy gave me a concerned glance and I realized that I'd made a mistake. The prospect of meeting customers, talking to strangers, was frightening to Dana. She wasn't ready for that, not yet.

What was I going to do? Franklin needed Margot and me over at his place and Dana needed Ivy up here. But somebody had to wait on customers.

Mom came to the rescue. "There's so much yet to do here," she said casually. "We've got twenty kits to cut and package before closing. Why doesn't Ivy go downstairs and work on the shop floor while Dana and I stay here and finish up?"

Ivy smiled. "Good idea. Sound all right to you, Dana?"

Dana nodded. She looked relieved. "Sure. Yeah. Virginia and I can do it."

Sure. Yeah. Virginia and I can do it. Eight words. That was six more than I'd ever heard Dana utter at one time. Maybe she would be all right.

After giving a few instructions to the others, Ivy followed me back downstairs. As we walked away, I could hear my mother's voice.

"Very nice, Dana. You're getting so much faster. Now, see if you can't ease up just a little on the pressure as you're cutting. It'll be a lot easier on your arm if you do. That's it. Wonderful! Dana, you're a natural!"

When he opened the door, Franklin looked tired—and relieved.

"I'm sorry to bother you, but I just couldn't wait until tomorrow. Abigail is beside herself. She won't unlock the door. I pleaded with her, begged her to let me in, but no matter what I say, she won't budge."

After my mastectomies, I'd fallen into a deep and dark depression, a situation not helped by the fact that I'd basically holed up in the small upstairs bedroom of Margot's house and refused to come out. Everyone—Margot, Charlie, Liza, and Abigail—had done everything they could to convince me to cheer up and get up, but no amount of tenderness and gentle encouragement could move me.

It wasn't until my best friend from Texas, Mary Dell Templeton, the host of the *Quintessential Quilting* show on cable TV, interrupted a taping to fly to New Bern and literally drag me out of bed that I'd stopped feeling sorry for myself and realized that breasts or no breasts, life not only goes on, it's well worth living.

I had needed someone to remind me of that, and while Mary Dell's tactics, like Mary Dell herself, weren't what anyone would call subtle, sometimes subtlety is overrated. Sometimes, the most caring thing you can do for a friend is give her a good solid kick in the behind.

I turned to Margot. "Margot, remember that part in the Bible where they lowered the paralyzed man through the roof so he could be healed?"

"Yes."

"Do you remember what Jesus said to him?"

"Sure. He said, 'Pick up your bed and walk.'"

Charlie was right. For some people, a nice quiet talk was a waste of breath. My dad had a word for those folks on whom subtlety and suggestion were wasted. He called them "two-by-four people"—as in, some people don't get the message unless you hit 'em with a two-by-four. It sounded like the paralyzed man was a two-by-four guy. I *knew* Abigail was.

My mind made up, I started up the wide staircase that led to Abigail's room, glancing over my shoulder at Franklin and Margot. "Well, it sounds to me like Abigail needs to do the same—pick up her bed and walk. Come on, you two. Enough pussyfooting. I think it's about time we had ourselves an Intervention."

Franklin cleared his throat before tapping on the locked door. "Abbie, Evelyn and Margot are here to see you."

"Tell them I'm not home," Abigail called out hoarsely. "I don't want to see them right now. I don't want to see anyone."

Franklin turned around and shrugged. "See what I mean? I think she's been in there crying. You know Abigail. She never cries."

I patted Franklin on the shoulder. Poor man. In spite of the fact that Abigail had been treating him abominably for the last few weeks, he wasn't mad at her. No matter how badly she behaved, he was too in love with her to be mad at her.

Well, that made one of us.

Don't get me wrong—I love Abigail, too. She's my dear, cherished, and forever friend, and no matter how badly she behaves, she always will be. But loving isn't the same as being in love. As Mary Dell had taught me, sometimes being a loving friend involves exchanging kid gloves for boxing gloves. Given Abigail's recent antics, it was an exchange I was more than ready to make. Bring it on!

But I couldn't confront Abigail through a locked door. How to get her to open it? I looked at Margot, hoping she might have a suggestion, but one glance at the lattice of worry lines tracing her forehead told me she had no more idea than I did.

Margot is good at any number of things. She can create and execute a marketing plan with one hand behind her back and recite whole passages of the Bible by heart—simultaneously. But conflict and controversy are not her strong suits. Nor mine. What was I going to do?

In this situation, what would Mary Dell do?

My eye fell on an antique bowfront hall chest that stood outside Abigail's bedroom door. It held a collection of very beautiful and, I was sure, very expensive porcelain and crystal collectibles, as well as a florist's vase filled with a stunning spray of white peonies.

"Where did these come from?" I asked Franklin.

"Byron. The wedding planner. They were just delivered."

"Very nice," I said, then pulled the flowers out of the vase and handed the dripping stalks to Margot. "Hold these."

"What are you doing?"

"I've got an idea," I answered as I poured the leftover water from the flowers into an exquisite crystal vase that was sitting on the table. "Trust me."

I pounded on the bedroom door. "Abigail, it's Evelyn. I want to talk to you. I know you're in there, so there's no use pretending. Open up."

"No!" came the emphatic answer from the other side of the door. "I already told Franklin, I don't want to talk to you or to anyone. Go home, Evelyn, and leave me in peace."

"Abigail, open this door. I mean it!"

No answer. All right, then, she'd had her chance. I picked up the crystal vase and lifted it high so I could look at the maker's mark on the underside.

"Abigail, I am holding a vase in my hand, a very beautiful one. It's crystal. Waterford. Looks like an antique, probably some kind of family heirloom."

On the other side of the door I heard the sound of chair legs scraping against wooden floorboards and of curious feet walking toward the door. She was taking the bait.

"Abbie," I said in a loud, clear voice, "if you don't open this door and talk to me, I am going to drop this fabulous family heirloom on the floor and watch it shatter into a million pieces."

A gasp from the other side of the door, the previously distant voice now very close. "You wouldn't dare!"

"Oh, yes, I would," I said gleefully. "And I will. In about five seconds. And after that, if you still won't come out, I'm going to start in on the rest of your bric-a-brac."

I turned to Franklin, tilted my head toward a porcelain teapot, gold rimmed and painted with delicate sprays of pink and white roses, and whispered, "Franklin? What is this?"

"Limoges."

"After the crystal, I'm going for the Limoges teapot, and then the cups and saucers, one by one, until you open that door."

"Great-great-grandmother Wynne's Limoges tea service!" Abigail cried. "Are you mad? Do you have any idea what that's worth? You wouldn't dare. You're bluffing, Evelyn. I know you are. Now stop this nonsense at once and leave me alone!"

I looked at Franklin and Margot and grinned. I was enjoying this, probably a little too much.

"All right, Abigail. I warned you. One, two, three, four . . ." I put the Waterford vase down on the chest and picked up the plain glass florist's vase that Byron's flowers had come in.

"Five!" I shouted and let the vase go. It fell to the floor with a wonderfully satisfying crash and shattered into a hundred pieces.

"My Waterford vase!" Abigail screamed from the other side of the door. "Evelyn! Have you lost your mind? Franklin, are you there? Do something! Stop her!"

Franklin, who was now smiling broadly, said, "I tried to, Abbie, but she's completely out of control. Nothing I can do. I think you'd better come out."

"I will not!" Abigail declared stubbornly. "I just want to be left alone. Go away! All of you go away and leave me be!"

"All right, Abigail. If that's the way you're going to be, you leave me no choice. Grandmother Wynne's teapot is next."

Abigail let out a little cry of disbelief. "Evelyn! Evelyn, you wouldn't. Please. Not my Limoges."

"Fair warning, Abigail. One, two, three, four, five! And liftoff!"

The door flew open. Abigail lunged for me. "Evelyn! Don't!"

Abigail stopped short, looked at me, standing among the shards of glass with my arms crossed over my chest, to the hall chest where her Waterford and Limoges stood entirely intact, and finally to Margot, who was holding the still-dripping bouquet of peonies with a slightly guilty look on her face.

Abigail's hair was disheveled and her blouse was untucked from the waistband of her wool slacks. Her eyes were wide with an uncharacteristically untidy smear of mascara below her lashes and an expression of panic that turned to anger as she took in the scene and realized she'd been duped.

"You! You!" she cried and held her breath, her face flushing red and furious as she racked her brain in search of a word bad enough to describe us. Being very intelligent and well read, she didn't take long to think of several.

"Traitors! Deceivers! Philistines!"

She spun to the left and pointed an accusatory finger at Franklin. "And you! You're the worst of all! My own husband! And you helped them! How could you? Collaborator!"

Abigail's temper has a short fuse, and it doesn't take much to set it off. I've seen Abigail angry on any number of occasions. I'm not sure why—maybe it was her tousled hair, or the way the wrinkled shirttail stuck out from under her cashmere sweater, or the fact that she was only wearing one earring, or maybe I was giddy from the emotional stress of this day—but suddenly this whole situation seemed very funny.

I started to giggle and then to laugh, and pretty soon Margot and Franklin started to laugh, too, which made everything seem even funnier. I began laughing so hard I cried, and pretty soon everyone else was doing the same. Everyone but Abigail, who was definitely not amused.

Red faced and sputtering, Abigail stomped her foot, smashing a few of the shards of the broken florist's vase into even smaller bits. "What *is* the matter with you? Are you all drunk or something?"

We were all laughing too hard to respond. Abigail belched an infuriated cry of indignation, spun around on her heel, and grabbed the knob of her bedroom door, ready to slam it and lock it behind her.

But Franklin, still laughing, stopped her. In three big strides he was at Abigail's side. In a swift and unexpected move, he wrapped his arms tightly around her backside and lifted her off the ground, leaving her feet dangling a good foot above the floor. Abigail wriggled like a fish on a line, but it was no good. She couldn't get loose.

"Franklin! Franklin Spaulding, let go of me this instant! This isn't funny! Seriously, Franklin, put me down. You mustn't exert yourself like this. Your heart!"

Franklin beamed up at his wife and squeezed her even tighter. "Don't worry about me, Abbie. I'm strong as an ox and you're light as a feather—and beautiful when you're mad. Have I told you that before?"

Abigail made a face. "Well, if it's true, then I must be gorgeous right now, because, Franklin, you're making me absolutely furious! Put me down!"

"I don't think so," Franklin said. "This is the closest I've been to you in weeks. I'm not letting you loose just so you can run back in your room and shut me out again."

Abigail, calmer now and somewhat resigned, growled in frustration. "I'm sorry," she said grudgingly. "I won't shut you out again."

"Really. You'll talk to me? Tell me what's troubling you?"

"I will."

"Promise?"

"Promise."

"Hmm." Franklin narrowed his eyes, feigning deep concentration. "Nope," he said brightly. "I don't believe you. You're just going to have to stay up there."

"Oh, Franklin!" Abigail exclaimed in exasperation. "Enough already! Put me down! Please."

"Ah, there's the magic word!"

31

Evelyn Dixon

Twenty minutes later we were all sitting in Franklin's library. There was a fire crackling in the hearth. Tina padded into the room and settled herself onto a big, red tartan dog bed with a contented sigh. Abigail, her hair recoifed, her face washed, her shirttail retucked, and now wearing two earrings instead of one, offered around tiny glasses of sherry and a bowl of salted almonds.

"Sherry is acceptable anytime after lunch," Abigail declared.

Even in moments of distress, Abigail is committed to observing the proprieties. But, our brief flirtation with hilarity notwithstanding, she was still distressed. I could see it in her eyes. So could Franklin.

He smiled his thanks as he took a glass from the tray. "Now sit down, Abbie. Talk to us." He patted the sofa and Abigail took a seat next to him. Franklin put his arm around her shoulders.

"Talk to you about what?"

I closed my eyes briefly, hoping she wasn't going to be like . . . well, like she was. Once, in reply to some question she considered entirely too personal, I'd seen Abigail lift her chin, look down her nose, and declare, "I don't think about things I don't think about."

Getting Abigail to talk about anything personal or emotional has never been easy, but in the years since she joined our quilt circle, where verbally sharing our lives, likes, dislikes, and loves gets equal time with actual quilting, she has gotten better at it. Not a lot, but some. However, watching her sit next to Franklin on the leather sofa, daintily sipping a glass of sherry, made me think she'd completely regressed. On another day, when I wasn't carrying around concerns of my own, I might have been more compassionate and understanding, but at that moment I was in no mood to extract information from Abigail like a dentist pulling an impacted molar.

"Knock it off, Abigail. You know what we're here to talk about," I said. "The wedding. And Liza. And why you've been acting like a complete . . ." An apt word came to mind, but I don't use that word. Also, I felt the reference might be an insult to Tina, whose big brown eyes were moving from speaker to speaker as if she were following the conversation very closely. I'd have to find another word. "A complete mobzilla."

Abigail turned to me, her expression offended and confused by turns. Margot asked the question Abigail wanted to.

"Mobzilla?"

"I think I just made it up. Kind of a mother-of-the-bride meets Godzilla thing."

Margot giggled. Abigail huffed indignantly.

"With a little touch of Tony Soprano thrown in," I added, meeting Abigail's steely gaze. "Seriously, Abigail. You have been impossible recently."

"I have not!"

Margot swallowed hard before saying in a quiet but slightly nervous voice, "She's right, Abigail. You have been a pain. A big one."

Abigail sat up a little straighter, taking a defensive posture, but I could see the doubt in her eyes. Margot would rather cut out her own tongue than say something the least bit critical about someone else, and Abigail knew it.

Nervous, Margot shifted her gaze toward me, lobbing the ball into my court.

"Abbie," I said, "when it comes to throwing a party, you can dance circles around me and I know it. That's why I decided to keep my mouth shut when Garrett and Liza announced their engagement and let you do your thing. I know how controlling you can be in these situations, and I was prepared for that—"

"I am not controlling!" Abigail exclaimed. I didn't respond, just gave her a look, daring her to prove me wrong. She colored a little under the heat of my gaze.

"But," I went on, "I wasn't prepared for the way you've gone around, hurting people's feelings, including Margot's and mine, bulldozing over everyone who gets in your way, even Liza! You're a strong woman, Abbie, and used to getting your own way, but I've never known you to resort to bullying, manipulation, and outright lying to achieve your ends. It's a lucky thing we are friends because if we weren't, I'd have given you a good slap across the face by now."

"I did not lie!" Abigail gasped before turning to Franklin for support. "When it comes to implementing my plans, I'm not exactly a shrinking violet, but I wouldn't lie! And it isn't like I was doing this for myself, after all. I was doing it for . . ." She paused for a moment, screwing her eyes shut as if she suddenly had a terrific headache. Franklin's eyes flashed concern and he leaned toward her, laying a questioning hand on her leg.

Abigail shook her head and held up her hand. She took a deep breath and opened her eyes, continuing in a deliberately steady voice. "I was doing it for Liza."

The look on her face told me that even she didn't believe that.

"And yet, somehow in this whole process, Liza—her wants and her wishes for this wedding—has gotten tossed aside. Which really isn't like you, Abigail," I said. "You're determined, probably more than anyone I know, but you always use that determination, not to mention your financial resources and personal contacts, to help and encourage others, not to hurt them. Especially not people you care about. You're an unusual woman, Abigail."

She puffed impatiently and dismissed my careful commentary with a wave of her hand.

"Oh, quit beating about the bush, Evelyn. If there's one thing I've always admired about you, it's your honesty. It's a quality in short supply these days, so don't abandon it now. Let's call a spade a spade. I am not 'unusual'; I am odd. I'm an oddball and we both know it." Abigail folded her hands primly on her lap. "Or, if you insist on being polite, you can call me eccentric. I believe that's the term usually applied to people considered too rich to offend."

"I don't know about too rich to offend, but you are pretty rich," I said truthfully. "But, Abbie, you won't be if you keep going on throwing away money like a drunken sailor on leave! I don't know what you've spent on this wedding so far, and I don't want to—"

"Well, *I* know," said Franklin. "And I can tell you, it's too much. You've always been generous with your wealth, Abbie, but you've never been foolish about it. And that's what this is—pure foolishness. What's worse, it's been getting in the way of you being able to devote your attention, time, and money to some causes that you care about very deeply. The library, the historic society, and even the Stanton Center and the New Beginnings program, more accurately known as the Spaulding Women's Center for New Beginnings.

"It's got your name on it, Abbie, and for good reason. You practically built that place single-handedly! Scarcely a year ago, you were all about blueprints and program plans. People in town were terrified to meet you on the street, knowing you were going to shake them down for another contribution toward the building campaign. And now, after all your hard work and effort, the new Stanton Center is finally open. Sixteen families of women who found the courage to escape from their abusive relationships are living in safety and comfort, thanks to your efforts. And also thanks to you, forging new careers and new lives for themselves and their children just got a lot easier. The New Beginnings program is finally up and running, offering career guidance to the women and enrichment programs for them and their families."

"That's right," I said. "Virginia's Mommy and Me quilting class at New Beginnings is completely full. Seven moms and seven kids signed up, including Ivy and little Bethany."

"How is Bethany?" Abigail asked, her expression softening. "I haven't seen her in such a long time."

Abigail had met Bethany when she was taking a tour through one of the apartments in the old Stanton Center. Bethany grabbed Abigail's hand and showed her around the tiny apartment that, to a little girl who had recently spent nights sleeping in a car, seemed like a palace. The minute that little hand had latched on to her big one, Abigail's formerly icy heart melted. The first quilt Abigail had ever made, and the only reason she'd accepted my invitation to become part of our newly forming quilt circle, was a present for Bethany.

"Bethany's fine," I said. "Bobby too. I can't believe how quickly they're growing up. Ivy brought Bethany to the shop the other day. They were picking out fabric for their class project and she asked about you. Seems you promised to take her and Bobby to the circus when it was in New Haven—but it never happened."

Abigail clutched at her throat with her hand as she recalled her forgotten promise and realized it was too late to do anything about it now. The circus had already left town, and even the wealth and influence of Abigail Burgess Wynne Spaulding could not convince it to return before next year.

"I can't believe I forgot," Abigail said weakly. "Was she terribly disappointed?"

"Well, yes," I said honestly. "She's never been to a circus. But I think she was more concerned about you than disappointed. She knows it's not like you to forget a promise."

Abigail let out a small sigh and bit her lip. "I can't believe I let Bethany down like that. I just . . . I've been so . . . so preoccupied. . . ." Her voice trailed off as if she was finally beginning to realize what an understatement that was.

Abigail was abject. Angry as I'd been with her over the last weeks, I took no pleasure in her misery. Part of me just wanted to pat her hand and tell her everything would be okay. If this had just been a case of a friend having been a little self-centered and needing to be straightened out, I would have. But it wasn't that simple. We really needed to get to the bottom of this. Abigail needed to get to the bottom of this.

To get her to open up and talk would require a serious dose of tough love. I knew that. So did Franklin.

"Abbie, it isn't just Bethany you've let down," he said gravely. "You've let down all those women at the Stanton Center too. With the New Beginnings internship program just getting off the ground, this is the time to be getting a positive buzz going about the program, generating publicity and community goodwill.

"The Grill, the quilt shop, and my law office are still the only companies in town who've agreed to participate in the program. A lot of the business owners are nervous about having victims of domestic violence working for them. They think they might be unstable, or unreliable—"

"That's ridiculous!" Abigail snapped, her spine stiffening with outrage. "These women will make outstanding employees. Outstanding! Each of them is carefully screened and evaluated before even being considered for an internship. Donna Walsh wouldn't let a woman take on an internship unless she was sure she was ready for it. Yes, at first they might require a bit more patience and sensitivity than some employees, but they're bright, dedicated, mature women, every one of them. And grateful for the opportunity to be given a chance!"

Abigail stabbed her index finger into her husband's chest. "Mark my words, Franklin! In five years' time the reputation of the women who come through our New Beginnings internships will be so stellar that we'll have business owners lined up around the block, *begging* us to let their companies be involved. Someone should explain that to them, Franklin!"

"I agree, darling. And I think that someone should be you. Except for Donna Walsh, no one is more passionate about this program than you are. And as a lifetime resident of New Bern with an unparalleled standing in the community, you are the ideal spokesperson. Donna thinks so too." Abigail was quiet, the flush in her cheeks fading as Franklin spoke, knowing what he was about to say.

"But when she called you last month and asked if you'd give an interview to the *Hartford Courant* about the program, and speeches at the Rotary Club and the Chamber of Commerce, you told her you were too busy with the wedding." Franklin paused a moment, letting this sink in.

"You let them down, Abbie. All those women who've come to the Stanton Center for help, many who've risked their *lives* in the hopes of making a fresh start, learning a skill, and finding a job that will enable them to support their families. They need you, Abigail, wedding or no. And they need you now."

Abigail lifted her chin and swallowed hard, the veins in her neck tightening as she struggled to keep her emotions in check.

"And you did lie," Franklin said quietly. Abigail turned her head away, avoiding his gaze. "You told Charlie that Evelyn wanted all those expensive hors d'oeuvres for the bridal shower, and she didn't. That was a lie and you knew it, Abbie."

Abigail shrank in her seat, shamefaced. "I just wanted the shower to be perfect. To be everything Liza could possibly want. I wanted it to be special."

"But it already was." Margot frowned, but her tone was more questioning than accusing. "Liza was very excited about the shower—the flowers, the balloons, the cupcakes. It was everything she wanted, but it wasn't everything *you* wanted.

"And what was it you wanted?" she asked. "Do you even know? Even after you waltzed in with your army of manicurists and masseuses and food we didn't need that cost—I don't know how much, but a lot—it wasn't enough for you, was it? You were nervous the whole time, fussing with the flowers and the table settings. What would have satisfied you? When would it have been enough?"

If anyone else had delivered this speech, laying out the case against her so starkly, asking such pointed questions, I suspect Abigail would have become combative, but Margot could get away with it. Margot never has a hidden agenda.

Margot is probably one of the only truly good people I've ever met. She'd argue with that, I'm sure. But not only does she never *do* anyone harm, I don't think she even *thinks* anyone harm. She is the genuine article. I know it and so does anyone who knows her, including Abigail, which is why she sat quietly under Margot's indictment, sinking lower and lower as Margot went on, wilting under the weight of her shame.

"It wasn't my intention to hurt anyone. Not you or Liza," Abigail whispered. "Truly. I am so sorry."

This was huge. Abigail is not the sort of woman who tosses off apologies lightly or frequently. "Never complain, never explain." That's Abigail's motto.

Her face still sober, Margot nodded. "Apology accepted. But that's not why we're here, Abigail. We're worried about you. Since Liza and Garrett announced their engagement, you've gone from being an everyday, run-of-the-mill overbearing mother-of-the-bride to someone we barely recognize."

Franklin smiled. "And I, for one, have been particularly distressed because I loved you the way you were."

Abigail emitted a derisive little laugh. "You mean stubborn, self-centered, intolerant, and pushy?"

Franklin reached up to run his hand over her perfectly smooth hair. "And stubborn."

"I already said that!"

"Yes, but in your case it bears repeating," he teased.

Abigail bumped him with her elbow.

"But, Abbie, you also have other qualities, good ones. You're intelligent, generous, energetic, especially on behalf of the many good causes you champion, beautiful—"

"Oh, what do you know? Isn't your vision about twenty/two hundred?"

"And, of course, witty. If not for you, New Bern parties would be incredibly dull. But, Abbie, this wedding has become an obsession with you. It's not about Liza anymore, if it ever was. So," he said quietly, "what is it about?"

"I don't know." Abigail paused for a moment. "Or I didn't. Not until today."

Abigail looked away from Franklin again, past Margot and me, and focused on Tina's fuzzy face, directing her confession to the tolerant gaze of those understanding brown eyes.

"This morning, at Byron's office in Manhattan, we were trying to choose accessories for Liza's gown. The jeweler sent over a selection of diamond necklaces and chokers for her to try on. I decided, as a surprise, that rather than just rent the jewelry, I'd buy it for Liza. A sort of pre-wedding present.

"But Liza said she didn't want it. She wants to wear some necklace that Garrett likes, one she made herself that she was wearing the night he proposed. Garrett asked her especially, but I . . . I'd made up my mind that she should wear diamonds. We argued. Heatedly. Liza accused me of doing this all for myself, of trying to engineer the wedding I wished I'd had but didn't. It isn't true. None of this has been for my own benefit, but . . . I've finally realized it wasn't for Liza's, either."

Abigail turned her gaze from Tina and looked into her husband's eyes, her composure crumpling like crushed tissue paper. "Franklin, I . . . I called her Susan. I called Liza Susan."

Franklin's face fell.

"Oh, Abbie. Abbie, come here." He gathered her in his arms.

Abigail collapsed on his shoulder and wept.

"Abbie, darling, Susan is gone. You can't . . ."

"I know," Abigail sobbed. "I know. She's gone. Nothing can change how I treated her when she was alive. The man I loved, loved her more than me. That's all. It wasn't Susan's fault. But I was so jealous, insanely jealous!

"She was my baby sister and she was alone in the world, broke, suffering, and Liza along with her. I could have helped her, but I didn't," Abigail cried. "I could have forgiven her, but I didn't. Not even when I learned she was dying. Not until it was too late to matter. I am a horrible, hateful person!"

Franklin shook his head. "Abbie, that's not true. You may not have been able to forgive Susan until after her death, but you did forgive her eventually. Some people are never able to do that. And your forgiveness has mattered, so much. Where would Liza be without you? She was angry, bitter, and heading down a dangerous path before you came into her life."

Abigail raised her head from Franklin's shoulder. Her eyes were red and there was a telling smear of mascara under her lashes. "Yes, and now she's angry and bitter again. I've made her that way. She hates me, Franklin. She hates me!"

Abigail's voice dropped almost to a whisper as she tried to stem her tears. "And I don't blame her. I didn't . . . it didn't start out like this. I love Liza as if she were my own. I love her the way I've never loved anyone, except Susan back when we were girls and she was as dear to me as my own heart. I took on this wedding out of a genuine desire to make Liza happy, but somewhere along the line, without realizing it, I forgot that. I started to confuse Liza and Susan, thinking that somehow, if I could just do enough or spend enough, I could make it up to Susan, to everyone. But the more I did, the more I felt the need to do more. It's not possible, is it, Franklin? There isn't penance enough in the world to expunge my sins."

"Abbie, don't. You've forgiven Susan. And God has forgiven you, long ago."

"I know," she said quietly. "I believe that. But I can't forgive myself, Franklin. God is great, but I'm not. I don't deserve to be forgiven."

"Abbie." Franklin's voice was hoarse and full of grief, feeling Abigail's pain as if it were his own. It was a sad scene but at the same time, beautiful.

And the two shall become one flesh. That's the way it's supposed to work. Two separate and wholly imperfect beings take a chance, make a pledge, and become one in body and in spirit, rejoicing in each other's successes, mourning each other's losses. That's what we all desire, someone who is so much ourselves and we them that the two halves become one, undistinguishable whole. We long to be known—physically, intellectually, emotionally, and spiritually—and to know another in return.

That is the bond every repetition of the marriage vow is supposed to create. Sometimes it does and sometimes it doesn't. I'm guessing that among those who know her, not many would have given odds on Abigail finding true love and making a successful marriage. There were times when I'd have been among them.

But looking at her now, weeping and in despair but doing so openly, enfolded in the embrace of a man who loved her beyond logic and in spite of her flaws, it was clear that Abigail and Franklin had found what I'd almost ceased to believe existed: true and lasting love, the kind that time could not tarnish and the cares and trials of life could not dissolve.

I was happy for them but, at the same time, I was also pierced with a stab of jealousy. That surprised me. And shamed me. I've never begrudged Abigail anything, not her popularity, or celebrity, or wealth. But that day, for a moment, I begrudged her the love that I longed for but no longer believed was possible, not for me.

As Abigail wept in her husband's arms and he wept with her, it was that jealousy and shame as much as the sudden sense that Margot and I were intruding on a moment of the deepest intimacy that caused me to tap Margot lightly on the knee and tip my head toward the open door.

Margot left. I followed her, closing the door softly behind me so as not to disturb Abigail and Franklin, though by that point I think they were beyond noticing.

Margot was misty-eyed as we headed toward the stairs.

"That was so beautiful. They're so in love. I only wish . . ." Margot sniffled and used the back of her hand to wipe the tears from the corners of her eyes. "Oh, Evelyn. I know you'll think I'm awful but, just now, I was jealous of Abigail. Isn't that terrible?"

"No. Why wouldn't you want what Abigail has? I do. We all do."

"Do you think we'll ever get it, a love like that?"

"Sure, you will," I said, excluding myself from the response. "It's just a matter of time."

"Do you think so?"

"Absolutely."

Margot smiled gratefully and hooked her arm through mine. We descended the stairs, intent on letting ourselves out, but met Hilda, Abigail's housekeeper, hurrying upstairs with a frightened look in her eyes.

"Oh, Ms. Dixon! Miss Matthews! Have you seen Mr. and Mrs. Spaulding?"

"Yes. They're upstairs, in the library, but I don't think they want to be disturbed. Is something wrong?"

Hilda bobbed her head. "Mr. Dixon is on the phone, Mr. Garrett. He's calling from a hospital in New York, from the emergency room. It's Liza. She collapsed on the street and was taken away by ambulance."

32

Liza Burgess

I had my hand on the doorknob, inches from a clean getaway, but Abigail, who swears she's getting hard of hearing but only seems to suffer from it at convenient intervals, heard my footsteps in the entryway and popped her head out of her office where she'd been poring over a seating chart for the wedding.

"Liza? Where are you off to, darling? It's nearly time for lunch."

"It's all right. I'm not hungry." Abigail looked concerned so I backtracked. "I'm not hungry right *now*. I had two waffles at breakfast. The weather is so nice that I thought I'd go for a walk. I'll have a sandwich when I get back."

She looked doubtful. I rolled my eyes. "Will you quit looking at me like that? I'm just not hungry right this second, all right? I'm sure I will be later, after my walk."

Her heels tapped on the wooden floorboards as she crossed the entryway and looked into my eyes to see if I was telling the truth, which made me feel terrible because I wasn't.

"Well . . . if you're sure nothing is wrong," she said. "If there is, you must tell me. Hold nothing back. I mean it, Liza. I'm always ready to talk. Always. Communication is so important in families. . . ."

I groaned.

Since I was released from the hospital—a stay that lasted barely twenty-four hours and probably would have been about twenty hours shorter if Abigail hadn't insisted that they keep me in for observation—and Abigail began seeing both Reverend Tucker to help deal with her guilt and spiritual issues and Camille Renfrew, a local therapist, to help her deal with . . . well, everything else, Abigail has been driving me crazy.

I'm glad all this is helping her, really I am. But just because Abigail is feeling the need to "get in touch with her feelings" doesn't mean everybody needs to go around talking about every single thought and emotion they have every moment of every day. But you can't tell that to Abigail.

Now that she's personally invented interpersonal communication, she's on a mission to win everyone on the planet, particularly me, over to her side. Personally, I prefer the old, caustic, pushy Abigail to this new sincere, sensitive, and touchy-feely Abigail. I told Franklin that, but he just laughed.

"Oh, don't worry about it, Liza. Your aunt is a woman of extremes, always has been. She's learning some new things about herself and how to relate to others, and that's good. But she'll settle down before long. Some of this newfound sensitivity will stick with her, I'm sure of it, but at the end of the day, Abigail is still Abigail. No amount of counseling is going to change that.

"Why, just last night, I walked into the bathroom and caught her with her face right up to the mirror, examining her wrinkles with a very displeased expression. When I asked her if she wanted to discuss her feelings about aging, she just glared at me and told me to mind my own damned business."

Franklin laughed again, showing all his teeth. It was nice to see him smile again.

"Trust me, Liza, Abigail will be back to her old self before you know it."

I hope he's right.

"Abigail, you've got to quit this," I said. "It's really getting on my nerves. I'm fine. I'm not mad at you. I don't resent you. I am not harboring any deep-seated emotional angst toward you or anyone else that I'm unwilling to discuss. I just want to go for a walk. When I get back, I'll eat something. I promise."

She smiled, finally satisfied that I'd make good on my promise.

"Liza, dear, when you get back, after you eat, I'm wondering if you'd like to take a look at the seating arrangements? That is, if you want to, if you're not too tired. I don't want to put any pressure on you. I just thought you'd be interested."

"Sure. No problem."

"Good! I'm just about finished with it, but if you don't like something, if there's anyone you'd like moved, then they *will* be moved. After all, this is *your* wedding, Liza. I want everything to be exactly how you want it."

She looked at me, expectantly. For a moment, I just stood there, forgetting what my line was. Then I remembered.

"It is, Abigail. Everything is exactly as I want it now. It will be a beautiful wedding."

Abigail beamed and then gave me a big, grateful hug. This is something else she's learned in therapy—hugging. Frequent, sincere, extended hugging.

Dear God, let Franklin be right. Let the old Abigail come back soon.

"Do you think so, really?" she asked and then answered herself. "Me too. So close to the big day now! Isn't it exciting!"

I told her it was and started to head out the door, but she laid her hand on my arm, delaying my exit.

"Liza, just one question. I was considering putting Judge and Mrs. Gulden at the same table with Margot and Arnie. Margot's been seeing such a lot of Arnie these days. Who knows?" she said with a meaningful lift of her eyebrows. "The next wedding might be theirs. If it were, then it certainly wouldn't hurt a young, up-and-coming attorney with a family to develop a good relationship with the most prominent judge in town. There's a rumor that Harry's being considered for a seat on the appellate court.

"On the other hand, I don't want it to look as if Arnie were trying to curry favor. But I don't think Harry would think that, do you? After all, I'm the one doing the seating arrangements, not Arnie. So what do you think, dear? Shall I seat Arnie and Margot with the Guldens?"

My eyes and mind glazed over about ten words into her soliloquy, but I refocused in time to say what I always say, "That's a great idea, Abigail. Let's go with that."

I submitted to one more hug before I finally walked through the door and down the sidewalk toward the village on this mid-May morning, six days before my college graduation and thirteen before my wedding.

After my little trip to Columbia Presbyterian Hospital, which Abigail continues to refer to as my "collapse," I woke to find a half dozen people at my bedside: a doctor, a nurse, Garrett, Evelyn, Franklin, and, of course, Abigail, who kept weeping and begging my forgiveness. Finally, the doctor gave Franklin a look and Franklin suggested that Abigail, and everyone else, go into the waiting room for a little while.

"That's better," the doctor said after they left, rubbing his chin while he perused my chart. "More oxygen in here now."

He finished reading and then looked up at me.

"Well, Miss Burgess, as far as I'm concerned, there's nothing seriously wrong with you. Your fiancé tells me you've lost a lot of weight recently, which isn't all that unusual for brides-to-be, but you've got to knock it off, all right? No more dieting."

I nodded compliantly. I hadn't been dieting, but why did he need to know that? It really wasn't any of his business, and if agreeing with him would get me out of there, then I was determined to be the most agreeable patient he'd ever met.

I picked up the can of liquid dietary whatever it was, the stuff that tastes like a chocolate chalk milkshake, and took a big drink. It almost gagged me but I got it down. The doctor smiled.

"Lack of food was what made you faint, but you also had a racing heart, sweating, overwhelming feelings of fear, right?"

"Uh-huh."

"All of which points to an anxiety attack, another ailment not so uncommon among brides-to-be. You're the third one I've seen this week. April is a big month for anxious brides, though the peak comes in May, right before all the June weddings. You're a little ahead of the curve."

He pulled a pad of paper out of his pocket and started scribbling on it.

"This is a prescription for an anti-anxiety medication. Take it until after the wedding. I don't think you'll need it after that. You seem like a pretty smart, together person," he said.

This was a big assumption, given that he'd only just met me and we'd only exchanged a dozen words, but I wasn't about to disagree.

"I think this will do the trick, but if you'd like, I can get somebody from the psych department to come down here and talk to you. Or I could give you a referral to an outpatient therapist?"

"No, that's okay. I think I've been a little too keyed up about the wedding."

"Yeah, that's what I thought." He tore the prescription off the pad and clipped it to my chart. "If your aunt wasn't quite so . . ."

"Influential?" I offered.

Knowing Abigail and the size of the donations her foundation made to just about every hospital on the eastern seaboard, I was pretty sure this doctor had already received a call from his hospital administrator informing him who I was and giving him instructions to make sure my influential aunt was very, very satisfied with my care.

"Yeah. Influential. If she wasn't, I'd let you go right now. But she's pretty insistent that I keep you here for a day. It's not such a bad place to spend a day. Rest, watch a little TV, and tomorrow, you'll be on your way. Just one word of warning: Stay away from the meat loaf. It makes the stuff they served in your high school cafeteria look like filet mignon." He winked.

"Will do, Doc."

He scratched his ear and hung the chart back on the end of my bed. "If you really want my advice, the best prescription I could give you would be an elopement, but somehow"—he glanced over his shoulder to the door Abigail had just exited through—"I get the feeling that isn't an option."

I shook my head. "Too late. If we eloped now, Abigail would be the one who'd need anti-anxiety drugs."

"Actually," the doctor said, tipping his head to one side, "that might not be such a bad idea. Just don't tell her I said so."

"Your secret is safe with me." I picked up the can of chocolate chalk and took another drink. The doctor winked again and waved as he walked out the door.

"See you, Liza."

"See you, Doc."

But I never did.

33

Liza Burgess

When I left the house that morning, I didn't precisely lie to Abigail, I just didn't tell her everything. I was going for a walk, but I didn't tell her my intended destination or that I wanted to talk to Reverend Robert Tucker, the man who'd be performing our wedding ceremony.

I'd already seen Reverend Tucker twice that weekend, once when Garrett and I went to his office for the second of our three premarital counseling sessions, and again this morning, when Abigail, Franklin, and I went to the early church service.

Garrett didn't go to church with us. After our counseling session yesterday, he left for New York and his bachelor party. He felt bad about leaving while I was still in New Bern, but I told him not to worry about it. We can talk tonight, after he's had some sleep. I bet he didn't get to bed until I was getting up. Besides, I'm kind of happy to be on my own this morning. For the last month, everybody has been hovering over me. I'm starting to feel claustrophobic.

Abigail calls at least three times a day, generally at mealtime, to make sure I'm eating. I've been seeing Garrett every weekend, either here or in New York, and on weekdays we talk at least twice a day. Franklin, and Evelyn, and Margot, and Ivy call too, not daily, but a couple of times a week. Everyone starts the conversation the same way, with hello, and a pregnant pause, followed by a concerned, "So how are you?"

I'm fine, already! Believe me! I'm feeling way better than I did back in April, so let's everybody just drop the subject, okay?

I don't like taking drugs; I don't even like to take aspirin, but the anti-anxiety medicine has helped. I don't feel as overwrought as before and I'm sleeping a little better. I've gained back about six pounds, which pleased Abigail and Byron but irritated Olga, who had to let the wedding gown out right after she'd taken it in. But the dress does look a lot better now and I like how I look in it, especially with my silver necklace, which Abigail insists I wear during the ceremony. No mention of diamonds has been made since the "collapse."

There have been other changes too. The weekend after I got out of the hospital, Byron came up to New Bern and we—as in me, Garrett, Abigail, Franklin, and Evelyn—sat around the dining room table and discussed how we could make the wedding, as Abigail put it, "Perfect! But," she said, raising her forefinger to underscore her point, "perfect for Liza and Garrett. This isn't about me, after all. This planning session is to be inclusive."

"Inclusion" is a big word with Abigail these days.

So, after some discussion, the Boston Symphony was told their services would no longer be required. Abigail sent a large donation to ward off any inconvenience or feelings of rejection. Now there will be a chamber orchestra for the ceremony and a dance band for the reception—the Tito Puente Orchestra—which will be fun, I guess. I'd never heard of them, but Abigail had and Byron thought they were good and Garrett likes Latin music, so when they asked me, I said, "Sure. Why not?"

Evelyn wondered if a seven-course dinner might be a little much. Garrett and Franklin backed her up on that and, once I saw which way the wind was blowing, I agreed. So, now there will be four courses instead of seven, with an "intermezzo," a little dish of sorbet, rhubarb flavor, to cleanse the palate between the fish and meat courses, which Abigail insists doesn't count as a course.

Fine with me.

See, that's the thing that really hasn't changed, the thing that nobody has picked up on. I'm eating better. And, thanks to the pharmaceutical industry, I'm less anxious and sleeping better. But even though I am now conscientiously consulted on all wedding decisions, I'm still doing what I did all along, agreeing with whatever anybody else wants. It's just that now I'm less obvious about it.

I listen, or appear to listen, to the options, but have you noticed that when people are showing you the options, they almost always, either directly or indirectly, make their preferences known? Well, trust me, they do.

Take the honeymoon.

While we were sitting around the table, Byron pulled a bunch of travel brochures out of his briefcase and handed them to me and Garrett. One was for Bermuda, of course; Abigail made sure of that. But I already knew how Garrett felt about that, so I put it aside right away. Then I just took a couple of minutes and leafed through them, watching Garrett out of the corner of my eye. He spent a long time looking at the Hawaii brochure. While he was flipping through the pages, he said, "Everyone says Hawaii is beautiful. Not as humid as the Caribbean."

So I knew what he wanted, and that was fine with me. Why not? How bad could an oceanfront suite in Hawaii be? But I didn't just say, "That's great. Let's go with that," the way I would with Abigail. Garrett would have known what was up. Instead, I looked through a few more brochures, came back to the Hawaii one, and said, "I've always wanted to go to Hawaii." Garrett grinned, agreed, and that was that. Simple.

Well, pretty simple. It made me nervous to watch Abigail sitting there with her lips pinched tight, forcing herself to keep silent about the wonders of Bermuda, but Franklin quickly suggested we move on and talk about the guest list, so we got past it.

The timing of my collapse turned out to be fortunate—just days before the invitations were to be sent out. At Franklin's suggestion, the guest list was cut in half, which was fine with me, too. Garrett and I have never met the governor, or the attorney general, or our senators, so why would they want to come to our wedding?

Franklin told Abigail that he thought meeting all those people would be too overwhelming. Instead, he suggested we only invite people Garrett or I have actually met at least once, which seems like a pretty reasonable standard. Abigail did mention that this would mean Garrett and I would get half as many wedding gifts, but Garrett pointed out that since we'll be moving into his one-bedroom apartment, he felt confident that we could live with only eight place settings of Juane de Chrome Big Bang Bronze china instead of sixteen, at least until we bought a house with a dining room.

A house with a dining room.

I don't know why, but ever since Garrett said it, I can't get that phrase out of my mind. Somebody who has a house with a dining room and a set of china that costs $170 just for the dinner plate sounds like somebody who ought to be a lot older than me, don't you think?

I mean, are we going to give dinner parties? The only things I know how to cook are French toast and ramen noodles. I know Garrett isn't going to suddenly expect me to turn into Betty Crocker, but I get the feeling he expects me to be something more than the girl who lives on ramen and loses the keys to her apartment at least a couple of times a week.

Our first meeting with Reverend Tucker went all right. He's really nice—glasses, big smile, good sense of humor. Everyone in town likes him. Even the atheists like him. After sitting us down in his study and chatting over coffee and cookies, Reverend Tucker had us fill out a compatibility questionnaire. Apparently we passed, even though it took me about three times as long to fill it out as it did Garrett. Looking over our answers, Reverend Tucker did say that it looked like I was someone who didn't always find it easy to talk about my feelings and that this was something we'd want to be aware of, that communication is so important in families. . . .

At that point, I kind of tuned out. I wasn't rude about it, but I've heard this same speech from Abigail about fifteen times, and she heard it from Reverend Tucker in the first place. If he'd asked me, I bet I could have repeated it word for word.

Our second meeting, yesterday morning, was a little different.

This time, after the coffee and cookie ritual, Reverend Tucker launched into a speech that he's probably given eight zillion times but that he managed to make sound totally off the cuff. He leaned in as he spoke and used his hands a lot, like he really wanted us to get this stuff because he genuinely wants to see our marriage work, which I believe he does.

He talked about the "Seven Fs" that can make or break a marriage: Friendship, Family, Faith, Finances, Fighting, Forgiving, and Fertilization.

"And when I say 'fertilization,' I'm not talking about sex," he said with an easy, unembarrassed smile. "I trust you two will be able to figure that out on your own. Though we will be discussing sex more specifically during our final appointment.

"What I'm talking about is fertilizing your relationship, making sure that you make time for each other. Today you're both fancy-free, relatively unimpeded by responsibilities and commitments, but before too long, especially if you have a family, you'll be just like everybody else, wearing too many hats, trying to keep too many balls in the air. It'll be harder and harder to make time for each other.

"When you do find a spare moment together, there can often be so many day-to-day issues to discuss, from budgets to bills and everything in between. If you're not careful, what little couple time you carve out for yourselves will deteriorate into something with no more intimacy than a meeting with your accountant, just one more thing on a to-do list that gets longer every day."

Reverend Tucker leaned in even closer than he had before, which was pretty close. I was thinking he'd slip off the edge of his chair and end up on the floor any second. "That's why it's so important to fertilize your relationship," he said. "Make time for each other every week and, if at all possible, try to get away for some kind of long weekend or retreat at least three or four times every year so you can . . ."

I lost him after that. I was too busy looking at Garrett. He was hanging on Reverend Tucker's every word and nodding, as if this all made complete sense.

Well. Maybe it does. Maybe this is what is supposed to happen after people get married. They go on their honeymoon, unpack their clothes and their sixteen place settings of china, buy a house with a dining room, and start making weekly appointments with each other. Reverend Tucker seems to think that's the deal, and he's been in the marrying business, and been married himself, for a long time. Judging from Garrett's expression, he seems to think this is all pretty normal. Maybe it is. How would I know? The only married couple I've ever seen up close is Abigail and Franklin. Their marriage seems about like Reverend Tucker described it: a lot of responsibilities, obligations, and schedules with a little bit of romance thrown in to make it more or less stick together. As near as I can tell, they seem happy. But they're both sixtysomething. When you're that old, you're ready for china patterns and dinner parties and having to coordinate calendars.

But is that what it will be like for us? Right away, I mean?

Other than getting to be with Garrett for the rest of my life—one of the few things in life I'm sure I want—I'm not certain what I really expected marriage to be like, except that . . . No. I can't even say that. I don't even know what I don't know.

That's why I wanted to get out of the house today. I want to talk to somebody about this, somebody trustworthy, somebody who is close enough to the situation to understand it but who isn't wrapped up in it emotionally. Somebody who won't think I'm crazy for asking questions and, most importantly, somebody who won't say anything to anybody else. Reverend Tucker is the only person I can think of who fits the bill.

I know some people would say I should be talking this over with Garrett, but I don't want him to think I'm getting cold feet. I just want to sort some stuff out in my mind.

Also, I don't want to talk to Garrett about the other thing that's been on my mind: the eight e-mails and five phone messages I've gotten from Professor Williams, wanting to know if I'm coming to Chicago or not. I should answer her. If she were in New York instead of Chicago right now, I'd have to. But she had some vacation time coming and was able to hand over her classes to somebody else in the department for a couple of weeks, until graduation.

I should call her back. Eventually, I'll have to. I should call her up and say, "Sorry, Professor, it was a really great offer, a once-in-a-lifetime offer. But I'm going to get married and live happily ever after and learn to make something besides ramen to serve on my Big Bang Bronze dinnerware when Garrett and I give dinner parties in our house with the dining room and all, so I guess I'll have to pass on Chicago."

That was a joke, okay? I was being funny. I won't say that.

But I'll have to say something. Whatever I say, it'll mean the same thing. I hate the idea of doing that, of closing the door forever. Sure, eventually it's going to close itself, but it won't be because of me, you know what I mean?

It's like all the wedding stuff. If I just lie back and let things happen, let somebody else take the lead, eventually all the decisions will take care of themselves.

Zoe kept nagging me about talking to Garrett, so I finally just told her I had. I don't like lying, but I had to get her off my back. I've intended to talk to Garrett. A couple of times I almost did. But then I chickened out.

Garrett is the best thing in my life, more important to me than any job could ever be. One half of my brain says that he'd be fine with the Chicago thing, that Garrett is an incredible, enlightened man who would want me to have everything I want. But another part of my brain remembers all the things my roommates said about even enlightened men being threatened by women who have powerful careers. I don't know which half of my brain to listen to.

If there's even a small chance that Garrett isn't as enlightened as I think he is, that this whole Chicago thing could end up coming between us, then why risk it? Especially over a job that I'm not certain I want, anyway?

A couple more weeks and it'll all be decided. The wedding will be over and my future will be set, so why take a chance on ruining everything?

Still, and despite my tendency to tune her out, too, Abigail's constant drumbeat on the importance of communication must be seeping into my consciousness. I should be talking all this over with Garrett, but I can't. It's too risky, especially so close to the wedding.

So this morning, after not being able to sleep again, even though I took my anti-anxiety meds, I've decided to talk things over with Reverend Tucker. It's the first real decision I've made for a long time. And as I'm walking up the street toward the church, under the shadowy canopy of spring green leaves, I feel pretty good about this.

When I turn the corner I can see that the second service is just letting out. Reverend Tucker is standing at the door, shaking hands with everybody as they leave. He waves at me and, for a minute, I feel like I'm going to throw up. My heart is pounding again, just like it did that day in New York.

I can't do it. I want to, but I can't.

And so, with sweat beading on my forehead and my pulse racing, I wave back, take a left at the corner, walk two more blocks, take another left, and end up back at the house, where I eat a turkey sandwich, stare at the seating chart, and tell Abigail that her arrangements look just great and we should go with that.

34

Evelyn Dixon

After figuring out that turning Liza's microwave sideways would leave enough room for her sewing machine, I pulled my head out of the trunk just in time to see my mother come out the front door of Liza's apartment building carrying a big cardboard box.

"Mom! For heaven's sake! Put that down! Are you trying to hurt yourself?" I ran over to her and tried to take the box away, but she sidestepped me and made a face.

"Evelyn, quit clucking. It's not heavy. The whole thing is filled with those microwave noodle thingies." Mom shook her head in disbelief. "Liza must have fifty packages of the stuff in her cupboards. No wonder she's so skinny."

Garrett came out the door, lugging two boxes with some loose items piled on top. He was sweating. Clearly his load *was* heavy.

Mom moved out of the way so Garrett could carry his burden to the car. She turned to me. "Maybe I ought to get Liza some cooking lessons as a wedding present."

"I heard that!" Grunting, Garrett put the boxes down on the sidewalk with a thud, then stood up and wiped the sweat from his face.

"I'm just saying," Virginia replied. "You're both too thin as it is. If all Liza knows how to cook is noodles in the microwave, then maybe a few cooking lessons would be a good idea."

"Grandma, Liza knows how to cook things besides ramen. She also makes a mean plate of French toast. Besides, I've been cooking for myself for the last four years. Just because we're getting married doesn't mean I expect her to suddenly don an apron and start making meat loaf. This isn't the fifties, you know."

"I'm just saying . . ." Virginia muttered again.

Garrett chuckled and looked at me with a "what can you do?" expression on his face. "We are in no danger of starving, Grandma. I promise. And, if it turns out we are, then I'll just invite you over for the afternoon and you can whip up a meat loaf, and maybe one of those strawberry-rhubarb cobblers you made for me last week. That'd pack on the pounds."

"Oh no," Mom said, completely missing the teasing tone in her grandson's voice, "I can't do that. As soon as this wedding's over, I'm going back to Wisconsin. I've been here too long as it is."

Garrett shot me a questioning look. I gave a quick shake of my head, signaling him to just let it lie. There is no point in talking about it; every time I do, Mom and I just end up arguing. She's made up her mind, and nothing I say seems to make any difference. I quickly changed the subject.

"Is that the last of it?" I asked, nodding to the boxes. "Where's Liza?"

"She'll be down in a minute," Garrett said.

He took the loose items off the boxes and laid them on the top of the car before wedging first one box and then the other into the backseat. "She's up doing the checkout with the super. The place looks pretty good. Thanks for helping with the cleanup. Liza shouldn't have any trouble getting her deposit back."

After shifting a few things to squeeze in the final box, Garrett slammed the car door hard to make sure the lock would catch.

"Good thing you two decided to stay in town for lunch and take the train home later. There's no more room. How was she able to fit this much stuff in a six-hundred-square-foot apartment split between four girls?" he said, scratching his head. "Thirty-eight pairs of shoes. Who needs thirty-eight pairs of shoes? I have three. Why do I have the feeling I'm about to be ejected from my own closet?"

Mom and I looked at each other and grinned. "Oh, Garrett," Mom said, "you don't know the half of it."

I walked over to my darling son and patted him sympathetically. "Wait until the wedding presents are all unpacked. You won't have room to change your mind."

Garrett frowned as he peered through the windows of the packed car. "Huh. Maybe we'd better give Wendy Perkins a call after we get back from Hawaii. We might need to buy a house sooner than I thought."

"Maybe. But, in the meantime, I can consolidate some stuff in the workroom cabinets. That should keep you in storage space for a while."

"Thanks, Mom." He smiled gratefully. "Well, looks like we're all set here. Now I just need my bride."

"What about that?" Mom asked, pointing to the top of the car.

"Oh! Thanks, Grandma. I can't forget Liza's quilt. She'd kill me. I'll lay it on the front seat so it doesn't get wrinkled. We're going to hang it in the living room."

Garrett carefully took the folded quilt off the top of the car and unfurled it, holding tight to the top two corners so he could see the full quilt. "It's beautiful, isn't it? Personally, I think she should have won first place."

Personally, I agreed with him.

Garrett stood quietly for a moment, a crease of concentration etched between his brows, looking at the quilted figure, the long-legged girl with the flowing hair and the transparent hands reaching out fruitlessly trying to catch hold of the thin silver threads before it was too late, before the flock flew past and the skies emptied.

"Mom? What do you think it means?"

Before I could say anything, a voice called out, "Hey! You there!"

We turned to see a woman with an angry expression and a head full of unruly curls that bounced as she trotted toward us, her arms pumping like a long-distance runner on the home stretch of a race.

"You! Who are you?" the woman demanded. "Where did you get that quilt?"

"It belongs to my fiancée," Garrett said, startled by this strange stranger. "She just graduated. I'm helping her move out of her apartment."

Garrett's explanation did nothing to mollify the woman. She marched up to him, practically nose to nose, and put her hands on her hips, glaring at my flabbergasted son.

"So! You're the fiancé." She shook her head, curls swishing left and right, and let out a harrumph. "So you're the Neanderthal who's ruining Liza's life! Forcing her to pass up a once-in-a-lifetime opportunity so she can iron your boxer shorts and cook your meals!"

"Oh, but Liza really can't cook," Mom said. She gave me a look and then shrugged, completely confused by this situation. That made three of us.

"Lady," Garrett said, annoyance beginning to creep into his voice, "I don't know what you're talking about. Liza hasn't said anything about—"

The woman puffed and held up her hand, waggling her fingers at him contemptuously. "Oh, don't give me that. If you insist on being a misogynistic jerk, at least don't be a lying misogynistic jerk. Liza told you about the job I offered her. She must have." She rose up on her toes so her face was even closer to Garrett's.

"Do you have any idea, *any* idea, what this could mean for her? She'll never get another chance like this. She could be one of the *youngest* curators in the country. You're a computer guy, aren't you? How hard would it be for you to do that from Chicago? Do you know how often an opportunity like this comes along in the art world? Do you? Never! That's how often. Especially for a woman. Believe me," she sneered, "I know what I'm talking about. And guys like you are the reason."

Garrett took a step back and folded up Liza's quilt. He was angry, I could tell, but he was working hard to keep it under control.

"Ma'am," he said evenly, "I don't know who you are or what you're talking about. If you'll excuse me, I've got to finish helping my girlfriend move."

The woman didn't budge. "You remind me of my old boyfriend. Calm and collected when there are people around, acting the part. But once the room clears you're all bullying and manipulation, controlling, forcing a woman to choose between love and a career. Well, I chose career, mister! And I've never regretted it. Not once!"

Lips pressed together, determined to ignore the woman's tirade or even look at her, Garrett opened the passenger door and carefully laid the folded quilt on the seat. Frustrated with his lack of response, the woman stomped her foot and then marched down the sidewalk and around the corner, but not before lobbing one final grenade at my son.

"Tell Liza that I wish she'd had the *courage* to call me up and actually refuse the job instead of avoiding my calls, but I understand. You can also tell her I hope she'll be very happy with you. But *somehow* I doubt it."

She marched down the sidewalk and turned the corner. Garrett shut the car door, locked it, and walked back toward the apartment building, saying nothing.

"Honey, what was that about? Who is that woman? Do you have any idea?"

"No," he said. "But I'm going to find out."

Grim faced, he kissed me on the cheek and Mom on the top of her head. "You two go on and enjoy your lunch. See you later."

I followed him to the door and stood on the stoop, watching as he walked through the lobby and up the stairs. I felt a hand on my elbow and turned around. Mom was standing on the step below, looking at me.

"Come on. Let's go eat lunch."

"But . . . don't you think we should wait here for a bit? To make sure everything is all right? Maybe I should go up there."

Mom shook her head. "No, Evelyn. Absolutely not. Garrett is a grown man. He and Liza are going to have to work this out on their own. I can't imagine it's the first argument they've ever had. And even if it is, it won't be the last."

I didn't move.

Mom's hand gripped me tighter. "Evelyn," she said in a warning voice. "Evelyn, don't. This doesn't concern you."

She was right. Garrett was an adult. He had to deal with this himself. I turned my back to the door.

"All right." I sighed. "I guess we should go. Charlie made a reservation for us at some new French place, not far from here. He said it's gotten wonderful reviews. It's about five blocks away. Shall we walk?"

Mom wrinkled her nose, rejecting this plan. "I don't want French food. Those rich sauces upset my stomach."

"No? What would you like instead?"

"A hot dog," she said in a tone that brooked no argument. "From one of those vendors in Central Park. Mary Flynn had one when she visited New York City with her daughter, and she said it was the best dog she ever had. I want mine with sauerkraut and plenty of mustard. And afterward, let's have ice cream. Come on."

Before I could say anything, Mom walked to the curb and hailed a passing cab like a seasoned city dweller.

"Central Park," she told the driver. I got in after her, but not before looking up at a third-story window and wondering what was going on behind the glass.

35

Liza Burgess

"That's ridiculous!" I countered. "The place is perfect. Cleaner than when I moved in. Why should I have to wait sixty days before getting my deposit back?"

Rick shrugged and scratched the side of his neck, slowly, which was how he'd done everything during the two years I'd lived in this apartment.

"Hey, whattaya gripin' at me for, huh? I'm just the super. I don't make the rules. You wanna gripe, call up the management company and gripe. I got a toilet to unclog."

He turned around and walked out of the empty apartment without saying good-bye, turning sideways to get past Garrett, who was just coming through the door.

I crossed my arms over my chest. "There goes the laziest building super in New York. But I'll get back at him. I'll have Abigail call him and his management company. It'd serve him right." I smiled at Garrett but he didn't say anything. He had a funny look on his face.

"Don't be mad, babe. It's not that big a deal. I'll get the check eventually. Let's go. I'm getting hungry."

"Liza, we need to talk about something."

His voice was low and serious. My stomach knotted, knowing something bad was about to happen but not knowing what.

"I was loading the last of the stuff into the car and this crazy woman saw me holding your quilt and she started going off about some big job offer in Chicago and how it was all my fault that you'd turned it down."

Professor Williams.

I'd expected to see her at graduation yesterday. Part of me had been relieved that we'd missed each other, but another part of me had been disappointed. I mean, she was my favorite professor. It seemed weird to leave without saying good-bye and also—well, there was no use thinking about that anymore.

The door was closed; my course was set. In a week, I was going to marry Garrett, go to Hawaii on my honeymoon, then come back to New Bern and start working in the quilt shop again.

Wasn't I?

Looking at Garrett's face, I started to feel scared. I'd never seen him mad before, not really mad. Even mad, he was still handsome but . . . Crap! I should have talked to him before. I should have! But I hadn't. And there was nothing to do about it now. I'd let it go too long.

"Liza, who was that lady?"

"Professor Williams. My art history teacher. The one I researched that paper for, the one who put my name on the article. I told you about her, remember?"

"Yeah," he said in that strange voice. "I remember. What I don't remember is you telling me about any job offer, not here and definitely not in Chicago. So, is it true? Did she offer you a job in Chicago?"

I nodded.

"Doing what?"

I looked at the wooden floor, keeping my eyes fixed on a black, quarter-sized knothole in one of the boards. "As an assistant curator at the Pinkham Museum. In the decorative arts division. She applied to be the new executive director, and the article I helped research kind of clinched the deal. She said I'd have to go to school at night, start working on a master's in art history, but that if I wanted it, the job was mine. I told her I needed to think about it."

I paused a moment, then whispered, "I told her I needed to talk it over with you." I lifted my eyes from the knothole to Garrett's face. His mouth was tight but he was breathing through his nose. His nostrils flared out and turned white when he was mad. I'd never known that before.

"When did you tell her that?" he asked.

I closed my eyes. They stung, the way they do when the optometrist puts in those drops that are supposed to make your pupils dilate. "Right before spring break."

"Spring break!"

He smacked his hand, palm open, against the painted wood doorjamb. I flinched, startled by the sound and the volume of Garrett's voice.

"Are you serious? You've known about this for two months. Two! And you've never even discussed it with me? Damn it, Liza!"

"I'm sorry," I said, knowing it was too late for that.

"How could you do that? Just cut me out of the loop like that? No wonder that lady thinks I'm some kind of throwback to the cavemen! She thinks I told you that you couldn't go to Chicago, told you to pass up the job of a lifetime . . . and it *is* the job of a lifetime, Liza! I'm no art critic, but even I can figure that out. She thinks I told you to pass all that up just so you could stay in New Bern and dust our apartment or something. No wonder she thinks I'm a misogynistic jerk! I'd think the same thing! Liza, why didn't you just talk to me about it? What did you think I was going to say?"

My eyes were stinging again, this time with tears. "I . . . I don't know. I was going to. I wanted to. But I was afraid. I was afraid you'd say no . . . or that maybe . . . I don't know. It didn't seem worth it. It's just a job."

"Just a job? No!" He shook his head furiously. "No, it's not! It's a great opportunity for you. What would make you think I'd say no to something like that? We could have moved to Chicago."

"But you love New Bern. So do I. And you're getting your business established. You've got all those new clients. . . ." Even as I was saying the words, I knew how stupid they sounded. As long as Garrett had a laptop and an Internet connection, he was in business.

"I was afraid to talk to you about it. I'd have to work a lot of hours and go to school at night too. And it would be very public, a lot of publicity and gallery openings and parties. I was afraid that even if you said yes, later you'd resent the job, resent me for taking it. Zoe says that even when they say they won't, men always end up resenting women who have careers that are more powerful than—"

Garrett looked ready to explode. "Wait a minute! Zoe said? You talked this over with Zoe? Probably Kerry and Janelle, too, but you didn't talk it over with me? I can't believe this!"

He clenched both his fists tight and let out a growl, as if the effort of not driving a fist into the nearest wall was almost more than he could bear. "Where have you been the last few weeks? Or months? Or years? Don't you know me better than that by now? Didn't you hear anything that Reverend Tucker said? A marriage that isn't based on friendship first doesn't stand a chance of lasting. And a friend is somebody you talk to, Liza. The people who you share your secrets with, those are your friends! You chose to share your secrets with your roommates but not with me. Think about what that says about me, Liza. About us!"

"I know . . . I should . . ." I stood there, trying to think of something to say that would make it all better, wishing there were some kind of time machine that would take me back a month. Or two. But there wasn't. I knew that. There aren't any do-overs.

"I'm sorry. It was stupid. *I* was stupid. Really stupid."

"Ya think?" he said caustically. "How about sneaky? And selfish? And while you're at it, why don't you add—"

"Hey! Knock it off!" I shouted. I could feel my cheeks flush with anger. "Remember what Reverend Tucker said about fighting fair. No put-downs and no name calling."

"Reverend Tucker? Since when do you care about anything he says? If you did, you'd have talked to me weeks ago." He threw up his hands. "This is ridiculous. I don't even know why I'm wasting my time. . . ."

He balled up his fists again, thumped one against his thigh, but not as hard as he had hit it against the door, as if he were giving up on fighting. Giving up on us.

"I've gone out of my way to win your trust, to support you, to listen to you. But it's no use. You don't even try."

Now it was my turn to explode. "Listen to me? Hold on right there! You haven't been listening to me. No one listens to me!"

"What are you talking about?" Garrett gasped. "Ever since you got out of the hospital, nobody has done anything but listen to you! People have bent over backwards listening to you, asking your opinions on everything from what kind of music the band should play, to what kind of filling they should put between layers of the wedding cake, to—"

"To where we should go on our honeymoon?" I asked.

Garrett stopped short, stared at me.

I let out a short, sharp laugh and shook my head. "In all this listening you and everybody have been doing, have you ever heard me say anything besides, 'Yes. Great idea'? Or words to that effect? That's my stock answer, Garrett. Nothing has changed. I just tell people what they want to hear."

"You said you wanted to go to Hawaii."

"No. I said I didn't know where we should go. I told you that I don't like making decisions. I told you that they terrify me. And they do."

My eyes started to fill again. I had to stop for a moment and catch my breath. Garrett was watching me so closely, listening so hard that I had to turn my head away.

"I'm so afraid of getting it wrong, of making a choice I'll live to regret. So I don't. I don't choose. I just let somebody else do it, like I did with the honeymoon. Or I wait until time makes the choice for me, like I did with the job. That way, if it all goes wrong, at least it isn't my fault."

He was still mad, but his voice was softer. He wasn't shouting anymore. "Liza, you could have told me. I'd have listened."

"But I *did* tell you. That night at the Café Carlyle, on the dance floor, remember? I told you that I didn't like surprises, that I wasn't ready. But you didn't listen. You just got hurt and walked off. I told you I was afraid, but you never asked why, you just tried to talk me out of it. You didn't listen, Garrett. I know you think you did, but you're wrong."

Garrett's fists opened. He lifted his chin, looked up at the ceiling, and exhaled a long, slow breath.

"I've got to go."

"What?" My stomach instantly clenched back into that familiar knot of fear. "Where are you going?" I reached out, tried to grab his arm, but he shook me off.

"For a walk. I need to think about . . . things. I'll be back." He turned around and walked out the door.

"When?"

"I don't know."

I followed him into the hall and watched as he walked down the stairs, diminishing inch by inch with each descending step until he disappeared.

The apartment was empty. There was nothing to sit on. No books or magazines. No TV or radio. Nothing to distract me while I waited for Garrett to return. My footsteps made a lonely echo as I walked to the window and looked out to see Garrett on the street below. His hands were shoved in his pockets and his head was down as he walked away.

When he disappeared around the corner, I turned my back to the wall and slid down until I was sitting on the floor, my arms wrapped around my calves and my chin resting on my knees, waiting.

There was a little pile of stuff sitting on the floor next to me, the final few things I'd gathered up before preparing to leave this apartment for good and drive back to New Bern and my new life with Garrett: my cell phone, my hairbrush—the good wooden one with natural bristles that I'd found again when we moved the dresser—a lime green mini stapler that I'd discovered in a kitchen drawer, my yearbook, and my diploma, the one they'd handed me yesterday, a million years ago, back when it seemed like everything in my life had been settled. Now I didn't know what was going to happen.

Overhead, I could hear the sound of footsteps, of somebody

playing a song by the Plain White T's, of laughter and chair legs scraping against the floor.

I picked up my diploma in its black leather case, flipped open the cover, and read the words inside.

LIZA CHRISTINE BURGESS
Is awarded this day, the degree of Bachelor of Fine Arts

There it was, in black and white, with a gold seal and a signature to make it official. I was a college graduate, twenty-two years old, and I still didn't know crap about anything that mattered.

When the Wizard of Oz gave the Scarecrow his diploma, he was just blowing smoke. A diploma doesn't make any difference. I was just as clueless today as I'd been the day before, maybe more.

I closed the leather case, laid it on the floor, and reached for my cell phone. I'd call Abigail, or Margot, or Ivy, or Evelyn. Well, maybe not Evelyn. She was probably mad at me. But I had to talk to somebody, ask someone what I should do.

I flipped my phone open and dialed the area code for New Bern, figuring that by the time I got that far, I'd know who to call. But my finger froze as I hit the fourth button.

No. It was time to stop this, time to quit asking everybody else what I should think and do and feel. I have to grow up someday, start figuring out things for myself.

After all, I have this diploma. It's time.

36

Liza Burgess

I heard footsteps on the stairs and I knew they were Garrett's.

I didn't get up. I just sat on the floor, waiting. I'd left the door unlocked. He opened it and called me. "Liza?"

He saw me sitting on the floor and smiled. He'd left his anger outside on the street, somewhere down the block and around the corner. His old face was back, the one I loved.

"Hi."

He sat down opposite me with his legs crossed and took my hands in both of his, like we were playing one of those mind-reading games you played at parties when you were in junior high. Except this wasn't a game. And I couldn't read his mind.

"Hi."

"I'm sorry I yelled at you. "And I'm really sorry I didn't listen. If it counts for anything, I thought I was. Guess I need more practice. I'm going to do better from here on out. Okay?"

"Okay," I whispered, feeling a small swell of hope. If he was talking about how he was going to do things from here on out, then that must mean he thought we had a future together.

"You know," I said, "on the scale of who screwed up worse than who, my side of the seesaw is definitely the one bumping the ground. If anybody should be apologizing, it's me. So here goes."

I took a deep breath. "I'm sorry, Garrett. I really am. I should have talked to you the second Professor Williams offered me the job. I should have been straight with you and trusted you about so many things. Maybe you didn't listen as well as you could have, but I didn't exactly make that easy for you. That was as much my fault as yours, probably more."

Being a Burgess, apologizing doesn't come naturally to me. I had been looking at Garrett's hands the whole time. But now I looked up at him from under my lashes.

"And I'm sorry I yelled, too. That wasn't fair. I wish I could promise I'll never yell again, but I know how I am and—well, if I promised that, I'd be lying, so I won't. But I promise I'll try. And I'll try to do a better job of talking things out and letting you know what I'm thinking and feeling. I know I can do better. From here on out, I will."

I waited.

"Okay," Garrett said simply.

"Yeah?"

"Yeah." Still holding my hands in his, he rocked forward and gave me a quick kiss on the lips.

The swell of relief became a flood. Everything was going to be okay. We were going to be okay. I couldn't keep from grinning.

"Hey! We just had our first fight—and lived through it. Pretty good, huh?"

"Pretty good," he said. "But I came awful close to punching a hole in your wall. For a minute I thought you were going to lose your deposit."

"You have amazing powers of self-control."

Now it was me who rocked forward to kiss him on the lips, but my kiss was not a quick one. I left my lips on his for a long time, opened them a little and then a little more, inviting his tongue to explore my mouth, extending mine into his, taking my time, running the tip of my tongue over the ridge of his perfect teeth before rising to my knees while putting my hands on his muscled arms, urging him to rise with me, wanting to feel the length of his body pressing against mine and know that all was forgiven and forgotten and that we would go on from here as though none of this had happened.

But when I tried to pull him up to me, he pulled back, put his arms on my shoulders, and pushed me away. I was sitting back on the floor again, close to Garrett but not close enough, breathing heavily.

"Whoa! Liza," Garrett said from his side of the floor, taking in a deep whoosh of air and then letting it out quickly, as if trying to catch his breath.

I frowned, feeling rejected and a little confused. "What? What's the point of fighting if you don't get to make up? That's the best part." I smiled, trying to tease him out of his serious mood, but it didn't work.

"But," he said, "we're not done fighting yet. I mean, we're done *fighting,* at least for today. But there are still a lot of things we need to talk about, things we need to figure out. All right?"

"All right," I said, but I said it with a pout. Personally, I could think of a lot better things to do than fight or even talk about fighting. But I had just promised I would be better about talking things out, so I was pretty well stuck.

Garrett scooted backward a little, increasing the distance between us by a couple of inches. Feeling chilled, I wrapped my arms protectively around my waist.

"Liza, when I was out walking, I came up with about a million questions I wanted to ask you. But after a while I realized it really comes down to one, the question I should have asked in the first place. What do you want? Out of life, I mean. Tell me. This time, I promise I'll listen."

I pressed my lips together. While Garrett was out walking, I'd prepared myself to answer any number of questions that might serve to explain my inexplicable behavior, but this wasn't one of them. Twisting the diamond on my engagement ring from the front to the back of my hand and back again, I realized how much that said. It wasn't the answers that explained me; it was the questions.

I looked up. "I don't know," I said. "Maybe that's the problem. Until five months ago, that question hadn't even crossed my mind.

And when it finally did, on the night you proposed, it caught me completely by surprise."

Garrett frowned, struggling and failing to understand how that was possible. "But you've always known you were going to graduate someday. Didn't you ever stop to think about what came after?"

"Not really. I know that sounds crazy, but it just seemed like everything would go on more or less like it always had. I would paint and live . . . somewhere." I shrugged. "I never thought about my options after school because it never crossed my mind that I really had any options, you know? It isn't like the Fortune 500 organizes recruiting fairs competing to snap up the most promising studio art majors. I figured I'd do what everyone else was going to do: find a job that would pay the bills so I could spend my free time painting. Knowing that I had a place to live and a job at the quilt shop waiting for me when I went back to New Bern made it even easier for me. I never had to think about my future. Not until New Year's Eve."

Garrett raised his eyebrows. "When I ruined everything by asking you to marry me?"

"Don't say that. You didn't ruin anything. You just surprised me, that's all."

"And you don't like surprises." There was no question in his voice; it was a statement of fact. I didn't try to deny it.

"Liza, I don't understand. You really were caught by surprise? That night, with the flowers and the car, the dinner and dancing—you didn't know I was going to propose?"

I shook my head.

"But didn't you know how I felt about you?"

"I knew you cared about me, even loved me, and I felt the same way about you, at least I thought I did. . . ." I tipped my head back, resting it against the wall, and looked at the ceiling. When I lowered my head, Garrett was staring at me and his expression was blank, as though steeling himself for some terrible disappointment.

I reached out and grabbed his hands. "Oh! Garrett, don't look at me like that! I'm not saying I didn't love you. I did love you! I do love you! But back then, I wasn't thinking about love the same way you were. I wasn't thinking love as in 'love and marriage.' I wasn't *not* thinking about it, either. I wasn't thinking at all. I was just living. Doing what I'd always done. Assuming everything would go on like it always had. Back then, if someone had asked me if I hoped you and I would get married, I'd have thought for a moment and said, 'Well, yes. Sure. Someday.' It never crossed my mind that you'd ask so soon. It just was so . . . so sudden. I wasn't expecting it.

"I felt like I'd been jolted awake in the middle of a dream. I didn't quite know where I was or what I was doing there. Suddenly, I had to start thinking about my future, and it just terrified me!"

Garrett was trying to keep his face neutral, but I could tell by the look in his eyes that he didn't really understand. How could I explain it to him?

"One of the great things about painting is that if I don't like how a canvas turns out, I can just paint over it and start again. Quilting is the same way. If the colors are ugly or the seams are crooked or the corners don't meet, you can just rip out the stitches and take another run at it. But life isn't like that. You've only got one chance to get it right. And that scares me, Garrett, because I want to get it right. I really do!"

I paused to give Garrett a chance to say something, but he didn't. He was listening, really listening, making no judgments, offering no solutions, just hearing me out.

"Next thing I knew, there were all these other decisions that had to be made, and they were all important too. Or at least they seemed like they were. After a while I couldn't tell the difference between the important choices and the trivial ones. Before long, deciding whether I should take the job offer in Chicago seemed just as overwhelming as trying to decide where we should go on a honeymoon. I was so afraid of getting it wrong! And it wasn't just the choices I had to make that were bothering me, but the things I was passing up. I told you that I don't know what I want, but that isn't quite right. I know what I want—everything! I want all of it! All the time! But," I said, "it doesn't work that way, does it?"

Garrett moved his head ever so slightly from side to side.

I sighed. "Yeah. I get it. It took me a while, but I get it. Eventually, you've got to choose. If you don't, then circumstances just choose for you. While you were outside thinking things through, I was sitting here trying to do the same. I didn't come to many conclusions.

"I still don't know if I want to go to a big city and be a world-famous museum curator or stay in sleepy little New Bern and be an obscure and underappreciated artist. Heck, I still don't even know where I want to go on my honeymoon. But, Garrett, wherever I go on my honeymoon, I want you to be there too. I don't know much, but I know that. For sure. I love you, Garrett. I always will."

He leaned down and bent his head over my hand, his lips so smooth that they felt like the caress of a soft sable brush. He looked up at me, still holding my hand in his, cupping his palms around it as though he were cradling a fragile blossom. And in that moment, seeing myself in the mirror of his eyes, I felt like exactly that: a cherished flower, beautiful and entirely loved.

"And when I go on my honeymoon," he said, "wherever it is . . . and whenever it is, I want you to be there too. There's no one else for me, Liza. There never will be."

My heart lurched.

Whenever it is? What's he saying?

I looked into his eyes and knew.

"Liza, don't! Don't cry! It's not what you think. I'm not breaking up with you. But we're not getting married. Maybe someday, but not next week. You're not ready. We're not ready."

I started to tell him he was wrong; I *was* ready. Maybe before I hadn't been, but now I *was*.

But I couldn't say any of that. When I tried to speak, nothing came out—not words, not sobs, nothing. Two tears traced a line from the corners of my eyes down my cheeks. Garrett reached out his hand, caught them on the bend of his knuckle.

"Liza, listen to me. This isn't an end to anything. If anything, it's a beginning. We're going to go back and do this again. Do it right. The way we should have from the first. We're going to take our time and give you time, time to find out who you are and what you want out of life, to realize a little bit of your own power, time to try things, succeed at some, fail at others, and *know* that it's not the end of the world! You need time to know how capable you are, and to learn how to choose, and fight, and tell people what you need. Time. Liza, you just need more time."

"You . . ." I sniffed and closed my eyes for a moment before trying my voice again. "You want to go back? I don't understand. You want a do-over?"

"Yeah," he said. "A do-over. Nothing has happened that can't be fixed. We were just rushing things. I was rushing things. Until today, I didn't realize it. It's my fault. I'm sorry, baby. You tried to tell me that you weren't ready. I didn't hear you. All I knew was that I wanted to marry you. As soon as possible."

He smiled. "On New Year's Eve, if somebody had told me the headwaiter moonlighted as a justice of the peace, I'd have tried to talk you into marrying me right on the dance floor. Sitting here looking at you, how beautiful you are, even with your eyes red and your nose running, I almost can't blame myself. But I should have listened better, been better, and stopped to think more about what you needed.

"I want to marry you so much, Liza. There are only two things I want more: for you to be happy, and for our marriage to last from 'I do' until death. And if pulling back and taking another run at this will make that happen, then I can wait. And if it never happens—if you're never ready—well, that's a chance I'll have to take. I don't want to, but I can and I will. You're worth waiting for, Liza."

The sun was streaming through the curtainless window, making my engagement ring blink a bright beam of light. The room was quiet. So quiet.

"Do you want this back?" I asked softly, nodding toward the ring.

"Do you want me to take it back?"

I bit my lower lip, thinking. "Maybe you could hold on to it for a while."

"I can do that."

"For how long?"

"Until you tell me that you're ready to take it back and keep it, forever."

I started to pull off the ring, but even though my fingers were thinner than they'd been when he first gave it to me, it caught on my knuckle. "What if I told you I was ready now?"

He raised his eyebrows, asking me to ask myself if that was really true, knowing I already knew the answer. The ring was a symbol of my love for Garrett and his for me, but in my mind, it had become something else as well, a safety net. As long as I was wearing the ring, a part of me would doubt that I could manage on my own, or take care of myself. I thought about everything that had happened today, about sitting alone on the floor, looking at my shiny new diploma, feeling as clueless and helpless as always. I thought about my resolve to quit being clueless or helpless, and to finally grow up. I brushed my finger across the angled edge of the diamond and knew what I had to do. I love Garrett, but it's time to be responsible for myself, and at least for now, that means working without a net.

On my list of hard days, really hard days, I number the day my mother died, the day I got arrested for shoplifting in New Bern, and the day Abigail told me the truth about the betrayal that came between her and my mom and tore our family apart for so long. And now this, the moment I tugged at my ring and gave it to Garrett for safekeeping.

But then I remembered something else.

All those terrible things happened to me? Those tragedies and trials and endings that, at the time, I was sure marked the end of the world as I knew it? They were awful, but that wasn't all they were. Each ending was also a beginning, a chance to grow up, to try again, to make myself over into someone a little bit wiser, braver, and better.

Garrett was right. This wasn't an ending. It was a beginning. Do-overs are possible, and this time, we are going to get it right. I'm sure we are. But that didn't mean I wasn't scared.

"So what am I supposed to do now?"

Garrett scooted around on the wooden floor so he was sitting with his back against the wall, next to me, and put his arm around my shoulder. "Whatever you want," he said.

I thought about Chicago and room after room of white-walled gallery spaces waiting for me to fill them with treasures of my choosing. I thought of my room back in New Bern, of light streaming through a south-facing window and painting whatever came into my mind, of sitting upstairs in the quilt shop on a Friday night, drinking good red wine. I thought of stories told, confidences kept, silences respected while we sat and stitched and figured out the meaning of everything, of walking through the woods with Garrett on a Saturday afternoon, of going to sleep and waking again and knowing he was only three blocks away. I thought of Paris, or what I imagine Paris must be like, city of lights and artists and scents and inspirations. I thought of being alone, and being happy being alone. I thought of painting in plein air on a beach, or a mountainside, or in a meadow among a cloud of butterflies. I thought about all the possibilities, of the things I know and the things I don't, and the things I've barely dared to imagine. And I thought of the doors, all the doors. . . .

"What if I don't know?"

"Then you'll figure it out," Garrett said in a voice so sure that I could just about believe he was right. "I'll help you. I'll listen. You talk."

So I did.

Facing the empty apartment with the bare walls and the naked floors, I looked beyond the boundaries of Sheetrock, brick, and mortar, and spoke of windy cities and quiet villages, of beaches and mountains, of friends and strangers. The words spilled out like paint on canvas, like handfuls of wildflower seeds scattered on a field, like rainbow yards of fabric laid out on a table, uncut, unbound, untraced—the stuff dreams are made of, ideas and inklings and desires that might yet be formed into anything imaginable.

Garrett listened and I talked, laying my head on his shoulder, opening my mind to the possibilities, embracing the choices, in love with my beloved, and for the first time ever, in love with my life.

37

Evelyn Dixon

Charlie was aghast.

"Seriously? You blew off your reservation at Maison La Mer so you could eat hot dogs in the park? Are you mad?"

Mom glared at Charlie through narrowed eyes. "I *like* hot dogs."

Charlie put his hand over his eyes and groaned. "I can't believe it. Brandade de morue for a starter, a spring salad with sherry mustard vinaigrette, moules frites, champagne poached pears for dessert or maybe strawberry napoleon. Or a hot dog with all the trimmings."

"And a Nutty Buddy ice-cream bar for dessert," Mom said proudly, which elicited a laugh from everyone at the table. "Don't forget that. It was delicious."

Charlie covered his face with both hands, as if it were all too much to bear. "Virginia, you are a mystery to me. As inexplicable as your darling daughter."

I gave Charlie a quick glance, wondering if this barb was in reference to my response to his many proposals, which would have been a violation of the six-month moratorium on proposals, but I could see that it wasn't. At the moment, marriage was the farthest thing from Charlie's mind. He was totally focused on trying to fathom my mother's plebian palate.

In fact, when it came to the moratorium, he'd been as good as his word. Since that day in the pizza restaurant, he hadn't uttered even the slightest hint of a proposal. Which, I'd just realized, was starting to annoy me. For a man who claimed to have been sick with love for the past three years, he seemed to have recovered awfully quickly.

No, no, I told myself. It was best this way. For the moment I had all the wedding worries I could handle.

In spite of Mom's assurances that Garrett and Liza were adults and could work everything out on their own, I couldn't help but worry about them. I hadn't heard a word from Garrett since we left Liza's apartment. It was everything I could do to keep from calling his cell phone. So even though I really should have stayed home and finished sewing the sample for the upcoming hunter's star table runner class, when Franklin called and said the whole gang was getting together for a late dinner at the Grill, I was quick to accept, eager for a distraction.

The big round table in the back was too small for our group. Charlie had pushed together a row of small tables along the wall to make room for himself, me, Mom, Franklin and Abigail, Margot and Arnie, Ivy, and Dana. Dana had barely said a word since she arrived, but she was smiling as she sipped her glass of wine and nibbled at a plate of crispy spring rolls. She appeared to be enjoying herself. I hoped so.

"Now, now, Charlie," Mom said soothingly, patting him on the arm, "don't take it so hard. I'm sorry you went to all the trouble of getting that reservation for nothing, but I really wanted to eat a hot dog in the park. It just seemed like such a New Yorky thing to do. Besides, why would I want to eat somebody else's moules frites when I can eat yours?"

Dana frowned as she crunched into another spring roll, looking a little confused by the terminology but saying nothing.

"Moules frites are mussels with French fries," Ivy explained.

"And a fabulous sort of garlicky mayonnaise to dip them in," Mom added. "What's that sauce called, Charlie?"

"Aioli."

"That's right! Aioli. It's wonderful! Delicious with the fries or the mussels. You should try some, Dana."

Dana covered her mouth with her hand and swallowed quickly, hesitant to talk with food in her mouth. "Oh. No, thank you. I don't like seafood."

Charlie made a noise and started to say something, but Mom cut him off.

"Neither did I, dear, not unless it was fried. But Charlie started encouraging me to expand my horizons. Now I like mussels, cod, haddock, and even calamari! That's squid. Never in a million years did I think I'd eat squid. And like it!"

Dana looked nervously down at her plate, as if wondering what frighteningly exotic ingredient Charlie might have snuck into her spring rolls.

"And before you know it, I'll have you eating oysters," Charlie declared.

Mom made a face. "Oh no. That's where I draw the line." Mom shuddered. "Oysters. Yech. They're so slimy."

"Now, Virginia, don't be like that. Haven't you heard? Oysters are an aphrodisiac."

"Aphrodisiac. Ha!" Mom said as she speared a circle of calamari with her fork. "Sure they are."

"They are!" Charlie insisted. "Isn't that right, Abigail?"

Charlie grinned at Abigail, who had just put a shell to her lips prior to slurping down the last of a half dozen oysters she'd ordered. "Since they got married, Abigail and Franklin have been going through oysters like nobody's business. At least a dozen a week—each! And look at them, Virginia. The picture of health and vigor, both of them. I'm telling you, if you want to put a spring in your step and a twinkle in your eye, not to mention add a bit of spice to your love life, nothing will do the trick like a nice plate of fresh oysters."

Franklin beamed at this teasing homage to his ongoing vitality and put his arm around his wife's shoulders. Abigail, however, was not amused. She lowered her oyster, uneaten, and put it back on the plate.

Charlie's grin faded. He'd known Abigail long enough to know when he'd gone too far. Margot, ever the diplomat, jumped in and changed the subject.

"Abigail, how are things going with the wedding? Arnie was just saying how much he's looking forward to it."

Arnie nodded. "Margot told me you're putting us at Judge Gulden's table. Thanks."

"Don't mention it. And, Arnie, if you'd really like to make a good impression on the judge, I suggest you develop a sudden interest in stamps. Harry is a collector." She rolled her eyes. "Personally, I can't imagine a duller hobby, but I suppose there's no accounting for taste."

"Actually," Arnie said, turning a little pink around the ears, "I collect stamps too."

"Really?" Abigail said without the slightest embarrassment about her earlier remark. "Well, that's perfect then, isn't it?"

Margot giggled and squeezed Arnie's arm. "I can't believe the wedding is just a week away! Do you need help with any last-minute planning or errands?"

"No, thank you. I'm happy to report that, at long last, everything is done. There was some fuss about getting enough sorbet cups to serve two hundred, but Byron called me just this morning and said he'd found a place in Westchester that had enough in stock. Of course, I had to buy them rather than rent, but that's all right. The supplier gave us a break on the price, and I'll use them again. They'll be perfect to use at the Stanton Center fund-raiser in the fall."

"That's right!" Ivy said. "Donna told me you'd agreed to chair the event after all. That's great, Abigail!"

Franklin squeezed Abigail's shoulders. "And did you hear about her idea? After doing the same event for seven years, the auction was beginning to lose a little steam. So Abigail proposed something new—an authors' luncheon. They're inviting four local writers from the area to read and talk about their work and then, afterward, they'll sign books, with all the profits from the sales going to the Stanton Center. I think it'll—"

"Really!" Dana exclaimed, interrupting Franklin and surprising everyone with her enthusiasm. "You mean we're going to have real writers at the Stanton Center? Who?"

Abigail closed her eyes for a moment and tapped her finger on the end of her nose, summoning the list of names from her memory. "Oh, now. Let me see. Janice Greenow, Phil Rensler, Dorothy Deloitte, and . . . who was that other one? Oh, yes! Estella Perez."

Dana's eyes widened. "Estella Perez! Estella Perez, who wrote *Comes the Morning*?"

"Why, yes. Estella and I are old friends. Do you know her work?"

Dana gasped. "I've read every one of her books five times! She's my favorite writer. I even wrote to her once. I was going to send her one of my poems but . . ." She ducked her head, embarrassed.

"Dana," I said, casting a quick glance in Abigail's direction, "I didn't know you were a writer."

"Oh . . . well, I'm not. I just scribble a little bit. Poems. A couple of short stories. Just for fun. It's not like I'm good or anything. I just . . ." Dana's voice drifted off. She looked down at her plate.

"Do you think," she said without looking up. "Do you think that maybe I could go to the luncheon? I couldn't afford a ticket, but maybe I could help out. Sell tickets or clean tables or something?"

"Oh," Abigail said casually, "I think we can do a little better than that. Ivy, I'd just been thinking that, after the luncheon, we might ask one or two of the authors to come to New Beginnings and give a little writing workshop."

She smiled and gave Dana a sideways glance. "Do you think any of the women might be interested in something like that?"

"I can think of a couple." Ivy winked at Dana, who was positively beaming. "But are you sure you have time to organize another event? I know how busy you've been with the wedding and all."

"I am *never* too busy to help support the Stanton Center," Abigail said haughtily. "But speaking of the wedding, where in the world are Liza and Garrett? I left a message with Hilda, asking them to join us when they got back home. Where can they be? I assumed they'd be here hours ago."

I started to say something about traffic when Garrett and Liza walked in the front door, holding hands and smiling. What a relief!

After our encounter with that strange woman and Garrett's stormy response, I'd worried that something terrible had happened, but obviously, I'd been worrying over nothing. Sitting across the table from me, Mom gave me a "what did I tell you?" look.

"Hi, everybody. Sorry we're late," Garrett said. "It took us a while to unload the car."

"It turns out I've got a lot more stuff than I thought." Liza laughed.

"Oh, that's all right," Abigail said magnanimously, getting up to give Liza a peck on the cheek. "You're here now, and that's what counts. Garrett, I bet you had a time carrying all Liza's boxes up the stairs to the apartment. You should have left it until morning."

Franklin nodded. "Yes, Garrett. It could have waited until tomorrow. Arnie and I would have given you a hand."

Garrett licked his lips nervously. "Well, we didn't exactly move everything up into my apartment. We took it all to your house."

"Our house?" Abigail clucked. "Why in the world did you do that? You'll only have to move it again in another few days."

Liza moved closer to Garrett and squeezed his hand. "Actually, he won't. He . . . I mean, we . . ." Liza took a deep breath. "Abigail, we've decided to postpone the wedding."

"What!" Abigail and I shouted simultaneously.

I couldn't believe it.

When Garrett stormed off to talk to Liza, I knew he was upset, but not that upset. Not upset enough to call off the wedding! I flopped back in my chair, stunned into silence, and looked at my son.

But Garrett didn't look upset. Not at all. Nor did Liza. In fact, they looked happier and more relaxed than I'd seen them in weeks. I didn't understand.

Like me, Abigail was stunned—but not into silence.

"What do you mean? You're postponing the wedding? Do you have any idea what you're saying? At this moment, ten cases of crystal sorbet cups are being rush delivered to New Bern so they'll be here in time for your wedding! Do you have any idea the lengths I had to go to *find* ten cases of crystal sorbet cups? And now, you just blithely walk in here and say you're postponing the wedding? Why?

Until when? And what in the world gives you the right to think you can just make that decision without consulting me!" she shouted.

And then, something wonderful happened. Liza shouted back.

With hands on her hips and fire in her eyes, Liza—the old, stubborn, firecracker Liza, the girl who had been missing for lo these many months—stood up to her aunt and shouted her down.

"You? This isn't your wedding! Since when do I have to consult *you?* Garrett and I have talked this over, and we've both decided that we're not ready to get married yet. Maybe someday we will. Or maybe we won't. When the time is right, we'll decide. *We* will! Not you, Abigail. It has nothing to do with you!"

Abigail started to protest, but Liza didn't give her a chance. "No! Don't say anything. Don't ask any questions. If something changes, then you will be advised on a need-to-know basis. Got it? And as for your rush delivery, well, that's your problem. Garrett and I aren't going to rush into marriage before we're ready just so you won't have to return two zillion crystal sorbet cups! There's a pretty long list of good reasons to get married, Aunt Abigail, but your sorbet cups don't even make it into the top five thousand!"

Liza stopped for a moment, breathing hard through her nose, and crossed her arms over her chest. "And if you'll think about it for a second, you'll see I'm right!"

That last statement pulled her up short. Abigail pressed her lips together before speaking. "And you're sure this is what you want?" she asked Liza and then looked at Garrett. "And you?"

"It's for the best," he said. "We were rushing things, and there was no reason to. We've got plenty of time."

I raised my eyebrows, silently testing Garrett's veracity. He gave me a quick nod and a little smile so I'd know he was all right.

Abigail's shoulders drooped, signaling her defeat. "Well. Obviously, if you're not ready to get married, then . . . you're just not. But, Liza, if you're not getting married, what are you going to do?"

Liza laughed, the first time I'd heard her laugh in months. "Anything I want! I haven't figured it all out yet, but I do know that, for a little while at least, it involves Paris." She leaned her head on Garrett's shoulder and gave him a questioning look.

"Oh, right," he said and turned to me. "Mom, would it be all right if I took a couple of weeks off? I'm going to Paris."

I smiled with relief. He really was all right. "Of course, sweetheart. Whenever you like. We can manage without you for a little while, can't we, Margot?"

"Sure we can!" Margot enthused and then sighed. "Paris. How romantic! I've always wanted to go to Paris."

Abigail scowled at Margot. "Well, isn't that just ducky! I'm glad everything has worked out so well for everyone. Why don't we all just drop everything and run off to Paris, hmm? Oh, wait! I can't. And do you know why? Because I've got two hundred two-pound lobsters on order from Maine and it's too late to cancel. Not to mention a full orchestra, a chamber ensemble, two hundred bottles of champagne, a six-layer wedding cake, and a small army of florists and a hairdresser—a *celebrity* hairdresser—all of which have been paid for in advance!"

She pointed at Liza and Garrett. "You may not be getting married on Saturday," she said, "but I have by gosh already paid for this wedding, and come Saturday at four o'clock, *somebody* around here is going to get married!"

She turned her laser-sharp gaze on Arnie and then on Charlie, both of whom had suddenly turned white and had definite deer-in-the-headlights looks on their faces.

"All right, gentlemen! Who is it going to be?"

38

Evelyn Dixon

When you're twentysomething, clear-eyed, fresh-faced, and slim-hipped, choosing a wedding gown isn't all that difficult.

Oh, I know Liza agonized over the selection of her dress, but let's face it, beautiful as she is, young as she is, she could have walked down the aisle swathed in a white sheet and still elicited murmurs of approval from the misty-eyed congregation.

But for a woman of a certain age, the range of options for bridal wear is narrow. The obvious choice is a simple ivory suit, perfect for a chapel, garden, or courthouse wedding but not really elegant enough for a big church ceremony. What to do? Too many ruffles or too much lace and you run the risk of looking precious; too many sequins or spangles and you'll look like you're playing the big room at the Bellagio.

However, on Saturday afternoon at a few minutes before four, in the bridal changing room of the New Bern Community Church, the full-length reflection in the mirror proved that beauty is ageless.

The dress was perfect in every detail, from the long, diaphanous slope of the bell sleeves, to the simple smooth fit of the bodice, to the soft shawl collar folded in the back, scooping down to reveal just a peek of shoulder blade before falling away gracefully into the sweeping skirt that barely brushed the floor, in layers of chiffon that whispered with every move and breath. Looking in that mirror, I saw a bride so beautiful and serenely happy that I had to blink to keep back the tears.

"Don't cry!" Abigail commanded. "It's almost time. You'll ruin your mascara. Margot, hand her a tissue, would you, please?"

"I can't help it," I said, dabbing my eyes. "Abigail, you look lovely."

She smiled gratefully and turned back toward the mirror.

"It is a beautiful gown, isn't it? Thank you, Virginia. I don't know what I'd have done if you hadn't been here."

"Oh, don't be silly," Mom said dismissively. "It wasn't just me. Everybody pitched in with the sewing."

"But it was your design," I said. "And it is absolutely perfect."

Liza sighed. "Abigail, you're so beautiful. You're glowing. Franklin is a lucky man."

She kissed Liza on the forehead before bestowing a beatific smile on all her attendants. "Thank you all. If not for you, none of this would have happened."

There was some truth in that.

The moments after Abigail tossed out her challenge to the potential grooms had been fraught with tension, drama, and romance, in exactly that order.

There was a pregnant pause as everyone waited for someone to say something.

After a long moment spent staring at my hands, my plate, my half-empty wine glass, I couldn't fight the urge to raise my eyes to Charlie's. He looked at me for a moment, pulled on the end of his nose, and said nothing.

I bit my lip, fighting back a surprising swell of disappointment before looking at Margot, who was looking at Arnie with flushed cheeks and a hopeful expression.

Arnie, in turn, gulped, turned an even whiter shade of pale, and quietly passed out, his eyes rolling back before his head lolled forward and fell into his plate of miniature crab cakes with a thump.

The silence was broken. The room suddenly vibrated with noise and confusion. Margot let out a little scream. Charlie grabbed Arnie's shirt collar and pulled his head up from the plate to check his breathing. Franklin jumped to his feet, scanned the crowd of Saturday night diners, and spotted Jeremy Bellow, a local endocrinologist, among them.

"Jeremy! We need a doctor over here!"

In an instant, Jeremy was at Arnie's side. Everyone moved back to give Arnie some air and watched nervously as the doctor checked Arnie's pulse and loosened his tie. Suddenly, Arnie's head jerked up and his eyes flew open wide, looking confused, as if he'd been jolted awake in the middle of a nightmare.

"What? What's going on?" he asked, scanning the ring of faces surrounding him.

"You passed out. What's your name? How many fingers am I holding up?"

"Arnie Kinsella. Three."

The doctor nodded, looked up at Franklin. "Pulse is a little fast, but he's fine. Might be a good idea for him to go home and rest for a little while, but I don't think there's anything to worry about." He turned to Arnie. "Have you been under an unusual amount of stress lately?"

"Apparently," Abigail mumbled under her breath.

Margot shot her a look. "Come on, Arnie. I'll drive you home."

The doctor went back to his table to finish his dinner. Charlie called over a waiter and told him to put Dr. and Mrs. Bellow's bill on the house tab. Arnie and Margot said good night and walked out the door, with Margot holding Arnie's elbow, just in case. Liza and Garrett took their now-vacant places at the table.

"Well!" Abigail said wryly. "This has been an interesting evening, hasn't it? Let's sit down and order our entrées before anything else happens."

"Too late," Franklin said.

And then, in the middle of the crowded restaurant, he got down on one knee, took his wife's hand, and said, "Abigail, my darling, would you do me the honor of marrying me, again?"

The pandemonium that broke out after Franklin's proposal and Abigail's joyful acceptance was even greater than after Arnie's fainting spell. The whole restaurant broke into waves of applause, whistles, and shouts of congratulations. Franklin ordered champagne for everyone and said they were all invited to the wedding.

"The wedding!" Abigail cried. "Oh, Franklin, it's only a week away! I've got to go home and start planning!"

"Abbie, what are you talking about? Everything is already planned. You've done nothing *but* plan this wedding for the last five months. I know it was all for Liza, but face it, sweetheart, you really put together the ceremony and reception that you'd want, or very nearly. I'm sure there's a little tweaking to be done here and there, but nothing that can't be easily handled by next week."

Franklin was right, but he was also wrong. Some changes would need to be made—actually more than Franklin realized—but it wasn't anything that couldn't be done in the next seven days, especially if you had a quilt circle in your corner.

I patted Abigail on the arm. "Calm down, Abbie. You're not going to be able to get anything done at nine o'clock on a Saturday night, anyway. Tomorrow, we'll all pitch in and give you a hand. Won't we, girls?"

Ivy, Mom, and Dana nodded in agreement. Liza said, "Sure we will. I'm out of school and unemployed. What else do I have to do? From here on out, I'm all yours."

"But I thought you were going to Paris."

"Paris can wait a week or two. It's not going anywhere."

Abigail smiled. "Thank you, Liza, darling. Would you be my maid of honor?"

Liza grinned. "I'd like that. I'd like it a lot."

It had been a busy seven days but, working together, we'd done the job. The next day, Liza, warming to her new role as maid of honor, called a meeting at the quilt shop and started handing out assignments. Everyone was there bright and early, including Margot, who, if she had any lingering disappointments over Arnie's fainting spell, didn't show it. In fact, she seemed delighted about the whole thing. She said her only regret was that she hadn't been there to see Franklin's proposal personally.

Knowing how busy we were all going to be over the coming

week, I called Wendy Perkins and asked if she might be willing to come in and help out in the shop. Fortunately for me, business at the real estate office was slow and she was happy to get the extra work. Garrett worked overtime, handling his job and a good part of Margot's. And Dana, who had turned out to be a very fast learner, took over most of the Internet and mail-order fulfillment from Ivy and even ventured downstairs to help Wendy out at the registers when she was shorthanded.

Margot called all the guests, informing them of the bride and groom substitution and reconfirming or canceling their RSVPs. The number of cancellations was nearly equal to the number of Franklin and Abigail's additions to the guest list, so it all worked out.

Liza was in charge of helping Franklin and his new groomsmen—Charlie as best man, plus Garrett, Arnie, and Judge Gulden—get their tuxedos ordered and tailored. She also got the bridesmaid dresses from her roommates and personally altered and hemmed them so they'd fit the new additions to the bridesmaid roster: Liza and I. While she was at it, she cancelled the Hawaiian honeymoon and booked a sumptuous oceanfront cabana in Bermuda, complete with dinner reservations, champagne and strawberries on arrival, a beachside couples massage, a guided tour of the island, a dolphin encounter, and a private scuba-diving lesson, as well as two first-class airline tickets.

None of this was easy to accomplish with less than a week's notice but, in true Burgess family fashion, Liza called in favors, dropped names, and pulled strings with a subtle surety that made her aunt proud. And when the flowers that had been ordered from Hawaii arrived in New Bern looking shriveled and lifeless, she took care of that, too, cutting gardenias from Abigail's greenhouse and arranging them into a beautiful bridal bouquet.

Under Mom's direction, I spent the week working on Abigail's dress. For all my experience as a quilter, it had been years since I'd sewn any clothing. But on Sunday, after Abigail called from Byron Dennehey's office, moaning that every dress she'd tried on made her look either dowdy or like an aging runway model gone badly to seed, Mom suggested we make the dress. Frankly, I had my doubts.

But Mom's expertise as a quilter was surpassed only by her draping and tailoring skills. It took both of us working almost round the clock, with extra help from Margot, Ivy, and Liza, to get it done, but we did, and the end result was more than worth the effort.

Wearing the dress we'd made, carrying the bouquet of white gardenias Liza had arranged, Abigail had never looked more beautiful. But it wasn't the dress that made her so.

Abigail, with all her faults and flaws and fears, had found love.

I had seen it when Franklin had had his heart attack, all those months before, when she'd sat by his bedside every day and when, in spite of his then poor health and the uncertainty of their future, she'd agreed to marry him at his hospital bedside. I'd seen it when Franklin, in spite of the slights and neglect he'd suffered at his wife's hands, had refused to give up on her or their love, had swallowed his pride and hurt feelings and helped her come back to herself. And I saw it again today as Abigail, eager and anxious as a girl of twenty, looked herself over in the mirror, running her hand over her hair one more time because she wanted to look her very best, not for the people in the pews, but for Franklin and Franklin alone.

That was the face of love, I realized, imperfect and sometimes unlikely, but unmistakable and true.

Abigail leaned closer to the mirror, examining her reflection with a critical eye, then drew her fingernail carefully across the edge of her lower lip, making sure that the line of her lipstick was absolutely even. When that was done, she glanced at the clock on the wall.

"Well, I suppose it's time," Abbie said. "Shall we?"

A knock sounded on the door. "Ladies? Are you decent?"

Liza opened the door. "Come on in, Byron. We're dressed and ready to get this wedding under way. Let's go!"

Byron made an apologetic little grimace. "Not just yet. We're going to have to hold for a few minutes." He looked to Abigail.

"Nothing to worry about. It's Arnie. He's feeling a little woozy. The sanctuary is a little warm. I think the heat got to him."

Margot, in an uncharacteristically irritated voice, said, "Oh, don't be silly. It's got nothing to do with the temperature, unless, of course, you're referring to the temperature of his feet—as in cold. And it isn't even his wedding! Argh!" Margot yelped with exasperation.

"Where is he?" she asked.

"In the pastor's study. Sitting with his head between his knees."

Margot sighed heavily. "I'll go talk to him, see if I can calm him down. And I know exactly how to do it too! I'll tell him I don't want to marry him, not now or ever! Why would I?" she cried. "Who would want to be married to someone who gets woozy over even the mention of matrimony?"

Margot lifted her chin and put her hands on her hips, blue eyes sparking with anger.

"When I marry—*if* I marry—it'll be because someone loves and wants me more than anything and because I feel exactly the same about him. It's not like I'm some charity case, you know! It's not like I *need* a man. I'm fine as I am. I've got a great life and wonderful friends, and I can take care of myself! I don't need Arnie Kinsella to be happy. I don't need *any* man to make me happy—not now, not ever! And I'm going to march over there and tell him so!"

And with her head held high, a transformed and newly defiant Margot swept past Byron and out the door to give Arnie Kinsella a piece of her mind.

Margot's exit was so sudden and so surprising that, for a moment, I was stunned into silence, but before Margot was even out the door, Mom started clapping her hands and said what we all were thinking: "Bravo, Margot! Good for you!"

"Yeah!" Ivy cried, joining in the applause with the rest of us. "You go, girl!"

"Woot! Woot!" Liza yelled, swinging her fist in a circle.

"Well done!" Abigail cried.

"That's right, Margot! You tell him!" I called out the door as Margot marched away, the sound of her high heels echoing an intrepid drumbeat as she marched across the lobby and took a left into the corridor that led to the pastor's study.

I turned around to face the others. "Did you see that? I'm so proud of her!"

"Well, it's about time," Abigail declared. "I was beginning to think she'd never see the light. A woman shouldn't need a man to feel complete. Especially a woman as lovely and accomplished as Margot!"

"But," Liza said, "don't you think it would be nice if she did find someone someday?"

"Only if he's the right someone," I said. "Someone who'll love her as much as she loves him."

"And definitely someone who doesn't get the vapors at the thought of marriage," Abigail muttered as she smoothed the sleeve of her gown.

"Marriage to a good man can enhance life," Mom said, "but it mustn't be a substitute for life. You've got to be happy with yourself before you can be happy with someone else."

"Hear! Hear!" Byron said. "Virginia, you're a very wise woman."

"Well." Mom laughed. "I'm a very old woman. If you live long enough, you're bound to pick up a few things."

Byron smiled and looked at his watch. "Ladies, I think I'd better go tell the musicians to play a couple more numbers. Hopefully, Arnie will be feeling better by then."

"Or not," said Ivy with a smirk. "By the time Margot's done with him, he may faint for real."

"Let's hope not. I won't be long." Byron left, closing the door behind him.

Abigail turned, trying to see the back of her gown in the mirror. "Liza, since we have a little extra time, maybe we should steam it again. I see a few wrinkles."

"All right. Ivy, could you plug the steamer in? I'll be right in. I just want to talk to Evelyn for a second."

Abigail went into the bathroom with Ivy and Mom trailing behind. Liza reached into the pocket of her skirt.

"I've been meaning to give this back to you," she said and pressed my grandmother's silver brooch into my hand.

I shook my head. "No. You keep it. I want you to have it."

"But I can't do that," she argued. "It's supposed to go from mother to daughter."

"I know. And it will. So you're not going to be my daughter-in-law. So what? Maybe you will be someday. Or maybe you won't. We'll see." I shrugged. "But no matter what happens, you'll always be like a daughter to me. You're my daughter in love. Nothing is ever going to change that."

"Oh, Evelyn!"

She put her arms around me, hugged me tight, and I hugged her right back.

Mom came back in the room and started rifling through her purse. "Liza, do you have any bobby pins? I seem to be all out. Abigail is worried that Emiliano didn't put enough spray in her hair."

Liza pulled away from my embrace. "For ten grand, you'd think the guy could afford some extra hair spray. Don't worry, Virginia. I brought some extra bobby pins, just in case. I'll take care of it." She smiled her thanks to me before heading to the bathroom.

"Liza's a wonderful maid of honor," Mom said approvingly. "Prepared for every emergency. Good thing for you to keep in mind."

"Mom," I said, the warning clear in my tone. "Don't start in."

"On what?" she said innocently. "I'm just saying. One of these days you *might* want to remarry. If you ever do, Liza would be a wonderful maid of honor."

"I see. Well, maybe I will. One of these days. Or maybe I won't. You said it yourself not ten minutes ago. A woman doesn't have to have a man."

"That's true," Mom agreed. "You've got to be happy with yourself before you can be happy with someone else, but I also said that the right man can enhance a woman's life, and she his. And from what I can see, Charlie is exactly that sort of man."

I raised my eyebrows. "Funny. I thought that about Rob Dixon too. As it turned out, I was wrong."

"Evelyn!" Mom clucked. "Is that what this is about? After all this time? For the last three years, Charlie has done nothing but try to show you that he's not like Rob. Are you punishing Charlie because of what Rob did almost five years ago?"

She moved her head slowly from side to side. "I'd never have thought it of you, Evelyn. You're being unfair. Worse than that, you're acting like a coward."

"Hey! That's not fair. I'm not cowardly. Just prudent. I don't want to rush into anything and I don't need to. Not until the time is right."

"I see," Mom said slowly. "So this is all an issue of timing? Then explain it to me, what's wrong with your timing? Charlie loves you, right?"

I nodded. He did and I knew it.

"And you love Charlie?"

"Of course I do. Very much. But it's not as easy as you make it sound. We've got businesses to run. We've barely got time to brush our teeth, let alone nurture our relationship. A good marriage takes more than love and good intentions, it takes time! Who would know better than me? All those years that Rob spent at the office and on the road? Maybe, if we'd spent more time together, things might have worked out. But after a while, we barely knew each other. Well, I'm not going to make the same mistake twice, Mother. I'm just not!"

"Well, good!" Mom retorted. "Glad to hear it. I'd hate to think I'd raised a stupid daughter. And you know what the definition of stupidity is, don't you? Doing the same thing over and over again and expecting a different result. So do it differently this time, Evelyn. Make time for each other!"

I wished Byron would show up, say it was time to go, and rescue me from this conversation. No such luck. The door remained firmly closed.

"Easy to say, Mom, but harder to do. Charlie said he'd sell the restaurant—"

Mom gasped. "He did! He actually said he'd sell the Grill? Oh, Evie. He *does* love you."

"I know," I said quietly. "But I can't let him sell. The Grill means as much to Charlie as the quilt shop does to me. He's put his heart and soul into building his business. It wouldn't be fair to ask him to give it up any more than it would be to ask me to give up the shop."

Mom looked at me, squinting, as if she were trying hard to put all this in proper focus. "But, Evelyn, surely there's another way. Almost every couple has to work. There's no reason you and Charlie shouldn't be able to. Why can't you just work a little less? Hire people to help you manage your businesses?"

"You think I haven't thought of that? I can't afford it. Even if I could, who would I hire? I'd need somebody with very special skills." I started ticking the list off on my fingers. "It would have to be someone with great people skills, who can answer customer questions, a good salesperson, who knows all about fabric and notions and how things are trending in quilting, *and* who can sew samples as well as teach all levels of quilters. That's a pretty tall order to fill. Especially if you're paying minimum wage."

"True," Mom said. "It's a big job. You'd definitely have to throw in some perks."

She narrowed her eyes. "Well then, here's the deal. Minimum wage, plus room and board, at least until I can find a place of my own, plus free fabric and notions, four weeks of vacation, and Sundays and Mondays off. I don't want to work on the Sabbath. You won't have to pay for my insurance because I've already got Medicare, plus my supplemental insurance with your dad's pension."

"What? Mom. What are you saying?"

She rolled her eyes as if wanting to take back what she'd said before, the part about me not being stupid. "I'm saying, if I'm going to take the job, I'd need minimum wage, plus room and board, fabric—"

I put up my hands to stop her. "No, no, I got that the first time." I laughed. "But . . . you're saying you'd be willing to stay in New Bern, permanently, and work as assistant manager for Cobbled Court Quilts?"

"I'm not particular about the title, but yes," she said. "That's what I'm saying."

"But before," I said incredulously, "you were dead set against staying in New Bern. What's different now?" Suddenly I was suspicious. "This doesn't have anything to do with Gibb Rainey, does it?"

"Gibb? Oh, heavens, no!" Mom exclaimed, coloring a little. "We're just friends. Not that it's any of your business, Evelyn, but there's nothing between Gibb and me and there never will be. He's a nice man, but compared to your father? I don't think so.

"The truth is, New Bern has grown on me. It's good to have friends again. More importantly, it's good to have a purpose again. Helping out at the quilt shop, teaching the next generation of quilters, all those young mothers-to-be and the little ones at New Beginnings? It's given me a reason to get up in the morning. I like feeling needed again. And when the one who needs you is your own daughter, the person you love most in the whole world? Well, that's just icing on the cake." Mom's eyes twinkled. She laid her hand on my arm and patted me affectionately.

"Now, don't you go marrying Charlie just to get me to stay in New Bern. I've pretty much made up my mind to stay anyway. I like it here. It just took me a while to realize it. But at least think about it, all right? No marriage is easy, Evelyn. But if you love Charlie and he loves you, then I think you're smart enough to figure out a way to make it work. Don't you? And if I can help you . . . Well, so much the better for all of us."

"Oh, Mom." I wrapped my arms around her and clung tight to her, just as Liza had to me.

Daughter-in-love can be an honorary title or a hereditary one, but either way, come age and arguments, fights and forgiveness, it's a lifetime appointment.

39

Evelyn Dixon

Mom and I were still laughing and wiping tears from our eyes when Byron tapped on the door.

"Margot is pacing in the vestibule, walking off a little steam while she waits for the rest of you. Arnie is standing up front with Franklin and the other groomsmen, looking pale and very repentant. I think we'd better have this wedding while he's still upright."

Three minutes later, I was lined up in the vestibule along with the others, nervously waiting for Byron's signal to go.

"Ready?" he asked in a quiet but steady voice. "Big breath, everybody. Evelyn, don't look so serious. You'll be fine. Smile, everyone! Here we go!"

He pushed open the double doors. A swell of violin music greeted us, filling the sanctuary and urging us forward.

In spite of Byron's reassurance, I was nervous. I stepped off on the right foot instead of the left and had to do a little hop step to get back on the correct foot. I hoped no one noticed.

I followed Liza down the aisle, past the pews filled with friends, toward Franklin, who waited at the altar with eyes only for Abigail. As I drew closer, I could not help but look past him to that stubborn, gruff-mannered, ill-tempered, giving, caring, darling man standing on his left: Charlie, who had eyes only for me.

Suddenly, my nervousness fled, leaving behind nothing but the wish that Charlie and Franklin might trade places, that when I reached the end of the aisle Charlie might be standing there, waiting for me.

And so later, after the vows were restated before God and the world and the dinners served, and the cake cut, and the champagne uncorked, and the speeches made, and toasts drunk, and when I was finally where I had wanted to be all along, dancing in the arms of my beloved, I wasted no time before looking up into that face I love above all others, and saying, "Charlie? I do."

"You do what?" His brow furrowed, confused, then unfurrowed with sudden understanding. His blue eyes lit up from the inside out.

"You do? You will?"

I nodded. "I do, Charlie. And I will. Forever and always."

40

Liza Burgess

My cell phone emitted an ominous beeping sound, the one that signals I'm about two minutes away from a dead battery. Fortunately, my call was about to wrap up.

"Great! Thank you so, so much, Professor! I won't let you down!"

"I know you won't, Liza. That's why I'm hiring you. Have a wonderful trip. I'll see you in August."

"Right, Professor. And thanks again. And don't worry, I'm going to make sure—"

She laughed, interrupting me. "You don't need to say it again, Liza. I believe you. I'm glad you're so excited. You should be. It's a great opportunity, for both of us. Now go on. Catch your plane."

"Okay. Good-bye, Professor."

"Liza? Just one more thing. Well, two. First, quit calling me Professor. I'm not your teacher anymore. Selena will be fine. Second, *please* tell Garrett I'm sorry about accosting him on the street that day. Now that you've told me the whole story, I can see what an enlightened, *supportive* man he is. I hope you know how lucky you are. Men like that don't come along every day of the week, *believe* me," she said. "Anyway, give Garrett my apologies and my best. Someday, I hope I get to meet him again. Under more cordial circumstances."

"Oh, you will, Prof—I mean, Selena. We've worked out a plan. He's going to visit me in Chicago every third weekend."

"Wonderful! Then we can all go out for dinner. My treat, all right? Now run and catch your plane, dear. Have a wonderful time. Give my regards to the Louvre! And Versailles! And the Bois de Boulogne! Ah, to be young and in love and going to Paris for the first time. . . . Enjoy it, Liza. Life is *short*. Enjoy every moment!"

"I will, Selena. I am. Thank you. Good-bye."

I reached out to press the End button just as the screen went blank, the battery spent. Good timing.

Garrett was sitting in the waiting area for our flight to Paris, his feet crossed and propped up on his backpack and his own phone still at his ear, just where he'd been half an hour before. I slipped my phone into my purse and walked back to our seats, thinking how cute Garrett was.

"Yeah. Okay, I'll tell her. Love you too. Bye. Don't worry, I will. Yes," he said with studied patience, "I promise. Grandma, I've got to go. It's almost time for us to board."

Actually, our flight wouldn't board for another half hour, but I couldn't blame Garret for stretching the truth a little. The way it sounded, it might take him that long to get Virginia off the line. I sat down next to him, pulled a plastic zipper bag out of my carry-on, and started stitching one of the quilt blocks I'd brought with me. After a couple more attempts and a couple more good-byes, he was finally able to sign off.

Yawning, he turned the power off on his phone, then laid his arm across my shoulders. "Sorry," he said. "It's not you. I couldn't sleep last night. Too excited, I guess."

"Me too."

"That's probably a good thing. We can sleep on the plane and when we wake up, it'll be morning in Paris. A whole new day."

"I never sleep on planes," I said. "While you're sleeping, I'll be quilting. I'd like to get the piecing done by the time we get back to New Bern. Virginia said she'd help me with the quilting later. The whole thing will be hand stitched," I said, smoothing the block down on my leg, trying to finger press the seam I'd just finished.

Garrett leaned over and peered at the block. "That's nice. Mom will love it. But you should at least try to sleep. You'll be jet-lagged if you don't. How was your call to Professor Williams? From the smile on your face, I'd say everything is still on track."

"The board met last night and approved all Selena's proposed hires—including me." I grinned. "You are looking at the Pinkham Museum's new assistant curator for the decorative arts. Should look pretty impressive on a business card, don't you think? By the way, Professor Williams, who I am now supposed to call Selena, sends her apologies and her greetings. She wants to take us out to dinner when you come to Chicago."

"Really? Well, that's certainly a turnaround from being attacked on the street and called a misogynist. Speaking of messages, you've got stacks of them. When people couldn't get through on your number, they called mine instead."

He closed his eyes and screwed up his face. "Let's see if I can remember them all. Grandma says to say hello, to watch out for pickpockets, not to drink the water, and to remind you to remind me to send her a postcard from the Eiffel Tower."

"Will do."

"Ivy says hi and to have fun and take a lot of pictures. Margot says the same and that everything is under control at the shop. She'd also like a postcard from Paris. Well, actually she'd just like some French stamps, to give Arnie for his collection."

"We can do that."

"Abigail and Franklin called from Bermuda. They're still loving it. Abigail wants to buy a condo there. Franklin talked her down from that, but they've already made reservations for next year. Abbie said to tell you that she called the credit card company and had them up your limit so you wouldn't run out of money in Paris."

I rolled my eyes. "She didn't have to do that. How many times do I have to tell her? I'm going to be making good money after August. Plus, I have plenty saved up from working at the quilt shop last summer. Doesn't she think I'm capable of taking care of myself?"

"I don't know," Garrett said, unsuccessfully trying to stifle another yawn. "I think it's just her way of letting you know she cares.

And, continuing on the list of people who care: Mom and Charlie called from London. Their flight to Dublin is delayed, so they had time to phone.

"Mom says to have a wonderful time. And Charlie says to make sure we have lemon tarts at Ladurée, and cassoulet at Allard, and baguettes at—"

"Okay, I get the idea." I laughed. "You don't have to go through the whole list again. He already wrote it down for me. How were they? Did they sound happy?"

"Very," Garrett said, raising his eyebrows. "At one point, Mom actually giggled."

"Oh, that's sweet," I said.

"Yeah, I guess so, but when it's your mom, it's a little weird. She said everything was wonderful. Charlie was wonderful. Their weekend in New York was wonderful. The flight to London was wonderful. I think she even thought their delay to Dublin was wonderful."

"Well, she's in love." I shrugged. "It just took her a while to realize it, that's all."

"I'll say. I knew Charlie was the right guy for her five minutes after I met him. Good thing Grandma pulled Charlie aside and told him to play hard to get for a while. Otherwise, who knows how long it would have taken her to figure it out?"

"At least once she did figure it out, she didn't waste time doing something about it. I've never been to two weddings in one week before."

Garrett smiled. "Yeah. That was crazy, wasn't it? But they did it right. Get the license and the ring, call up the minister, arrange for a quiet little ceremony at the church, followed by lunch for a few friends and family at the Grill, and then fly off to Ireland for the honeymoon. Simple. And I thought it was just as nice as Abigail and Franklin's wedding."

I nodded. "I agree. There's only one downside. When Abigail finds out that they got married without her, she's going to blow a gasket." I looked up from my quilting, worried. "You didn't say anything to her, did you?"

"Are you kidding? And risk her reaching through the phone line to strangle me? I'm not stupid. Mom and Charlie can detonate that bomb on their own, thanks. I'm nobody's stooge."

Garrett leaned his head back, closed his eyes, and said in a wistful voice, "Babe, if we ever do decide to get married, do you think we can pull a Charlie? Just run off, get married, and tell Abigail about it later?"

I laughed. "Tempting, but no. We can't leave Abigail out of the picture. She'd never forgive us."

"I was afraid of that." Eyes still closed, he shrugged. "Oh, well. It never hurts to dream."

I put down my stitching, reached out to hold Garrett's hand, and leaned my head on his shoulder. "Nope. It never does."

The flight was nearly full, but Garrett and I had an extra seat in our row. Even so, we sat side by side, me in the window seat and Garrett in the middle, stretching his long legs to the left, taking advantage of the empty space next to him.

He was asleep before we'd even left the ground, his head lolling on my shoulder, which was kind of nice.

The air-conditioning was going full blast, so the plane was chilly. I wished I had my Star-Crossed Love quilt with me, the one that was supposed to be my wedding quilt but that the quilt circle had agreed could be my bon voyage quilt instead. It was big, too big to put in my carry-on luggage, so I'd had to check it. It took up a lot of room and I'd had to leave behind some extra clothes to make room for it. Garrett thought I was crazy to bring it, but there was no way I was going to Paris for a month without it. No matter how far I was from home, when I snuggled up under my quilt, blanketed under those beautiful stars, I felt surrounded by friends.

I pulled one of those cheap little airline blankets out of a plastic bag, covered my legs with it, and scooted a little closer to Garrett as the plane climbed.

There was a movie on a big screen at the front of the plane. I glanced at it now and again but didn't put on my headphones, preferring to enjoy the stillness, the steady white whoosh of engine noise, while I worked on my quilt blocks and Garrett slept.

Having finished one block, I reached into my bag to pull out another but realized they were all done. All I had to do now was stitch together the separate blocks, quilt the top, and bind the edges, and the wall hanging, my wedding present to Evelyn and Charlie, would be finished.

Moving slowly so I wouldn't wake Garrett, I put down my tray table and laid out a few of the blocks so I could get an idea of how the finished wall hanging would look.

Two painted doors of the quilt shop and the restaurant side by side, one red and one black, flanked by a generic background of shop doors and windows, patched from fabrics of gray and charcoal, a New Bern streetscape silhouetted against a cerulean sky that darkened in layers, from sapphire to indigo to midnight, as my eye rose past rooftops and treetops and into a miniature firmament of tiny stars in bright, bold colors, each one separate and distinct from the others but also in harmony with the whole, like brilliant hues in a little girl's paint box, untouched but full of possibility.

It would look beautiful when it was done. Evelyn would love it. She would understand it.

And while I was thinking this, the separated blocks moved closer and closer together, becoming one seamless whole, the entire scene flawlessly stitched and perfectly joined just as it had been when I first bought the fabrics, laid them out on the table, side by side by side, and imagined what they could become.

It was all there, just as I'd seen it in my mind's eye. With one addition.

On the left side, about a third of the way up between the rooftops and the midnight sky, there was a flight of birds, ghost white against the darkening sky, flying in formation to an unknown destination. I hadn't sewn those birds, not in this quilt anyway. At least I didn't remember doing so. How had they gotten there?

"What would you like to drink?"

I looked up. A flight attendant was standing in the aisle, smiling, her hands gripping the handles of a completely empty beverage cart without a can, bottle, or even a pitcher of water on its surface.

"Well . . . I don't know. What do you have?"

"Anything. Anything you can imagine. Well, almost anything. Here," she said, reaching down into a square opening in the top of the cart and pulling out a green glass bottle with a gold label, "try this. It'll help you sleep."

"But I'm already asleep," I said, accepting a glass from her hand and taking a sip of the wine, deep red, complex, and quenching.

"Yes, of course you are," she said. "But this will help you stay asleep, at least for a little while, so you can get some rest. It's good to dream, Liza. It's even better to live."

I finished the wine while the woman looked on approvingly. Leaning down to take my empty glass, she saw the quilt lying on the tray table.

"That's lovely! You made it, didn't you? I can tell. It has your mark all over it, your voice, your touch." She leaned closer to get a better look.

"There's just one thing missing. You need some silver thread, don't you? For the birds. Let me see if I can find some." She reached into the cart again. When her hand emerged, she was clutching a collection of beautiful threads in her hand, shining and smooth and thin, cobalt and salmon and celadon and pearl, every color you could imagine, every color but silver.

"Oh," she said softly, a little crease of disappointment appearing between her brows, in exactly the same spot it did when I was disappointed, which I suddenly realized I was.

"I thought you said anything I could want is in there."

"Almost everything. Some things you have to find for yourself. Wait a minute!" she exclaimed, her features brightening. "Of course! I should have remembered. You don't need me to get you the thread. You can do that for yourself. See?"

She smiled and pointed to the window. I looked out and saw them, a flight of birds, each one holding a silver thread in its beak, each thread attaching itself to some point on the wing of the plane, one thread for each person inside.

"There's yours," she said, pointing to the thread nearest my window. "You can reach out and clip off as much or as little as you need."

I turned from the window. "But if I do that, won't I run out?"

She laughed. "No! Of course not! Your thread is always as long or as short as you need it to be."

"Are you sure? How do you know? And how do you know which one is mine?"

She tipped her head to the side, as if trying to understand how I had failed to grasp something so obvious. "Well, *I* don't, Liza. Only you know that. After all, it's your thread. It's your choice. I'm just glad you finally made one."

"But that's what's had me worried. How do I know I'm making the right one?"

"You don't." She laughed. "Not for sure. But don't worry. It's not like there's only one right thread. If you find your thread is taking you somewhere you don't want to go, you can always grab hold of another. You'll have many threads, many choices in your life. Some will be better than others. But all of them, every single one, has at least the potential for good. You'll see," she said and reached her hand to run her finger tenderly along my cheek, a touch I remembered from other dreams and other days.

"The main thing is not to be afraid."

"I'm not. Not anymore."

"Good for you. You're going to be fine. I always knew you would be. Just keep reaching out and grabbing hold. The thread may look thin, but it's stronger than you think. You'll see. You're stronger than you think too."

She smiled again and held out her hand. I looked up at her, handed her the empty glass, and saw the name printed on her name tag: Susan.

She grabbed hold of the cart handle. "It's time for you to wake up now, Liza. But I'll see you again," she said as she walked down the aisle, pushing the cart ahead of her.

Garrett stirred next to me, yawned.

I yawned, too, opening my eyes and blinking a few times before turning first to the left, toward the empty aisle of the darkened plane, filled with sleeping travelers, then down to my lap, where the unstitched patches of my quilt block still sat, and then to the right.

Looking out the tiny oval window, I saw the velvet-black night studded with pinprick stars in a sky that began in the mind of God and ended at the edge of dawn, to a thin silver thread of morning arcing across the horizon, stretching as far as I could see and farther still, a shining path that could lead me anywhere.

Anywhere I choose.

A READING GROUP GUIDE

A THREAD SO THIN

Marie Bostwick

ABOUT THIS GUIDE

The following questions are intended to enhance your group's reading of A THREAD SO THIN.

DISCUSSION QUESTIONS

1. One of the recurring themes in *A Thread So Thin* is that women have many and varying choices today: to marry, not to marry, to have children, not to have children, to pursue a lucrative field or one that is fulfilling but does not provide financial security. Liza said, "The way I see it, the older you get, the more chance there is that the choices you make now will screw up the whole rest of your life." Why do you think Liza had this outlook on life? Do you agree with her? Like Liza, have you faced a crossroads in your life when you had a difficult decision to make about your future? Did the decision turn out right for you? If not, did it or did it not impact the rest of your life? Looking back, would you make the same decision?

2. Both Garrett and Liza had lost their fathers due to betrayal, yet one of them lived life with a positive outlook, and the other seemed to continue to suffer from the betrayal. What do you think led to this difference?

3. When Liza's mother died, her mom's attorney, Franklin, gave her some of the support her mother would have provided had she lived. In your life, has there been an adult other than your parents who helped you through tough times and helped you celebrate your successes? Who is that person, and what did he or she do to help you?

4. After Liza was forced to move in with her aunt Abigail, she set out to make Abigail's life hell. Do you recall a time in your life when, in rebellion, you gave your parent or guardian similar grief? Why do you think you did this? Later, how did you feel about your attitude? Did you change your attitude, and why?

5. Liza loves New York City—the ambience, the art, the food—especially the people. How would you characterize the people where you live? Are they generally friendly or standoffish? Why do you think the local populace has this kind of attitude?

6. Garrett is an optimistic person. What is your outlook on life? Are you, like Garrett, confident that, one way or another, everything will work out and that the best is yet to come? Or do you find that you generally expect the worst to happen? Why do you think you have your attitude? Has your outlook been influenced by turns of events in your life, or do you think this is just a part of your inherited tendencies? Do you think a person can change his or her outlook on life? If so, how?

7. Abigail and Liza mended the rift between them, aided by their shared involvement in quilting. If you have mended a broken relationship in your life, share how the mending began and what brought you back together.

8. When Liza was trying to make up her mind what to do about Garrett's proposal, she surveyed her friends and acquaintances about their attitudes toward marriage. Do you think marriage is as relevant to women today as it was fifty, even twenty-five, years ago?

9. Why do you think it took Evelyn so long to say yes to Charlie's proposal? Was that wisdom on her part, or fear, or some of both? Have you, or has someone you know, faced similar difficulty in responding to a proposal? How does time and age change what women want or expect from life, marriage, and career?

10. One of Charlie's favorite sayings about a person who possessed a certain skill was, "You don't just lick it up off the

rocks," meaning that a lot of the talents we think of as belonging to us alone are actually inherited. What talent or special skill do you have that you think you inherited from a member or members of your family?

11. After Liza did not immediately say yes to Garrett's unanticipated marriage proposal, and she witnessed his abrupt change in demeanor, she decided that the idea of being responsible for someone's happiness isn't any more comfortable than the idea of being responsible for someone's misery. Have you ever felt you were forced to "own" someone's happiness or misery? If so, did you convey that this was not a weight that should be put on your shoulders, and how did you accomplish this? How did the person react to your assertion?

12. Evelyn was thrilled that every woman in the new quilting class taught by her and her mother left with at least one new friend. She allowed that new friends are the kinds of treasures that don't show up on a balance sheet but do add up to the best sort of payday. Especially considering what Evelyn has been through in her marriage and her health, what does this attitude say about Evelyn? How do you think her attitude has contributed to or detracted from her happiness and success?

13. Why do you think Evelyn reacted negatively when she first learned about Garrett and Liza's engagement? Can you remember a time when you wished you could have taken back a response to someone's news?

14. What impact did Liza's father's betrayal have on her concept of family? How did this affect her ability to commit to Garrett?

15. Liza was profoundly touched by the beautiful quilt her friends and relatives made for her as their wedding gift. Have you

ever received a gift that touched you similarly? If so, tell the group about it and the people who gave it to you.

For more information about *A Thread So Thin* or Marie Bostwick, visit www.mariebostwick.com or follow her on Twitter, @mariebostwick.

Dear Reading Friend,

It has been such a joy for me to serve as your guide on this, our third visit, to New Bern. Three books in to the Cobbled Court series of novels (and already working on book four, which I believe you'll see in the late spring or early summer of 2011), I can honestly say that I find this little village and these characters as compelling as ever. I hope you feel the same.

When I sat down to begin working on *A Single Thread,* the first Cobbled Court novel, I had not considered it to be the first in a series. But by the time I finished writing it, I very much wanted to return to New Bern, so I asked readers to write and let me know if they felt as I did.

You did write, by the thousands, and I am so grateful.

Your enthusiasm for these characters and their stories, and your openness as you shared how these books have made you laugh, cry, think, and even make important changes and decisions in your own lives, convinced me that it was important to return to New Bern. I have done so with pleasure.

Every e-mail and letter I receive from readers is a huge encouragement. I do read every note, and every note receives a response—not always as quickly as I'd like, and it does take me much longer to respond to letters than e-mails, but I do my best to keep up. (If you don't hear back from me, please double-check to make sure you've included a correct return mailing address or e-mail.)

If you'd like to write to me, you can do so at the address given below, or you can drop by my website, www.mariebostwick.com, and send me a note via the contact form. While you're there, you can also read excerpts from all six of my other novels and check out the Recipe of the Month, my Latest Crush, my blog, or my upcoming appearance schedule.

Also, if you register as one of my Reading Friends (click on the Become a Reading Friend box on the left of the home page to begin), you'll have access to special content; be registered in my monthly Readers' Contest; receive personal invitations to my appearances in your area; and have the opportunity to connect with other readers in the online forum, as well as download free goodies such as the Broken Hearts Mending quilt pattern from *A Single Thread* and printable recipe cards for the dishes that were featured in *Snow Angels*.

AND, as a special thanks to my registered Reading Friends who are also quilters, I'm delighted to offer a new quilt pattern from *A Thread So Thin*! Famed quilting teacher and designer Deb Tucker, of Studio 180 Design, has created a beautiful table-runner pattern based on Liza's Star-Crossed Love quilt that I think you'll love. Reading Friends can download the table-runner pattern free for their personal use, but **please remember: *This gift is available only via computer and only to registered Reading Friends.***

Thank you again for visiting New Bern. I hope you enjoyed this trip as much as I did. Until we meet again . . .

Blessings,

Marie Bostwick
PO Box 488
Thomaston, CT 06787
www.mariebostwick.com